Murderous Intent

Murderous Intent

Keith Littler

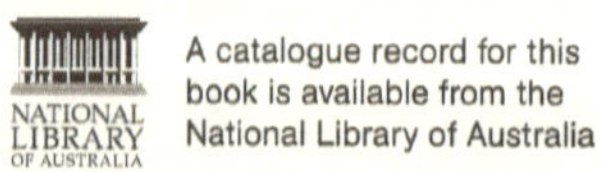

A catalogue record for this book is available from the National Library of Australia

Published By: Keith Littler
Cover Design By: Richard Littler
Editor: Eddie Albrecht, Pickawoowoo Publishing Group

ISBN: 978-1-7638114-0-9 (Paperback)
ISBN: 978-1-7638114-1-6 (E-Book)

Printed & Channel Distribution: Lightning Source / IngramSpark

CONTENTS

Where's Cassie?

2023

Part One

John McGuire sat listening to the music, tapping his fingers on the top of his steering wheel as he patiently waited for the temporary traffic lights at the road works to change. He then turned right into Collins Street. As he looked left, he could see Tesco car park. It looked extremely busy; people manoeuvring shopping trollies, some piling bulging shopping bags into their car boots, mothers dragging toddlers along, one hand on the heavily laden trolley, one hand on the arm of a screaming youngster. Further along he saw the dilapidated ruins where the Regal Cinema once stood proud. The cinema had been an integral part of the Chamesly community for as long as he could remember. He had been brought up in Chamesly and well-remembered the Saturday afternoon matinees at the Regal. Sadly, it had finally succumbed to the changing habits of the population and had closed. It looked a sorry sight; the once grand entrance and the ornate windows now boarded up. The Art Deco frontage was still covered in posters advertising forthcoming films, now torn and defaced. Several construction vehicles were parked on the forecourt as the demolition began to take place.

John was glad to be back in Chamesly. As a teenager he had left the town to pursue his studies at Uni where he'd graduated as a geologist. His career had, until recently, involved flying the world. Those first few years had been a fantastic experience, and he could look back with pride on achieving most of his career goals; travelling to different countries, the extraordinary people he'd had the privilege to work with and the life-long friends he made. The time he spent away had been rewarding, but exhausting. He was now back in Chamesly – with a desk job.

John McGuire was a thirty-eight-year-old geologist of worldwide reputation. He was tall, with a thick head of silver hair. He'd been married to Pam for eleven years. She was an independent, practical woman and worked as an advisor at a finance company in the city. John and his wife had moved back to Chamsely three years ago. They'd settled well into the community. They lived in a large, detached house, enjoyed two holidays abroad each year, dined in the best restaurants and swapped their cars every two or three years. Life was good!

John was employed by Evolva Exploration. He'd successfully negoti-ated several tough interviews and was now senior project manager, re-sponsible for numerous geological exploration projects around the UK. Evolva were exploring the possibilities of mining gold in Devon and Cornwall. Should they be successful the next project was looking for gold in Cumbria. He was glad to be back in Chamesly, away from the muck and dust of field work in the hotter, drier regions of the world.

Evolva's current project was a £165 million coal mine on the Cum-brian coast. It was almost complete and was ready for production when it had suddenly flooded. Teams of workers were already on site to assess the damage and undertake repairs. Unfortunately, it was going to take weeks or even months before the mine could be re-started. It would be an expensive set-back! The two gold mine projects in the south-west had juddered to a halt as the local councils involved were being put un-der pressure from the local community and environmentalists to reverse their decision to allow mining. On this occasion it appeared there was a legal argument and John knew, from bitter experience, that legal arguments could drag on for years. He'd spent several long and exhausting hours in meetings with Evolva's legal team to decide the next move. He knew if the appeal were too drawn out it could scupper the viability of the mines.

Yes, it had been a bloody awful week, and he couldn't wait to get home to enjoy a relaxed weekend. Go out for dinner with Pam and catch up with some friends.

John turned the last corner into Rabbit Close, an exclusive estate of only twelve houses, all detached, all different. John and Pam lived at number seven. The front garden had a weeping willow to one side, and a row of standard rose trees in front of the bay window. He gave a deep sigh of relief to be home – *what a bloody awful week!* He pressed the remote and the garage door slowly lifted. Strangely Pam's car was not in the garage. He glanced at his watch, six o'clock! She should be back by now.

He let himself in via the door from inside the garage which led into the kitchen. It seemed strangely quiet. The kitchen was tidy, no pots were in the sink. He quickly looked up at the clock just above the units. Five past six!

'Pam! I'm home!' He called. He put his briefcase down on the floor and went through to the lounge. Thinking Pam may have gone for a nap, which is something she wouldn't normally do, but it was worth a check, he climbed the stairs and looked into their bedroom – no Pam. He shouted again. 'Pam!' He popped his head into the bathroom; she wasn't having a shower. He walked over to the window which overlooked the rear garden – maybe she was taking five minutes out and having a quiet pre-dinner drink on the patio – No! If she went out she would always leave a note. There was no note.

Worst-case scenarios were running through his head. *Has she had an accident? Was she lying somewhere in severe pain? Had she been kidnapped?*

An hour later Pam still hadn't arrived home. He now began to panic. A cold shiver shot down his spine. His mind went blank, he couldn't think straight. *Where the hell is she? Why hasn't she phoned me?* He sat in the kitchen on one of the high stools that butted up against the central unit and went over in his mind the conversation they'd had at breakfast. *Did she say she was going somewhere and he hadn't been listening properly?* His mind eventually slotted into gear. He jumped up and picked up the phone. He phoned Pam's sister. 'Hello, is that Josie? Hi it's John. I'm just wondering where Pam is. She's not there is she? She hasn't arrived home yet and it's nearly seven. She's normally home just before six. Oh, right. If she contacts you, can you phone me? OK, I'd appreciate it, thanks.'

He slumped back in his seat. *What next? Ah, friends!* Lying on the unit was Pam's mobile. *Why would she have gone out without that?* He turned it on and searched through her contacts list, many of the names he recognised. One by one he contacted them to no avail. No point in phoning her mum as they'd been estranged for years. Pam had never explained why. She used to say she *'didn't want to talk about it'.* Panic wasn't normally part of his make-up, but it certainly was now. He was hitting dead-ends whichever way he turned. His next step was to phone all the hospitals in the area. One by one he went through the list. No luck. No one had been admitted under her name. Her phone ringing made him jump. Maybe this was Pam! Maybe her car has broken down!

'Hello, Pam?'

'Hello, is that Mr McGuire?'

'Er, yes.'

The person on the other end hesitated for a nanosecond – they clearly hadn't expected Pam's husband to answer. 'Oh, hello. Is Pam there?'

'Er, no. Who is this?'

'Sorry, I should have said, it's Candice...a work colleague of Pam's. I was just checking that she's okay.'

John's mind was going into overdrive. 'And why shouldn't she be?' he queried, rather more abruptly than he intended.

The other person was now even more hesitant. 'Well, I know she was having a few days leave, but she promised to drop a report off to the office this afternoon, one she'd been working on at home. I was just phoning to see if she was okay because she never came in.'

'Sorry, but she's not here. I don't know where she is. I came home a couple of hours ago and she hasn't come back yet.'

'Oh, okay. Can you ask her to phone me when she turns up?'

'Yes, of course.'

He slowly put the phone down and slumped into his chair. He was distraught. Tears were forming in his eyes. He realised his hands were shaking. *Where the hell is she?* He ran from room to room once more to check and double-check if he'd missed anything. He hadn't. At ten o'clock he decided to call round at the police station. The station was a twenty-minute drive away on the other side of town. It was housed in a typical 1960s concrete block together with the library and the Citizens Advice Bureau. He parked in the visitors' bay then ran up the steps, two at a time into the reception area where a large officer with a walrus moustache, watery eyes and a bulbous nose loomed from behind the high counter.

'Good evening sir. Can I help you?'

John wiped the sweat off his forehead and stammered incoherently, 'Yeah, er, yeah. My wife hasn't come home.'

'Let's just stay calm sir and tell me what this is about.'

John shook his head and tried to regain some composure. 'Yeah, sorry. I want to report a missing person.'

The officer bent down to retrieve a large pad from beneath the counter. 'I'll just collect a few details sir. Name?'

'John McGuire.'

'No sir, the missing person's name.'

'Oh, right. Pamela McGuire, she's my wife.'

Walrus moustache slowly wrote Pam's name down. 'And how long has she been missing?'

'Well, just this evening. She hasn't come home from work...in fact apparently, she hasn't been in to work today. Her boss phoned to ask how she was...she was due to deliver a report, you see.'

'I assume you've checked with friends, relatives, contacts?'

John nodded furiously. 'Yes...all those and the hospitals too.'

'I'm assuming she's over eighteen?'

John looked puzzled. 'Yeah.'

The officer looked as though he'd heard it all before. 'She could be anywhere sir. Decided to have a night on the town by herself, maybe. Or just wanted time to herself perhaps? Until she's been missing twenty-four hours I cannot record her as a missing person.'

John looked exasperated. 'Surely you can do something.'

'I'm sorry sir.' He looked genuinely sorry; he could see John was pan-icking. 'You're welcome to come back here if she doesn't come home by tomorrow.'

John thanked him and feeling totally dejected, left the station. He sat in his car for twenty minutes mulling over where she could be. He didn't come up with any answers so drove home hoping she'd have re-turned. She hadn't!

He stood in a daze in the lounge scanning the room for any clues. Nothing! Then suddenly he had a thought and shot up the stairs two at a time to the bedroom. He yanked open her wardrobe door and felt sick. Gone was her pink suitcase and several sets of clothes. Empty hang-ers swung on the rail.

He sat on the edge of the bed, head in his hands, when he had an-other frightening thought. Quickly reaching across to her bedside table he pulled the drawer out and tipped it on the floor. Her passport was also missing!

After a sleepless night, copious amounts of coffee and checking his mobile every few minutes, he returned to the police station the follow-ing evening, having waited precisely 24 hours. They were the most frus-trating and draining 24 hours of his life. This time the desk was manned by a tall cadaverous officer with sandy hair and a wispy moustache.

'Good evening sir. How can I help you?'

John quickly related the details of his earlier visit the previous evening. 'But she still hasn't returned...or made contact.'

The sergeant referred to the notepad which he retrieved from underneath the desk and flicked through a couple of pages. 'Ah, yes. It's all down here.' He lifted his head and looked John directly in the eyes. 'And you say there's been no contact since?' John shook his head. 'Have you re-checked with any friends or relatives to see if they've heard from her?'

John shook his head once more. 'They all know to phone me if they hear from her.'

The officer took another pad from beneath the desk. 'I'll formalise her disappearance. Can you give me a full description of your wife...colour of hair, weight, height, what she might be wearing?'

John gave as much detail as he could then he produced a photo from his wallet. 'Would this help?'

The officer nodded and took the photo. 'Thank you, that's a great help. May I keep this?' John nodded. 'Does your wife have a car?' John nodded again and gave the officer a description. 'It's a navy BMW SUV, reg 5829 NF.' The sergeant dutifully wrote it down.

'Is anything missing... passport, clothes?'

'Yes. Her passport is missing, a soft pink suitcase and clothes.'

The officer placed his hands flat on the top of the desk. 'I have to ask you, sir, did you have an argument before she disappeared?'

John shot back. 'No! Absolutely not.'

'Are you aware that she might have been having an affair?'

John sounded exasperated at all the questions. 'No! Everything was fine between us.' He pleaded, 'can you do something to find her, please! Issue her photo, ask for information.' He threw his arms in the air in frustration, 'I don't know, whatever you do in these cases. Please, do something!'

The officer nodded, 'I know it's frustrating for you sir, but I will issue an alert with the patrols in the area. I'll also contact all airports and ports. If her passport is missing, she may have planned to go abroad.' As an afterthought he added, 'does she have any contacts abroad?'

John dropped his shoulders and shook his head. 'No,' he said completely exhausted.

'Leave it with us sir. In most cases of this type, they eventually turn up. We'll keep in touch with you.'

John turned to go. 'Thank you.'

PART TWO

Fifteen Years Earlier

2009

Cassandra 'Cassie' Mellings had just come out of the shower when she heard a familiar plop through the letterbox. Rushing down the stairs, at the same time trying to wrap a towel around her head, she stumbled into the hall just as her mum was picking up the mail. Recognising one of the envelopes, Cassie held her hand out. 'Please, mum.'

Her mum pretended to prevent her from taking the mail. 'Breakfast first, Cassie.'

Cassie playfully buffeted her mum and grabbed the envelope. 'Fingers crossed mum.' She trotted down the hall and into the kitchen, plonking herself onto one of the stools up against the central unit. She skillfully flicked open the envelope with her manicured nail. After carefully reading the contents, she leapt from her stool and pranced around the kitchen waving the envelope in the air. 'Yes, oh, yes, oh yes oh yes.'

Her mum continued to pour out a coffee. 'Good news, then?' she inquired nonchalantly.

Cassie stopped in her tracks, her eyes sparkling, a broad grin across her face. 'Straight As mum. Straight As.' Her A-level results had arrived.

Her mum went to hug her daughter. 'Congrats Cassie. Well done, you deserve it. You've worked so hard.'

'Edinburgh Uni, here I come!' Tears rolled down her cheeks. 'I don't believe it! I'm in! They wanted two A's and a B, and I got all A's. Brilliant.'

'Toast, Cassie?' asked her mum, determined that she should eat.

'Oh, I'm too excited to eat anything'.

Her mum was insistent. 'Come on Cassie, you need something otherwise you'll feel sick from hunger rather than excitement.'

Cassie reluctantly agreed. 'Shall I phone dad at work?'

Her mum had a broad smile across her face. 'Go ahead. I'll make you some toast. Phone your dad.'

She phoned her dad with the good news and he told her how proud he was of her. 'Brilliant Cassie. Maybe we go out for dinner tonight. Tell your mum not to prepare anything for tea. I'll organise it.'

Cassie sat quietly re-reading the letter and smiling to herself. 'I can't wipe the smile off my face mum.'

Her mum smiled back. 'Are you going to phone Amanda?'

'Oh yeah, I said I would once I got my results.' She bit her bottom lip, 'what shall I say if Amanda hasn't got the grades?'

Her mum tilted her head to one side. 'It's up to you Cass, but calm your enthusiasm, just in case she's feeling disappointed, but you won't know if you don't phone.'

Amanda Wallis and Cassandra had been close friends since infant school. They'd gone to secondary school together, were in the same class, both passed O levels with flying colours and socialised together. They were very different. Cassie had to work hard to achieve. She was the quieter of the two, less impulsive, more measured. Amanda on the other hand was more adventurous. Passing exams came easily to her. She was more carefree, impulsive. She had once been threatened with expulsion from school because she'd been discovered handing out cigarettes to other pupils. She was a party girl!

Cassie flicked open her mobile, dialled, then waited for a few seconds, then, 'hi, Mand, got them?'

Cassie's mum could see Cassie nodding her head furiously and trying to control a broad grin creasing her face. 'Brill Mand, brill. How about a catch up for a coffee this morning?'

She turned her phone off and smiled at her mum then blurted out. 'She got straight A's too. Thank God for that.' Cassie looked thoughtful for a few seconds then. 'I'm glad she did mum, it means we'll be at Edinburgh together. I feel better for that. We'll be there to support each other whilst we're away from home.'

Her mum nodded. Although she knew Amanda was a bit of a tearaway, she was happy that Cassie would settle in better having someone she knew close by. Both girls were going to Edinburgh in a few weeks' time to undertake Business Studies. Cassie was well liked by her peers. She had long blonde hair and blue eyes. She was one of those fortunate people who had no trouble in keeping her figure. Although it was never said, she was the envy of her friends. University life would suit her fine; she would fit in well. She would be a good friend to have around and help keep Amanda's feet firmly on the ground.

* * *

The academic year was to start on the eighteenth of September with a Welcome Week commencing on the eleventh. The day finally arrived. It was the beginning of a new life for Cassie, no longer within the comfort of the family home. She would be independent. Who knows where it would lead? She was feeling excited, but very apprehensive. It was a big step, a leap into the unknown. A few days prior to the start date Cassie and her parents drove to Edinburgh, via the M6, across the border through Jedburgh and into the capital. 'It'll be good for you to have a few days to settle in before the start of the academic year.' Her mum was twisting round from the front seat to speak to Cassie, who was stretched out on the rear seat and being unusually quiet.

'I'm getting butterflies now mum.'

Her mum laughed. 'That's normal love. Everyone else will be experiencing the same feelings.' She quickly switched the subject. 'By the way when is Amanda coming up?'

'Day after tomorrow.'

'At least you'll have someone to pal up with once she arrives.'

Silence followed for the next thirty miles.

Dad began to slow down. 'Coffee? Anything to eat?'

Cassie and her mum replied in unison. 'Yes please.'

Over coffee and a tuna sandwich in a service station, mum re-visited the conversation of Cassie settling into her new surroundings. 'We want to make sure you're okay with your room in the halls of residence. Remind me again which one it is.'

'Blair House, it's part of the Pollocks Hall site.' Cassie sounded upbeat in an attempt to dispel the butterflies in her stomach, which she hoped would soon learn to fly in formation! 'It's only a twenty-minute walk into town and the same to the campus.'

They finally arrived in Edinburgh.

Edinburgh: a beautiful city with majestic architecture, most of which was constructed from grey sandstone. The old town was a jumble of cobbled streets, narrow wynds and ginnels. Overlooking the town was the formidable Edinburgh Castle perched high on a hill at the far end of Princes Street. The street was the main shopping thoroughfare and home to the grand monument built in 1840 of Sir Walter Scott, writer and proud Scot. Edinburgh is built on an extinct volcano and, for the more energetic, can be climbed via Arthur's Seat, 250 metres above the city. The city is also boasts The Palace of Holyrood House built in 1671, the residence of King Charles III when visiting the area. The only image of Edinburgh that Cassie had ever seen was the Edinburgh Tattoo on television.

As they drove through the city centre on their way to the halls of residence, Cassie was impressed with what she saw. 'It looks lovely mum. I'm sure I'll be okay once I've settled in. I'll be glad when Mand arrives. Apparently next week they have a Welcome Week, not sure what that entails but it sounds good.'

They found Blair House without any difficulty, were welcomed by a friendly receptionist and shown to the accommodation which she would be sharing with Amanda.

Cassie's parents scanned the room and nodded in approval. Her dad was keen to leave Cassie and her mum to sort out the accommodation and decided to take a walk around the grounds. Her mum smiled. 'Well, it's clean.' It was always her first criteria as she opened and closed various cupboards and bedroom doors checking everything was in order.

Cassie flopped onto the bed; concern spread across her face. 'I do hope I cope.'

Her mum sat down beside her and tried to reassure her. 'Of course you will. It'll all feel a little strange to start with.'

She jumped up patting Cassie on the knee and headed for the fridge. 'You can help me unpack some goodies I've brought for you to fill your fridge and cupboards to start you off.'

Cassie enthusiastically unloaded the bags whilst her mum put things away, calling out as she went through the bags. 'Coffee, tea, milk. Ah, Weetabix, rice, pasta, tins of soup.' She looked at her mum in appreciation. 'This is like Aladdin's cave, thanks mum.'

Her mum lifted an insulation bag onto the unit. 'You won't starve – yet!' She proceeded to unload several frozen meals. Her mum looked at her disapprovingly. 'These are just to start you off, don't live on frozen foods.'

Cassie laughed and gave her mum a hug. 'I won't, promise.'

Her dad re-entered the room having had a saunter around the building. 'I'm impressed,' he said, 'security looks good.' He casually leaned against the door, 'the three years will soon go you know. Before you know it you'll be home for Christmas,' he pushed himself off from the door, 'come on you two, we need to book into the hotel, then we'll have dinner. How does that sound?'

'That sounds great dad, thanks.'

Before Mr and Mrs Melling departed for home the next morning, they called back to Blair House to check on Cassie. She opened the door, half-asleep, surprised to see them.

'Oh, hi, come in.'

'We thought we'd catch up before heading home.'

'Thanks for coming round, can I get you a coffee?'

'Yes please,' her mum replied, 'I'll make it.'

Cassie put her hand on her mum's shoulder and pushed her down onto the sofa. 'No! I'll make it! You're guests,' she insisted.

Eventually her dad made the move. 'We'll have to go Cass, it's a long drive home.'

Cassie nodded, tears in her eyes, she knew this moment would eventually arrive. Her dad kissed her on the cheek, then her mum held onto her for as long as she could. 'Look after yourself, Cass.'

Cassie couldn't look her parents in the eye, nodded and tried to hold her tears back. 'I will.'

Once her parents had left Cassie sat on the bed and sobbed her heart out. She felt so lonely and lost; frightened of the unknown. She didn't know how long she'd sat on the edge of the bed but eventually spoke sharply to herself. 'Get a grip, Cass. Mand will be here tomorrow.'

On the drive home Cassie's mum was quiet and quickly teared up when thinking of Cassie being alone, although she was aware Amanda would be arriving the next day.

'You okay?' Cassie's dad asked, glancing sideways as he drove, 'you're quiet. Cass will be okay you know,' he reassured her, guessing why she was quiet, 'Amanda will be there tomorrow.'

She gave a weak smile. 'I know Amanda is arriving tomorrow...I have concerns about Cassie being around her.'

Mr Melling looked sideways once more. 'Amanda?'

His wife nodded. 'She's a bit of a tearaway. I just hope Cass doesn't get sidetracked. Amanda's been in a few scrapes over the years.'

Her husband nodded thoughtfully but remained silent.

* * *

Mandy arrived with her parents just after lunch the next day. The two girls hugged each other. Cassie was relieved to see a friendly face and Mandy was pleased that someone she knew was already ensconced, albeit it had only been for one day. Amanda's parents took them both for lunch in town then said their goodbyes, leaving the two friends to explore the campus.

The following day they went to the main Uni building and picked up an itinerary. It was headed *Welcome Week*, which the Uni had thoughtfully produced for the freshers. Over a coffee they checked over the itinerary. Cassie put her cup down and pointed to the top of the list. 'Intro by the Dean in the main hall Thursday morning. We'd better have a wander over there this morning, so we know where we're going on Thursday', she scanned further down the list, 'then we're split up into courses and welcomed by the head of department. From there we're given a tour around the campus to show us where everything is, then after lunch an intro to the lecturers.'

Mandy stood up. 'Another coffee Cass?'

'Er, yeah, please.' She continued to wade through the document until Mandy returned with two cups of coffee. Mandy sat down and lit up a cigarette. Cass looked shocked. 'How long have you been smoking?'

Mandy blew smoke into the air. 'A few months. I met a lad in The Oasis, he got me started again.'

The Oasis was a popular disco in Manchester city centre. When Cassie had been revising and laboriously burning the midnight oil in preparation for her A levels, Mandy had been gallivanting around the discos in the city centre. She'd pestered Cassie to join her, but Cassie had reluctantly declined knowing she had to put the effort into her studies. Mandy pulled the itinerary around on the table to face her. 'There's a map on the back showing the layout of the campus, that'll be useful...it shows us where the students' union is, a priority when you're at Uni,' she added with a mischievous smile.

Cassie thoughtfully sipped at her coffee, not responding.

* * *

The formal welcome to Uni was a friendly and, thankfully, brief affair.

Once all the freshers were assigned to their various course groups, they were given a whirlwind tour of the campus by third-year students: the refectory, counselling rooms, sick room, the students' union – which appeared to create the most interest– and the gym. They were then left to roam the campus to investigate the several marquees that had been set up on the lawns. Each marquee had staff and students encouraging the new students to join the clubs they represented: the debating society, chess club, line dancing, drama group, astronomy, the choice was endless. Cassie and Mandy returned to their rooms without having committed to any of the extracurricular activities.

The weeks went by reasonably smoothly, although from time to time there was friction between Cassie and Mandy. After all the years of knowing Mandy, Cassie hadn't realised how untidy Mandy was. She had a habit of leaving clothes lying around, dirty pots were left in the sink or on the kitchen unit whilst she swanned around titivating her hair or make-up. On several occasions Cassie had come home from classes to find Mandy still in bed or sprawled out on the sofa reading a magazine. 'Mand! You've got to pull your weight. The place looks a mess! I can't keep tidying up after you.'

Amanda would often dismiss Cassie's grumbles with a, *You worry too much, Cass, relax. Chill out.*

On one of the few days they attended lessons together, Mandy tentatively made a suggestion to Cassie. 'I got talking to one of the third year's who's organising a pub crawl for some of the freshers. He's invited me, are you coming?'

Cassie was non-committal. 'I'll see, I've got assignments to do.'

Mandy responded showing her exasperation. 'Cass, you've got to go out sometime! You can't just sit in the room working...come on, you'll enjoy it.'

Cassie sighed and forced a laugh. 'You're right Mand. OK, I'll come. It'll do me good.'

Mandy slapped her on the back. 'Good for you, it'll be a good night.'

* * *

On Saturday night, they met with several others in the students' union for a few drinks before embarking on the town centre pub crawl. First on the agenda was The Laird, then The Renfrew in Cowgate, quickly followed by The Castle in Princes Street and, lastly, The Sporran in Forsythe Street.

Three hours of drinking had made Cassie feel noticeably unwell, unsteady on her feet, slurring her speech and, uncharacteristically for her, argumentative.

'Come on, Cass, I'll get a taxi. You can't get on the bus like this.' Cassie didn't want to be fussed over and through half-closed eyes, told Mandy to leave her alone, that she was perfectly capable of getting on a bus.

Just as she felt she was about to vomit, she turned to Mandy. 'Thanks, Mand, I think I will get a taxi.'

The next morning, in fact it was nearer lunchtime, Cassie slowly walked, bleary eyed into the kitchen where Mandy was enjoying a quiet coffee and bacon sandwich. 'Cass! You okay? You weren't too good last night.'

Cassie shook her head and sat down. She looked accusingly at Mandy. 'How come you feel okay? You had as much to drink as me.'

Mandy rose and picked up the coffee pot, waggling it at Cassie. 'Practice, Cass, practice.'

Cassie shook her head in frustration. Mandy seemed to be able to get through life without any effort. She often missed classes and yet managed to score high marks...and could drink most of her peers under the table. Mand was definitely a party girl! 'Live for the moment' was Mandy's mantra.

Although Cassie felt rough the night after the pub crawl, she admitted to herself that she'd enjoyed letting her hair down. On reflection there was more to life than assignments and revising for exams.

The end of year exams were due in a couple of months and would be upon them before they knew it. She needed to get her act together and concentrate on finishing the first year of her studies on a high note.

Mandy had met a boy on one of her frequent visits to the students' union. 'You'll like him Cass. He's from Manchester!'

'Manchester?' cried Cass.

'Yeah. I saw him in the union and thought I recognised him from The Oasis, caught his eye, started to chat and we clicked. I've been seeing him for a couple months now.'

Cassie looked askance. 'What course is he on?'

'Sociology.'

Cassie harrumphed, clearly unimpressed.

'He's got a car,' Mandy said to try to convince Cassie he was okay, 'he always seems to have plenty of money and he's a good laugh.'

'Name?' asked Cassie abruptly.

'Aaron, Aaron Crossly.' She sat down beside Cassie. 'Look, he's invited us to a party on Saturday night in Leith. Why don't you come?'

'Cos I've got assignments! And in any case isn't Leith a bit rough?'

'Cassie, we'll be with Aaron and his mates, we'll be okay.' Mandy let it rest for a few moments then spoke as if she was speaking to a five-year old. 'You used assignments as an excuse the last time before the pub crawl, remember? and you enjoyed it. You can't keep stopping in night after night, you've got to get out occasionally and enjoy yourself,' her voice rose an octave, 'it's one night! You can do as much assignment work as you want on Sunday. Come on Cassie,' she pleaded, 'it'll be a laugh.'

Cassie shook her head, sighed then reluctantly relented. 'Okay, I'll come.'

Aaron picked them both up on Saturday night in his car. Mandy introduced them to each other. Aaron twisted round in the driver's seat and shook hands with Cassie. 'Good to see you Cassie, I've heard all about you,' he said in his flat Manchester accent.

'All good I hope,' replied Cassie for something to say.

It didn't take long to reach the tenement block in Leith. Aaron stopped the car, pulled on the handbrake then reached over to the glove box. He took out a plain paper package which he unwrapped. He handed a couple of white pills to Mandy and the same to Cassie. Mandy swallowed them straight down; Cassie held them up. 'What are these?'

Aaron held his hand up. 'Sorry Cassie, I should have explained. They're just a couple of pills to keep you awake. It'll be an all-nighter.'

Mandy reassured her friend. 'It's okay Cass. I've taken them several times; they just help you stay awake.'

Cass looked at them hesitantly. 'Er, okay,' then reluctantly swallowed them. As they got out of the car Cassie looked up at the building. It was a five-storey tenement in a row of similar buildings which looked as though they had previously been used for warehousing for the docks a stone's throw away. The once beautiful grey sandstone stonework was now black, the result of many years of industrial smoke. She followed Aaron and Mandy, who seemed very familiar with the building, through a badly scarred door and up cold concrete steps, worn smooth over the years, and made their way to the third floor. The dim lighting on the stairs and landings made for an uncomfortable atmosphere. The walls between floors were dirty and missing plaster in several places. She tugged Mandy's jacket and whispered. 'I don't like this, Mand. It feels iffy.'

Mandy slowed and tried to reassure her. 'It's okay, promise. I've been to parties here a few times and it's been fine. Stick with me Cass.'

Cassie resigned herself to having to stay and make the best of it. She didn't know how to get back to their halls of residence even if she'd wanted to, so dutifully followed Mandy into the flat. It was heaving with bodies and pungent smelling smoke. There were bodies everywhere, some lying on the floor, some dancing, some smooching, some appearing to be having normal conversations, if indeed it was possible to have a conversation. The music was deafening. Mandy nudged her and smiled as if to say, *'Isn't this great.'*

She sat on a couch whilst Mandy and Aaron were dancing in the limited space available, when someone sat next to her. 'Cassie, isn't it?'

She glanced at the newcomer and half-smiled. 'Yes.'

He held his hand out. 'Hamish...I'm a mate of Aaron's. He pointed you out. Fancy another drink?' he asked noticing her empty glass.

She relaxed slightly and nodded. 'Yes please, a beer.'

He was back in seconds with two beers and sat down beside her. 'Mandy tells me you've been mates for years.'

She nodded. 'Yes.' She looked askance at Hamish for a second then queried, 'are you a student at the Uni? You look older than all the rest of us,' she added as a way of explanation for her question.

He chuckled and shook his head. 'No. I work.'

'Doing what?'

He rocked his head from side to side. 'This and that.'

She smiled to herself and thought, *what a smart arse!*

Glancing at her watch she was surprised to see the time – midnight! The pills Aaron had given her really worked! Cassie didn't remember arriving home from the party and woke up to find she was still dressed and lying on the sofa. Mandy was standing by the kitchen unit. 'Great night Cass?'

Cassie nodded and fell back to sleep.

* * *

College life continued over the weeks with classes, studying and parties. The Christmas break had come and gone. She'd enjoyed being home for the vacation, but she was glad to be back in Edinburgh; she was getting used to the independence and the partying lifestyle. Her college work was beginning to suffer. She'd missed deadlines for a couple of assignments, failed and was forced to re-do the assignments. As a result of the late-night partying she had also missed a few classes, mainly accounts, which had been scheduled for early mornings. As she hated accounts she didn't have a guilty conscience about it. However, on occasion she heard a voice in her head saying – *Get your act together Cass, you have one chance at Uni to set yourself up for the rest of your life.* Nevertheless, her new party image was slowly taking over. She had been seeing Hamish for some time now. Her common sense told her to ditch him – he was too much of an enigma. She still didn't know exactly what he did for a living, how he made his money – which seemed to be in plentiful supply, but life felt good. Having the freedom away from home was something new for her, and she loved it.

The occasional friction between herself and Mandy still showed its ugly head from time to time. Mandy was still annoyingly untidy, didn't do her fair share of the work in keeping their room respectable and often didn't come home, only to admit later she'd stayed at Aaron's. More irritating was the fact that completing and passing assignments seemed so easy to Mandy. She was incredibly bright, and academia seemed second nature to her, whereas Cassie still had to graft and burn the midnight oil.

On the other hand, Cassie was grateful that Mandy had dragged her out to parties and clubs, often reluctantly to start with but which, if she was honest, she enjoyed. Cassie was the new party girl on the block, she was still getting mainly Bs for her course work and was happy to accept second best and enjoy the party life and club scene.

'New club in town Cassie. Saturday night, no argument! Aaron and Hamish will be there.'

Saturday night came around. Whilst Cassie was completing one of her assignments, for Mandy, the afternoon was spent carefully applying make-up, trying several options with her hair before deciding on a pony-tail. The club, Mango's, was in a cellar down a cobbled side street and illuminated by a yellow flashing sign. It was in stark contrast with the street during the daytime when it looked dark and dingy. They arrived at the same time as Aaron and Hamish. 'Sorry we couldn't pick you up girls, we've been out of town on business.'

The bouncers on the door were letting in small groups of three and four people at a time. Finally, the foursome headed down the stairs into the darkened cellar and into deafening noise and a haze of smoke. A DJ was shouting his banal spiel from the far corner, quickly followed by some pounding music as they made their way to the bar. Having had a few sips of their drinks, Aaron and Mandy joined the throng in the middle of the dance area and moved with the flow. Hamish excused himself from time to time to chat to various people and Cassie questioned herself yet again why she'd allowed Mandy to persuade her to come to the club. If the truth be known she had now started to hate the clubs, the atmosphere, the noise, the fact that it was impossible to have a conversation. She tolerated the noise, the music and the crowd until she couldn't stand it anymore. Once the others had returned to their seats she announced. 'I've had enough, guys, I'm making for home. I'll grab a taxi.'

Hamish offered to accompany her to a taxi rank on the next street.

As he walked her down the road he suddenly stopped her.

'Hold on a sec Cass. I've just seen someone who owes me money.'

He approached a man who was standing by the edge of the pavement lighting a cigarette. Cassie couldn't see him clearly in the street lighting, but she could see that the stranger was tall and thin with long straggly hair. By their arm gestures and aggressive body language the two men were obviously arguing. She suddenly saw the flash of a knife. She couldn't believe her eyes! Hamish had pulled a knife from inside his jacket and was threatening the other man! What happened next was all too quick. The man pushed Hamish away and ran across the road to escape. Hamish took chase only to trip on the kerb on the other side of the road, his knife scooting across to the centre of the street. The man stopped and saw Hamish lying in the road with blood pouring from his head.

The stranger and Cassie locked eyes.

The blade of the knife sparkled on the wet road.

Both knew what the other was thinking.

Both were equidistant from the knife.

Both knew what the next move was.

Both ran for the knife.

Cassie shot across the road; her agility surprised even herself as reached the knife a second before the stranger. At the same moment as she grabbed the knife the stranger grabbed Cassie around the neck. With one almighty effort Cassie lunged back and stuck the knife into the stranger. The man collapsed. Cassie stood with the knife in her hands looking down at a man she'd never met, bleeding copiously from his stomach. She dropped the knife and ran. Someone coming out of the club must have seen the altercation and phoned for an ambulance and the police.

As Cassie ran aimlessly down another dark side street, she saw a taxi dropping someone off. She hailed it and gave the driver her address, the distant sound of sirens in her ears. Once home she quickly paid the taxi driver and dashed into her room. She immediately stripped off to have a shower, dumped her clothes in the linen box and scrubbed her skin until it hurt. *Christ! What have I done!*

She was sitting in her pyjamas in the dark when Mandy arrived home. Her hair was still wet and she was clutching a glass of wine. She had a wild look in her eyes. Mandy panicked when she saw the state Cassie was in. 'You okay Cass? You look terrified.'

Cassie looked up at her, then burst into floods of tears. 'Mand, I've done something dreadful.'

Mandy slowly made her way over to the kitchen unit and poured herself a wine. Leaning back on the unit she shook her head at the state of Cassie. 'What happened? You look awful!'

Cassie took a long swig of wine then looked at Mandy, pleadingly. 'You've got to help me. I think I've killed someone.'

'What!' she shrieked, 'tell me you're kidding.'

Cassie shook her head, and the tears ran faster. Her friend put her arm around Cassie. 'Tell me what happened.'

Cassie tried to tell the story in between deep sobs. 'It happened outside the club'.

Mandy put her hand to her mouth in shock. 'Oh, no! When Aaron and I came out of the club the street was full of cops and an ambulance.'

Cassie nodded and went on to explain what had happened. 'It was all over in seconds, Mand. I thought whoever it was, was going to stab Hamish so I reacted.' Mandy was lost for words. 'Mand, what am I going to do? The cops will be looking for me!' Cassie burst into hysterical sobbing once more.

Mandy went to pour another glass of wine for herself. 'Let me think.'

The silence seemed to go on for ever, until Mandy broke the impasse. 'Listen to me Cass', she hesitated before she continued, 'listen carefully, Aaron and Hamish were involved in drugs.'

Cassie stared at her friend not comprehending what she was saying. 'What do you mean?'

Mandy spoke slowly and clearly. 'Where do you think they both got their money from?'

Cassie looked down at her shaking hands. 'Oh my God. What am I going to do?' She straightened up with some resolve, 'I need to go to the police. Tell them everything. It was an accident.'

Mandy panicked. 'Whoa there. You can't go to the police. They'll link you to Aaron and Hamish,' she let that gem of information sink in.

'Look, leave it with me, I'll have a word with Aaron. He's got contacts. They'll know what to do. Try and get some sleep, we'll sort it out tomorrow.'

EDINBURGH TIMES
Last night there was an altercation in the club area of the city. It is reported that two men were seen arguing when one of them pulled a knife. A witness said a woman was also involved. It is not known whether she knew the two men but police are asking her to come forward. One of the men was declared dead on arrival at St Joseph's. The second man was admitted to the hospital with head wounds. Police are waiting to speak to him. They are asking for anyone with information to please contact their nearest police station.

* * *

PART THREE

At breakfast the next morning Cassie slowly trudged into the kitchen, dark shadows around her eyes from lack of sleep. She sat down and acknowledged Mandy with a wan smile. Mandy sat down next to her traumatised friend. 'Cass,' she said slowly, 'I've spoken to Aaron, and he's spoken to one of his contacts,' she bit the inside of her lip before continuing, 'they've suggested we get you out of the country. They can't risk you being interviewed by the police; it would put a lot of people in danger.'

Cassie suddenly woke up to what was being suggested. 'Out of the country! Where? Where would I go? I can't just leave the country. What about my parents; what do I say to them?'

Mandy patted her hand. 'Aaron has it all in hand. He's coming over this morning.'

The atmosphere between the two girls was subdued. The silence was interrupted by a sharp knock at the door. Cassie looked terrified. 'Who is it?' she asked Mandy, her eyes darting wildly around the room.

Mandy spoke softly to reassure her. 'Don't worry, it'll be Aaron.'

She answered the door and Cassie could hear a muffled conversation in the hallway before they both entered the lounge. Aaron tried to sound up-beat. 'Hi, Cassie, how are we this morning?'

Cassie gave him a weak smile. 'Not good. I know Hamish is in hospital and I hope he's not too badly hurt, but this is all his fault. If he hadn't produced that knife, none of this would have happened.'

'I know, I know, and I'm sorry Cassie. I understand the predicament you're in,' Aaron exchanged eye contact with Mandy before explaining the plan, 'the cops will be looking for you now; there were witnesses. If you are identified it's inevitable that you'll be linked to me and Hamish.'

She interrupted him. 'How is Hamish?'

Aaron stifled a laugh. 'He'll live. Anyway,' he continued, 'we need to get you out of the country until it all dies down.' He took a large brown envelope from his inside pocket and tipped a sheet of paper out onto the coffee table then turned it round to face Cassie. 'This is the plan. By the end of the week I'll have all the relevant documents you'll need, new passport, money, etc. During the week get your hair cut short, dyed, anything to change your appearance. On Sunday you'll fly to Holland, change at Schiphol airport and catch a flight to Singapore, then on to Perth, Australia. I've got friends who will put you up for a few days, then it's up to you to find a job and accommodation so you can blend into the community,' he passed her another piece of paper, 'this is my friend's address and contact number in Perth, it's in Northbridge. It's a multi-cultural area. There are lots of cafés and restaurants in the area, so finding work shouldn't be a problem.' He could see the horrified look spreading across Cassie's face and tried to reassure her. 'It'll only be until the hoo-ha dies down, then you'll be back.'

During the week she reluctantly cut her hair short into a bob as best she could and dyed it dark brown. She looked at herself in the mirror and cried. This wasn't who she was. By the end of the week she was Pamela Jenks, backpacker, a student taking a gap year out to tour Australia and south-east Asia. Cassie felt physically sick at the immensity of the task ahead: travel to the other side of the world, stay with people she didn't know, find work in an environment that was alien to her.

Oh my God, what will mum and dad say when they find out I've dropped out of Uni.

* * *

DI Bill McClean stood in front of his team, his DS, Shirley Dantzig, standing next to him. They had been allocated a temporary briefing room whilst the main station was having a safety check after asbestos had been discovered in the roof. The room was cramped, dusty and had a smell which McClean couldn't quite put his finger on.

DI McClean was due for retirement next year. He had been a dedicated police officer all his life and was looking forward to his pending retirement, when he could spend time listening to jazz and getting lost in his beloved greenhouse. He'd done his bit, joined as a cadet aged eighteen and successfully moved up the promotional ladder and was now DI of a dedicated murder investigation team. He was a rotund gentleman with bright ginger hair, extrovert, and famous for his outrageous ties. He was also a DI who everyone wanted to work with. He had a formidable track record and reputation.

He lifted himself up to his full height, albeit not very tall. 'Thank you everyone for being on time. We have a murder on our hands and someone still in hospital with a severe head wound. Last night there was an altercation between two men in Canal Street in the heart of club land. The man who died is a Trevor Moffat, a petty thief on the periphery of the drug scene and well known to the police. The man who is still in hospital is Hamish McGonnal, also known to the police.' He scanned the group. 'DC Jones and Kershaw, would you go and interview the bouncers at Mango's and the other clubs along Canal Street. I know they won't want to talk to us, but we need to ask the usual questions.' The two DCs duly nodded, clicked their pens and made notes. 'Mallard and Prescott, check along the street, see who's got CCTV. Have a look see if they show us anything. Shirley and I are going to check out Moffat's and McGonnal's families. Any questions?' He received no response so closed his file and the briefing. 'Right, back here tomorrow afternoon, four o'clock, Okay?'

* * *

By 4.15pm the next day, everyone was seated in the cramped briefing room as best they could. McClean brought everyone to order. 'OK everyone. Grab a coffee if you need one before we start.' There was a scraping of chairs as one or two left the room for their hourly fix. Once they were all back, McClean looked around the room. 'Right, what have we got?'

DCs Jones and Kershaw predictably got nothing from any of the bouncers. Alan Jones chuckled. 'It's amazing boss. All the clubs down Canal Street, each with one or two bouncers on the door, and nobody saw anything, surprise, surprise.'

McClean nodded. 'I know, it's a cultural thing. Shirley and I also hit a brick wall. Neither of the two men involved lived at home, neither were married; both lived in flats at opposite ends of town. I'll organise search warrants for both properties.' He moved his gaze to DCs Mallard and Prescott. 'How did you two get on?'

DC Julie Prescott spoke for the pair. 'We managed to get hold of some very interesting CCTV footage. A company just across the street from Mango's, a clothing importer, has had several break-ins over the last couple of years, hence the CCTV. When we looked at it, it shows

McGonnal confronting the victim. You can see McGonnal pulling a knife then there's a scuffle. It's very clear. The footage shows McGonnal falling and the victim running across the road to escape. That's where the footage fails, there's no coverage once they cross the road, but there was something else boss. The footage also shows a woman who was at the scene, but it only shows her back, she's not identifiable.'

McClean was now feeling more upbeat. 'No matter, it's all useful, we've now got something to work with. Well done you two.'

DC Mallard added, 'Sir, the other bit of info we managed to get was that McGonnal was already under observation from the drug squad. They've been watching him for some time. They believe him to be the intermediary between the main drug honcho and the people who distribute it on the streets. We'll interview him once the hospital gives us the okay.'

* * *

Cassie braced herself then phoned her parents from Edinburgh airport. She told them she had dropped out of Uni and was taking a gap year to 'find herself'. Her explanation sounded so pathetic, but that's all she could think of. She knew they would be devastated. They had such high hopes for her to achieve and make a great future for herself.

* * *

Cassie was in tears as she heard the public address system call for the Singapore flight via Schiphol. She held her passport ready to board, under her new identity – Pamela Jenks, aged 20, student. She hated herself for having got herself into such a mess and imagined the conversation her parents would be having after receiving her phone call.

'Where did we go wrong? Has she been caught up in some strange cult? Is she pregnant? Why would she give up a golden opportunity to do something with her life? Was Amanda Wallis behind all this?'

Cassie's mum picked up the phone and called Amanda's parents. They were no help. They hadn't heard from Amanda in weeks and assumed everything was okay with them both.

Cassie sat on the plane to Holland in a state of panic! She felt lost, frightened, isolated. She'd never been by herself on a plane before, never mind the distance she had to travel to her ultimate destination. Who was waiting at the other end? She remembered feeling lost when she first arrived at Edinburgh Uni; how in the early days she was constantly on the verge of tears. At least when she was at Uni her parents were only a phone call or a train journey away, but this was very different. The flight to Schiphol airport was, thankfully, a comparatively short one. There was a half-hour lay-over, with no disembarking before continuing the journey to Singapore. She had a two-hour lay-over at Changi Airport so wandered around aimlessly in and out of the many shops, stopping for a bite to eat before re-boarding for the last section of her long journey to Perth, capital of Western Australia. She'd always wanted to visit Australia – but not under these circumstances.

The plane finally touched down in Perth. She could see from her window seat that Perth was living up to its reputation. The sky was deep blue, not a cloud in the sky, no wind, not a branch on the trees moved as the plane slowly taxied to the terminal. After the inevitable wait whilst some passengers slowly gathered their bags from the overhead lockers and shuffled their way to the exit, she felt the hot air drifting into the plane. The panic returned! What a mess she'd got herself into! She prayed she would remember that she was no longer Cassandra Melling, she was now Pamela Jenks. *What were these people like she had to contact? Were they involved in drugs? It was highly likely if they were friends of Aaron's. How would she find a job? Would the UK police eventually find her? They'd certainly keep looking, after all she had murdered someone!*

Outside the airport she grabbed a taxi and gave him the piece of paper Aaron had given her. 'It's in Northbridge, apparently,' she offered in a confident tone.

He turned to the rear seat. 'Yes, I know.' She was taken aback at his brusque response. He turned back to the front, pulled into the taxi exit lane and never said another word – she guessed because he was Iranian, or certainly Middle Eastern and was struggling to understand her. Finally, he announced their arrival. 'This is it. Thirty dollars, please,' he said as he pointed to the meter mounted on the dash.

She paid him, then found herself on a pavement outside a strange building in a strange city. It was stiflingly hot, the heat from the concrete pavement seeping through the soles of her shoes. It was a two-storey wooden building, probably built in the mid-nineteen hundreds and looked as though it could do with a complete rebuild. The paint was faded, peeling in places, the wooden surrounds rotting, the side path had become home to two derelict vehicles, one without wheels. Faded curtains hung loosely from some of the windows. She pulled the piece of paper Aaron had given her out of her rucksack to check she was at the right address, 47 Simpson Street: Sadly, she was. She tentatively pushed open the shabby door which led into a dark hallway. The inside was in a worse state than the outside. It smelled musty and dust mites floated through the air highlighted by the sun streaming through a tiny side window. There was no reception desk or bell to ring so she stood there for a moment wondering what to do, when a door opened and a young girl emerged. She had spiky hair and was wearing a pair of dungarees. She nodded a brief acknowledgment to Pamela and made to walk past her. Pamela held up her hand. 'Excuse me. I'm looking for a Tony Melody.'

The girl pointed to a door at the other end of the corridor. 'End one on the right.'

'Thank you.' Pamela walked to the door the girl had pointed to and gave a gentle knock. It was immediately opened by a middle-aged man. He was short, swarthy and wore an earring in his left ear. She noticed a tattoo on the back of his hand. With his hand leaning on the door jamb and his facial expression looking as though he was annoyed at being disturbed, he abruptly asked. 'Yes?'

'Tony Melody?'

"Yes,' he replied, accentuating the word with a note of caution, 'who wants to know?' She detected the trace of an Italian accent.

She held her hand out. 'Pamela Jenks. A friend of Aaron's from the UK.'

Melody relaxed. 'Ah, he did contact me, said you needed a place to kip down for a couple of nights.'

She nodded nervously...*only a couple of nights...?* 'Er, yeah. I've nowhere to stay.'

He nodded and invited her into his room. 'It can only be for a few nights; I've got people coming and going all the time', he said in an abrupt manner. He picked up on her panicked expression and tried, unsuccessfully, to reassure her. 'Don't worry. You can stay until you find your feet.'

'Oh, right, thank you.'

He opened the door again. 'Come, I'll show you your room.'

She dutifully followed him back down the corridor, up the carpetless stairs onto the first-floor landing where he swung open a door and motioned for her to enter. She stepped in and was instantly horrified. The room was almost bare. It had a single bed with sheets containing stains of a dubious origin draped across it, an easy chair, the fabric in urgent need of a degrease, a wardrobe with only one door and faded curtains. In one corner was a unit containing a sink, a small hob, a cheap kettle and toaster to one side.

She was massively disappointed. This was not what she had expected, or was used to. Her mind flicked back to her previous lifestyle and the aspirations she held, and then mused over what she had now. Melody's voice snapped her out of her brooding. 'Okay, I'll leave you to it.' With that he turned and disappeared out of the room.

She flopped down onto the bed, stared up at the ceiling, tears running down her cheeks. She didn't dare phone her parents and tell them the mess she was in. *No doubt there'll be a warrant out for my arrest*!

Slowly she unpacked her case and hung some of her clothes in the wardrobe. She didn't unpack everything as she had no intention of staying in this dump. Tomorrow she planned to go into the centre of Perth, find a job and move on. 'Come on Pammy,' she muttered and smiled inwardly at how easily she referred to herself as Pam. It was a question of self-preservation.

* * *

Early the next morning, after a restless night, she purposefully strode out of her lodgings, then turned left into a newsagent's store. 'Do you have an A to Z of Perth please?' After she'd made her purchase, she asked a stranger the way into the city centre and was directed over the railway horseshoe bridge and into a large square, Forest Chase. Settling into one of the numerous cafes, she ordered a croissant and a coffee whilst she studied the A to Z. According to the map there were two main shopping streets, Hay and Murray. Saint Georges Terrace was obviously where the business end of Perth was located. She wandered up and down the main streets and through the various arcades linking them. Feeling more comfortable in this small, clean and hospitable city she began to relax a little. Maybe this is where she could start a new life, away from the hurly burly of the UK. She looked up at the sky, a bright blue, and still no clouds! What a difference to the daily drabness of the UK where the constant low cloud was so oppressive. She strolled down to the River Swan. It was a wide expanse of clear water, sparkling in the early morning sun. She wandered along its banks to the jetty area where one or two restaurants and cafes lined the river. Sitting on a bench overlooking the river she watched the people passing by on the narrow footpath in front of her. Some were on their way to work, smartly dressed carrying take-away coffees. It was obvious some were overseas visitors from the clothes they wore, whilst others were either jogging or ambling along, taking time to enjoy the peace and slow life of Perth. Heading back toward the centre, she made it her business to search out employment agencies. A job! Her own flat! A new life! New friends!

Despite the warm sunny weather, a dark cloud constantly followed her. *I killed someone! I could be arrested!*

She approached an office building across the road from a shopping mall. She read the list of names on the side of the main entrance wall within the four-storey block. Pushing her way through the heavy double glass door she confidently strolled past reception before taking the lift to the third floor where she found Western Employment Agency. Double doors slid back as she approached. She immediately felt the cold air conditioning, which was very welcome after her stroll around town. A woman in her mid-thirties with immaculate make-up, wearing a light-weight white top and navy slacks was sitting at the reception desk. Her name badge pinned to her blouse collar said 'Nicola'. She greeted her with a smile and a strong Aussie accent. 'Good morning, how can I help you?'

Pammy smiled back. 'I'm new in Perth. I'm looking for some work.'

'Sure. Would you like to take a seat. I'll get one of our advisors to see you. 'Could I have your name, please?'

Pam coughed slightly. 'Pamela Jenks.'

'I shan't be a moment,' the receptionist replied and disappeared into a large open office behind her whilst Pamela Jenks sat down and looked around. On the walls hung black and white photos of old Perth. *Old!* Pam said to herself with a smile. *I've got relatives older than Perth!*

The receptionist soon re-appeared. 'Sonia will see you soon.'

Pam was still looking around the reception area when she heard a voice calling her.

'Pamela?'

Pam nodded and stood. 'Would you like to come through?' Sonia beckoned her through as she opened her office door. Sonia wore carefully applied make-up and sported unnaturally white teeth. Pam followed her to the far side of the open office and into a glass cubicle. 'Please take a seat.'

Pam sat down and looked around the office as Sonia organised herself with pad and pen. The corner office overlooked the Swan River which was flat and blue. One office wall was lined with filing cabinets and a large abstract painting. 'Can I get you a coffee or a tea?' Asked Sonia.

Pam shook her head. 'No, thank you.'

Her interviewer smiled and picked up her pen. 'I just need to take a few details from you. Could I take your name?'

Pam nodded her consent. 'Pamela Jenks.'

'Are you currently registered with us?'

She shook her head. 'No, I've only just arrived in Perth.'

'Address?'

'I've got a room at 47 Simpson Street, Northbridge until I can find somewhere more permanent.' She hoped Sonia didn't know the building.

'Have you emigrated or are you visiting?'

'Visiting.'

'Gap year?'

'Yes.'

Sonia put her pen down and leaned back in her chair, a look of curiosity forming across her face. 'What are you studying?'

'Er, law.'

Sonia's smile broadened. 'Congratulations. I've got a law degree, from some time ago I might add,' she joked.

Damn!

'Where are you studying?'

Pam answered in a confident voice. 'Edinburgh.'

Sonia pointed to her chest. 'Melbourne.'

Pam tried to look impressed then Sonia continued. 'So Pam, what work are you looking for?'

'I don't really mind. I just want to get myself into the community. Hopefully find a place of my own - perhaps waitressing or reception.'

Sonia nodded. 'Okay,' she said as she made some notes, 'do you want to stay in Perth or are you happy to go further afield?'

'Either I don't mind.'

Sonia leaned forward on her desk. 'Are you up for an interview this afternoon?'

'Er, yes.'

Sonia picked up the phone and spoke to someone. Pam could hear only one side of the conversation but it was obvious Sonia was giving her details to someone else. 'Thank you, Rachael. Two o'clock. Thanks.'

She turned back to Pam. 'That was an old friend, Rachael, we were at Uni together. She now runs the personnel department for a resort up north.'

Pam looked puzzled. 'Up north?'

'Yes, it's a beautiful resort in Broome, very up-market.'

'Broome? Where's that?'

'Broome is up in the north-west. A two-hour flight from here. Rachael is currently in Perth recruiting for new staff for the resorts. She's looking to recruit a receptionist. Would you be up for an interview?

Pam was taken aback; it was all happening too quickly. 'Yeah, that would be great.'

Sonia pushed a piece of paper across the desk. 'That's where you need to be for the interview, the Metropol, 2.30. Do you know where the Metropol is?'

Pam slowly shook her head; this was all too much. 'No, I don't, sorry.'

'Hay Street, that's the main shopping street. The Metropol is at the top end.'

'Okay.' She then hesitated. 'I haven't got any clothes with me suitable for an interview.'

'Don't worry, I told Rachael you'd just arrived in Perth, and in any case, if you do get the job, you'll be supplied with a uniform.' Sonia stood up and held out her hand. 'Good luck with the interview.'

Pam stood up, dazed. 'Thank you.'

She arrived at the Metropol, still in a daze at the speed things were moving. Within ten minutes of arriving, she'd had a positive interview with Sonia's friend, Rachael, who offered her a position working on reception at The Dolphin Resort. Pam immediately accepted the job.

'I'll organise a flight for you up to the resort. I'll leave the tickets with Sonia. When you arrive, you'll have an orientation day. You'll be supplied with a uniform and shown your quarters.' She smiled looking at Pam's confused face. 'A roof over your head and meals is part of the package.'

'Thank you, thank you very much.'

* * *

The Dolphin Resort was paradise. Pam couldn't believe she'd struck lucky at her first interview. A minibus met her and several other potential new employees at the airport. On arrival at the famous holiday destination they were met by Jason who took them through to a small room behind reception and welcomed them to the resort.

'Welcome to you all. We're a friendly bunch and so are our visitors, mainly because they are on holiday,' he said with a wry smile. 'Some visitors you may see on a regular basis as they have work commitments in the area. Today you'll be shown your quarters. You will be sharing with someone else.' The group cautiously looked around wondering who they would be sharing with. 'Tomorrow you'll be given a tour of the facility so I'm not going to overload you with information today. You'll need to be familiar with the layout of the twenty-six acres of gardens, which includes the many paths bordered by exotic plants and various options for visitors to spend their leisure time. You will be asked numerous questions from visitors about attractions available outside the resort, and you will be expected to know the answers. All the information you need to know will be covered in your tour tomorrow. Are there any questions before I continue?' He looked around the group, but got no response. 'Let me give you a snapshot of the history of the resort and of Broome. The resort was built in 1972 by an English businessman, Sir David Whitnom. Cable Beach was chosen because of the twenty-three kilometres of pristine white beaches. Cable Beach was so named because of a communication cable that was run under the ocean in 1889 and came ashore here, on Cable Beach. Broome itself was settled by Malays who started the pearl industry in the area, the quality of the pearls are respected worldwide...'

Pamela's mind began to wander.

Will I be safe here? Have the Edinburgh police identified me? Can I blend into the community?

Pam found herself sharing with Natalie, a New Zealand girl, taking a gap year. She was studying to be a vet, following in her father's footsteps. Natalie was an effusive, open-minded individual. Pam steered clear of any deep discussion about her own reasons for taking a gap year. Pam was happy to be in employment and an additional bonus was the fact that Broome was, in her mind, a million miles from anywhere and hopefully out of the reaches of the Scottish legal system.

That night she phoned home and tried her best to sound positive, confident and in control. 'Don't worry, mum, I've got myself a reception job way up north in the Kimberley in Western Australia.' She couldn't risk telling her parents exactly where she really was. 'But I'm moving on soon.' She laughed, hoping she sounded convincing. 'The sun shines every day. I'm really enjoying it here and I've made some good friends.' She put the phone down and sobbed. She felt so far from home and vulnerable. Having to lie to her parents made her feel ashamed, but it was better than telling them the truth. She told her parents she was moving on soon in the hope that they wouldn't try to trace her.

The following day was the tour of the resort. The new group, twelve in all, gathered outside the reception area to wait for their guide, Heidi. Pam's mind was wandered again, back to Edinburgh. *What was her friend Amanda doing right now? Was she still with Aaron? Had she heard what the police were doing? Did she dare contact Amanda? Had they interviewed anybody for the murder?* Heidi, their guide, was a bright cheerful individual. She was German and spoke fluent English with a captivating accent. 'Welcome everyone. My name's Heidi. Please follow me and I'll point out the various activities that are available to our visitors. Please ask questions as we go.' After a few moments of trooping along winding paths lined with palm trees and exotic plants she stopped at a statue of a leaping dolphin and asked everyone to gather around her. 'This,' she said, affectionately stroking the concrete dolphin, 'is your saviour – your guide. If you get lost wandering around the facility you will always be within a short distance of a dolphin. The statue always points in the direction of the reception area, so, follow the dolphin and you'll arrive back at reception. It's a useful guide in your early days here, and for any guests who may be lost.' She went on twisting and turning along the paths and pointed out several pools, the mini-golf, the gym, spa and beauty salon. Interspersed amongst all the leisure facilities were a number of restaurants including a large pavilion-style breakfast room. 'Please note the breakfast room, which, as you can see, overlooks the beach. It fills up very quickly first thing in the morning because many visitors want to make sure they gain a good view of the train of camels arriving which give rides up and down the beach.' Heidi scanned her little group. 'Any questions?' She smiled mischievously. 'No? Then I'll leave you to find your own way back to reception.' She pointed to the exit of the breakfast room. 'First test! There's a dolphin just outside, it's your guide back to reception.' With that parting remark she grabbed a cup, filled it with coffee and sat down at an empty table. Whilst she had been on the tour Pam had noticed the lightweight, summer clothing everyone wore. She couldn't wait to earn some money and buy some new, more suitable clothes.

* * *

Pam had been a receptionist at Dolphin Resort now for nearly twelve months and loved it. Every day the sun shone. Her colleagues were great, particularly, Natalie, who was proving to be a great friend. On their days off they would go into Broome town and have a lazy day shopping or having lunch.

On one of the main back streets there were many shops specialising in the much sought-after gems. On a couple of occasions they'd been to the open-air cinema, the oldest in the world, where the audience sat in deckchairs to watch the movies under the stars. Another day they went to experience the local crocodile farm.

* * *

The weeks and months rolled by. Her images of that fateful night in Edinburgh were slowly receding, although on occasions she would wake up at night in a sweat.

During the mid-morning lull she would always scan the visitors who were due to book in the next day. The resort was almost full so she knew there wouldn't be many new arrivals until the following week. Looking down the list on the desk computer at tomorrow's arrivals she noted:

Mrs and Mrs Taylor

Mr and Mrs Khan and two children

Mr D Peters – *a regular*

Dr Cunningham

Dr Stevenson

Dr Bailey – *all the doctors were here for the seminar*

Mr J McGuire – *regular*

Mr and Mrs Smith – *yeah, right!*

Ms Moston

Mr P Mossley

That evening Natalie announced that she would be leaving the Dolphin. 'The whole purpose of my coming to Oz was to travel round, so, by the end of the week I'll be off to Darwin. I'll stop there a couple of months then I'll travel onto Brisbane.'

Pam was sad to hear of Natalie's intentions, the fear of being alone returning, but Pam couldn't blame her as she wanted to do the same. 'I'll be sorry to see you go, Nat, but good luck. Before you go we need to have a night out.'

'We will!'

When Pam retired to her bedroom at the end of her shift she typed a letter to her parents.

Dear mum and dad

I'm having a great time; Perth and Broome were lovely places and I'm sorry to leave them, but I must. I made a great friend from New Zealand; we go around together on our days off. The whole purpose of 'finding myself' was to travel and experience as many things as I could. I believe it will make me a better person.

I've just arrived in Darwin and immediately got myself a job in a bar. I travelled with a friend of mine so it would be safer. From Darwin I'm going to Queensland, then down to Brisbane and then... I'm not sure yet, maybe Indonesia. I want to experience south-east Asia.

Will keep in touch before I leave Darwin. Love Cassie

She felt guilty about lying to her parents, yet again; they didn't deserve what she was putting them through. For all she knew the police may have already been around to see them. She couldn't leave a trace. Pam sealed the envelope and called Natalie who was in her bedroom.

'Can I ask a favour, Nat.'

Her friend poked her head around the corner of the door. 'Sure.'

Pam handed her the envelope containing the letter to her parents. 'Would you post this for me please, when you get to Darwin.'

'Of course.' Nat popped it into her rucksack. 'No problem.'

Pam smiled. 'Thank you.'

She had no intention of going to Darwin, but if the police had been in touch with her parents the letter would give them a false trail.

The next day she was back on reception. The early mornings were always busy with guests settling their bills. The day passed slowly until mid-afternoon when various flights began to arrive at the town's small airport.

First through the doors were the three doctors. 'Good afternoon, gentlemen.' They all nodded politely. 'Welcome to the Dolphin Resort. Would you please fill in this form.' She pushed three forms over the desk. 'Are you here for the seminar?'

They all responded with a 'yes'. She pointed over to her right. 'That's the seminar room where you'll be tomorrow.'

They thanked her and trundled off with their cases. Only moments later Mr and Mrs Khan arrived with their two children. Pam went through the same rehearsed procedure for what seemed like a million times a day. In the brief moments she had between guests arriving she checked the computer and saw that Mr D Peters, a regular, had cancelled and pushed his booking to the following week. Mr and Mrs Taylor then arrived, were quickly dealt with, then Ms Moston, who needed to know if they had a beauty salon. Pam pointed her in the right direction. Mr Mossley arrived and met up with some colleagues waiting in reception. Mr and Mrs Smith arrived and appeared to be a legitimate couple. Pam scolded herself for being so cynical when reading the guest list. The only one outstanding was Mr J McGuire, a regular. She knew his plane was running late and wouldn't be arriving until late afternoon.

Towards five o'clock Mr McGuire arrived looking harried, it had obviously been a stressful flight over from Melbourne. Pam courteously passed over the paperwork and welcomed him to the resort. 'It's good to see you again, Mr McGuire.'

'Thank you. And how are you?'

'I'm well thank you. Enjoy your stay.'

He smiled back. 'Usual?'

Aware of other members of staff close by her yes was an imperceptible slight nod. She watched him move off in the direction of the lifts and looked forward to catching up with him later.

* * *

EDINBURGH

DI Bill McClean stood in front of the team who had been working all the hours God sent in order to gather information which would allow a cohesive argument to be put together for the CPS.

'As you know we've identified the man with the knife as being Hamish McGonnal. We're still assuming at this stage that the altercation and subsequent killing is related to drugs. Yesterday the hospital informed us that he was being discharged this morning so I arranged for uniform to pick him up as he left the hospital and he's on his way here as we speak. The woman who appeared to be following McGonnal across the road has not yet been identified. I hope I'll have more to tell you once I've interviewed McGonnal. Thank you.'

* * *

McGonnal was placed in the interview room; a room with which he was very familiar. He'd been picked up on numerous occasions in relation to drugs. He sat on a hard plastic chair, legs outstretched, arms folded. A solicitor equally stony faced was sitting to his left. McClean entered the room with DS Dantzig. Both smiled at him as Shirley turned on the recorder and the DI pulled out a chair.

Dantzig spoke formally to McGonnal. 'Both your body language and your verbal responses in this interview will be recorded.'

McGonnal made no acknowledgment; he'd heard it all before. He sat stony faced in front of the DI. McClean opened a file then turned to McGonnal. 'Mr McGonnal, could you tell us where you were on the evening of the second of September?'

'No comment.'

'Do you know a gentleman called Trevor Moffat?'

'No comment.'

'Do you know the Mango club in Canal Street?'

'No comment.'

The two officers exchanged glances then the DS turned her laptop toward McGonnal. 'Do you recognise the two people in the video?'

'No comment.'

The DI sat back in his seat and gave a stifled grunt. 'Well, I'm surprised. One of them is you and the other is Trevor Moffat.' The DI continued. 'If you look at the video we can see a woman following you across the road. Was she with you?'

'No comment.'

'Do you know the woman?'

'No comment.'

DI McClean closed the file, stood up and put his chair straight. 'Thank you, Mr McGonnal. No doubt we'll speak to you again when you're in a more cooperative frame of mind.'

The two officers made their way down into the bowels of the station to the canteen.

The DI came to where Shirley had settled with two coffees and a bag of crisps. 'So, what do you think?'

'Well, the facts are, we can see McGonnal with a knife. He threatened Moffatt and Moffat ends up dead. Is that enough for the CPS?'

McClean slowly and thoughtfully nodded. 'Probably, but I don't think it's the whole story.'

'What do you mean?'

'Not sure. I'd be happier if we could identify the woman and bring her in for questioning. Then we might get a fuller picture. We didn't see what happened across the road.' He tapped his fingers on the table. 'But who is she? I'll have a word with the press officer to see if we can get the video on Crimewatch. See what response we get. You never know, someone might recognise her clothes.'

Shirley chuckled. 'There'll be the usual raft of nutters!'

'I know, I know, but it's worth a try.'

That evening the video showing the altercation and the back of the woman was shown on Crimewatch. DI McClean made the appeal:

'Last week we had a tragedy occur in the club land area of Edinburgh where a man was stabbed and subsequently died. We have made an arrest. However, we are keen to identify the woman shown in the video. If anyone watching this programme can identify her, can you please phone the number at the bottom of your screen. Thank you.'

The response desks were overwhelmed with phone calls, all claiming they could identify the woman in the video. The information was passed on to the various detectives who meticulously followed them up; all to no avail.

A week went by with no new leads, then, one sunny Tuesday morning the officer at the front desk phoned the DI who was in his office revisiting all the statements that had been taken. 'Morning boss. There's a gentleman down at the front desk wants to show you something regarding the stabbing. It's a Mr Wagstaff.'

'Right, thanks, I'll come down.'

Sitting in the front desk area was a well-dressed man in his mid-fifties, wearing a suit and impossibly shiny shoes. McClean pushed his way through the office door into the public area. 'Mr Wagstaff? I believe you have some information for us.' The gentleman half rose and nodded. 'Please come through.'

Mr Wagstaff followed the DI into a soft interview room. 'Please take a seat. Can I get you a coffee or a tea?'

Mr Wagstaff raised his hand and shook his head. 'No thank you.'

The DI sat opposite the man, who looked quite nervous. 'What information do you have for us?'

'I saw that video of the woman. The one you wanted information on.'

'Yes.'

Mr Wagstaff handed over a camera chip. 'I was parked on the street at the time of the incident. It's from my dashcam, it shows the woman clearly.'

The DI eagerly took it and slotted it into the machine at the end of the table. 'So, you know the woman?'

Wagstaff shook his head. 'No, but it shows her face distinctly. Someone may know her if you show it again.'

The video played and the woman's face was as clear as daylight. It showed her picking up the knife and struggling with Moffat. A broad smile crossed McClean's face. 'Thank you. It's most helpful.' He hesitated not wanting to put a damper on this good citizen's valuable contribution. 'Could you tell me why you hadn't brought this to our attention earlier.'

The man blushed and looked sheepish. 'When I was parked, I was er, with someone who I shouldn't have been with, sorry.'

The DI smiled. 'I'm not here to judge. Thank you again. This is really helpful.'

The next briefing was more positive. 'We now have an image of the woman we want to speak to. I'm going to release the image on posters to distribute throughout Edinburgh. Universities, shops, council premises, pubs, you name it we'll saturate the town with her face, see what we get.'

They didn't have to wait long. A phone call to the police reception desk from a lecturer at Edinburgh Uni positively identified the woman in the video. 'It's Cassandra Melling. She was in my Marketing class, but hasn't been to class recently. No contact, just hasn't turned up.'

'Do you have an address?'

The constable could hear the rustling of paper down the phone then a voice read out Cassandra's address. 'I think that's her parents' address.'

'Thank you.'

The desk sergeant quickly ran down the corridor to McClean's office and gently knocked on the door.

'Come!'

She spoke excitedly. 'Sir, we've got a name and an address regarding the clubland killing.'

McClean read the piece of paper she'd handed to him and beamed. 'Brilliant! This could be the breakthrough we need.'

* * *

DI McClean and DS Dantzig, were relieved that they'd now got a lead. Next morning they enthusiastically shot off to the address in Manchester the lecturer had given them. It was a long, tedious drive, stopping off for the obligatory comfort break. There was very little small-talk. Neither of them was prone to idle chit-chat. What conversation they had revolved around what leads, if any, they had and what, if anything, they'd missed.

They eventually arrived at a secluded cul-de-sac. A large, detached property set in a leafy environment. 'Number 14, Shirley.' She neatly parked outside and both glanced sideways weighing up the house; the one they were hoping would lead them to Cassandra Melling. They walked up the drive; Shirley glanced at DI McLean, then looked straight ahead and rang the bell. A deep bark could be heard from somewhere inside the house. Both officers raised their eyebrows, neither were dog lovers. The door was opened by a smart looking woman. She was wearing a pair of jeans and a T-shirt top. 'Yes?'

Both officers flashed their warrant cards. The woman paled. 'Is it Cassie?'

'Mrs Melling?'

'Yes.'

'May we come in?'

She stepped back to allow them in and asked again. 'Is it Cassie?'

'We just need to ask you a few questions as to her whereabouts.'

She relaxed, but only slightly. 'Please come through.'

The DI and DS followed her through to the large, expensively furnished room overlooking a pristine back garden. She beckoned them to take a seat on one of the two sofas. She sat opposite, perched on the arm of the sofa opposite, hands clasped together. 'What's this about?'

'As part of an investigation we'd like to interview Cassandra. Do you know how we can contact her?'

Mrs Melling gave a short laugh. 'She's somewhere in Australia.'

'Australia! We understood she was attending Edinburgh University.'

Mrs Melling looked uncomfortable. 'She was! Then I had a phone call out of the blue to tell me she was dropping out, taking a gap year to,' she used finger quotes, 'find herself, whatever that means.'

'Do you know exactly where she is?' asked DS Dantzig.

Mrs Melling wrung her hands. 'No, I don't. She wrote to me from Perth, said she was going to work her way up to Darwin via the north of WA then south-east Asia.'

McClean pulled a face at being thwarted. It was proving to be a bit trickier than he'd hoped. 'Do you have a recent photo of her we could use to try to trace her?' Mrs Melling leaned over to the sideboard and lifted a small photo of Cassie.

'She had that taken a week before she left for Uni.'

McClean took it and carefully placed it in his briefcase. 'Thank you. If she makes contact would you let us know please.' He stood up. 'Thank you for seeing us, we'll show ourselves out.'

Cassie's mum opened the lounge door, then called to them as they went down the hallway. 'You will let us know as soon as you hear anything won't you? You've not told me exactly what it's in connection with?'

McClean turned, his face apologetic. 'We're investigating a murder.'

On the drive back to Scotland McClean declared, 'First job when we get back, I'm going to contact the Australian police in Perth. I'll send them her photo, see what they can find out. Check with her fellow students - she might have kept in touch with one or two. See if it prompts any of them to come forward.'

EDINBURGH GAZETTE

Where's Cassie?

The police are asking for information as to the whereabouts of Cassandra Melling. She was, until recently, a student at Edinburgh University and has since disappeared. The photograph below shows a recent photograph of her. Her last known contact was from Perth, Western Australia, but she may have moved on to south-east Asia. If anybody has any information as to her whereabouts, please contact your nearest police station.

Many weeks went by, but there were no further sightings of Cassie, either in the UK or in Australia. Perth police had drawn a blank, which wasn't surprising as they were looking for a Cassandra Melling with long blonde hair.

* * *

Pam thought back to when she first met John McGuire. Nearly twelve months ago now. He was a regular visitor, flying into Broome International airport initially once a month and, more recently, every two weeks. He'd often spend a few minutes chatting Pam up and eventually asked her if he could take her to dinner in one of the resort's restaurants. She had to explain that the staff were not allowed to fraternise with the guests, so she had, sadly, declined. On his next visit he suggested that she meet him in the public car park after her shift and they would go for dinner in Broome town centre. He knew a good Chinese restaurant, The Golden Dragon.

Their relationship became more intense over time. They had grown much closer, and it had eventually developed into an intimate relationship.

One evening around seven o'clock he sat in his hire car waiting for Pam.

He'd planned a special evening. She arrived on time, jumped in the car and they drove off to Broome town centre. 'You seem in a good mood tonight, John.'

He laughed. 'Yeah. I had some good news today I'll tell you all about it whilst we're having dinner.'

She looked at him curiously a crooked smile across her face. 'Good news?' she asked excitedly, 'tell me.'

'No. I'll tell you when we're having dinner.'

The restaurant was quiet; it was after all, mid-week and out of season. He called a waiter over to their table. 'A bottle of Moet, please.'

Pam looked surprised; John looked devious. The waiter arrived and allowed John to taste the champers. After nodding 'okay' the waiter poured out two glasses then backed away from the table. John raised his glass and Pam followed. They chinked glasses. Pam still looked curious.

'Pamela Jenks,' John said, tipping his glass towards her. 'Pamela Jenks', he said again, hesitated then blurted out, 'I would like to make you Mrs Pamela McGuire.'

Her eyes opened wide, she laughed and was lost for words for a few seconds, then accepted. 'John, I would love to be Mrs Pamela McGuire.' She took a long drink from her glass. 'Was that the surprise?'

He chuckled. 'Well, the main one, yes,' a mischievous smile crossed his face, 'but I do have some other good news,' he held his hand up to stop her interrupting, 'I won't be flying in and out of Broome every couple of weeks.'

She leaned back in her chair, flummoxed. 'That's the good news?' she said disappointment showing in her voice.

He shook his head. 'No. I've got a new position within the company. I've been promoted. I've got a desk job. No more flitting from one mine site to another. I'll be in one place with just the odd visit here and there.'

She shook her head trying to take it all in. 'Here, in Australia?'

'No, back in the UK.'

Pam's heart stopped. 'Where will you be based?'

'Manchester. I've already got a house in Chamesly which I currently rent out,' he chuckled, 'it's in Rabbit Close. We'll move into that.'

Her stomach did a double somersault and she felt sick. Chamesly was only ten minutes from where she grew up.

What were the chances of her bumping into her parents after she'd been lying to them since she left home? Were the police looking for her? Should she tell John about her deceit, her offence? Would he believe her side of the story? Will her change in appearance be enough to keep her safe?

'You okay, Pam? You look pale.'

She smiled as best she could. 'I'm fine. I think you took me by surprise, that's all.'

He laughed it off. 'That was the whole point,' he looked serious for a moment, 'I'm so glad you said yes.'

She nodded and took another sip of champagne.

* * *

Chamsley, England

The McGuires moved into Rabbit Close. John allowed Pam to have a free rein with the décor. She decided on a minimalist approach with lots of white and space. Pam successfully obtained a post as an advisor within a finance company. It scared her sometimes on how easy she found it to scam her way into various positions. She still worried that

John didn't know about her background – there never seemed to be a right time.

They generated a good circle of friends, organised dinner parties, and generally had a good life. She became so entrenched in the community, helping to organise local events and volunteering, she would sometimes forget her sordid background, but not for long. Over dinner one night John informed her that a new guy had started in the office. 'He's a really nice guy, Ken; knows his job well. He and his wife are new to the area. He's been working in South Wales,' he poured Pam another glass of wine, 'I've invited them for dinner on Saturday night. Hope that's okay with you?'

'Oh, fine. What's his wife's name?'

He thought for a moment, then. 'Ah yeah, I think he said his wife was called Marie. Ken and Marie Tuffnel.'

John saw the car headlights flash through the lounge window as it came to rest on the drive. Moments later the front doorbell rang. 'I'll get it,' John shouted up the stairs to where Pam was getting ready.

'Right. I won't be a sec.'

By the time Pam descended the stairs Ken and Marie were in the hallway shrugging off their coats. They turned as Pam came down ready to say hello. The two girl's eyes met. Pam's stomach turned. Her head was spinning. She thought to herself – *Marie! Like hell it is! It's Amanda!* Then she remembered Amanda's middle name was Marie after her grandmother. *Damn! What the hell do I do now?*

Pam smiled. 'It's nice to meet you both.' She quickly grabbed Marie's elbow. 'Marie, would you like to come into the kitchen with me, I'll show you what I've been busy with today.'

Marie nodded her head. 'Thank you, Pam, it'll be nice to talk.'

Once in the kitchen, Pam gently closed the door then turned on Marie. 'Don't you dare say a word. John doesn't know about my background.'

Marie mutely nodded. 'Okay. Just a friendly word though. The police are still looking for you,' then sniggered, 'I have to say the short hair suits you,' she conspiratorially put her finger to her lips, 'Mum's the word.'

The dinner went as smoothly as John had hoped, and as smoothly as Pam had prayed for. They caught up with Ken and Marie on a regular basis and Marie kept her word.

* * *

Pam had a few days leave owing, so decided she would take a few days mid-week for some retail therapy, treat herself to a leisurely lunch in town and spoil herself. She had also promised to take a report into the office that she'd been working on. She'd wandered around Clements, the department store, tried on a few things and decided on a new skirt, a sweater for the upcoming winter and a pair of warm boots. Sitting in a coffee shop enjoying a few minutes daydreaming, she was suddenly aware of a man across the café staring intently at her. She turned away and made to leave. As she stood and gathered her shopping bags, she suddenly remembered she was supposed to drop a report into the office, but she was distracted as the man approached her. He wasn't threatening, in fact, he was well dressed and had a warm smile. 'Excuse me. Are you Cassandra Melling?'

Pam looked at him defiantly, going weak at the knees. 'No, I'm not.'

He tilted his head slightly and apologised, 'I'm sorry. I must be mistaken.'

Pam quickly hurried out of the shop and headed for the car park. Unknown to her, the stranger in the coffee shop followed her at a discreet distance.

He turned the ignition on his car at almost the same time as Pam. She sedately pulled out of the car park and drove home. The man followed, stopping several houses away from where he saw Pam turn, open the automatic garage doors and drive in. He made a note of the number of the house.

That evening Sharon McClean was studying her husband's face. They were having dinner and he hadn't spoken since he'd arrived home. 'Bill?' she said slightly exasperated, 'you've not said a single word. What's on your mind?'

He looked up his shoulders sagging. 'Not sure.'

'Not sure about what?'

Bill McLean and his wife Sharon had moved to the Manchester area from Edinburgh to be near their daughter, who had been going through a messy divorce. Bill had been a successful detective inspector in the Lothian Police service. The last case he'd been involved in before his retirement was the killing of Trevor Moffat. Although some of the evidence had pointed to Hamish McGonnal being the perpetrator, McClean was not convinced. He had been keen to identify and interview the woman in the video, but that hadn't happened. By the time the woman had been identified, by a university lecturer, that bird had flown. It was assumed at the time that she had gone to Australia, but police In Perth – the last place she was known to have been – drew blanks. From that day Bill McClean had been frustrated he'd not been able to wrap up his last assignment.

He gave a deep sigh. 'Sharon, remember my last case, the clubland killing in Edinburgh?' She nodded. 'Well, at the time I was concerned that we didn't have the full picture before the CPS gave the okay to charge Hamish McGonnal. He was tried, found guilty and is still in jail, but I never got to interview the woman who was in the video.'

Sharon nodded slowly trying to recollect the finer details of the crime. 'And what's triggered this?'

He put his elbows on the table and placed his chin in his hands. 'I think I saw her today.'

His wife frowned. 'But I thought you never interviewed her; how do you know what she looks like?'

'At the time I had a photo of the woman, Cassandra Melling. The woman in the coffee shop is older, of course, and her hair was dark and short, but I'd place bets that the woman I saw is Cassandra Melling. I followed her home and got her address. I'm going into the local nick to-morrow. I'm going to ask them to have another look at the case.'

The next morning Bill McClean went into the local police station and spoke to one of the homicide detectives. 'I'm absolutely sure it's her. I've got her address. It wouldn't be difficult to identify who lives at that address.'

DS Kevin Malpas nodded. 'No problem. I'll get it done now whilst you're here.' As the current and the retired cops discussed the case over a coffee, a constable was busy searching for the old file. The canteen was noisy and buzzing. Bill realised he missed the camaraderie and excite-ment.

Bill looked straight at Kevin. 'I'm sure it's her. We think she fled to Australia, but she couldn't be traced. It's frustrated me from the day I retired.'

The constable was back sooner than either officer expected. Kevin was impressed. 'That was quick, thank you,' he said as he took the pa-perwork from the constable.

Bill sat back in his chair and smiled contentedly. 'I know it's her Kevin. See if her current employer has a photo, they might have taken one for employment purposes. Compare it with the photo her parents gave me at the time. Let's see what she looks like.'

Kevin pushed his chair back. 'I'm happy to contact Lothian Police and ask them to re-open the case.'

Bill hesitated then plunged straight in. 'Kevin, I want in on this, please! It was my last case; I want to finalise it.'

'I'll have a word with my boss. It's not unheard of to take on an 'old bloke' like you on a consultancy basis.' He winked at Bill. 'Leave it with me.'

Bill stuck out his hand. 'Thanks.'

Kevin finally said 'Be aware, Bill, my boss is away until next week and we're all under the pump with other jobs so it could be a few days before we follow up.'

Bill nodded; he understood the pressures the homicide squad was under since a more violent culture had imposed itself on Manchester. 'That's okay. I'll look forward to you contacting me.'

Had Bill waited another thirty minutes outside Pamela McGuire's house after he had followed her home, he would have seen the garage door glide up, Pamela reverse hastily down the drive and shoot off down the road. In the boot was her hastily packed suitcase. She made sure she had her passport with her. She didn't have any intention of returning any day soon. She drove to the airport, parked in the long-stay car park then grabbed a taxi outside the terminal. 'Manchester Piccadilly Station please.' She caught the train with only ten minutes to spare. She sat back breathing shakily. She didn't even notice the scenery, she simply let the train take her all the way to Edinburgh. She felt sick at the thought of leaving John behind without a word. He didn't deserve that, but she couldn't risk letting him know where she was. And, she certainly couldn't explain to him why she had left.

She retrieved her mobile from her handbag, rang a B&B which she knew from the old days and hoped it was still in business. It was, albeit under different ownership. She booked for two nights. She arrived in Edinburgh late in the evening. When she stepped out of Waverley Station it was raining; the street lights along Princes Street reflecting on the wet roads, the brightly lit shop windows a blur as the rain obscured her view. She didn't mind the rain, she loved Edinburgh; she felt at home. Towing her pink suitcase behind her it was only a ten-minute walk from Waverley Station to The Heathers, in Carstairs Street.

Bill and Sharon were watching a documentary on the Scottish Highlands when the phone rang. Bill looked at his watch, 8.30. 'It's probably Kevin, he may have some news for me.' He pushed himself out of his easy chair and ambled along to the phone in the hallway. 'Hello'?

'Hello Bill.' It was Kevin. 'I've got some news, it's not good.'

Bill didn't comment so Kevin continued. 'Your Pamela McGuire has just been reported as a misper. She's flown Bill, I'm sorry.'

Bill's heart sank. 'D'you reckon I frightened her off? If anything, it probably confirms I was right.'

Kevin filled him in with further details. 'Her husband reported her missing a couple of days ago, so it probably happened shortly after you approached her. He came home from work and she'd gone. No note, no phone call, nothing. He did tell the desk sergeant that her passport was missing so that's the first place we looked, the airport, then the Channel tunnel route. Uniform eventually found her vehicle in the long-stay car park at the airport. Either she's gone abroad, or the airport is a ruse.' He hesitated for a second. 'Look Bill, do you think you could come in to-morrow to give us any more info you may have?'

'Yes, of course. What time?'

'Make it around nine-thirty; I've got a briefing until then.'

'Will do. Thanks for phoning.'

Bill slowly walked back into the lounge a concerned look on his face, and sat down without saying a word. Sharon muted the TV. 'What's up, Bill? More bad news?'

He took a deep sigh and shook his head in frustration. 'Yeah. That was Kevin. Cassandra Melling aka Pamela McGuire, has fled – again.'

'So, what now?'

'I've got a meeting with Kevin tomorrow to bounce a few ideas around.'

Sharon nodded and turned the sound back on the TV.

The next day the weather was as depressing as Bill's mood as he ran up the steps to the police station. He couldn't believe he'd been so close to closing the case and now he'd lost her. Kevin met him at the front desk and took him to a side office. 'Come in here, Bill, we'll get some peace and quiet.'

Kevin left to grab them both a coffee from the canteen. Although it took longer, it was better than the sludge from the machine on the corridor.

'Right Bill, any thoughts as to where she might be?'

'There're two obvious destinations. Australia is a good option for her because presumably having lived there for some time she will have made contacts. I think you need to re-contact Perth police with an up-dated photo. The other option is Edinburgh.'

Kevin repeated Bill's suggestion. 'Edinburgh, why Edinburgh?'

Bill leaned back in his chair, coffee cup in one hand. 'She was at Uni in Edinburgh when this tragic event happened. She may know people there. She knows the area. Have you contacted her parents in recent times?'

'Tried to, sadly they both died in a car crash six months ago. They're both buried in Langham Road Cemetery. Apparently, according to neighbours, they hadn't heard from Cassandra for years; a quick note from when she was in Perth and that was it.'

'I'm sorry to hear that. It's sad to think they died without ever knowing what happened to their daughter.'

Kevin nodded solemnly and quickly moved back to the purpose of their meeting. 'I'll get the updated photo printed today. Once we're okay with it I'll email both Oz and Lothian who will then print it off and distribute it.'

'Good. Let me know if it brings a result.' He remained silent for a second then, 'Kevin, remember, I do want to be in on the interview if she's brought in.'

Kevin chuckled. 'I know, Bill. I hadn't forgotten. You'll be in when the time comes.'

Thanks to Bill McLean's description of the woman he saw, and Pamela McGuire's workplace providing a reasonably current photo of her, the poster being distributed across two major police regions showed a good likeness of Cassandra Melling aka Pamela McGuire.

LOTHIAN NEWS

WHERE'S CASSIE?'

Police are asking for the public's help in locating the woman in the photo. She's been missing for a week and no contact has been made. She is Pamela McGuire aged thirty-five. She is also known as Cassandra Melling. She may be travelling under an assumed name. If anyone recognises the woman in the photo or knows her whereabouts, please contact your nearest police station.

* * *

Pam looked out of the window of her bedroom at the Heathers B&B, her arms folded across her chest, tears in her eyes. It was raining and people were hurrying along, dodging each other with their umbrellas to avoid a soaking. Once more she felt vulnerable and lonely. She sank back onto the bed. How much longer could she keep running? She was devastated to think of how John was managing without her. He wouldn't even know why she was running; she'd never had chance to tell him what happened in Edinburgh. *I'm free, at the moment. I've managed to avoid that cop who recognised me. I'm too good for them! Who am I kidding? I'm sick of this. I want it all to end. To tell everyone what happened. To own up to it all. Should I go and hand myself in? After all it was self-defence; Moffat had me by the neck! My God, what will John say when he finds out?*

She shook herself out of her negativity, rolled onto her side and fell asleep. She had a restless night and was down for breakfast at seven o'clock. 'Early bird?' said Mrs Connors, the landlady, 'people to see, places to go?'

Pam smiled. 'Yes, I've got a busy day ahead.'

Pam briskly stepped out into the street. The rain had stopped, but the low clouds were laden with a threatening downpour. She knew the city centre well and where the cafés and restaurants were. That's where she'd planned to look for a job. She needed to be earning. Several of the cafés she walked past had signs in the windows 'We are Hiring'. She made a note of which ones were busy, which ones were well fitted out, what the clientele were like. Sitting on a park bench and looking at her notes she decided to approach a café that was positioned in the business area. It had bay windows and space for outside seating. It was called The Coffee Pot. Obviously, someone didn't have much of an imagination when it came to choosing a name for their business. She pushed open the door and could immediately smell the aroma of freshly made coffee and home baked cakes. A well dressed and neatly coiffed woman in her mid-forties approached her and smiled. 'Good morning. May I help?'

Pam returned a warm smile. 'Yes. I'm enquiring about the position you are advertising.'

The lady nodded and smiled even broader. 'Ah, yes, please come this way.'

She took Pam into a rear office which was just as pleasantly appointed as the café itself. She held her hand out. 'Natalie Beattie. Please take a seat.'

Pam shook her hand before sitting down. 'Kirsten Horrocks.'

'Well Kirsten, what were you looking for?'

'I'm new in town so I'm trying to get myself established. I only arrived a couple of days ago from north Wales. I've booked into a B&B whilst I have a look round. I need to orientate myself.'

Mrs Beattie pondered something for a second then asked. 'Have you somewhere to stay yet, I mean other than the B&B?'

Kirsten shook her head. 'No, not yet.'

Mrs Beattie smiled, then said tentatively, 'I have a room above the shop I'm looking to rent. It may be of interest to you.'

Kirsten nodded enthusiastically. 'That sounds good.'

'Come,' she said pushing back her chair, 'I'll show you the room now. See what you think.'

Kirsten followed Mrs B to the rear of the kitchen then up the staircase. She pushed open a door and ushered Kirsten through. 'It's two rooms. The main room is the lounge and there's a bedroom off to the side. There's a small kitchen along the landing. There would only be you up here; you don't have to share.'

Kirsten wandered through the two rooms which were also well-appointed, then strolled along to the kitchen. It was small, but sufficient for her needs.

'It looks lovely Mrs Beattie.'

'Natalie, please.'

Kirsten tilted her head in deference. 'Natalie', then creased her brow, 'but how much will it be?'

The figure Natalie suggested was within Kirsten's budget. It also meant she wouldn't have to travel to work if she were offered the full-time position in the café.

Natalie continued. 'Weekends are our busy time so your days off would be during week days. I do have a couple of part-timers who fill in as and when.'

The deal was done. Kirsten, aka Pam aka Cassie, moved in the following day and started work the day after. On her second day she was horrified to see two police officers enter the café. She approached them. 'Do you need a table or is it take-away?'

The female officer smiled kindly at Kirsten. 'Are you new here?'

Kirsten replied, her heart in her mouth, 'Yes.'

'Two flat whites to go, please.'

Kirsten retreated behind the counter. 'Certainly. It'll be a couple of minutes.'

The officers then grabbed their coffees and left.

Two weeks later the same officers came in for their take-aways. The female officer asked to speak to Mrs Beattie. Kirsten was beside herself and tried not to show the panic she was feeling. She did her best to sound calm. 'Yes of course, I'll just get her.' She found Mrs Beattie in the office surrounded by paperwork. 'Erm, sorry to interrupt, there are a couple of police officers at the counter. They would like a word.'

Mrs Beattie immediately looked concerned and headed for the café. The female officer handed a poster to Mrs Beattie.

'We'd appreciate it if you could put this poster in your window. She's missing, and Manchester police are trying to locate her.'

Mrs Beattie agreed. Kirsten arrived with the two take-aways.

Several customers were seated in the alfresco area of the café – although it was dull and threatening rain some customers needed to smoke. As Kirsten was re-entering the café after delivering a couple of friands and a pot of tea to a table, she noticed the poster in the window. She was horrified! It was her! She didn't dare remove the poster for fear it would prompt suspicion from her employer.

Kirsten Horrocks had been at The Coffee Pot for a few weeks. Natalie Beattie picked up the phone and dialled.

* * *

Bill's wife Sharon was in town meeting a group of friends for coffee. Bill was in the garden when he heard his name being called. He looked up from tending his tomato plants to see Kevin peering above the side gate. 'Bill!' he shouted, 'got a minute?'

Bill laughed. 'Of course, come in.'

Bill went to unlock the gate then took him inside. 'Coffee or a beer?'

Kevin responded predictably. 'It'll have to be a coffee, I'm on duty.'

Whilst Bill was opening and closing cupboard doors to grab mugs and coffee, he spoke over his shoulder. 'Haven't seen you for a few weeks. Hope you've got some good news for me.'

Kevin didn't reply until Bill had placed two mugs on the table with a plateful of ginger biscuits. 'Excuse me,' he said as he dipped a ginger biscuit, 'couldn't resist.'

Bill followed suit. 'So, what's new?'

Kevin looked smug as he took his first sip. 'We think we've found your runaway.'

Bill looked elated. 'No! Tell me more.'

Kevin settled back in his chair. 'Let me start at the beginning and I'll give you a blow-by-blow account.' He took another sip. 'Lothian Police had a phone call yesterday from a lady in the city centre who runs a coffee shop, The Coffee Pot. She thinks she has Cassandra Melling working for her. She's now using the name Kirsten Horrocks. It appears that our Mrs Beattie had a few doubts soon after this Horrocks girl started. Anyway, the other day when Horrocks was serving in the cafe, a young cheeky lad asked her for her name, she immediately replied 'Pamela', then quickly said 'no, actually it's really Kirsten.' To cover her embarrassment, she told him that her middle name was Pamela, the name her mum used. She seemed distracted and was unusually quiet for the rest of the shift. Our Mrs Beattie had another close look at the poster she'd put in the window, and she's convinced Kirsten Horrocks is your Cassandra Melling. The other thing that concerned Mrs Beattie was that Kirsten said she was from Wales, but when Mrs Beattie asked her specific questions about her background, she was always vague. Mrs Beattie then phoned the Lothian HQ in Edinburgh. They arrived at the café to talk to Kirsten and asked her for her name. She gave the name Kirsten. She then excused herself saying she had to get some stock from the kitchen. It was flight or fight. She chose flight and ran into the kitchen and out of the back door, only to be apprehended by a female police officer. She's being held at HQ as we speak.' Kevin had a broad smile across his face and leaned back in his chair. 'You up for travelling to Edinburgh tomorrow?' His smile abruptly stopped, then he mischievously suggested, 'of course, if you're too busy I'll go by myself.'

Bill flicked a crumb across the table. 'Don't you dare!'

'One last thing, Bill, I don't think she knows her parents are no longer alive. She distanced herself from them. You'll need to tell her.'

Bill solemnly nodded. 'I will.'

* * *

They caught the early morning train, had breakfast from the buffet car, then settled down to plan their interview with the individual who would, hopefully, turn out to be Cassandra Melling. Kevin suggested that Bill take the lead. Kevin was keen for Bill to be involved. 'It's your case Bill, you finalise it. And in any case, you remember the detail from all those years ago.' He chuckled. 'I'd only just joined the force at that time as a brand-new rookie, straight out of training school!'

Bill nodded and agreed. 'I'll start the interview using the name under which she was picked up which is Kirsten Horrocks. I'll ask her if that's her real name. I'll ask her if there's anything she wants to tell us about her past, see what she says. Then I'll explain why we're talking to her and, if she hasn't already done so, I'll mention the murder. At that point I'm hoping to get her to confirm she's Cassandra Melling. Any stalling from her and I'll show her the video from the dashcam which clearly shows her committing the offence.'

Their arrival at Waverley station coincided with lunchtime and an unwanted downpour. 'Every time I come to Edinburgh,' complained Bill, 'it rains.'

'It's good for your skin,' was Kevin's helpful reply.

The Central Lothian Police HQ was situated on the edge of the city alongside a busy main road. It was an uninspiring 1970s Lego box-type construction of three storeys and metal window frames. A car park abutted on three sides. On getting out of the taxi they both looked up at the building and raised their eyebrows. 'Come on, let's get on with it.'

They introduced themselves to the desk sergeant who buzzed them through to a DS who, in turn, took them along a narrow corridor to the interview room. 'Can I get you anything to drink?' Both declined. 'Okay, I'll bring Miss Horrocks along, give me a minute.' He was true to his word, as no sooner had Kevin and Bill settled themselves down, than the door opened and Miss Horrocks was shown in. She looked nervous and looked around the room.

Bill commenced the interview. 'This interview is being recorded. In the room is myself, Bill McLean and,' he looked at Kevin for his response, who replied, 'DS Kevin Malpas.' Bill continued 'Miss Horrocks, can you please state your name for the tape?'

She replied nervously 'Kirsten Horrocks.' He opened his file and looked up 'Miss Horrocks,' he started, 'we would like to ask you a few questions regarding an investigation we're conducting.' He referred to the file in front of him. 'We understand you were a student in Edinburgh in...er 2008, is that right?'

She didn't respond, but continued to look down at her hands which were tightly clasped on her lap. Bill pushed. 'You were a student in Edinburgh in 2008, weren't you?'

She briefly nodded without giving him eye contact. Bill continued. 'Can you speak it for the tape please?

She weakly said, 'Yes'.

'Would we be correct in assuming that in 2008 you were known as Cassandra Melling?'

This time she did look up and tears were forming in her eyes. 'Yes.'

'Do you remember an incident one night, near the Mango night club where a man was killed?'

She nodded.

Kevin broke in. 'For the tape please Cassandra.'

'Yes.'

'Did you know the man who was killed?'

She shook her head.

'For the tape please.'

'No.'

'Do you know the man who he had the altercation with?'

'Yes.'

'Who was that man?'

'Hamish McGonnal.'

'Were you out with Mr McGonnal that night?'

'Yes.'

'Can you tell us what happened?'

Cassandra spoke quietly and slowly. 'We were on our way home when Hamish, er Mr McGonnal saw a man who owed him money. He went to talk to him, Mr McGonnal produced a knife, then they got into a struggle. The man Hamish had been talking to ran across the road to get away. I saw a knife, but then Mr McGonnal tripped and the knife skidded across the road when he fell.'

'What did you do?'

She remained silent. Bill let the silence become invasive. Cassandra finally broke the silence. 'I thought the man was going to pick up the knife and stab Hamish. I ran and picked the knife up.'

Bill let the silence continue.

'I picked it up,' she repeated, this time in tears, her words struggling to come out, 'but the man grabbed me by the neck...' She was now sobbing loudly. 'I pushed my arm back to free myself, then I'm not sure what happened.'

Bill turned his laptop round to face her. 'Maybe I can help.' He flicked the video from the dashcam on and watched for her response. She was clearly shown falling and the knife going into Moffat.

She almost collapsed. 'I didn't mean to do it,' she pleaded in panic, 'it just happened...I promise, I didn't mean to hurt anyone.'

Bill let her compose herself then continued. 'Then what happened?'

'I was encouraged by Aaron somebody, I didn't know his full name, to leave the country as Ham.., Mr McGonnal, and the others were involved in drugs and didn't want any involvement.'

'Where did you go?'

She was now talking more rationally. 'Australia.'

'Did you travel under the name Cassandra Melling?'

She looked down and shook her head. 'No.'

'Who then?'

'Pamela Jenks.'

'How did you obtain a passport in that name?'

She looked shocked at the question knowing she was about to get other people into trouble. 'Er, Aaron arranged it.'

'Was anyone else involved?'

'Yes, my friend Amanda Wallis. Her middle name is Marie. She's married to a Ken Tuffnel. Her husband works for my husband, John.'

The thought of John's name coming up panicked her again. 'Does John know what's happened?'

Bill reassured her. 'No, not yet, but I need to go round to see him and explain. He still believes you're missing.'

Cassie nodded and dabbed her eyes.

Bill remained silent for a few moments then gently spoke to her. 'Cassandra, I need to tell you, both your parents died in a car crash some months ago. I'm so sorry for your loss.'

She looked at him but didn't respond.

'Cassandra Melling, would you please stand up.'

Cassandra went cold, and obediently did as she was told.

'Cassandra Melling, I'm arresting you for the manslaughter of Trevor Moffat on November nineteenth, 2008. You don't have to say anything...'

Cassie fainted. When she'd recovered, she was taken back to her cell. Bill and Kevin took a taxi back to Waverley station for their journey home.

'Well Bill,' Kevin stated, 'you've managed to close your last case, after all these years.'

Bill looked exhausted but satisfied that he'd finalised the last case he'd been involved in before his retirement. 'It'll be interesting to see if the CPS will want to up it to murder.'

Kevin nodded and patted him on the shoulder. 'A beer?'

'I reckon so.'

The next day Bill kept his promise and went to see John McGuire. John opened the door.

'Mr McGuire, I'm a former police officer that's been assisting with an old case. As it turns out it's linked to your missing wife. I wonder if I might have a word. May I come in please?'

'Yes, of course.' Whilst John showed him into the lounge, he was firing questions at Bill. 'Have you found Pam? Is she OK? Please tell me she's safe.'

McLean looked serious and from the look on his face John feared the worst. 'Is she dead?'

'No, Mr McGuire. The good news is that we have found her, and she's quite safe.'

'Oh, thank god. Can I see her?'

Bill continued, 'I'm afraid not at the moment. She has been arrested. I've been investigating a murder that took place in 2008 in Edinburgh where a man was killed after an altercation. We believe it took place because of a drug debt.' He took a deep breath before continuing. 'I'm sorry to tell you that your wife Pamela, her real name Cassandra Melling, has been linked with the man's death. She's actually been charged with manslaughter, but I have to warn you, the CPS may increase the charge to murder. I'm sorry, Mr McGuire.'

EPILOGUE

Cassandra Melling was charged with manslaughter, found guilty and sentenced to ten years imprisonment.

Marie Tuffnel (Amanda Wallis) and Aaron Crossly, her boyfriend at the time of the offence, were both charged with procuring false documents and sentenced to seven years imprisonment.

Hamish McGonnal, already serving time, was charged with drug dealing, found guilty, and sentenced to five years imprisonment.

He appealed his initial sentence for murder after the conviction of Cassandra Melling. The appeal was upheld.

John McGuire took the news badly. He couldn't get the thought out of his mind that he'd been duped by Cassandra. He filed for divorce. Within two years he'd met someone else, Fiona Drew, got married and lived a very happy and contented life. John still experienced moments of acute anger and depression due to the way Cassandra had lied to him. *How could he have been so naïve? Were there any red flags? Anything he could have seen to give him a clue as to her Walter Mitty existence?* Still, he was grateful for his now, contented, comfortable life.

Bill McClean, the hard-bitten cop of thirty years also had a compassionate side. It constantly nagged at him that Cassandra's parents had died not knowing where their daughter was. One bright sunny morning he had an idea. He contacted Cassandra in prison. She agreed to his suggestion. The next day he went into town, bought a beautiful bouquet of assorted flowers, and drove to the cemetery where Mr and Mrs Melling were buried. He placed the flowers on their grave. The card read:

Love you mum and dad.

Sorry. Cassie

2 |

The Weak Link

2023

Callum Forsyth stood and called out over the hubbub of conversation between the group that was gathered in the room. They were upstairs in the function room of the Moss Trooper pub. This was where the Courston Book Club held its monthly meetings and of which Callum Forsyth was the self-appointed leader.

It was almost 10.00pm, the agenda of the evening had finished, and everyone was enjoying a sociable get-together with a cup of coffee.

Raising his voice, he pleaded, 'one moment please!' The talk died down and everyone turned to hear what their leader had to say.

Callum was an innocuous looking man. He was an English lecturer at the local FE college. As was his want, he wore his usual Viyella check shirt with a beige V-neck sweater, oatmeal plaid tie and brown cords. As he called for the attention of the group he twizzled his rimless spectacles in his right hand.

'Please, one moment. Thank you, as usual, for coming and contributing this evening. I'm sure you'll agree our book for tonight, *Homo Deus*, gave us all pause for thought.' There were murmurings of agreement. It did indeed give pause for thought and had generated some interesting discussion. The book by Yuval Noah Harari, flagged up the world's projects, dreams and, more importantly, the potential nightmares of the 21st century. It suggested how the world needs to protect itself from its own power and how this could be achieved. Undoubtedly some ideas suggested were good for humanity, if somewhat mind blowing. As an example, the book highlighted advances in medical science, such as the cosmetic procedures that had initially been developed to help those who were disfigured during the world wars, but had now developed into a fashion accessory for the vain and wealthy. Technology had become an everyday part of our lives, for good and evil. The book quoted, as an example, that in the US there is now a chain of pharmacies that no longer employ humans. The patient inputs their symptoms into a computer, the 'electronic doctor' diagnoses the problem and dispenses a prescription, all undertaken with no human intervention.

AI is creating uncertainty. It prompts the question, does the public really know what is real news and what is fake news? How will this easily available propaganda tool be used by tyrants throughout the world to serve their own ends?

A general agreement during the discussion, was that technology was a little like a coin: it had a head and a tail. The head, the good, showing itself in the medical world, communication and manufacturing efficiency. However, there was a consensus among the group that the population was being dragged, by the scruff of the neck, technologically, to somewhere they weren't sure they wanted to go – this was the tail of the coin.

Callum continued. 'If you remember, we analysed his book *Sapiens* a couple of years ago which was also a thought-provoking read.' He pushed his floppy fair hair out of his eyes then held up a book. 'This is for next month. Have any of you read any of Patricia Highsmith's books?' One or two said they'd read *The Talented Mr Ripley,* but most of the group had never heard of her. He continued, 'The Mr Ripley series is very good and no doubt some of you are aware that Netflix have made a TV series of the book. This book,' he emphasised, holding it higher, 'is her very first novel, *Strangers on a Train.* Written in 1950 and made into a film by Alfred Hitchcock in 1951. This is your project for next month.' He smiled and looked around the group. 'Thank you, see you next month. Enjoy.'

Having said their goodnights, they all trooped out to make their way home.

Marlene Drinkwater sat in her car deep in thought for several minutes whilst the car park cleared. The full moon was showing through the bare branches of the silhouetted trees and casting shadows across the car park. A wind suddenly whipped up from nowhere and blew litter across the open space. It wasn't just the *Homo Deus* book that prompted her dark thoughts – it was the Patricia Highsmith book which was the assignment for the next meeting.

Marlene Drinkwater: fifty-two years old had a reputation for being a little brusque and, on occasions, downright rude. She was the manager of the Personnel Department of a coffee bean importer in nearby Scafford. She and her husband of twelve years lived in a large detached, non-descript house with an equally large garden that backed onto Scholes Park; Its only obvious features from the outside was a double garage and a concrete gnome and water-well on the left-hand side of the front lawn, both looking a little worse for wear. She was a little on the plump side and had salt and pepper hair, now more salt than pepper. Her dowdy appearance and brusque manner didn't help people warm to her. She was married to Frank and was bored with her marriage. Frank was an easy-going character, too easy-going some might say, with a conservative view of life. Marlene thought he had no oomph, no get up and go – after all, he was an accountant and a local council accountant at that. What did she expect! They each had a car, went on holiday, albeit to Wales, each year, and occasionally went to conventional restaurants where Frank invariably had a meal of roast beef and two veg; he didn't like foreign food. She wanted more, some excitement, maybe an affair; that would add some spice to her dull, boring life with Frank. She longed for a thrill – something that she could look back on and say, 'Wow, I did that!' Maybe a bungee jump, scuba diving, climbing Mt Everest, or as an assistant in a knife throwing act. Whatever it was, she wanted something to relieve the daily boredom. Maybe it was her age that had made her sit up and realise her life was quickly passing her by. Her friends all seemed to have full lives: hobbies, holidays abroad, a taste for foreign food. She had been married before and her first husband, Tom, had died under suspicious circumstances. As in most spouse deaths, the other partner was the prime suspect. For months she came under intense scrutiny from the police. Almost every week the investigating detective would contact her with more probing questions. The police interviewed her children, neighbours, friends, relatives, work colleagues from her office, all to no avail. It was embarrassing and never-ending. No evidence led back to Marlene. Eleven years on and the case was still open, now firmly tucked away in the cold case files. No one has ever been charged. Marlene sat in her car. She was not going to be the centre of a murder investigation again...ever!

No, what triggered Marlene's dark thoughts as she sat alone pondering in the now empty car park was the subject of next month's book – that, and the discussions she'd had with her work colleague, Irene Hamilton. She turned on the ignition just as the patter of rain spread across her windscreen to blur her vision. As she drove home a plan was developing in her mind.

Twelve Months Previously

As Marlene entered the office canteen, she saw Irene Hamilton sitting by herself, an empty plate and coffee cup in front of her. She was staring aimlessly out of the window, a shrub outside the window tapping against the pane. Irene was the antithesis of Marlene. Irene worked in the Administration Department. She was above average height, had shoulder length blonde hair and blue eyes. She dressed smartly. She was one of those lucky women who looked great even without make-up. Marlene, having purchased a coffee and a sandwich from the counter, made her way over to her and sat down. 'You okay Irene?' Irene must have been miles away as she initially ignored Marlene, only the scrape of a chair and the rattle of the coffee cup made her turn to face her. Irene looked embarrassed. Marlene was shocked. 'What happened to your face?'

Irene forced a smile, reddened and at the same time ran her hand gently over her black eye. 'Oh, it's nothing, I tripped at home.'

Marlene didn't believe her and pushed for a more convincing explanation. She paused before she again asked, 'come on, what really happened Irene?'

Irene looked away again and Marlene saw tears forming in Irene's eyes. 'Everything okay at home?'

Irene shook her head. 'No. It's Jeff, when he drinks, he gets angry.' Immediately she wished she'd not said anything.

Over the next few months, Irene slowly but surely, confided in Marlene about how difficult her marriage was. Her husband was a drinker and a gambler, dangerous traits in any husband. 'Why don't you just leave?' suggested Marlene.

Irene shrugged her shoulders. 'I don't know. I think I'm afraid of the consequences. The fact is I shouldn't have married him.' Marlene slowly nodded. She wasn't sure what was worse, having a violent husband, or one that constituted a big zero in one's life, like her Frank.

* * *

One morning Marlene wandered into the canteen for a well-earned break. She was surprised to find that Irene was not in her usual place. Marlene nevertheless sat down, then scanned the canteen in case Irene had decided to sit elsewhere. She couldn't see her. On her way out she bumped into Annie, a colleague of Irene's. 'Irene not in today?' she asked nonchalantly.

'Er, no she phoned in this morning. She's not feeling too good.'

'Did she say what was wrong?'

'No,' she answered curtly. Annie had arrived at the counter by now and ordered her coffee and toast.

Marlene returned to her desk, promising herself that she would call on Irene on her way home.

It was an extremely busy afternoon, which meant that Marlene was forced to stay late until the work had been completed. Eventually her desk slowly cleared. She shrugged on her coat and make her way out to her car. The evening was now drawing in and Marlene began to have second thoughts about popping in to see Irene. She knew there were road works en-route to Irene's which would have delayed her even more, but she finally resolved to call in to check if Irene was okay.

Irene lived in a reasonably up-market area. Her house was of mock Tudor design with a double garage. On either side of the bright red front door were two terra-cotta pots containing trailing red geraniums. She gently knocked on the door hoping Irene and her husband were not in the middle of their evening meal, or worse, in the middle of an argument. There was no response, so she knocked a little louder, but there was still no response. Leaning to one side she could see through the window that the lounge light was on. In the dim light she could see Irene sitting motionless on an easy chair, staring at a blank television screen. Marlene rapped smartly on the glass, to which Irene suddenly jumped up and, on seeing Marlene, held up her hand in acknowledgement. She reluctantly opened the door; Marlene was horrified. Irene's face was swollen to almost twice its size, streaks of blood still evident down one side of her face.

'What the hell has happened?'

Irene silently turned back into the hallway and headed into the lounge; Marlene assumed she was expected to follow her. Irene slumped once more into her chair whilst Marlene stood at the lounge door. 'Was it Jeff...again?' she asked accusingly. Irene nodded. Marlene shook her head in disgust. 'You're foolish to put up with this. Move out. You've always been too weak.'

Irene looked up at her, anger in her eyes. The last thing she needed was someone to tear her to shreds in her hour of need. But that was Marlene. She was well known for having very little patience. 'Leave me alone...now!' she barked, a little more aggressively than she intended.

Marlene was taken aback by her outburst and quietly got up. 'I'll let myself out,' she said pointedly as she closed the lounge door, then, determined to have the last word added, 'I'd think about a divorce if I were you.' Irene waited until she heard the front door click, then gave a loud scream of frustration. Thank goodness Marlene doesn't work in admin.

Irene had encountered Marlene's hostility over the years. She reminded herself that Marlene had latched on to her, not the other way round. Irene was quite happy to sort out her own problems, not with someone who had a reputation for being dogmatic and totally lacking in empathy. Why had she confided in Marlene? She felt so stupid at being so weak. She snatched a magazine that was lying on the coffee table and irritably began to flick the pages, then immediately threw it down again. Why was Marlene Drinkwater taking an interest in me? We've never been close friends. She doesn't seem to have her own close friends at work. Why now? Then it hit her. Of course! The rumour mill at work said that her own marriage was not good. Of course! She wanted a kindred spirit. Someone she could confide in.

* * *

The Present Day

Marlene sat in the lounge, a book open on her lap, her husband was upstairs updating his stamp collection. She wasn't reading, she was mulling over the thoughts she'd had on the evening of the last book club meeting.

The latest project, Patricia Highsmith's book, had set the grey matter working overtime. Although she hadn't seen Irene to talk to at work, particularly after the little contretemps as the result of her home visit, she had nodded to her across the canteen. However, she did clearly remember the conversations they'd had over the months in relation to Irene's abusive husband. She had come to the conclusion that Irene wanted out, but was afraid of making the first move. Maybe Irene Hamilton might be the perfect 'partner'. She heard Frank clumping down the stairs which snapped her out of her reverie, and she dropped her head to concentrate on her book.

'Good book, is it?' asked Frank indifferently as he went into the kitchen. 'Cup of tea?'

'Yes please,' she shouted with little enthusiasm. 'And yes, it is a good book, very thought-provoking.' She turned to the outside cover and smiled to herself. *Strangers on a Train*.

* * *

The day had been a bloody awful start for Marlene – the coffee machine at home had been playing up and she could see from the kitchen window that next door's cat had dug up yet another plant. She shouted up the stairs as she opened the front door, 'I'm off to work.'

He urgently shouted back down to her, 'Hang on, remember I'm taking the car in for its service today. You're following me then taking me to work.'

She glanced at her watch and gave an exasperated sigh. Christ! Yes, she had forgotten. 'Well hurry up, I'm running late as it is,' she shouted, drumming her fingers on the half-moon hall table. Frank came scurrying down the stairs desperately trying to get his arm into the sleeve of his sports jacket. He reversed his car out of the garage whilst she impatiently sat waiting by the kerb revving her engine. The trip to the garage then onto Frank's place of work was completed in silence, at least on her part. However, Frank spent some time explaining to her that he'd read an article about some Rhodesian stamps produced in the sixties, some of which had less perforations in them than they should have had, i.e. they were a misprint and therefore worth a lot of money.

'That's what I was doing last night, counting the little perforations.'

Marlene yawned before asking. 'Find any rare ones?'

'No,' he said rather disappointingly, then added enthusiastically, 'I did check them all twice, in case I'd miscounted.'

She almost screamed in frustration. Give me bloody strength! I can't take any more of this. I need out! I need to get a life! She agreed to pick him up later to take him back to the garage. 'I may be late though; I've got a lot on today.'

'Don't worry,' he said picking up his thermos flask and sandwiches. 'I'll get a lift from someone at work.'

'Right' she said and drove off almost before Frank had time to close the car door. The journey to deliver Frank to work had taken her out of her way and no sooner had she got back on the main road, she hit road works, the temporary traffic lights on red. She drummed her fingers on top of the steering wheel whilst constantly checking the clock on the dashboard. Damn! She was running even later than she'd expected and she had a lot of work to get through today!

Quickly parking her car in her usual spot, she ran into the building saying an abrupt, 'morning' to the receptionist and made her way down the corridor to her office. The pile of papers she'd left on her desk the previous evening which she had planned to wade through this morning, had a yellow memo sticker attached to the top file. She snatched it up and quickly read it. Meeting. Boardroom. Ten o'clock. 'Bloody hell!' She checked her watch. Five to ten! *They'll have to wait for me, I need to grab a coffee.* Throwing her coat onto the hat stand she then shot back down the corridor to the tiny kitchen where she made herself a strong coffee. She barged into the boardroom, coffee in one hand a pen and pad in the other to find most people already there, including the chair, Kathy Zeigler. 'Morning,' she gasped breathlessly to the others.

The meeting was to discuss the new intake of staff, in particular the interviewing, selection and training.

At eleven-thirty the meeting was thankfully over, and Marlene shot back to her office having grabbed another coffee on the way back. She'd just opened the first file when the phone rang. 'Hello? Right, leave it with me. I'll phone you back this afternoon.' Then a knock on her door interrupted her concentration. She looked up to see Mary Constance looking apologetically at her.

'Have you got five minutes?'

'No, I haven't at the moment,' she answered abruptly. 'I'll see you this afternoon...if I get chance.'

Will people just leave me alone to get on with my job! Her staff had picked up the warning signs that she was not in a good mood and kept their distance. They knew from experience that she could be aggressive and rude, even obnoxious when she was stressed. When she handed out work to them, they would reply with mono-syllabic responses. She wasn't well liked, and this was reflected in the high staff turnover. By late lunch time she'd cleared most of the work from her desk. She was desperate for a break, so made her way down to the canteen. *Give me a break. Just five minutes!*

Frank was bad enough, but work is almost as bad.

Whilst queuing for her standard fare of coffee and a tuna mayo sandwich, she noticed Irene sitting by herself. Marlene wandered over and sat opposite her. At the same time as opening her sandwich she ventured to initiate a conversation. She was still wary after her visit to Irene's home. 'Busy in your department?'

Irene looked up and gave a wan smile. 'Of course, isn't it always. You?'

Marlene tilted her head in acknowledgment and laughed. 'Of course.'

Irene continued the conversation. 'We're really busy because of the new computer systems they're putting in.'

Marlene shook her head in frustration. 'We're interviewing for twelve new positions.' She looked directly into Irene's eyes. 'Two for your department, plus six for the IT section, one receptionist and three for the warehouse. It's time-consuming checking their CVs then organising the interviews.' Marlene continued stirring her coffee for something to do.

'I know, I've just been informed by Kathy. I'm glad I'll have two new members of staff; we've been run off our feet for the last twelve months.'

Marlene nodded in acknowledgement, then tentatively broached the elephant in the room. 'Are you okay at home, Irene?' Then, putting on her concerned face said, 'I've been worried about you.' Silence descended at the table for several minutes then Marlene decided to push a little harder. 'No movement on a divorce?' Irene mutely shook her head, so Marlene continued. 'Do you ever think what it would be like if you got a divorce?'

Irene smiled at the thought. 'Don't tempt me,' she laughed. 'Life would be so different.'

Marlene nodded. 'How?'

Irene paused to put some thought to her answer. 'Well, no more bullying or violence, no more stress...and I'd be free to marry my childhood sweetheart.'

Marlene stopped with her coffee cup halfway to her mouth. 'Wow! Childhood sweetheart?'

Irene didn't know why she was opening up to this woman sitting across the table from her. She didn't even like her. But somehow it felt like a weight was being lifted from her shoulders just to talk. 'Well, not quite childhood. We were at secondary school together. Did O and A levels together, then I went to the local FE college and he went to uni. From there we drifted, maybe understandably.' She leaned back in her seat, a broad smile crossing her face. 'Anyway, about twelve months ago I'd been over to see my sisters in Moreton and by chance, I met him in a coffee shop in the main street. It was great to see him after all those years. The connection was still there. We got talking and we've caught up on a regular basis ever since. It's as though we'd never been apart.' Her serious face returned. 'However, he's married, I'm married...but if we weren't, things would be so different.' Marlene nodded, her plan could, perhaps, be implemented sooner rather than later. She moved some used plates and cups to one side and leaned across the table.

'I'm in the same position,' she confided, 'I'm married and desperate to get out.' She was about to say something else just as several staff returning from their lunch break passed the end of the table. She waited until they were out of earshot then continued. 'I've got a plan...which would benefit both of us.' She smiled reassuringly, 'And...you could reunite with your childhood sweetheart. Look, why don't we catch up in the pub after work and I'll fill you in?'

Irene nodded, still asking herself why she was getting involved with this woman. 'Okay,' she whispered still a little reluctantly. When they both got up to go, they realised they were the only ones left in the canteen. Simultaneously they both looked at their watches.

'Oh no, it's quarter past two,' they said in unison. They hurried out of the canteen leaving the canteen assistants tidying the tables. Marlene turned left to go to the Personnel Department and Irene turned right to the Admin Department. Irene sat at her desk pondering the conversation of the last hour with Marlene. So, the rumours are true, she's not happily married. Why would she unload to me?

* * *

They met in The Lavender Bush a few miles out of town. It was a quaint pub with small, cosy rooms, low beams and gentle background music. It was a little too early for most patrons, which meant the pub was relatively quiet. Two men stood at the bar and two couples were sitting on the far side of the room. The pub lounge was reasonably quiet, which meant the two women could converse without fear of being overheard. Marlene ordered them both a glass of white wine then directed Irene to a small table in the corner. 'Have you been here before?'

Irene shook her head. 'No,' she looked around, 'but it looks very nice.'

Marlene raised her glass to clink with Irene's. 'It's one of my favourites. They do a very good lunch by the way; you should try it sometime. Cheers.'

Marlene wasted no time in explaining. 'I wanted to explain my plan...I'm sure it would help us both.' She paused before continuing. 'Are you still keen to distance yourself from your husband...and make a new life?' Irene nodded then took a sip of her wine. Marlene took a deep breath. 'Do you know of the author Patricia Highsmith?' Irene shook her head. 'Well, she wrote a book in 1950 called *Strangers on a Train*. I'm a member of the local book club and it's this book that's up for discussion at the next meeting.' She took a long swig of her wine. 'I've not finished the book yet, but I do remember seeing the film they made based on the book many moons ago. It was a Hitchcock film. I seem to remember it was on TV in the days they used to show black and white films on a Sunday afternoon. Anyway, if I can explain the gist of the story to you it will help explain my plan.' She was just about to enlighten Irene when they both heard a vaguely familiar shrill voice and looked up.

'Oh my god, what are you two doing in here?' It was Simone Peters, an old work colleague from three or four years ago. She looked like she'd had a difficult life since then. Her face was lined, made worse by having no make-up on. She had sunken cheeks, dark rings under her eyes, her hair was unruly and her clothes decidedly the worse for wear. She continued, much to Marlene's chagrin. 'How are you both? Long time no see.' To their dismay she grabbed a chair and sat at the table. 'Still busy?' They both responded with a short answer hoping to curtail her stay.

'Yup, very busy.'

She'd worked in Irene's department so Irene took the lead. 'So, how are you Simone, what have you been doing?'

Simone pursed her lips for effect. 'It's a long story. If you remember I moved south to marry Conrad, the bastard. He bled me dry, cheated on me, you name it he did it. I eventually got a divorce, had to sell the house and I've moved back up north. I've been back in the land o'plenty for three weeks now; still finding my feet, looking for a job.' Her eyes lit up momentarily. 'I see your company is recruiting. Anything going that would suit me?' Both women looked non-committal.

Feeling uncomfortable with their curtness Simone looked for a way out and waved to someone standing by the bar. 'Sorry ladies, must go, I'm meeting someone. We must all catch up.' She slipped a piece of paper over to Irene. 'I'm staying with my mum, that's her phone number, you can get me there. Ciao.'

'Ciao.' Marlene shook her head in frustration as she watched Simone sashay over to her friend, relieved she'd moved on. 'Thank God she's gone. Now where was I? Oh yeah, *Strangers on a Train*. If I can remember correctly, two guys meet on a train. They get chatting and find they would both like someone close to them to disappear.' She used her fingers as quotes around the word disappear. 'They knew how investigations worked...the spouse is always the top of the suspect list.' Marlene leaned closer in order to confide further information. 'I've already experienced that, and I don't want to go down that road again.'

Irene raised her eyebrows at this extraordinary admission. 'You?'

Marlene nodded then carried on. 'In a nutshell, they agree to get rid of each other's 'problem' and by doing so provide no direct evidence between the perpetrator and the victim. Clever, isn't it?'

'Murder?' she barked. Irene had raised her voice louder than she intended, causing several people to look in their direction, including Simone, who stared at them.

'Shush for goodness' sake, someone will hear you.' Marlene stood up. 'I'll get us both another drink, then we can put some detail together.' On Marlene's return carrying the two glasses Irene leaned in close to her and in a low, panic-stricken voice, whispered,

'You...you want me to murder your husband?'

Marlene nodded and held her hands palm up, to placate her. 'Just listen, please. It's a one-off job. We both come out of it with what we want. I get rid of a boring-as-hell husband and you get rid of a violent thug, then you're free to be with your lover. Neither of the murders can be linked to us because we'll have alibis. What's his name, by the way?'

Irene looked away from Marlene. 'It doesn't matter...it would certainly solve my problem.' She bit her bottom lip before relenting. 'So, what is your plan? How do we avoid being caught?'

Marlene took a sip of her wine. 'We each need to do it at exactly the same time. We pick an evening when both men are not at home. Mine goes out on a Friday night to the Philatelic club.' Irene interrupted, now feeling more positive toward Marlene's plan, 'Mine's out on a Friday night...with his mates in the pub.'

'Okay. Next we need to decide how we do it. Each, ahem, method of disposal needs to be different – if they were identical on the same night that would be too much of a coincidence. Then we need alibis. The police will initially interview us...as I said, they always suspect the spouse first. I know my sister will swear blind I was with her. What about you?'

Irene nodded. 'My mum would give me an alibi. I don't think I could say the 'M' word to her. I would have to come up with another reason for his disappearance. She never wanted me to marry him in the first place and knows I've been beaten up on occasions.'

'Good. So, time, place and means.' Marlene took out her phone to check her calendar. 'Let's tentatively put in a week on Friday, but we need to check with your mum and my sister that they are available to give us an alibi.'

Irene nodded taking it all in. 'And what about the means?'

Marlene leaned back in her seat. 'That's the difficult one. It depends on what you're comfortable with.' She then spoke as if creating a shopping list. 'Could be a whack over the head, a knife, run down by your car, although someone might see and take the registration number so that's high risk.'

Irene finished off her glass of wine then thoughtfully offered her contribution. 'I'd prefer to whack someone. I don't think I could put a knife in someone,' she then added, with a cynical smile, 'but I'd be happy for you to knife my husband...it would be revenge for all the beatings I've had to take.'

Marlene thought for a few moments then nodded in agreement. 'I'm okay with that.' She sat back with a satisfied smile. 'Just think, two more weeks then you'll be free to start a new life.' Irene half-nodded and stared into the distance. Marlene panicked for a second. Was Irene having second thoughts? She placed her hand on Irene's. 'Are you still comfortable with this?'

'Yeah, yeah, I'm okay,' Irene replied distractedly. She turned to Marlene and gave a reassuring smile. 'I'm just worried. There's a huge amount at stake, and if something does go wrong, we could end up in prison – for life.'

Marlene nodded. 'I understand what you're saying, but don't the benefits outweigh the risks?' The pub was filling up and the noise level increasing. 'Let's call it a day. I'll see you at work on Monday, but in the meantime lock in your mum for an alibi and do a recce on the Philatelic club.' She reached into her handbag and retrieved a pen and pad. 'Here, this is the address of my husband's club, it's in the civic hall behind the library. He gets there about seven-thirty. I'll do a recce on your husband. Which pub does he go to on a Friday night?'

'The Mulberry on Clifton street.'

Marlene nodded knowingly. 'Yeah, I know it.'

They both rose and pushed through the crowd to the car park at the rear of the pub. 'Stay positive, Irene. Another two weeks and you'll be free!'

Irene smiled and got into her car.

* * *

Marlene rang the doorbell of her sister's home, a modest semi on a modern estate. The hall light flicked on in response. Her sister, Jan, answered the door. 'Well, what a surprise, my big sis, come in.' Jan was a slim, petite woman with dark hair and sparkling hazel eyes. She wore navy tailored trousers and a pale grey sloppy Joe sweater, quite the reverse of her older sister's frumpy appearance.

'Mike not at home this evening?' Marlene began.

Jan switched on the coffee machine then leaned on the central unit. 'Away in Leicester until next Tuesday. Biscuit?'

'No thanks.' Marlene wanted to get through the small talk before asking the big favour.

'How's work?

Marlene tried to sound upbeat. 'Oh, same as usual, boring as hell.'

The machine finally stopped spluttering and Jan expertly poured out the coffees. They both trooped into the lounge and flopped down into easy chairs.

'So, to what do I owe the honour?'

Marlene hesitated for a few seconds then ploughed into an explanation for her unannounced visit.

'I need you to do me a big favour. What I'm asking is, if the police happen to come sniffing round, and I'll explain why in a minute, that you'll give me an alibi; say I was here all evening until late. Say something like, I came for my tea and left at nearly eleven.'

Jan pulled a face and took a deep breath. 'Whoa! That's some ask.' She took a sip of her coffee to give her time to think. 'Why on earth would the police come round asking questions?'

'Look Jan, you know I've not been happy with Frank for some time.'

'Yes, of course I do.'

'Well, I work with a colleague and she's not happy with her situation either, her husband beats her up when he's drunk.'

'What's that got to do with anything?'

Marlene took a deep breath before launching into an explanation. There was no other way to take her sister into her confidence without giving her the whole truth. 'We have decided to sort out each other's husbands, i.e. get rid of them, one way or another.'

Jan had her arms folded, a shocked expression across her face. She didn't want to hear what was coming next. 'Sort out?'

'We've agreed to get rid of each other's husband. That way any suspicion is directed away from the obvious suspect – the spouse.'

Jan stood up and began to pace the room. 'Sis, are you joking? Have you gone mad? Think of the consequences if it all goes wrong. Life in prison.' She stifled a cynical laugh. 'I've got to say, if I was married to Frank I'd want a way out...but this! It's mad. Can't you just walk out on him?'

Marlene didn't respond, but let Jan ponder on what had been said. Jan eventually stopped pacing and looked to Marlene for further explanation.

Marlene grabbed her sister's hands. 'It would allow me to do the things I've always wanted to do...travel, move to the country, be my own boss, come and go as I please. I can't do that if I simply leave him. I'd probably end up in some pokey flat on a housing estate struggling to pay the bills.' She took a pause then pleaded, 'I've got to do it. I want to have a life other than conversations about bloody stamp perforations.'

Jan looked aghast, banged her cup down and started pacing again. 'I can't believe I'm hearing this.' She stopped pacing and folded her arms in a defensive position. 'And what about your partner in crime? What does she get out of it?'

Marlene leaned forward in her chair. 'She will avoid the beatings every time her husband is drunk. She also tells me she's been having an affair with a childhood sweetheart for the past twelve months. If she's free of her bum of a husband, she can start a new life with her lover.'

Jan nodded solemnly. 'I get it. But what if it rebounds on me?' she asked slowly coming round to the idea.

'That's the great plan of 'swapping' crimes, neither of us would be a prime suspect...and we'd have alibis.'

'Oh sis, this sounds really desperate, but if that's what you've got planned, I'll back you all the way, you know that. Just don't drag me in any further than providing the alibi. Giving a false alibi can send me to jail.'

On the way home from her sister's Marlene detoured via The Mulberry pub and checked out the car park. It was perfect. Dark, secluded and lined with large overhanging trees. Plenty of cover.

While Marlene was checking out The Mulberry pub and convincing her sister to give her an alibi, Irene was doing the same.

Irene's mum was eighty-six. She lived in a terraced house on a cobbled street and had done so for more than fifty years. It was in an older part of town and over the past ten years had slowly become gentrified as young couples moved in and renovated the houses. It had become a sought-after area in which to live. Irene went around the rear of the house, along the back passageway and into the back yard via a large green wooden gate. She knew the back door would be unlocked and gently knocked so as not to alarm her mum.

'Hello mum, it's me.' She opened the door to be met by the elderly woman wiping her floured hands on a towel.

'Oh, hello love, it's good to see you. I'm just making a cake. Cup of tea?'

She was a grey-haired lady, physically infirm from arthritis which made her unstable when walking, but her mind was as bright as a button. They sat in the small lounge where there was a large oak table, a matching sideboard and two easy chairs. One of the chairs nearest to the television was now never used – it had been Irene's dad's, who had died nearly ten years ago. Her mum just couldn't bring herself to get rid of it. 'It's lovely to see you Irene, have you come for anything in particular?'

'Yes, I have mum.' She wanted to keep the sordid details from her mum so told her a shortened version of what had been planned. Irene took a deep breath before she began. 'You know I've not been happy for some time, don't you?' Her mum nodded, grim faced, wondering what was coming next. 'Well, I've decided to distance myself from him.'

'Good, about time.'

'Well, a friend and I are going to make him erm... go away.' She cringed at the ridiculous words she was using. 'Please don't ask me to explain. I just want to let you know that I'll finally get rid him for good soon.' Her mum looked even more grim. Irene looked away from her mum hoping she'd told her enough and that her mum wouldn't ask any questions.

Her mum took several seconds before responding to Irene's words. 'Listen love, if it means giving you peace of mind, away from that...that evil man, who I've never liked, then I'm happy for you.'

Irene felt a load being lifted from her shoulders. 'Thanks mum.' She took her mum by both hands and made direct eye contact with her. 'I promise I'll be safe. I promise. Oh, by the way, I'm going to a restaurant for a meal with a friend on Friday night. A girl I knew from school.'

Once she'd left her mum's house, she parked the car and dialled a number.

It was answered almost immediately. 'Hello, Ferguson's restaurant?'

'Ah, hello. My name's Irene Hamilton, can I book a table for two for Friday night, please, seven o'clock. Great, thanks.'

Ferguson's restaurant was a converted barn in Skelfold, twenty miles away from the potential crime scene, far enough away to be an alibi for Irene. She then dialled another number. 'Hi, Chloe? It's Irene. Yeah, fine thanks. I'm giving you a ring to see if you're free Friday. I had a table booked at Ferguson's and my friend has just phoned to cancel. Some family problem I gather. So, are you free Friday...my treat.'

Chloe couldn't believe her luck. 'Wow, that would be great, thanks. It's been some time since we caught up, so we'll have lots to talk about.'

'Wonderful. I'll pick you up around six-fifteen if that's okay.'

'Fine, see you Friday.'

The second part of her alibi was locked in.

On her way home, feeling relieved having got the difficult face to face chat with her mum over with, she checked out the civic hall behind the library. Marlene would need to know she'd checked it out, so she needed to sound knowledgeable.

* * *

At work on the Monday Irene received an email from Marlene.
Lunch, canteen, one-ish?
Irene replied. *Fine.*
Irene started the conversation. 'Did you clear it with your sister?'
Marlene nodded. 'Yes, I did. Slight change of plan though. Jan's coming over to my house rather than me going there, that way she doesn't have to explain anything to her husband.'
'Good. I spoke to my mum and implied I was planning something... obviously not the details. She's never liked Jeff and to be honest I don't think she cares what I've got planned as long as he's out of my life. She doesn't need to give me an alibi for later as I've arranged to meet a friend at a restaurant on Friday night. Also, I checked out the library. The rear car park is limited; however, it'll serve my purpose.'
 Marlene pushed her empty plate to one side. 'So, are we good to go on Friday night?'
'Yes, we are.'
Marlene hesitated slightly then said, 'Just to confirm their arrival times... Frank will arrive at the club around seven-thirty, seven forty-five.'
Irene nodded and smiled. 'I'll be there, in which case I'll be home by eight thirty-ish. You need to be at The Mulberry by seven-thirty.'
Marlene nodded. 'Good luck.'

* * *

Friday night. D-day

Both women were nervous, but with the detailed planning and the thought of the rewards that lay ahead, they were psyched up.

Marlene saw her husband off to the Philatelic club, then ran upstairs to get ready. She donned black trousers, a black polo sweater, black Chelsea boots and a black jacket, scraped her hair into a ponytail, then sat on the edge of the bed and rehearsed in her mind the next few hours. She had a photo of Irene's husband to make sure she would be targeting the right man as the car park was, for the most part, in darkness. *Arrive seven-twenty, park up, do the deed, home by eight-eight-fifteen.* She glanced at her watch. Time to go! She went back downstairs and removed a knife from the block on top of the kitchen unit. It felt heavy in her hand. It gave her confidence. More than enough to do the job.

She arrived just as she'd planned, at seven-twenty and parked under the lowest hanging branches of the surrounding trees so as to be hidden from the casual observer. She looked steadfastly through the windscreen, her eyes locked on the car park entrance awaiting Jeff Hamilton's blue and white ute. She imagined Irene arriving at the library car park at the same time as she'd arrived at the pub. No doubt Irene would park in the darkest corner, next to the skip which always seemed to be there. Frank would arrive totally unaware of what fate awaited him. It would only be a few minutes before Irene had successfully completed her half of the deal and Marlene would be a free woman.

At seven thirty-five, Irene's husband's Ford arrived at the pub and parked two car spaces away from her. Marlene checked the registration number Irene had given her and the photo of her target. Yes, this was him. *Now, move fast before he enters the pub.* As he blipped his doors to lock them, she climbed out of her car and approached him. 'Excuse me, you don't have a torch with you, do you?'

He turned to face her not sure if she was directing her question at him. 'Er, yeah, I have. Why?'

'Sorry to bother you, but I stumbled getting out of my car and dropped my keys. I can't see them anywhere, it's so dark where I've parked.' She scoffed apologetically. 'And I've got a bad back so if they've gone under the car, I'll never be able to bend down and retrieve them.' She moved back towards her car. 'Would you mind?'

He shrugged his shoulders. 'Sure, not a problem.' He went to the rear of his vehicle and unlocked a silver toolbox fastened in the rear of the ute. He produced a heavy torch and came over to where she was standing. 'Where did you drop them?'

She pointed down to the underneath of the car. 'Somewhere down there.' He switched on his torch and bent down to allow the light to illuminate the underneath of the car.

'I can't see anything.'

She suddenly began to panic. The discussions she'd had with Irene in the comfort of the work canteen whilst enjoying a coffee suddenly came into stark focus. *What the hell am I doing! It's too late, I mustn't let Irene down.* At this point Marlene's heart was beating so fast she thought she was going to faint. She took out the knife she had concealed inside her jacket and plunged it into Irene's husband's neck. He immediately collapsed, grabbed his neck and made the most awful blood-curdling noises. It was if he was trying to speak. Blood spurted everywhere. She reached down and grabbed him by his jacket collar and slowly dragged him away from the car door and into the even darker gloom of the overhanging tree branches. She had no idea a body could weigh so much. Several more people were arriving at the pub and parking their cars. They were in deep conversation with each other so didn't notice what was going on at the rear of the car park. She quickly jumped in her own car, turned the ignition and drove out onto the main street and headed home. She was shaking uncontrollably.

Her sister had a glass of wine ready for Marlene when she arrived home. Once Marlene stepped in through the front door, still shaking, Jan raised her eyebrows and nodded down to Marlene's clothes. 'Oh my God, you did it then. Let's hope no one saw you. I think you'd better get changed. Give me your clothes and I'll get rid of them.' Marlene looked down and was horrified to see her trousers and shoes spattered in blood.

Almost at the same time Irene and Chloe were enjoying a meal and catching up on old times. They were old school mates, and in those days went everywhere together. Once they'd left school, as usually happens, they went their separate ways, Irene to the local FE college and Chloe landed a job in the marketing department of an events company. They finished off their evening with an espresso coffee then Irene drove Chloe home, arriving back at her own home around ten o'clock. She smiled to herself as she put her key in the front door lock. An evening well spent!

Marlene stripped off her clothes. She washed her shoes under the tap and put them in the wardrobe. Whilst she had a shower her sister collected them and put them in a metal container in the back garden and collected some garden rubbish to place on top. It was left for burning the following day.

Feeling much better after a hot shower, she returned to the lounge where her sister was patiently waiting for her. 'Had a good scrub sis?'

Marlene nodded. She was still in a daze over what she'd done. 'Yeah, thanks. I'm glad it's all over. Irene will be relieved she no longer has to suffer the violence that's been dished out to her over the years.'

'And you are free of Philately Frank the Boring,' said her sister, raising her glass.

Marlene laughed and slumped onto the sofa. 'Yeah. At last. Just think, I no longer have to put up with long-winded accounts of counting bloody perforations on stamps.'

Jan chuckled. 'Yep.'

Marlene looked at the time then half-rose from her seat. 'Coffee before you go?'

Jan nodded. 'Of course.'

They both went into the kitchen and chatted whilst the coffee machine did its job. She'd just poured out two cups when a noise stopped them both in their tracks. She frowned at Jan and her stomach somersaulted.

'What was that?'

Jan shook her head. 'It sounded like a key being put in the front door...but that's impossible, right?' Before Marlene had time to respond the kitchen door opened and a man appeared.

'Hello, you two, you look as though you've seen a ghost.'

'Oh, Frank, I wasn't expecting you...yet,' she stammered, then glanced at her watch in an attempt to divert her surprised look. 'Oh, is it that time already.'

He smiled. 'I'll leave you two to chat, I'm going for a shower.' They waited until they could hear the shower being turned on.

'Oh God!' Marlene growled, 'what's going on? He shouldn't be here.' She picked up her mobile from the unit and shakily dialled Irene's number. Without any introduction she hissed down the phone. 'What the hell's happened? I've kept my part of the bargain, what's going on?'

'Sorry Marlene, I couldn't do it. I don't want to talk,' and slammed the phone down. Marlene slowly put her phone down. She'd been betrayed. A flood of emotions hit her. She was angry, panic-stricken and so disappointed at the thought of her dream being shattered. She stared into space. Jan could see the devastation in her sister's eyes.

'What the hell has gone wrong?' Marlene turned her head to look at Jan and answered her robotically. 'She's reneged on the deal, said she couldn't do it. Where does that leave me? I've got rid of her husband, but she hasn't got rid of...' she pointed with her forefinger in the direction of upstairs.

* * *

The next day the local newspaper and the television news reported the murder of Irene's husband.

The Northern Herald
Man murdered in pub car park.

Late last evening a man was found bleeding heavily in the car park of The Mulberry pub in the town centre. An ambulance was called, but he died on the way to hospital. He has been named as Jeffery Hamilton, a thirty-two-year-old electrician.

'We don't know of a motive at this stage,' a police spokesman said. It was a particularly vicious killing, and the police are asking the public if anyone has any information to contact their local police station.

Irene's mum watched the television news with alarm, and concern for her daughter. She phoned Irene.

'No, I'm okay, mum. I told you I would be. A police officer came round to the house late last night to inform me of his death. They want me to go into the police station this morning to formally identify him. They want to interview me, just routine questions.'

Her mum sounded distressed. 'Why would they want to interview you. Surely you had nothing to do with his murder? I know you said you were going to distance yourself from him but...well, I don't know what to think.'

Irene tried to reassure her. 'I'll be okay, don't worry. They have to interview me, I'm next of kin. And the spouse is always top of the suspect list. I was out with Chloe last night so she'll confirm where I was, and the restaurant will confirm what time I arrived and what time I paid the bill. Don't worry.'

Her mum was silent for a few seconds then. 'Let me know how you get on tomorrow.'

'I will, promise.'

Irene arrived at Citrus Street Police Station and explained to the desk sergeant why she was there. The sergeant was a bulky man who, by the scars on his face, appeared to have encountered his fair share of affrays during his career in apprehending villains. His paunch wobbled over his trouser belt suggesting to Irene that it was doubtful he was now in any fit state to chase villains. He directed her to a hard plastic chair, one of four lined up against the wall. She sat feeling daunted by the unfamiliar surroundings. Eventually a side door opened, and a young woman emerged. 'Irene Hamilton?'

Irene stood up. 'Yes. One of your officers asked me to come in.'

The female officer gave a welcoming smile and held her hand out. 'DI Sylvia Marchant. Please come through.' Sylvia was a no-nonsense officer, well known for being firm but fair. 'I know this is going to be extremely difficult for you, but we need you to formally identify your husband. Are you OK with doing that?' Irene nodded. She was then taken down a narrow glass-panelled corridor past offices crowded with people busying about, some in uniform, some presumably plain clothes detectives. She was escorted out of a rear door of the station and into the 'next-of-kin suite' within the mortuary which was located to the rear of the police station. DI Marchant stopped and opened a door waving Irene through. She was led into a small, well-furnished room with a sofa and armchairs. The walls were painted a light grey with a light oak coffee table. There was a viewing window across which a curtain had been drawn. DI Marchant looked at Irene and asked, 'Are you ready? Do you need some more time?' Irene shook her head, and the curtain was drawn back. On seeing her husband's body, she gasped.

'Yes, that's my husband.' She did her best to look distraught and grabbed a tissue which was lying in a box on the coffee table.

Once identification had taken place, DI Marchant took Irene back into the station, along the corridor and into one of the interview rooms. The room was small, dismal and smelled of sweat. To the right of the DI was DS Michael Bond. The DI opened a manila folder in front of her then looked up. 'First of all we'd like to say we're very sorry for your loss.'

'Thank you.'

The DI continued. 'I know it's a very difficult time for you, but we do need to ask a few routine questions at this stage Irene.' She paused then asked, 'can I call you Irene?'

Irene nodded and dabbed her eyes trying to look as distraught as expected when someone has lost a loved one.

'Can I ask where you were last night?'

Irene sniffled. 'Ferguson's restaurant in Skelfold.'

'Can anyone corroborate that?'

Irene nodded and wiped her reddened eyes again. 'My friend Chloe.' She gave a weak smile. 'An old school friend.'

'What time did you arrive at the restaurant and what time did you leave?'

'I'd booked a table for seven and left around ten-ish.' She rummaged in her handbag. 'I think I've still got the receipt showing what time I paid.'

The DI held her hand out. 'I'd like that please. And we'd like the full name of your friend and her contact details.' Irene dutifully handed her the information.

Then the DI changed the subject. 'Did your husband always go to The Mulberry on a Friday night?'

'Yes, he did, he liked to catch up with his mates.'

'Do you know of anyone who would want to hurt him?'

Irene was on the verge of saying 'I DO' in a very loud voice but stayed in control. 'No, I don't, he got on with all his mates.'

Sylvia hesitated then asked, 'And you? Was everything okay at home?' Irene silently nodded. Sylvia stood up. 'That's all for the present. Thank you for coming in. If there's anything we can do, please let us know.'

Irene left the police station and went to her favourite coffee shop, Tinkers, hoping her guilty conscience hadn't betrayed her.

* * *

Marlene arrived for work after an intense weekend of jangled nerves and sleepless nights. She ensconced herself in her office, having first been to the tiny kitchen to make a cup of coffee. She found it impossible to start the day without one. She could imagine the whole company would be abuzz discussing the events of last Friday evening. It was a small town and news travelled fast. Having closed her office door, she picked up the phone to speak to Irene at home, determined to give her a piece of her mind and insist they meet up. She was fuming and desperately needed an explanation. She would demand one! She picked up the phone and dialled. 'Hello?'

'Irene?' Marlene didn't recognise the voice.

'No, it's her sister. Irene's gone away for a couple of weeks. She wanted to get away from all the dreadful events of the weekend.'

I bet she bloody did! thought Marlene

'If she contacts you, can you please tell her Marlene from work phoned.' She put the phone down and sat back in her chair, biting her bottom lip. She thought, *Surprise, surprise, she's buggered off!*

* * *

Immediately Irene had left the police station, DI Marchant took the short walk to return to the forensics lab and pushed open the double doors leading to the reception. She gave a smile and a wave to Sadie, the receptionist, who returned the greeting and clicked open the door that led to the labs. The labs were based in an old building which at one time had been part of the town hall. They were promised some time ago a purpose-built structure, but that seemed to have been shelved due to budget cuts. Sylvia found the team leader, Monica Sutcliffe, sitting in her office studying some paperwork. Monica was a refined lady in her early sixties. She wore rimless glasses which were hung round her neck on a red cord. She looked up as the DI gently tapped on her door. 'Come in Sylvia. How are you?' They went back a long way and trusted each other implicitly. Sylvia made herself comfortable in a chair on the opposite side of the desk.

'Have you got anything for me from The Mulberry?'

Monica nodded. 'I think we have. Not much, but it might give you something to work with.' She pushed a report sheet across the table to Sylvia and began to explain the content.

The DI laughed and put up her hand. 'In plain English Monica...if you don't mind.' Monica chuckled knowing she could easily confuse Sylvia with 'path' speak.

'I'm coming to that. We found blood on the floor which matches that of the deceased and some tyre tracks across the blood pools. Checking our database for tyre treads it's likely that they are maybe from a Volvo, but nothing more specific. If you could find the vehicle then maybe it could still have blood on the tyres that matches the deceased. We found no weapon, sorry.'

Later that evening in The Lavender Bush, Simone Peters ordered a white wine whilst she waited for her friends. It didn't seem that long ago she was in this pub when she had bumped into Marlene and Irene. She also remembered how annoyed she was with their 'brush off' which was totally uncalled for. She looked around the room registering the table where she had seen Irene and Marlene. Something in the back of her mind nagged at her about that meeting. Her friends arrived and ordered their drinks then they all wandered off to find a suitable table. They met up once a month for a catch up.

'A lot has happened for me since we were in here last,' said Carly looking around the room, 'I've got a new job, and I've met a new bloke.'

'Hey, that's great. A new job? Where? Doing what? And who's the new guy? Give us the nitty-gritty and leave nothing out.'

Carly had a smug smile across her face. 'Supervisor in the IT section at Harpers,' she added. 'More money and not as far to travel.' There was applause all round and a raising of glasses.

'Congrats Carly, good for you, you deserve it.'

Simone leaned into the group. 'More importantly. The new bloke?'

Carly had an even bigger smirk across her face. 'His name is Callum.' This prompted an overtly female 'ooh' from the gang which she ignored and carried on with her description. 'He's thirty-five, divorced and a sales rep.' This was followed by more 'oohs'.

'Where did you meet him?'

'He does business with our company, saw me in reception, we had a chat, he invited me out for lunch and, hey presto.' They all took a long swig of their drinks then the conversation became serious.

'What about last weekend. The murder at the back of The Mulberry?' interjected one of Simone's friends.

Simone jumped in. 'I used to work with his wife, Irene Hamilton.'

'Oh, really? It must be terrible for her,' someone interjected.

Simone continued in a low voice. 'From what I hear he was a bum. A violent one at that. He used to beat her up.' There were tuts, shaking of heads and disapproving comments about anyone who had to put up with a violent spouse. They quickly changed the subject on to lighter things – clothes, films, what they'd seen on streaming-TV channels and good and not-so-good restaurants they'd visited.

The background hum of noise in the pub slowly diminished as customers made their way out, some decidedly worse for wear. Simone checked her watch. 'Oh, my God, look at the time, it's nearly closing time.' They gathered their handbags and coats and pushed their way out into the cold air. The forecast had been for severe cold weather and the pavements were already tinged with sparkling frost.

'See you all next month. Same place?'

'Yeah, see you then. Stay safe.' They jumped in their respective cars and exited the car park. All except Simone. She sat in her car in the gloom and mulled over the events of her previous visit when she'd bumped into Irene and Marlene. What was it that was nagging her? *Was I imagining what I heard Irene say? It sounded like genuine distress at the time. Maybe that's why they were so cool with me; they wanted me to move on because they had personal issues to discuss.*

* * *

DI Marchant de-briefed the rest of the team. They were in the briefing room on the third floor of the building. For such a small team there was ample room. It had been the IT room before they were transferred to the prestigious new building at the opposite end of town. It was a stark contrast to the rather shabby and dated pathology lab next door, which was linked via a purpose-built corridor. It suited Marchant perfectly. There was room for two whiteboards and, most importantly, the automatic coffee machine. It had been abandoned by the IT Department in favour of the new super-duper Italian frothy machine that had been installed at their new abode. The DI tapped on the table with her Texta to grab everyone's attention.

'I spoke to the victim's wife earlier and at this stage she's not a priority suspect. On the night in question, she was out with a friend in Skelfold. Her alibi has been confirmed with both her friend and the restaurant, Ferguson's. They were able to confirm that she and her friend arrived at seven and, according to the till receipt, it was paid at nine-twenty. I estimate that Irene Hamilton would have arrived home around ten. This puts her outside the timeframe the murder took place. According to Mrs Hamilton her husband had no enemies that she was aware of. I've got a list of his friends that need be interviewed.' She held the list up. 'DCs Cranbrook and Brown, take this list and work through it, thanks. DS Bond, you're with me. We'll go and have a word with some of her workmates. You know how workmates gossip, there just might be something. Back at four for a debrief. Any questions? No? Right, see you later.'

The interviews with Jeff Hamilton's mates didn't reveal anything. The general consensus was he was a great guy, good for a laugh and the life and soul of a party.

At Irene's workplace one member of staff suggested they have a word with Marlene Drinkwater as she was often seen having lunch Irene. The DI knocked on Marlene's office door. Marlene looked up from what she was doing and suddenly felt nauseous. 'I'm DI Marchant and this is DS Bond. Mind if we have a word?'

'Er, of course, come in.' Had the DI detected the tremor in her voice?

'We're investigating the murder of the husband of one of your colleagues, Irene Hamilton. I believe you know Mrs Hamilton?'

Marlene nodded solemnly. 'Yes. It was a terrible shock. Do you know what happened?'

The DI smiled. 'That's what we're trying to find out. We understand you were close friends.'

She shook her head. 'No, not really.'

'Oh, I see. We understand from a member of staff that you often had lunch with Mrs Hamilton, is that so?'

'Yes, we did sometimes.'

'Did she ever mention if her husband had any problems?'

'Er, no she didn't.'

DS Bond was making notes as the conversation continued. 'Were you made aware if Mr Hamilton had any enemies? Did Mrs Hamilton ever discuss what the situation was like at home? Were there any problems?'

Marlene slowly shook her head. 'I didn't know her that well. We never discussed personal things. It was mainly work chit-chat.' The DI finished her questioning, and the DS put his notepad and pen in his jacket pocket. 'OK, that's it for now. Thanks for your co-operation. If you think of anything, anything at all, please let us know straightaway. We'll see ourselves out.'

Marlene watched them leave then put her head in her hands as she leaned on her desk. *Oh, my God. I'm in deep... Wait till I get my hands on that bitch...leaving me to pick up the pieces.*

The DI and DS sat in their car and pondered the interview with Marlene Drinkwater. 'What d'you reckon Michael? Do you believe her?'

The DS shook his head. 'There's something she's not telling us. I was studying her body language. I can always tell if someone is either lying or hiding something.'

The DI turned the ignition. 'I agree. We'll probably end up having another word with her.'

Marlene wandered back to her desk after having watched the police car exit the car park and turn left in the direction of the police station. She sat at her desk, not sure whether she'd convinced the officers of her innocence. The paperwork in front of her just became a blur. She couldn't concentrate. *How, why, did I get myself into this mess? I need to get hold of Irene Hamilton.*

* * *

The team was already in the debriefing room awaiting the DI. She had to inform them that very little progress had been made. 'Of all the people we've spoken to we've got no leads. Even with the newspaper coverage no members of the public phoned in...not even the nutters. DS Bond and I interviewed Marlene Drinkwater this afternoon and we both feel she's not divulging all she knows. We need something to turn this investigation around. It looks like I'm going to have to do a TV appeal. I'll have a word with the Super to get the okay. Somebody out there knows something. I need to find out what it is.'

The TV appeal was broadcast the following evening.

Many of you will know from the media coverage over the past few days, that last Friday evening a thirty-two-year-old male was viciously murdered in the car park of The Mulberry pub. As usual, the pub was busy that Friday evening. Somebody must have seen something, know something or suspect something. The police are asking for anyone in the community who has information which could help us apprehend the perpetrator, to please come forward, however insignificant you may think the information may be. His family need closure on this horrendous crime. Thank you.

The following day, DI Marchant was sitting at her desk reviewing the information on the interviews that had been completed. Had she missed something? She was still uncomfortable with the response her and DS Bond had gleaned from Marlene Drinkwater. The woman appeared too nervous. As she pondered on the type of approach to take, a constable knocked on her door. 'The front desk has just received this ma'am. Someone phoned in after your TV appeal,' he said as he handed her the piece of paper.

'Thank you.' She read the scrawled note. A Simone Peters had phoned to say she had something that may be relevant. At the bottom of the note was Simone's work phone number. The DI picked up the phone, praying the next few minutes would be productive.

'Hello?'

'Is that Simone Peters?'

'Yes.'

'Good morning, this is DI Marchant. You left a message saying you may have some information regarding the recent murder that could be helpful to us.'

'Er, yes. I don't know how useful it will be, it's something I heard in the pub.' She explained she'd been in The Lavender Bush a couple of weeks prior to the murder and saw Marlene and Irene sitting together. 'I used to work with them both,' she explained. 'Anyway, I had a quick chat then moved on as I got the impression they didn't want to be interrupted. I joined my friends at the bar and then later we all heard a sharp cry from either Irene or Marlene, I don't know which, but one of them cried out 'murder' in a very loud voice. Everyone in the pub stopped talking and turned round.' Simone paused, then, 'That's it, really. We all thought it odd and then two weeks later Irene's husband is killed.'

Marchant continued making notes then thanked Simone. 'That's really helpful. Thank you for coming forward.'

She put the phone down then called to DS Bond in the next office. 'Michael, get your coat.' As they hurried out, she stopped at the desks of DCs Cranbrook and Brown. 'Can you two get over to Irene Hamilton's place. I think she's taken leave from work so could be anywhere. Her sister's staying at the house and her mum lives not too far away. Whatever, find her somehow. Phone me as soon as you've located her, then DS Bond and I will go and see Marlene Drinkwater to ask her the same question. It's important we speak to them at the same time. What I want to know is: What were they discussing to warrant one of them shouting out 'murder' in the pub? I want to see if their explanations tally, OK? As soon as we've asked the question and got their answers, I'll see you back here.'

DCs Cranbrook and Brown contacted Irene's sister, who reluctantly gave them the number of where Irene was staying.

As DI Marchant and DS Bond arrived at Marlene Drinkwater's place of work it had started spitting with rain and a stiff breeze had set in, forcing them to turn up their coat collars as they ran through the main doors. They found her in her office and knocked on her door. 'Mind if we come in, just a couple more questions to clarify one or two points.'

Drinkwater's face suddenly looked ashen, but she put on a confident façade. 'Certainly, come in. How can I help you?' Her voice didn't sound as confident as she would have liked.

The two officers remained standing. 'We have a witness who says that a couple of weeks prior to the murder at The Mulberry, you were seen with Irene in the Lavender Bush pub, when one of you suddenly shouted out 'murder'. What had you been discussing?'

Marlene sat back in her chair and laughed. 'Oh, that! We were talking about a Netflix film we'd seen the previous night.'

'Ah, right. What was the name of the film?'

Drinkwater pursed her lips in deep thought. 'Ooh, I can't remember, sorry. It was one of many true crime programmes we'd both watched.'

Marchant smiled. 'That's okay. If you do remember, can you let us know.' Once more Marlene nervously watched them exit the building, climb in their car and disappear up the road. Panic set in again. Who heard them and told the police? What did they really want? Were they closing in?

Marchant and Bond checked their answer from Drinkwater with the response Cranbrook and Brown had gleaned from Irene Hamilton.

Brown provided Irene's side of the story. 'We managed to speak to her over the phone. Her sister gave us a contact number where she's staying with friends in Peterborough. Her explanation for shouting murder, and it was her by the way, was that they were discussing who was the last woman in England to be executed for murder.'

The DI chuckled. 'She must be a very quick thinker to come up with that one...incidentally, it was Ruth Ellis in 1955. The fact remains that their explanations are miles apart which signals a red flag. I know Hamilton has a solid alibi for that evening, so it forces us to look more closely at Drinkwater. I'm going to apply for a search warrant for Drinkwater's home.'

The search warrant was issued. DI Marchant organised forensics and several uniformed officers to be available for a 6.30am visit. Dawn was just breaking and doing its best to brighten the day with a promise of some wintry sunshine. Dead on the dot of six-thirty Marchant smartly rapped on the door. After several seconds they saw an upstairs curtain move then eventually the front door being unlocked. Marlene wore a pink floral wrap-round quilted housecoat tightly pulled around her body. She was wearing no make-up, and her hair was badly in need of some TLC. Frank Drinkwater hovered in the background looking equally unkempt and bleary-eyed. 'Wha...what's going on Marlene? Who is it?' She ignored him concentrating on the officer in front of her.

Marchant held up the warrant. 'Good morning, Mrs Drinkwater, I have a warrant to search these premises.' She stepped over the threshold forcing Drinkwater further into the hallway. 'Would you please sit in the lounge whilst these officers carry out the search. We also need to search your car so can you open the garage please.' The officers piled in knowing exactly what was expected of them. Forensics made directly for the garage and the car.

Frank looked bewildered. 'What's going on? Why are you doing this? We've done nothing wrong. You must have the wrong address.'

All Marlene could say was, 'Shut up Frank.'

'Please take a seat with your wife,' Marchant calmly advised.

As they sat on the edge of their seats, upstairs they could hear drawers being opened and closed and hangers of clothes jangling against the rails. Downstairs, the kitchen was being thoroughly checked and they could see the block of knives being taken away. They took computers from the lounge and both mobile phones. Monica, who was heading up the forensics team tapped on the lounge door and motioned for Marchant to join her in the hallway, her white suit rustling on the door frame. Inside the evidence bag she was holding, were a pair of black Chelsea boots which she upended to show Marchant. The soles had obvious signs of mud and blood.

'We'll check the blood against the victim and the mud against that in the pub car park.'

Marchant smiled and nodded. 'Good work Monica.' She pointed to the evidence bag. 'Soon as, please.'

'Would tomorrow suit?'

'Perfect.'

True to her word Monica had the results by the following day and phoned Marchant mid-morning. 'Good news for you. The blood on the soles of the boots match that of the victim and the mud matches the car park. It tells us that at some time she'd been in that car park when there was blood on the floor. In addition, there were traces of blood on the door sill of her car. Again, it tells us that she may have stood in that blood after the event and transferred it as she got into her car.'

'Thanks Monica, it's a big step forward.' She put the phone down and put her head in her hands in frustration. Bugger, it was still only circumstantial evidence. It was promising, but nevertheless not quite enough. She grabbed the file which contained the initial interview with Marlene Drinkwater and quickly scanned the pages knowing what she was looking for. Ah, there it was!

In Drinkwater's original statement she stated categorically that she was at home...all evening, with her sister. Why would she lie? I'll need to bring her in, put her under a bit of pressure. One more thing to check.

She picked up the phone and phoned traffic. 'Hi, it's DI Marchant. Can you do me a check on a white Volvo, registration number 5829 NF. Was it picked up anywhere on ANPR around town in the evening on the 14th of this month?'

Within an hour traffic had phoned her back with a positive sighting.

'Hi, it's John Robb, Traffic. The car was picked up on Bangor Road, twice, once at seven-eleven and again a seven forty-six. Hope that helps.'

'Great, thanks John.' Marchant did a mental high five. Yes! Correct road, correct time. And she said she was at home all evening!

* * *

In the Drinkwater household the atmosphere was tense. At breakfast Frank was still complaining about the search and why they had been targeted. Marlene informed him she was as much in the dark as he was as to why the warrant had been issued. She had endured his questions and general complaints all morning and she wanted to scream. She jumped up. 'I'll have a quick shower then I'll go into town. I'll phone work to tell them I'm not going in today.'

Frank continued chewing his toast and stared out of the window. 'Right.'

By eleven-thirty Marlene was back from her shopping trip laden with several branded bags. As she went in the front door Frank was coming out carrying two suitcases. She was taken aback and slowly watched him. A puzzled look on her face. He headed for his car, put the cases in the boot and climbed in the driving seat. She suddenly realised what was happening and ran after him. 'What do you think you're doing? Where are you going?' He wound the window down at the same time as switching on the ignition.

'I'm leaving you,' Frank said stridently.

She took a step back from the car, 'Leaving?'

'Yes, I've been having an affair for the past twelve months and Irene and I have decided we want a life together.'

Her mouth gaped open then, suddenly, the penny dropped. In a shrill voice she shouted, 'Irene?'...... Irene Hamilton?'

'Yes. She's free now her husband has gone.' With that he put the car in gear, clicked off the handbrake and reversed down the drive.

Marlene stormed into the house, slammed the door making a vase on the hall table rattle. She ran down the hall sobbing and cursing in equal amounts and used the landline to phone her sister.

'Jan? It's me. Frank's gone,' she wailed, struggling to get her words out.

'Gone? What d'you mean?'

Marlene shouted hysterically, 'Gone! Gone as in left me.'

Her sister spoke in a low voice, 'But isn't that what you want? You wanted him out of your life.'

'Yes, but he's been having an affair...with that woman!'

'Slow down sis, what woman?'

'Irene bloody Hamilton,' Marlene shouted even louder in frustration, 'that bitch!'

Her sister's voice rose a couple of octaves, 'Irene Hamilton! You've gotta be joking. The one whose husband you got rid of?'

'I'm not joking. I've been conned...shafted by that woman. She got what she wanted, her husband out of the way, but I'm the one who is out in the cold having murdered her husband. I've been had! She reeled me in good and proper. I tell you, if the cops come knocking, I'm going to take her down as well. Tell them the whole story. If I'm going to jail, so is she.' At that moment the front doorbell chimed. 'Hang on, there's someone at the door.' She placed the handset on the hall table and made her way to the door, still ranting and raving. When she opened it, she was faced with two police officers, DI Marchant and DS Bond. At the end of the drive, she could see a yellow and blue chequered police car and an officer leaning against the rear door.

Marchant was grim faced. 'Mrs Drinkwater, we'd like you to come down to the station for a more formal interview.'

Marlene nodded but looked confused, 'I'm sorry there must be some mistake.'

Marchant stepped forward and took her by the arm and placed the phone on the back on its base, 'I'm afraid not.'

She was marched down the drive only to see, to her embarrassment, Mrs Chivers across the road who'd stopped to see what was going. David Crosby, who was walking his dog, almost walked into a lamppost as he gawped at the scene. How humiliating! Seeing her being helped into the rear seat of a police car.

Back at the station Marlene was placed in an interview room and left for half an hour. She sat frozen in time staring at the cold metal table. *I'm trapped! Was this really happening to me? It had all seemed a good idea at the time and it's all backfired.*

Marchant and Bond entered the room and sat down. Marchant opened a file and Bond switched on a tape recorder. Bond waited a second then said, 'Present in the room interviewing Mrs Marlene Drinkwater are DI Marchant and DS Bond.' Bond prompted Drinkwater with a nod in the direction of the machine, 'Please state your name.'

'Marlene Drinkwater.'

Marchant started the interview. 'Do you know why you've been arrested?' Marlene nodded with a frown across her face, 'Yes, I think so.'

'We'd like to ask a few more questions in relation to the murder of Jeffery Hamilton.' She pretended to scan her notes, 'Forensics found a considerable amount of blood at the scene which was subsequently identified as the blood of the deceased. We also found the same blood on the door sill of your car. Can you explain how it got there?'

'No.'

'Okay. More worryingly, we found the same blood on the soles of your boots. Any idea how it got there?'

Marlene mutely shook her head.

'For the tape please.'

'No.'

Marchant again referred to the file. 'You said in your statement that you were in all evening on the night in question. Is that correct?

Marlene responded more defiantly this time. 'Yes, I was. I told you to check with my sister.'

'Did anyone borrow your car that evening?'

'Er, no'

'Then can you explain why your car was picked up on our ANPR at...' she checked the file once more '...at seven-eleven and seven forty-six, very close to The Mulberry? Do you have any explanation?'

Marlene felt trapped. She started to perspire. She coughed to clear her throat. 'Er no.'

Marchant let the silence continue for some time then in a more friendly voice continued.

'Marlene, it's not looking good for you. The evidence against you is stacking up. If a court finds you guilty, you'll be spending a long time behind bars. Your only hope is to help us. Be up front. Tell us the whole story. Maybe then we can put a good word in for you, tell the court you co-operated.' She let the silence hang in mid-air again to give Marlene a chance to absorb the seriousness of the situation. Tears were now running down Marlene's cheeks, her hands were shaking, and she was hyperventilating.

'Mrs Drinkwater, would you like to take a break?'

Marlene shook her head and began to regain some control, 'No, I'll give you the whole story.' She took a deep breath before continuing. 'Irene Hamilton was my accomplice.' Her words interrupted by her sobbing.

Marchant and Bond looked at each other at this revelation, 'Irene Hamilton? But she had a solid alibi for the evening in question.'

Drinkwater shook her head vigorously, 'No, no, not on the night. She was supposed to have been getting rid of my husband at the same time. She was part of the bigger plan.'

'I think you'd better start from the beginning.'

She leaned back in her seat and hesitated before she continued.

'The plan was for Irene and I to kill each other's husbands...to divert any suspicion away from us. You see, it's usually the spouse who's the main suspect in these sorts of crimes isn't it? Irene wanted her husband out of the way because he was so violent and I wanted mine out of the way because, well, he was so boring and I wanted a new life, where I could be me. If I'd simply left him, I wouldn't have any money to start my new life.' She blew her cheeks out, relieved that she'd got everything off her chest and had implicated Irene Hamilton in the process. Marlene was filled with venom and spat out 'I kept my side of the bargain, Irene didn't. And, she's been having an affair with my husband for a year.'

The DI gave an imperceptible nod to her DS who immediately left the room and organised DC's Cranbrook and Brown to find and re-interview Irene Hamilton with a view to arresting her for conspiracy to murder. Marchant turned back to Drinkwater.

'Please stand up.' Marlene reluctantly pushed back her chair and stood. 'Marlene Drinkwater, I'm charging you with the murder of Jeffery Hamilton on the fourteenth of October. You don't have to say anything but anything you do say may be taken down and used in evidence against you. Do you understand?'

EPILOGUE

Marlene Drinkwater was found guilty of murdering Jeffery Hamilton and sentenced to twenty-five years imprisonment. She was also found guilty of the conspiracy to have her husband Frank Drinkwater murdered and was sentenced to a further ten years imprisonment.

Irene Hamilton was found guilty of conspiracy to murdering Frank Drinkwater and to having her husband murdered. She was sentenced to twelve years imprisonment.

Drinkwater's sister, Jan, was found guilty of supplying a false alibi on behalf of her sister and was given a twelve-month suspended sentence.

No evidence was found against Frank Drinkwater of having any involvement in the conspiracy. He continued to live in Irene's house awaiting her release from jail.

3

The Shrove Tuesday Incident

February 13-14, 2024
Shrove Tuesday and Ash Wednesday
Ashbourne, Derbyshire

It was a bitterly cold day. The wind from the east came directly from Siberia, putting an extra chill in the air. The low black clouds were threatening snow or, at the very least, sleet. The locals were scurrying along the pavements, their collars turned up. They were attempting to complete their essential shopping before the severe weather arrived.

'You okay there?'

'Aye, just to your left a bit.'

Two pairs of ladders were propped up against the wall of Neville Gibson's newsagency. He and his brother-in-law, Dave Mitchell, were boarding up the windows. The sound of their drills pressing home the screws into the window frame stopped the conversation for a minute whilst they concentrated on the job in hand. Once back down on terra firma they stepped back to look at their effort.

'I don't want a repeat of last year.' Dave pointed across the road. 'I see Boots has already done theirs.'

Neville shook his head in frustration. 'Aye, last year they had both windows stoved in.'

Shrove Tuesday in Ashbourne was an important day in the town's calendar. In preparation for the big day, shops and car parks were closed and warning signs were placed at the roads leading into town, advising visiting motorists the dangers of street parking. It was THE football match. The boarding up of shop windows was not a reaction to the possibility of a visiting team causing trouble – the collateral damage from the Shrove Tuesday football match was all home grown. This was a match when the whole community took part, several hundred of them!

* * *

The now famous match goes back to 1667. This is a match that uses the whole town as its pitch, the goals being set three miles apart. The teams are the Up'ards - those born north of Henmore Brook and the Down'ards - those born south of the Brook. The aim of the Up'ards was to score a goal at Sturston Mill and the Down'ards to score at Clifton Mill. Neither mill still existed, the goals being represented by a rock plinth on which the goal scorer has to tap the plinth three times. The ball is a hand-sewn leather ball, larger than the traditional football, similar in size to a medicine ball. It is filled with cork so it would float, and hand-painted in the likeness of the person, otherwise known as 'The Turner Up', who would be chosen to 'kick off'. The usual choice was a local dignitary.

Dead on two o'clock, 'kick-off' time, the 'Turner up' would throw the ball into the crowd who would then fight to take control of the ball and pass it overhead towards their targeted goal. The main street, side streets, fields and rivers were all acceptable routes to the goal. Cemeteries and churchyards were out of bounds. The match would go through until ten o'clock at night. It would then be repeated all over again on Ash Wednesday. The teams became just a mass of people who would use any means at their disposal to gain control of the ball. It was common to see eye gouging, elbowing, twisting of arms, kicking and thumping. According to the medieval rules violence was frowned upon, although not forbidden! However, murder and manslaughter were definitely not on the agenda. Once the game was under way, the crowd (teams) moved as one, swaying this way and that along the length and width of the streets leading to the goals; in and out of rivers and across muddy fields. The ball would be thrown and bounced or kicked, by the teams. The crowd had once been likened to a flock of starlings that, when flying, suddenly changed direction as one. Those of the local population who didn't take part in the annual scrum watched from the safety of upstairs windows. They would point out people they knew and where they saw violence taking place. As the teams moved to the left and then to the right the main street would be empty for a few minutes before the opposing team was able to gain traction and move back toward their own goal.

On one such break from the cacophony of noise generated by the shouts of encouragement, a woman hanging out of the upstairs window of the ironmongers spotted a man on the floor lying against the kerb. He'd been trampled by the crowd. 'Oh, my God. A man's been hurt!' she cried and immediately phoned for an ambulance, hoping they could arrive before the crowd returned, pushing in the opposite direction. The ambulance arrived with only minutes to spare before the crowd filled the road again. The paramedics knelt by the man and checked his vitals before moving him. Sonia the lead paramedic pointed to the man's right side.

'Tony, look!' Her partner looked more closely to see the man had been stabbed under his left arm. They stemmed the bleeding and urgently put him on the gurney and into the ambulance, but sadly he died on the way to hospital.

* * *

DI Tom Brindle stood at the front of the briefing room acknowledging his team as they entered the room, some with take-away coffees in hand. His DS, Jen Morecroft, was busy at the whiteboard, pinning up a photo of the man who'd been stabbed at the football match, then writing his name underneath with a red felt-tipped pen.

Tom Brindle was a newly promoted DI and had worked for Derbyshire police since joining as a cadet, more years ago then he cared to remember. He was a short, stocky man, with dark hair and a well-trimmed beard. Today he wore a navy suit, light blue shirt and a conservative navy and red striped tie.

His DS, an attractive thirty-something woman, had decided on a career rather than motherhood. Through her dedicated commitment to the job, she had risen through the ranks and had been earmarked for further promotion. Jen Morecroft was petite, but tough. She was like a dog with a bone, leaving no stone unturned and was particularly good at diffusing potentially violent situations. She had dark hair, cut in a bob and had dark brown eyes. Her smile was captivating, even to the most hardened criminal.

The DI pointed to the whiteboard. 'This is the man who was tragically stabbed today at the football match. We're not releasing his name to the public until the body is positively identified by a member of his family. Once that's happened our first part of the investigation will be to talk to people who knew him; friends, relatives, associates. Did he have any enemies?' He paused, waiting for any questions, then directed his gaze over to his DS. 'Jen will provide you with a list allocating jobs to each of you. Please liaise with Jen regarding your tasks. Back here tomorrow, four o'clock for a debrief. Thank you.'

* * *

ASHBOURNE GAZETTE
February 15th

The annual Shrove Tuesday Football match was marred this year by the tragic death of one of the participants. It appears that in the rough and tumble of the melee, one man was pushed over and trampled on. Although an ambulance was called immediately, he died on the way to hospital. Police are not releasing the name of the man who died until further investigations have taken place. Event organiser Norris Forbes said 'This was a sad day for what is normally a time for the local community to get together and enjoy the day. Our condolences go to the unfortunate man's family. In the four hundred years of staging the event, only two deaths have occurred, one in 1860 and sadly, this one.'

* * *

Several weeks earlier:

Cyril Prosser turned into the drive of his home in the up-market suburb of Upper Blestone, a stone's throw from Ashbourne town centre. He pressed the automatic garage door opener. It slowly opened whilst Cyril patiently waited in his new BMW SUV. Once the door was fully open, he took his foot off the brake and eased the car into the double garage. His wife's BMW SUV was already parked to one side. His and hers! Both with personalised number plates! He reluctantly eased himself out of the car and entered the kitchen directly from the side door within the garage. He could have sat in the BMW's comfortable seats all day,

'De, I'm home.'

His wife Deirdre staggered into the kitchen, a wine glass in one hand a cigarette in the other. 'Hi, doll, had a good day?' She was a woman in her mid-fifties, more than a little overweight and over-bearing to those who knew her. She was wearing a tightly fitting, turquoise sweater and white joggers. Her hair was sprayed to the point of defying even the most ferocious of gales. Her make-up was as overdone as was her general appearance sporting a slash of vivid red lipstick and bright blue eye shadow. 'Sis came round this afternoon, so we had a little drinky poo,' she slurred. Cyril pecked her on the cheek. He was accustomed to seeing her in this condition.

'You look good babe. How's your sis?'

She belched before replying, 'she's fine.'

Cyril and Deidre were a pair alike. They would have spoiled another couple if they hadn't been married to each other. Cyril was a short, round, balding man with a greasy comb-over. He constantly sweated and was always seen in a shiny brown ill-fitting suit. People who knew them were constantly surprised at how they managed to have, what appeared to be, an extravagant lifestyle. They had two holidays a year, both had new cars and demanded the best service whenever they visited restaurants. Unfortunately, it was obvious to everyone they both, sadly, lacked taste on a personal level. Their lack of dress sense and occasion was only outdone by their poor choice of décor for their home. Cyril had left the décor to Deidre, the result being cheap prints hung on the walls, a glass cabinet filled to the gunnels with knick-knacks and copious amounts of bling. They epitomised the phrase, "money can't buy taste". They were overly ostentatious!

Cyril was the Contracts Manager for Derbyshire Health Authority. He was responsible for awarding contracts to companies who supplied the hospitals and clinics throughout the county. The contracts included all the health authority's drugs, uniforms and equipment, from the smallest of scalpels to large X-ray machines. Until recently, he'd been the deputy manager to the long-standing and well-respected John Wild. John had been ill for some time, two years in fact, and eventually had succumbed to his illness. When John had finally died, the local authority, desperate for a replacement – some would say too desperate – expeditiously passed the baton over to Cyril. He was an obnoxious character and was disliked by all who had to do business with him. He would sit behind his large desk and appear superior, looking down on anyone who was sat opposite him in the small chair, making sure they were fully aware who was boss, who called the shots. He had also recently been appointed as a councillor in Ashbourne, thanks to an extremely generous donation to the mayor, and could be seen strutting around town, as much as his portly figure would allow him to, making himself appear convivial, but, as usual, over-doing it. He was an arrogant, conceited man. To sum up, he was a pompous buffoon.

* * *

Geoff Marsden was the Managing Director of Cope and Marsden, textile manufacturers. There was no Cope in the business since the last member of the Cope dynasty had died four years previously. They specialised in uniforms and workwear for industry. They were the 'go-to' company and currently supplied engineering companies, hospitals, garages, supermarkets and many others. They employed two hundred workers in their purpose-built factory situated on the Hardman Industrial Estate and imported cloth from all round the world. Geoff was the grandson of one of the founders, Josiah Marsden, who in 1910 went into partnership with Arthur Cope to form the company. The last director to die was Marlon Cope who had no children to pass the business to, enabling the Marsden family to buy out the Cope share in the business.

The company quickly grew in its early days, partly due to supplying uniforms for the forces during WWI and again in WWII. In the 1950s and 60s they further developed their business, which brought the company to where it was today – a highly successful organisation. Geoffrey Marsden, who had originally been the overseas sales director, was now managing director and had held the post for the last four years.

Geoff was forty-four, a tall dark-haired, rather cadaverous-looking man, who had the habit of constantly pushing his spectacles up the bridge of his nose, especially when stressed. However, behind his mild demeanour lay a determined, motivated individual.

There was a gentle tap on his door and his secretary entered. 'Good morning, Geoff, how are you this morning?'

He smiled at Monica who'd been by his side in business for 7 years and knew him better than anyone. 'Good, thank you Monica. What exciting things have you got for me today?'

She stood by his side and flipped open an appointments book. 'Four appointments today...I have emailed them to you.' She pushed the appointment book in front of him. 'Just in case you haven't checked your emails this morning. I know you prefer to read a hard copy,' she said pointedly as she ran her finger down the list, 'all straightforward.' She stood back with a teasing look across her face. 'At the end of next week, you've got something to look forward to.' Geoff frowned at her curiously as she began to make her exit. Monica spoke over her shoulder as she made for the door. 'Friday, ten o'clock, your mate Cyril Prosser!'

He put his head in his hands. 'Oh, no! Bloody hell, I can't stand the bloke. What does he want?'

'The contract is up for renewal.'

He looked surprised. 'Already?'

She nodded. 'Five years soon goes when you're busy doesn't it?' He threw a balled-up piece of paper at her and smiled, where would he be without her? He'd had a few run-ins with Prosser and didn't look forward to Friday's meeting. It was always somewhat daunting as Prosser always entered his office ready with some overtly aggressive, verbal sparring. It was well-practised, and Marsden had to be on his toes.

Monica, a super-efficient secretary had been his 'third arm' from his days as sales director and had never faltered. She was organised, tactful on the phone, white-lied when she had to and most importantly, she had a cheeky sense of humour. She and Geoff worked well together. Monica Collins was a woman in her mid-forties with a head of premature silver-grey hair and unusually long, slim fingers.

Geoff drove home that evening pleased with himself. Today he had finalised a massive contract for a garage chain with nearly one thousand outlets across the country. He'd been chasing the business for nearly two years and today it came to fruition. Tonight, he could justify a small celebratory drink.

He lived in the same leafy suburb as Cyril Prosser. Thankfully Prosser lived at the opposite end of the suburb. As he drove home, he pondered over his Friday appointment. It was always a worry when contracts were due for renewal, as it always involved awkward financial negotiations, and this year may prove even more difficult. Geoff Marsden was having to increase his prices and knew Prosser wouldn't like that.

He arrived home and parked his Jaguar on the drive. He clicked his key in the front door and stepped in, picking up a leaflet from the floor as he entered. He read it as he strolled along to the kitchen. *An invitation to a church meeting.* He balled it up, opened the kitchen door and dropped it in the waste bin. 'Hi, darling.'

His wife wiped her hands on her mini apron and greeted him with a wide smile. 'Hi, sweetie, had a good day?'

He nodded and gave his wife a hug. 'Yes, it was really good. We finally got the Horizon garage chain contract.'

'That's great news! You've worked hard for that.' She quickly whipped off her apron.

He raised his eyebrows and laughed at the same time. 'Hey, don't stop!'

Susie gave him a sideways glance, 'Cheeky!'

Geoff added, 'the staff will be pleased with the new contract. They'll have the opportunity for lots of overtime to meet the order.' Susie grabbed a couple of glasses and poured them both a white wine before they headed for the lounge.

His wife, Susie, was a lecturer at the local FE College where she taught economics. She was an outgoing woman; strong, positive, generous with her time and very attractive. She had been likened to Natalie Zuev, a famous model who seemed to appear on the front page of every news stand on a regular basis. Susie was tall with long black hair and coal black eyes. People couldn't believe she'd chosen teaching economics over a life in the modelling industry.

As in the Prosser household, the décor in the Marsden household had also been left to the woman of the house. However, Susie took a different approach to the decor. The Marsden home was bright, light and minimalist. The large lounge which overlooked the large, manicured garden, had two, white, three-seater leather sofas. On the black and white rug was a glass and brushed chrome coffee table. On the wall hung two original watercolours, one a Lowry. Their home was the antithesis of the Prosser household. No bling in sight! Susie came into the lounge carrying the opened wine bottle, poured them another drink then sat beside Geoff. 'Cheers, congratulations on the new order.' They chinked glasses.

* * *

Cyril Prosser kissed his wife goodbye. 'I'll see you later. I won't be late.'

Deidre stood at the front door still in her short, faded floral housecoat, her hair dishevelled which was now free of the hardened hair spray, her eyes still getting used to the early morning light. With coffee in hand, she limply blew him a kiss as he reversed down the drive.

Prosser had a busy day ahead. From time to time, he would visit the various depots throughout the county, allegedly checking that suppliers were delivering exactly what had been negotiated and agreed. Most of the contracted supplies would be delivered to a central warehouse in Bispham Road, before being allocated to the various hospitals and clinics. He smirked to himself as he thought about the free lunch he would get at the main depot.

The central warehouse was a single storey building tucked away in the industrial estate surrounded by a high mesh fence and thick shrubbery. He nodded to the man on the gate who waved him through, followed by a one finger wave once Prosser's back was turned. He parked his car in front of reception, grabbed his commodious briefcase and purposefully strode into the building. He was met in reception by Bryan Withers, the Warehouse Manager. Bryan was in his forties. He had a head of thick, white hair and sported a goatee beard. Bryan offered him a coffee before he and Cyril started the rounds. Cyril declined with a wave of his hand wanting to appear that he needed to get on with more important things. Prosser was at the warehouse to check that recently delivered stationery had been printed with the correct updated information, uniforms had the correct logos, drugs were packaged as agreed and there was no out-of-date items still in storage.

Prosser proceeded to dismiss Withers with the brusque suggestion, 'I'm sure you've better things to do than wander around with me. I know my way around. I'll pop my head round your office door when I've finished.'

Withers inclined his head. 'Well, if you're sure. I do have things to do.' Withers wandered back to his office with relief, the last thing he wanted to do all morning was play babysitter to Prosser the Poltroon. Prosser made his way to the storage section, let himself in via his security tag, then, working his way round the aisles of fixtures studiously checked the stationery first: letterheads, admission forms and leaflets offering patients advice on their impending stay in hospital. He took his time, not wanting to appear to be rushed. Next, he moved to the uniforms section where he checked the right size range had arrived, logos were in the right position on the garments and there was no variation in the fabrics being used. He took a deep breath. The next section was why he was really here. The drugs section. He looked up and down the corridor to check the coast was clear, then quickly entered. He knew exactly which drugs he was looking for, where they were kept and had a keen eye as to which boxes had already been opened. Taking a felt-tipped pen from his outwardly bulky, yet empty briefcase, he diligently changed the number of 'contents' on the box to show what was in the box after having removed the quantity he needed. He emptied the wastepaper out of his briefcase and stuffed the items into it. He had entered the building with an empty briefcase, but was now leaving with a substantial stock of very saleable commodities.

Withers looked up as Prosser knocked on his office window. 'I'll have that coffee now, if it's still on offer.'

Bryan jumped up, pleased that Prosser was at the end of his visit. 'Yeah of course, give me two minutes.' He was soon back with two coffees and a plate of biscuits. For twenty minutes Prosser voiced his opinion on how the warehousing could be improved, Withers nodding in agreement when he thought it appropriate. On the floor in plain sight between the two men was a bulging briefcase.

* * *

Geoff Marsden was at his computer, mapping out his plan for the forthcoming appointment with Cyril Prosser. He knew Prosser would be difficult, so preparation for the potentially protracted negotiations was vital. A fact Geoff couldn't get away from was the price increases in production that were coming from all directions: fabrics, energy costs, freight and staff. He identified the final increase he needed to pass on to Prosser, guessed what Prosser would knock him down to and, between the two of them, they would arrive at a figure that would hopefully be acceptable to both parties. Negotiation was an integral part of business. He brainstormed, trying to think of any other criteria on which he could negotiate other than price. He might be able to negotiate extended delivery dates, or perhaps payments. He tried to think of any elegant tradables he could think of. He typed a list with a heading Elegant Tradables, underlined it, then racked his brain as to what he could offer. These were the items he could offer which would be of minimal cost to himself, but worth a good deal more to Prosser. A recent example was when he and Susie had made a complaint at a local restaurant and the waiter had offered them a free coffee. It was minimal cost to the restaurant, but of value to the customer. Sadly, under the circumstances, he couldn't think of any to offer Prosser. More importantly, he had a 'walk-away figure', critical in any negotiations, although he appreciated it would be difficult to walk away from the lucrative contracts he had with Prosser. He had a business to run, staff to keep employed. He also needed to pay his own suppliers. He looked up as Monica tapped on the door then stepped in.

She placed a brown file in front of him. 'A few letters to sign.' She peered at his computer screen then smiled. 'I see you're working on your plan for the District Health Authority.'

He leaned back in his chair, his hands around the back of his head and chuckled. 'It's worth the effort Monica. I've learned over the years if you fail to plan you plan to fail.'

She laughed. 'You're right of course. I'm sure it'll go OK...coffee?'

'A large black if you don't mind, thanks.'

* * *

Friday came all too quickly. It was a dull drizzly day and, according to the weather forecast, there was no chance of a let-up for the next few days. Geoff had had a busy week, tiring but lucrative. He'd picked up some useful contacts and two firm orders, one from a security firm and one from a chain of bakeries.

He arrived at the Derbyshire Health Authority's headquarters in plenty of time for his appointment. The building was a modern, three-storey glass edifice surrounded by well-manicured grounds. It crossed his mind that money always seemed to be available to maintain bureaucrats in luxury, whilst at the same time pleading poverty when it came to funding projects which would benefit the masses. He found these meetings with Cyril Prosser tiring because Prosser seemed to go out of his way to make life difficult. Geoff thought about his other customers who had successful businesses and were pleasant to deal with. It's not difficult for both parties to establish a good rapport. Any useful relationship with Prosser was a non-starter, mainly due to his aggressive negotiating technique. Checking his briefcase and running through his presentation, adding a few comments in the margins as reminders, he took a deep breath, climbed out of his car, flipped the locks and made his way to the main doors. They automatically opened at his approach and funnelled him into reception. He was met by a young woman. According to her name tag she was called Chelsea. She greeted him with direct eye contact and a well-practised broad smile. 'Good morning, how may I help you?'

Geoff returned the smile and handed her his business card. 'Good morning, I'm here to see Cyril Prosser. I have an appointment.'

She picked up the phone and at the same time offered him a seat whilst he waited. The reception area was a large and well lit, the walls showing photographs of the achievements of the DHA; lots of hand shaking with politicians of all persuasions. Plastic potted palms stood to attention in corners and recesses.

"Mr Marsden!' Geoff looked up to see Prosser waddling across the reception floor with his arm outstretched to welcome him. 'Mr Marsden, how are you? Please come through,' he said in his usual bonhomie manner. Geoff wasn't fooled by the effusive welcome from the man in front of him.

'Fine and you?' he asked insincerely.

'Fine also.' Prosser buzzed them through a security door and along a corridor passing employees wandering about with bits of paper. 'Please, come in,' said Prosser, standing to one side to allow Geoff to enter his inner sanctum. 'Take a seat.' Geoff ensconced himself in a chair whilst Prosser sat on the opposite side of a large walnut desk. It had a poise lamp to one side, several photos of, Geoff assumed, his wife, two trays containing files and a grubby mug out of which stuck several pens and pencils. Prosser reached for one of his trays and retrieved a manila folder in front of him which he flicked open.

'Ah, yes, Cope and Marsden. Your contract is up for renewal.' He looked at Geoff and smiled a wolfish smile. 'I hope you're going to pleasantly surprise me with your new proposal.' Geoff smiled back rather weakly.

'I think so. I thought I could save you some time by summarising the main points, then I can leave the full proposal with you to read at your leisure.' He lifted his briefcase onto his knee, clicked open the clasp and took out a bound sheaf of papers. He handed the proposal over to Prosser, followed by the single page summary. Prosser put the bound papers to one side and studied the single page.

'Hmm, I see your prices are up.'

'Yes,' Geoff responded, 'there're a couple of items I'd like to highlight, the cost being one. Sadly, the increase in cost is down to criteria that everyone is battling with at present, the cost of fabrics, energy, staffing and so on. What would help is for us to discuss the delivery arrangements.'

A frown crossed Prosser's jowly face. 'Deliveries?'

Geoff continued. 'Yes. Currently you receive two bulk deliveries from us each year. One at the beginning of the new financial year, 1st May, followed six months later by completion of the contract. It would be helpful to us if the deliveries could be spread equally over twelve separate deliveries.' Before Prosser had time to respond Geoff continued. 'If we could deliver monthly, we could even out our production and the holding stock level for you. This would allow us to deal more effectively with our financial obligations.'

Prosser sat back in his chair, ignored Geoff's points and pursed his lips. 'Hmmm. I do have to tell you that we are also talking to one of your competitors.' He looked to Geoff for a reaction. Geoff remained stony faced. Prosser continued. 'I know we've dealt with you for quite a number of years, and,' he held his palms up in apology, 'we've always been happy with you, but circumstances are changing.'

'So, what are you asking for?' Geoff responded. What are your priorities?'

Prosser leaned forward on his desk. 'Well, my job is to persuade the powers that be,' he pointed toward the ceiling, 'that Cope and Marsden are still our preferred supplier.' He took a deep breath and stared Geoff directly in the eyes. 'I have other suppliers that have hit the same problem, and they have, somehow, managed to…' he looked up thoughtfully as if looking for the right words. '…well, managed to incentivise my efforts in persuading the powers that be that price isn't the be all and end all and to continue with them as one of our preferred suppliers.'

Geoff was stunned at what he thought he was hearing and let it race through his mind. Before he had time to respond Prosser placed his hands on his desk and stood up. 'Well, I'll leave you with that thought. Let me know if you can see a way around our little dilemma. Thank you for coming in.'

Geoff thanked him, shook hands and left. He sat in the car park and mulled over the brief, but disturbing meeting he'd just experienced.

Was Prosser asking me for a bribe? Did I mis-hear? Has he taken this approach with all his suppliers? A bribe! Really!

He phoned Monica in the office. She thought he sounded subdued. 'Oh, hello Geoff. How did you go on with old Prosser?'

'I'll tell you on Monday. I just phoned to say I'll call at Jessop's Mill whilst I'm in the area then I'll go straight home. Can you lock up for me and I'll see you on Monday.'

Monica became concerned. 'Of course.' She hesitated. 'You okay, you sound a bit cheesed off?'

He tried to laugh off her concerns. 'I'm okay, see you Monday. Have a good weekend.'

'Bye, Geoff.'

He turned the ignition, drove out of the car park and headed for his favourite coffee shop in town. He had no intention of visiting Jessop's; he just needed some time to mull over what he thought he'd been asked to do.

The coffee shop was situated on the edge of the market square, nestled between a dress shop and a book seller. He was a regular and was welcomed with a broad smile. 'Good morning, Geoff, what would you like? The usual?' He nodded, relieved to be in a neutral environment.

He laughed, 'Am I that predictable? Oh, and I'll have a friand, please.' He grabbed a seat at the back of the café where he could mull over what he thought he'd understood to be Prosser asking for a bribe. *Why now? After all the years we've dealt with DHA.* Dealing with Prosser's predecessor had always been so straightforward. The coffee and friand arrived.

'Enjoy.'

'Thank you.'

None of the conversation with Prosser was clear-cut. He hadn't been specific, and he was expecting Geoff to read between the lines. The time spent in the café helped him to rationalise the situation. He finished his coffee and made his way home.

* * *

He arrived home as Susie was seeing a friend, Collette, out of the front door. Collette waved a hello to Geoff as she climbed into her car and drove away.

'You're home early?' queried Susie. He forced a wan smile, gave her a peck on the cheek and went inside. She closed the front door and followed him into the lounge, detecting some unease. Geoff wandered into the lounge, flopped down on the sofa and stared out of the window. Susie quickly joined him. 'I take it your meeting with your pompous friend didn't go too well.'

'I think I was being blackmailed today,' Geoff blurted out.

Susie swivelled in her seat to face him. 'Blackmailed!'

He nodded. 'Prosser implied the only way to renew the contract was to bribe him. He didn't use the word bribe, just...implied. He implied we would only be able to maintain the contract if we provided him with a financial 'incentive'.' He relayed the whole conversation he'd had with Prosser.

'Will you go over his head to the Health Authority Committee?'

Geoff looked at his wife. 'And tell them what...I think I was manipulated for a bribe. It's his word against mine.'

'So how will you respond?'

He was quiet for a few seconds then. 'I don't know. I need some time to think it through.'

On Monday morning Geoff had the same conversation with Monica.

'That's where we're up to. If I don't go along with his plans it puts our business in a very precarious position. If we don't get the DHA business, and, as you well know, they're our largest customer, it leaves us vulnerable. DHA is the volume business that covers a lot of our expenses. If we go under it'll cause a domino effect. We've got the staff to think about as much as our customers...and our suppliers.' He stood up and paced in frustration then suddenly stopped. 'I'll make us a coffee; it'll give me something to do.'

* * *

Saturday night was the wedding anniversary of Susie and Geoff's closest friends, Pete and Mel. They had been married for twenty-five years. Susie had arranged for them to meet at the restaurant on the far side of town.

Geoff hadn't been privy to the plans so asked, 'Where are we going?'

'Jean-Pierre's. We've been there before, remember?'

'Who's driving?'

'I'll drive there, you drive back,' Susie replied.

'Right.'

They were looking forward to seeing the happy couple as it had been some time since they'd last caught up. 'Last time we saw Pete and Mel was when we had that weekend up in the Lakes,' said Susie as they turned onto Chisholm Road. It was the ring road around Ashbourne which would take them to the old mining village of Cumpsty. 'It's a pity we have to drive through this type of area to get there.'

Geoff glanced out of the passenger window at the dark side streets and seedy pubs, and responded, 'It's not so bad during the day, but on the way back we need to keep the doors locked, there's been a few incidents over the past few months.' She silently nodded and kept her eyes on the road. Geoff was silent for a few miles then asked, 'How long have you known Mel now?'

'Since Uni. We both studied economics.'

Pete and Mel were already seated at their table when Geoff and Susie arrived. After much hugging and kissing there was the usual – 'haven't seen you for ages' and 'hope you've both been well, it's great to catch up...'

The restaurant was as busy as always on a Saturday night and bookings were usually made many weeks in advance. The ambiance of the restaurant was helped by the dimmed lighting and soft accordion music in the background. Several 1930s posters hung around the walls, mainly advertising Moulin Rouge, Le Club de Solace and Le Coq D'or. The waiter approached them, poured water into their glasses and handed them each a menu. 'Can I get you drinks?'

Pete looked up at the waiter. 'A bottle of Moet please.' He looked at Susie and Geoff. 'My treat. Our anniversary.'

The menu was as enticing as the last time they were here. After much deliberation they each gave the waiter their choices from the menu. Pete and Geoff ordered pork terrine as the starter and coq au vin for the main, the ladies ordered goats cheese soufflé for the starter and moule mariniere for their main.

'So, what have you two been up to?' asked Pete. 'Anything exciting?'

Both replied in unison. 'Busy with work, as usual.'

The evening seemed to go too quickly; they had so much to catch up on. Both Geoff and Pete restricted their intake of alcohol. Already they were onto the desserts, crème brulee all round. Mel looked at her watch. 'You two have a fair drive ahead, maybe we should make tracks.'

They all agreed. Geoff and Pete sorted the bill, exchanged a few kind words with the maître d' and reluctantly made their way to the car park.

'Must do this again soon,' grinned Geoff knowing that's what everyone said after a thoroughly enjoyable evening.

'Yes, we must,' laughed Pete from the open car window, then he and Mel drove off.

The journey home had a different feel. On driving through the rougher area, the maze of back streets seemed darker, more threatening. There were some bright neon lights flashing on and off which emanated from the various seedy clubs along the way. The odd police patrol car flashed past, sirens and lights urgently encouraging people to get out of the way. 'Lock your door, Susie.'

She placed her hand on his knee as reassurance. 'It's already locked.' The traffic suddenly slowed as a melee outside a fish and chip shop spilled across the width of the road. Eventually the traffic stopped.

'God! This is all we need!' They came to a standstill across the junction of one of the side roads. As they waited Geoff glanced up and down the side streets looking for potential trouble. A group of young lads, obviously intoxicated, swayed across the road throwing bottles at other pedestrians. 'Put your head down Susie in case one comes through the window.' She eased herself low down in the seat. The melee continued, the louts creating even more havoc. Geoff continued glancing left and right, up and down, hoping the traffic would move before they got entangled in some sort of incident. Susie was still cowering as low in the foot well as she could when she heard Geoff gasp. 'Bloody hell! I need to check this. Hang on Susie.' He turned the steering wheel sharply to the left and shot down the side street. 'I thought it was, bloody hell!'

Susie whispered to him. 'What? What have you seen?'

Geoff ignored her question. 'Have you got your mobile with you?'

'Of course, why?'

'Sorry, Susie, I'll have to ask you to sit up and get your mobile ready.'

She did as she was asked and rummaged through her handbag for her phone. 'Now what?'

'I'm going to drive slowly past the next car parked by the kerb, it's a BMW SUV, take a video of the guy looking this way and what he's got in his hand. If you get a chance, keep it going so you can get a view of the guy he's talking to.' Geoff drove slowly past whilst Susie, trying to stay low in the passenger seat, held her phone up to the window and started the video on her mobile. Geoff then looked at her. 'Well? Do you know who that was?' She shook her head. 'Poncy Prosser, and it looks like he's dealing drugs.' Geoff changed gear. 'I'm going round the block so we can get a second chance to get more footage of him.' He drove round the block into an even seedier road and back on to the street where he'd spotted Prosser. The BMW had moved. 'Damn! Hang on, his car has just moved further up the street.' Geoff drove to within three car lengths of the BMW then stopped. 'It's him alright, CP number plate. Whoa, this is too good Susie. Keep the video running.' The BMW had stopped, and a woman was leaning on the side of the car obviously talking to the driver. Within seconds she had climbed into the car and was driven away.

'Got it!' shouted Susie in delight.

'Brilliant! Let's head for home. A good night's work, don't you think?'

They drove home shocked at what they'd witnessed. Once in the house Susie asked. 'Do you want to talk about it?'

Geoff shook his head. 'No. I think I want to sleep on it first.'

Susie nodded in agreement as they both climbed the stairs.

* * *

Sunday breakfast in the Marsden home was always a relaxed affair, particularly if they'd both had a stressful week. Geoff sauntered into the kitchen in his Liberty dressing gown, yawning and scratching his head.

Susie was already busying herself setting up the coffee machine swaying to some Spotify music that was playing in the background. The kitchen had a long central unit and fitted cupboards all round. All the appliances were stainless steel and of German design. 'Morning, hon! Have a good sleep?'

She turned from the kitchen unit. 'Yes thanks.' She poured him a cup of coffee. 'Just to let you know, I've downloaded that video from my phone to your laptop. When you're ready you can view the footage even more clearly.' He picked up his cup and wrapped his hands around it.

'Thanks. Breakfast first?'

The footage on his laptop was indisputable. Cyril Prosser was clearly seen handing someone small white packets and receiving what looked like money. Further into the footage a woman, who appeared to be a prostitute, was having a conversation with the driver of the BMW before climbing in. Geoff looked at Susie, for once lost for words. She broke the silence. 'So, what are you going to do with it?' Geoff sat back with a smug grin across his face.

'I'm due for an appointment with him in the next couple of weeks. I'm going to present him with this footage and that should twist the pompous bastard's arm into renewing our contract.'

Susie remained silent, but with a smile fixed firmly on her lips. Geoff picked up on the silence and looked at Susie in a slight panic. 'What? What?'

She said as gently as she could, 'Think about what you're about to do.' She pushed her cup to one side and leaned on the table. 'You're going to present footage of Prosser's extracurricular activities, with an inbuilt threat to expose him, for your own personal gain...' She sat back in her chair. 'Now then, what does that sound like to you?'

Geoff's enthusiasm suddenly deflated. 'Oh, bloody hell, that's blackmail, isn't it?' She nodded without saying a word. Geoff thought for a few minutes then spoke. 'But this is too good to ignore, isn't it?' Susie nodded again in agreement. 'So, if I showed it to him but didn't make any demands...hmmmm, this needs thinking through, doesn't it?' Susie nodded again. Geoff ran his hand through his hair and began to slowly voice his thoughts. 'If I did show him…he's not likely to report me, is he?' He took a sip from his now cold coffee. 'I've got to do it, Susie. If I don't and we don't get the new contract we're up the Swanee. Think about all the staff we're responsible for…our suppliers…us!'

* * *

Half-way through breakfast the following Thursday morning, the phone rang. Susie looked up at the kitchen clock. 'That's early. Very few people phone us at this time, particularly on the landline, it's probably my mother.' She put the coffee pot down and went into the hall. Geoff could hear a short, muffled conversation before Susie returned to the kitchen and whispered, 'It's your favourite customer.' Geoff drained the last bit of coffee from his cup and went into the hall.

'Hello. Ah, Mr Prosser. Yes, ah-ha. Yes, I have put some further thought to your suggestion at our last meeting. Yes, sure. No, next Wednesday's fine. Ten-thirty.'

When Geoff came back into the kitchen Susie raised her eyebrows. 'Well?'

'Ten-thirty appointment, next Wednesday morning. It's crunch time.'

* * *

As Geoff drove into the DHA car park, he felt buoyant. He strode briskly across the car park, into the reception area and informed the receptionist he had an appointment. Within seconds of him sitting down, Cyril Prosser waddled through the door, his hand outstretched. 'Good morning, Mr Marsden. Please, come through.' Once in his office Prosser placed the palms of his hands on top of his desk. 'Now then, Mr Marsden, have you put any more thought to our last discussion?'

Geoff smiled an indulgent smile. 'Indeed I have.' He reached into his briefcase and pulled out his laptop. He silently opened the lid, clicked a few buttons then without saying a word turned the computer round to face Prosser. He watched as Prosser followed the footage, his face turning red, sweat began to roll down his cheeks. His jowls shook as he looked up at Geoff. 'What's the meaning of this?' He was raging.

Geoff tilted his head slightly as if in apology. 'I would have thought it was self-explanatory.'

Prosser put his head in his hands, then defiantly stared Geoff in the face; his voice quiet, but clear. 'Okay, what do you want?' Geoff remained silent to let Prosser continue. 'Ah,' he said condescendingly, 'you want your contract renewed, am I correct?'

Geoff leaned forward onto the desk. 'It's not as simple as that Mr Prosser.' Prosser raised his eyebrows questioningly, so Geoff continued. 'No doubt you've tried your disgraceful tactics on other suppliers.' Prosser was shaking as he demanded to know exactly what Geoff wanted. Geoff closed the computer down and returned it to his briefcase. 'Can I leave this with you?' he said handing Prosser a USB, 'it's all on there if you'd like to view it at your leisure.' He stood up. 'In the meantime,' he said theatrically, 'I bid you a good day.'

Prosser was sitting at his desk, panic and anger were coursing through his veins. His face was bright red as his blood pressure hit the roof. He could see his world collapsing in on him...and his wife Deidre. *Oh my God! Deidre! She'll never cope with this! Not Deidre! She was too settled into their easy, comfortable lifestyle! She'll kill me*! At the thought of Deidre's reaction, he jumped up from his desk, popped his head around his secretary's door and informed her he had a family emergency and he was going home.

* * *

Still in a panic, Prosser arrived home to find Deidre lying on the sofa, wine glass in hand, smoking a cigarette. Netflix was playing on the widescreen TV. She jumped up spilling her wine on the beige carpet as Prosser came through the door. 'Bugger,' she screamed, 'Cyril! You scared the living daylights out of me.' She suddenly noticed the dishevelled state he was in, the top button on his shirt undone, his tie askew, his comb-over flapping about. He was sweating profusely. 'Christ Cyril, what's happened? What are you doing home? You look as though you've just run a marathon.'

He shouted back. 'We need to talk. And turn that bloody thing off,' he bawled, pointing at the television.

He was breathing heavily as he started to explain what had happened at the office. 'Bloody Geoff Marsden. Somehow, he got footage of me selling the drugs.' He didn't mention the part regarding the prostitute. 'We've got a problem De, a big one. If he forwards the footage to the Authority we're done for.'

'What do you mean done for?' Deidre shouted as she struggled with her cigarette lighter that refused to work. She threw it on the sofa and grabbed a box of matches. 'I'm not with you.'

Prosser threw his head back in exasperation. 'Bloody hell, Deidre,' he waved his arms around the room, 'how do you think all this was paid for? The holidays, the cars, your bloody dresses and shoes, bottles of the best wine...where do you think all the money came from?' He stood up and paced round the room before starting again. 'We're in trouble. Not just from losing all this,' he said, waving his arms around again, 'but with the law. I'll serve time.'

Deidre suddenly realised the seriousness of the situation and began to cry. 'Don't say that Cyril, it won't come to that.'

He screamed again. 'Why won't it? I've broken the law. For God's sake woman wake up.'

He sat down again and softened his voice. 'Look, I've got meetings all day tomorrow, but when I come home, we'll have to talk about how we're going to deal with this. And it WILL have to be dealt with.'

* * *

February 13th

Shrove Tuesday

The next day Cyril left without breakfast. His stomach, which was usually ready for anything going into it, particularly if it was free, was in no mood for food. He had to prepare for several meetings which would take up his whole day and he left Deidre at the breakfast table still in her faded floral short house coat, her eyes red from crying all night. She looked round the kitchen then strolled into the lounge and took in all the expensive things. She burst into tears. *No, no, no. I can't give all this up! It's not fair! I just can't! And I won't!*

* * *

Deidre had made up her mind. She looked around at all the beautiful things they had amassed, the lifestyle, the large home, the massive TV, the full wine rack, a wardrobe full of designer clothes, her own car in the garage. It reinforced her determination. Her mind suddenly went back to her childhood. In those days she had none of these luxuries, no holidays, meagre Christmases, no treats. Her parents both had menial jobs. Her dad worked in the council depot and her mum cleaned offices – money was always short. *No, I can't let all this go!* Lifting a kitchen knife from the block on the unit she slipped it inside her anorak. Holding back tears, she then made her way into the garage, climbed into her car, slowly reversed out of the garage and out of the cul-de-sac. She was on auto pilot. Her mind couldn't comprehend losing all she now had. Within ten minutes she was outside Geoff Marsden's house. She remembered where he lived after Cyril had taken her on a drive around the estate when they'd first moved in. Geoff Marsden's end of the road was almost the same as theirs. However, the houses at this end were larger, with more grounds around them. It had always rattled Deidre and Cyril that, at the time, they couldn't quite afford one of the larger homes. She remembered Cyril saying to her, 'that's the sort of house we deserve, Deidre. By hook or by crook we'll get one.' They never did manage to buy one, due mainly to Deidre's regular shopping sprees and her insistence on exotic holidays.

She parked several houses away and waited, not sure what her next move was. She didn't have a plan, only a burning anger and an urgent need to protect her lifestyle. After fifteen minutes and several cigarettes she saw the front door open, and Geoff Marsden came out. He was dressed casually in a maroon rugby shirt and jeans and carried a jacket which he threw onto the back seat of his Jaguar. She could see him wave to his wife who was standing at the bedroom window. He reversed down the drive and headed in the direction of town.

As she followed him at a discreet distance, she noticed groups of men walking in the direction of the town centre, chatting and laughing. *Why weren't they at work?* Then it struck her! *Of course, of course, it's Shrove Tuesday. The football match*! That explains Marsden's casual dress. That explains why all these groups of men would be heading to join the rest of the townsfolk, ready for the kick off at two o'clock. She continued to follow him until he turned into the car park of the King's Arms pub and park close to the pub's rear entrance. He locked his car, waved to a couple of people he knew and disappeared into the pub. Several raucous groups of people came and went whilst she waited. The King's Arms was obviously the pub for the pre-match catch-up. This was a big day in the town's diary. An hour later Marsden reappeared. This time he was with a group of four other men as they headed in the direction of the town centre. No cars were allowed in the town centre on Shrove Tuesday, so parking at the pub was a good move. Deidre did the same and parked as close to the exit as she could. She then gathered her belongings, making sure she had her cigarettes and mobile with her and followed the group on foot.

* * *

The town was heaving with eager participants raring to start the annual pushing and shoving over the three-mile pitch. *Perfect!* She thought. *I can push through the crowd and wangle my way close to Marsden, I won't be noticed among the crowd. I'll be hidden in plain sight. Perfect!*

There was a massive roar from the crowd as the Turner Up threw the ball into the crowd. Immediately there was a mad scramble to obtain possession of the ball as it was kicked, bounced and thrown over the tops of the teams. Voices were raised, elbows were thrust, fists were flying, feet were kicking, and the general mayhem of the match was well under way. The two hundred plus willing participants were determined that the ball should stay within their own side and were ready to do battle to achieve that aim. The two teams moved and swayed first in one direction then the other as they moved up the main street, spilled over down the side streets, along the banks of the river and occasionally in it, on their way to the goal.

Slowly but surely, Deidre pushed her way through the mob to find herself side by side with the unsuspecting Geoff Marsden. Stealthily she slipped the knife from beneath her jacket and, firmly gripping the handle, she forcefully stuck the blade into Marsden. It entered his body under his left armpit. He immediately dropped to the floor as Deidre sidled away and mingled among the crowd. In her rush to get away she was jostled about and dropped the knife. She couldn't stop to pick it up so had to leave it and continued to push her way out of the melee, which was still pushing and shoving. She kept her head down as she slowly inched her way out of the crowd. As she reached the perimeter of the crowd, she heard someone shout, 'Call an ambulance.' She quickly walked back to her car, then, unable to stop herself from shaking, she drove home. On arriving home, she quickly changed out of her trackies and Nike trainers and poured herself a generous glass of red. She lit a cigarette, but on this occasion, it took both hands to hold the lighter steady. As soon as she sat down on the sofa, she realised the gravity of what she'd done. *Oh, my God! I've killed someone*! Then she attempted to rationalise what she'd done and why, and finally convinced herself she had no choice. *I had to do it. Our life would have been destroyed if Marsden had made the footage public. No, I did the right thing because I had no choice.*

Cyril arrived home after a day of incredibly boring meetings. He'd found it difficult to concentrate; his mind was elsewhere. *What was he to do about Marsden?* The 'what to do' was taken out of his hands when he arrived home that evening and Deidre told him what she'd done. 'You've done what?' he screamed, 'you must be mad! What possessed you?'

Deidre burst into tears. She was almost incoherent as she tried to explain how and why she'd done it. 'I had to Cyril, for us,' she sobbed, 'he could have ruined our life.' She reached for the wine bottle. 'All that we've worked for...all gone. I had to do something.'

Cyril paced up and down the lounge, almost lost for words. He was furious. 'What do we do now?' he barked, 'what if someone recognised you!' Cyril suddenly stopped pacing and looked her directly in the eye. 'Where's the knife?'

She shook her head and sobbed even more. 'I dropped it.' She looked at him for forgiveness. 'It was knocked out of my hand in the crush,' she pleaded.

He sat down with his head in his hands. 'This is a bloody nightmare!' Deidre put her arm around him and tried her best to placate Cyril.

Her voice softened, 'I'm sure no one saw me do it. Everyone was more concerned with where the ball was. I doubt anyone could say who they were stood next to at any one time.'

Cyril stood up, looking even more dishevelled, poured himself a wine and said venomously, 'I hope to god you're right.'

Two Days Later

DI Tom Brindle welcomed the team back as they came into the briefing room.

'We seem to be making some headway. We've now been able to positively identify the victim at the football match. Mrs Marsden has formally identified the body. He's Geoffrey Marsden. He's the same Marsden of Cope and Marsden, the textile company on the industrial estate. I've got Christine Harding, our FLO, staying with Mrs Marsden. One of our first tasks is to identify if he had any enemies or had upset anyone recently. We dropped in lucky with the weapon. It was found near the victim and was, fortunately for us, picked up by an off-duty police officer based at this station. It was bagged and taken directly to the path lab.' He smiled smugly, 'and we've got a match. The prints are of a Deidre Prosser. She was picked up last year for causing an affray in The George and Dragon on Stamford Street. The blood on the knife matches Mr Marsden's. DS Morecroft and I will go and have a word with Mrs Prosser this morning.'

The two officers knocked on the door of the Prosser household and it was immediately opened by Mrs Prosser.

'Mrs Prosser?' asked the DI, flashing his warrant. 'Mrs Deidre Prosser?'

'Yes.' She was wearing a light turquoise set of trackies, an oversized T-shirt and beige mules. She had a glass of wine in her hand.

'May we come in?' She stepped back to allow them in and led them through to the lounge. The DI introduced himself and DS Morecroft, then explained why they were there. 'We're investigating the murder of Geoffrey Marsden. He was killed at the football match two days ago.' He paused to see her reaction. Nothing, apart from her reaching down to her cigarette packet on the coffee table and offering them to the officers. They both declined. 'Do you know Mr Marsden?'

She took a deep drag. 'I know of him, of course. He's a businessman in town...my husband has dealings with him.'

'In what way does he deal with your husband?'

'He supplies uniforms and pharmaceutical goods to the DHA, my husband's the Contracts Manager.'

Brindle changed tack. 'Can I ask you where you were on Tuesday between two and three in the afternoon?'

She looked up, pretending to think, then, 'I was here, having a lazy day.' She then added with a smile, 'I watched TV.'

'And you were here all afternoon?'

'Yes.'

'Have you had anything go missing in recent weeks?'

Deidre frowned at the odd question. 'Er, no. I don't think so.'

'You're sure?'

She shook her head. 'No, nothing. Why?'

'Mrs Prosser, we retrieved the knife that killed Mr Marsden and it has your prints on it. Can you explain that?'

She tried to look shocked. 'No, I can't,' she replied, her face ashen.

'Whilst we're here could we check your knife block please?'

They followed her through to the kitchen where she held her hand to her mouth and uttered a stifled shriek. 'Oh yes, I remember now. One of the knives is missing.' She turned to the officers and pointed. 'Look, see, that's where it should be. I've no idea where it went.'

'Has anyone other than yourself and your husband had access to your kitchen?' She vigorously shook her head. Brindle smiled and tilted his head. 'Thank you, Mrs Prosser, you've been most helpful. We may want to talk to you again.' He turned to leave the kitchen. 'We'll see our-selves out, thank you again.' Back in the car Brindle looked at More-croft. 'Well?'

'She's definitely lying.'

Brindle turned the ignition. 'I agree. Next stop let's talk to her hus-band. Did she say he worked at DHA?'

'She did indeed, boss.'

* * *

They arrived at the DHA headquarters and asked for a Mrs Comp-stall, who was head of the Authority. She was a stout woman. She wore a heather-coloured tweed jacket and skirt, brown walking shoes and a man's heavy watch. The DI introduced himself and his partner.

'What can I do for you fine officers today,' she asked, 'it isn't often we get a visit from the constabulary. Please come through.' It was a large square office with an expansive window overlooking the new skate park and tennis courts. Along one side of the room were several heavy grey filing cabinets.

'So, what can I do for you?' she repeated as she clasped her hands in front of her.

'Do you have a member of staff answering to the name of Cyril Prosser?'

'Why?'

'We're investigating the murder of a participant at the football match on Tuesday, and we'd like to talk to him.'

She suddenly looked worried, not sure if she should say what she was about to. 'Do you mind if a colleague sits in with us?' she quickly added. 'Ken Harvey, our head of security.'

The two officers looked at each other, then Brindle nodded. 'Okay.'

Mrs Compstall picked up the phone and made the request for Ken to come to her office immediately. A few seconds later there was a knock at the door and a tall, broad-shouldered man appeared. He looked at the two officers and held his hand out.

'Ken Harvey,' he said with a smile, 'I used to be in the Force.'

He settled himself into a chair whilst Mrs Compstall quickly explained the reason for the officer's visit.

'Could you explain to the officers why their investigation into the murder on Tuesday may link to your own investigation Mr Harvey?' Harvey nodded and turned to the officers. 'Prosser has been under surveillance for some time. We have reason to believe he's been pilfering drugs on his so-called check-up visits, and we think he's selling them on the streets. Our depot manager, Brian Withers, meticulously takes a tally of the drug stock immediately before and after Prosser's visits. We've generated a substantial tally of what has gone missing and are slowly putting a case together.' He paused then continued. 'We've no hard evidence yet. We thought, perhaps he has a bad debt to pay off or it could be financing his opulent lifestyle. Do you think there's a link between him stealing the drugs from the depot and the murder?'

The DI nodded. 'Maybe.' He referred his next comment to Mrs Compstall. 'We would like to talk to him now please.'

Compstall picked up the phone once more and spoke directly to Prosser.

'Would you pop up to my office Cyril.' Harvey got up to go.

The DI thanked him for his input. 'We may need to talk to you again, thanks for your help.'

As Harvey exited the room Prosser entered. He looked quizzically at Harvey as they passed each other; he started to sweat as he entered the office. Mrs Compstall introduced the two officers. 'They'd like to have a quick chat to you, Cyril.'

Prosser sat down; his face starting to glow as beads of sweat popped out on his forehead. 'How can I help?' His voice showed signs of a tremor.

Brindle smiled to put him at ease. 'Could you tell us where you were on Tuesday between two and three o'clock?'

Prosser relaxed slightly. 'I was here. In meetings all day. At least a dozen people could corroborate that. What's this all about?'

'We've spoken to your wife this morning. It appears that a knife is missing from your knife block. Do you happen to know where it's gone?'

He shook his head vigorously. 'No, I don't. Look, why do you need to speak to my wife? What has she got to do with anything?'

'We're making enquiries regarding the murder of a Mr Geoffrey Marsden. We're speaking to a number of people; just routine you understand. You've been extremely helpful Mr Prosser; thank you for your time.' Brindle and Morecroft rose, thanked Mrs Compstall and left.

Back in the car the DI had his usual question. 'Well?'

Morecroft smiled. 'Definitely shifty boss. That was useful info Harvey provided us with regarding the thefts. Do you think there's some connection between Prosser stealing drugs and the murder?'

The DI thought for a moment. 'Could be. We need to get hold of Prosser's bank accounts and both Marsden and Prosser's computers. See if either can shine any light.'

The Prosser bank account showed high expenditure. A large, detached house, two new cars, holidays abroad, personal shopping. 'They seem to have a good lifestyle Jen,' observed Brindle, 'Could that lifestyle be supported by the salary that a contracts manager would earn?'

'Don't know, we need to get information on his salary from Compstall.'

'I agree, although companies are often reluctant to give out personal info.'

'Even though they are investigating him themselves and he's the main suspect in a murder enquiry?'

'Let's ask. If you don't ask you don't get.'

When they got back to the station there was a message for them to phone the FLO, Christine Harding, who was staying with Mrs Marsden. Jen Morecroft phoned her immediately then reported to DI Brindle.

Jen's eyes twinkled. 'You'll love this boss. We need to go over to the Marsdens – like now.'

The FLO, on hearing their car roll up on the drive had opened the door before Brindle and Morecroft had time to knock. 'Come in boss. Mrs Marsden has something she needs to show you.' They followed her into the lounge and introduced themselves to Susie Marsden who was sitting on the edge of the sofa looking forlorn. She smiled weakly as they came in.

'We're so sorry for your loss Mrs Marsden. We're doing all we can to find out who did it.' She indicated for them to sit down. They then looked at Christine the FLO in anticipation. Christine sat down beside Susie Marsden.

'Susie, can you show the officers what you showed me earlier?' She nodded and picked up a laptop that was sitting on the coffee table. She flicked the lid, clicked a few buttons then turned it round for them to see. It was the footage of Prosser, not only dealing drugs, but also apparently procuring a prostitute. Brindle tried not to show his excitement at seeing the footage.

'Please may we take this away with us. I promise we'll get it back to you as soon as we can.' Susie silently nodded. 'Thank you.' As they reached the front door to leave, the FLO filled them in on the additional information obtained from Mrs Marsden.

'Apparently Prosser was pushing for a backhander from Marsden in relation to renewing Marsden's contract. As a counter threat Marsden showed Prosser the footage.'

Back in the car Brindle smiled at Morecroft and tapped the laptop. 'This hopefully confirms what Harvey at the DHA thought was happening to the stolen drugs.'

This was dynamite! This was the clincher they had been looking for.

* * *

Brindle and Morecroft sat in the police canteen savouring a well-earned coffee break. 'I've put the evidence to the CPS, and they reckon the evidence against Deidre Prosser regarding the fingerprints and the missing knife is conclusive and we've been given the go ahead to charge her with murder. The CPS have suggested we leave the case against Cyril Prosser for the Health Authority and the drugs squad to deal with. I think we need to pay Mrs Prosser another visit.'

When Deidre Prosser opened the door the defeated look on her face indicated that she was half-expecting them. 'Come in.' Once in the lounge the DI and DS remained standing. Mrs Prosser took a deep breath, tears forming in her eyes. 'Can I phone my husband? ...he's at work.'

'I'm afraid not. He's being arrested at his place of work as we speak.'

She broke down and slumped onto the sofa. The officers gave her a couple of minutes to compose herself then she was read her Miranda rights. 'Mrs Prosser, would you please stand up.' She did so leaning unsteadily on the arm of the sofa. 'Mrs Prosser, I'm arresting you on suspicion of the murder of Geoffrey Marsden on Tuesday 13th February 2024, you do not have to say anything but anything you do say will be taken down and may be used in evidence against you. Do you understand?'

'Yes,' she quietly replied.

'Please come with us.' She was led outside and placed in the rear seat of the police car. As they drove down the street, she tearfully watched her comfortable lifestyle disappearing in the distance.

EPILOGUE

Deidre Prosser was found guilty of murder and sentenced to life imprisonment.

No evidence was found against Cyril Prosser that he'd coerced his wife into committing the murder.

Ken Harvey, Derbyshire Health Authority's head of security had been assisting the drugs squad. Several other contractors were contacted to ask if they had also been approached by Prosser relating to bribes. The information gathered was subsequently passed to the CPS for their consideration. They agreed to lay charges against Cyril Prosser. He was charged with stealing, dealing drugs, and procuring a prostitute, for which he was sentenced to 12 years imprisonment. He was also charged with malfeasance, acting illegally in an official capacity, and was sentenced to a further 5 years imprisonment.

Susie Marsden became MD of Cope and Marsden. In addition to the company's manufacture of uniforms, she developed the business into a manufacturer of fashion goods supplying own brand department stores throughout the UK.

Cope and Marsden is now listed on the stock exchange.

4

The Rise and Fall of the House
of Quilley

2003

There were dark clouds forming in the distance and an easterly wind was picking up as Patrick leaned on the farm gate. To the right he could see the outline of the Jodrell Bank radio telescope beyond the rolling fields of Cheshire. To his left he could see the heavily wooded area around the perimeter of Barnstock Farm that he'd worked day and night for more years than he cared to remember. Patrick was well into his seventies now, but continued to complete a day of hard graft. With his arms resting on the top of the gate and his left foot resting on the bottom rung, he surveyed what was in front of him. Acres and acres of potatoes, their deep green leaves swaying in the wind. He had a weathered face and a cigarette was expertly clamped in the corner of his mouth. His battered, but favourite cap was askew on his head. He wore a waterproof gilet over a flannelette blue check shirt, baggy corduroy trousers and overly large boots.

'Your breakfast is ready Patrick,' came a shrill call. He always made a check around the perimeter of the farm before sitting down to breakfast. Satisfied that all the fences were in good order, no crops had been trampled on by escaping cattle from nearby farms and no trees had come down, he was then ready to sit with his wife of forty years and enjoy his hearty breakfast. His wife, Teresa, walked up to the farm gate, stood behind him and placed her hand on his shoulder. She repeated her request for him to return to the farmhouse and have his breakfast. Patrick Quilley turned and leaned backwards on the gate toward the farmhouse.

'Aye, I'm ready for my breakfast.' He smiled at his wife and put his arm around her. 'Forty odd years we've lived in that house,' he said nodding in its direction. 'It's where we brought Declan up, and built this business into a successful enterprise; the biggest in the north-west,' he added proudly. 'Biggest and best.' Teresa mutely nodded and squeezed his hand in agreement. Patrick pushed himself off the gate. 'Come on then, breakfast. Let's get the day rolling.'

It was a large five-bedroom farmhouse set on two hundred acres. The land had been given over largely to produce potatoes, with a small acreage which Patrick leased out to local farmers for their cattle. The processing shed and the fleet of trucks had been built up since Patrick became the steward to carry the Quilley name forward. There was an unspoken family mantra that the Quilley name should continue at all costs. Quilley Potato Merchants became a by-word for reliability and quality.

A couple of hundred yards to the left of the farmhouse the workers were beginning to arrive. Patrick had built a massive processing shed where the workers would sort, wash, bag and label tons of his own and other farmers' potatoes daily. The precious cargo would then be distributed by Patrick's fleet of trucks to supermarkets and large organisations, such as hospitals and prisons. As Patrick and his wife strolled back to the farmhouse he reminisced. 'Look at all this Tess, and to think there had been years of the Quilley family suffering abject poverty. My family worked hard to get themselves out of poverty, to what we have here.' He smiled at her, spreading his arms in front of him. 'It won't be long before we pass all this over to our Declan,' he crossed his fingers and added, 'if he manages to stay out of trouble.'

Their son, Declan, had been a wayward teenager. He was expelled from school and sent to boarding school, where he was even more disruptive, and was subsequently threatened with expulsion. He was eventually accepted by Leeds Uni to study Business Studies, during which time he was arrested for various drug offences. He dropped out after two wild years, then came home to help run the farm and, much to his parents' surprise, did a reasonable job. Maybe he'd settled down at last.

As Patrick and his wife crossed the farmyard, several chickens scuttled across in front of them as a large truck arrived having delivered its load to the large sorting shed. Patrick waved to the driver who had been on the road since 4.30am picking up potatoes from several farms for Quilleys to wash and bag on their behalf. The outlying farmers were happy with the arrangement as they got a better deal from Patrick than the supermarkets. They didn't have the restrictions placed on them that the big retailers imposed. As the driver jumped down from the cab Patrick called out to him, knowing he'd been up since the early hours. 'There's some breakfast here, Jack.' Jack gave Patrick and Teresa a thumbs up and ran over to them.

* * *

1845-1851

The Great Irish Famine

The Great Irish Famine caused the death of one million people and another million took flight to other countries to escape the poverty, but it could have been avoided! The disaster can be placed firmly at the feet of the British government and the nobility – the infamous 'absentee landlords'.

The short-term cause was the failure of the potato crop, especially in 1845 and 1846, because of the fungus known as potato blight. The potato was the staple diet of the rural Irish community, and its failure left millions exposed to starvation and death from sickness and malnu-trition.

The crisis was compounded by the social and political structure in Ireland in the 1840s. At that time, the agricultural labourers lived at a subsistence level and had little or no money to buy food – they relied on growing their own staple diet of potatoes. Food was widely available in Ireland at the time, but the communities at the bottom of the so-cial structure, could not afford it. At the same time, they were expected to pay rents to their absentee landlords. Failure to do so resulted in en-forced eviction, worsening an already dire situation.

From 1840 to 1845, the population of Ireland had increased from four million to eight million, the infant mortality rate having dropped dramatically due to the increased use of inoculation against disease. Consequently, this resulted in more people consuming potatoes. Other than Ulster, which had a growing linen industry, the rest of Ireland was agricultural. It had not undergone the industrial revolution to pro-vide employment for the expanding population and were still dealing with subsistence living. The agricultural land was owned mainly by Protestant, absentee landlords, who did not live in Ireland and left their managers to look after their lands. There was no shortage of food pro-duction during this time, but any surplus was designated for export to England. So valuable was the stock, that England sent soldiers to Ire-land to guard the warehouses should the starving masses raid them. It became a perfect storm. Due to the potato blight, unscrupulous land-lords increasing the rents, subsequent evictions, and surplus crops sent to England, the Irish rural communities starved.

In 1847 the British government set up soup kitchens in Ireland to help alleviate the starvation. However, they were concerned that the three million people using the kitchens would soon become dependent on food handouts and eventually they cancelled them. In the same year the government decided to cancel all financial assistance which had been put in place to alleviate the famine, and pushed the tax burden back on to Irish taxpayers, who were mainly landlords. However, many landlords did not pay the levy. Furthermore, the government compounded the problem when they used the Gregory Clause by which a tenant with more than a quarter of an acre was deemed not to be desperate and, therefore, not eligible for relief. The result of these combined decisions resulted in a catastrophic outcome. Up to 15 per cent of the population died and many more emigrated ostensibly to England and America, particularly to Liverpool and Boston respectively. The population of Ireland declined from eight million in 1840 to four million by 1900 and it never recovered. The mass starvation was not caused by malice from the British government, but from appalling neglect, ideological blindness and the assumed superior attitude of the English over the Irish.

* * *

1850

Limerick

The steady drizzle was mixed with the tears cascading down Seamus Quilley's cheeks as he stood by his mum's open grave. The priest had performed his duties and disappeared, eager to get out of the inclement weather. The relatives and friends, those still around or fit enough to attend the funeral, had rushed off at the onset of the heavy rain. The gravediggers were sheltering under a spreading elm tree whilst waiting to fill in the grave. Seamus's sister Dervla, stood next to him, linking his arm. Their father was too ill to attend and was waiting at home for their return.

Their mother had deteriorated significantly over the last three months before finally expiring. There wasn't a family in Ireland that hadn't been touched by the Great Famine. In many towns up to 25 per cent of the population had died.

'Come on, Seamus, there's nothing more to be done.' She gently pulled him away from the grave side. They arrived home to find their next-door neighbour, Mrs Donovan, comforting their father. She stood up as they opened the door. 'I'll put the kettle on.' They could hear her busying about in the kitchen whilst they sat silent, the curtains drawn. An air of misery pervaded the atmosphere. Almost everyone in the village had experienced loss within their families. Losing a loved one was becoming a daily occurrence. Mrs Donovan came in carrying a tray with a teapot and three cups. 'I'll leave you now, call me if you need anything.' Seamus silently thanked her with a nod and a hand gesture, then poured out three cups of strong tea.

Seamus was twenty years old. He was a tall, wiry individual, with black hair and deep blue eyes. Life on the small plot of land where they grew potatoes and kept three pigs, was all he knew. His parents leased it from a distant landlord.

A few days after the funeral Seamus sat Dervla down. 'I need to talk to you. It's important.' She sat down and readied herself for whatever news Seamus was about to impart. He coughed and cleared his throat. 'Dervla,' he began nervously, 'I'm going to England.' She looked at him and opened her mouth to speak, but he held up his hand to stop her. 'I'm going to find work.' He looked pleadingly at her. 'I can't stay here. I want to find work and send money home. That's the only way to keep our small family going.'

Dervla had tears in her eyes. 'I've been half expecting this. I understand why you need to go; we can't carry on as we are, but I wish there were some other way.'

Seamus felt a deep sadness as he looked at Dervla. 'Will you be able to manage things whilst I'm away?

She knew she had no choice. 'Don't worry, Dad and I will manage things until you return.'

Many of Dervla's friends had taken the decision to emigrate. Some had decided on Boston in the US and many, like Seamus, had decided on England. Staying in the Emerald Isle was no longer an option. Families had been decimated by starvation and death. Emigration seemed the only way out. Seamus looked to her for support. She smiled, which gave him comfort. She moved to his side, put her arm around his shoulder and kissed the top of his head. 'You go Seamus. You show the English what the Quilley family is made of.'

He nodded and squeezed her arm. 'Thanks, I'll do my best.'

* * *

Liverpool

Seamus stepped down the gangplank along with dozens of other Irishmen trying their luck in the country that had been the cause of all their problems. Over his shoulder he carried a backpack he'd managed to scrounge off a distant cousin; it was a shabby, faded blue, with straps missing. He'd packed one extra shirt, a pair of trousers and a small, framed pencil drawing of his mum.

Nervous, but excited, Seamus, placed his feet on English soil. The docks were busy; large ships were unloading and loading. Carriages waited patiently for the wealthier passengers to hire their services and be whisked away, no doubt to some comfortable home that was warm and had copious amounts of good quality food. He had the address of an acquaintance who had made the same journey several months earlier and where he'd been promised a bed and a contact at the docks for a job. He carefully unfolded the piece of paper and read the address out loud to himself, *1524 Scotland Road, Bootle*. Turning the paper over, there was a crude sketch of the directions. It showed an arrow opposite St Joseph's church indicating the location of the address. It was sandwiched between a Chinese laundry and pawnshop advertising for forfeited pledges.

Seamus boldly put one foot in front of the other and made his way out of the docks and onto Scotland Road. It was hectic. The noise of the clip clopping of horses' hooves and the metal wheels of the carriages created a cacophony of noise he wasn't used to. On the pavements were throngs of people going about their daily lives – this was a busy and crowded city! The noise, the people! It was so different from his quiet life in the Emerald Isle. Would he settle or even fit in? Would he find a job which would pay well enough to send money home? By the time he'd pondered all the questions rushing through his mind, he found himself outside St Joseph's. He checked his piece of paper then looked across the road. It was a sorry sight. The building he was heading for was a four-storey building with shops on the ground floor and goodness knows what waiting for him on the upper floors. The shop frontages were covered in dirt from the wet and manure-strewn road which had sprayed onto the windows as the horses and carts passed. The paint-work was peeling, and dubious characters were coming in and out of the nearby pawnshop. With trepidation he navigated his way across the wide road in-between the endless flow of carriages. He hesitated at the door, which was hanging off its hinges. There was what appeared to be old envelopes sticking out of the letter box and a strong smell which Seamus recognised as cabbage being boiled to within an inch of its life. He slowly inched his way up the stairs, several steps creaking as he went. The lighting was poor and the décor almost non-existent. He reached the first floor just as someone came out of one of the doors. Seamus assumed he was Irish by the ashen face, the freckles and dark hair...and his Irish lilt as he nodded 'good morning' to Seamus. He responded, feeling more at home having heard an Irish accent and politely asked, 'I'm looking for Ardle Doyle?'

His newfound acquaintance gave him a broad smile. 'New to the country, are you?' He stuck his hand out. 'Liam Kelly.'

Seamus stuck his hand out in response. 'Seamus Quilley.'

Liam pointed along the landing. 'Last door on the right.' He continued down the stairs shouting back, 'See you around Seamus!' Seamus edged his way along the landing, noticing the damp patches on the walls and the crumbling plaster, before tentatively knocking on the door Liam had pointed out. It was opened by a face he recognised.

'Ah! Seamus, you made it!' Ardle welcomed Seamus into his room. 'Come in, come in. Cup of tea?'

'Yes, please.' Seamus knew Ardle from Limerick. Ardle was a cousin of Seamus's mum's auntie. He had been in Liverpool for just over a year for the same reasons as Seamus. They sat together over the cup of tea and reminisced over their times in Limerick. Whereas Seamus had been a product of the farming community, Ardle had worked in a factory processing wool from the surrounding sheep farms. The Great Famine had not only decimated the population, but it had also impacted employers in the area. They were unable to recruit sufficiently capable people to work in the shearing sheds and packing warehouses. The wool factory had closed, and Ardle's family had suffered the same poverty as everyone else.

'It's good to see you Seamus. You can have a room here. I know the owner and I've already okayed it with him. Come, I'll show you your room, then we'll talk about getting you a job.' He looked apologetically at Seamus. 'It'll be in the docks, there's no farming jobs around here.' Seamus nodded and followed him out of the room. Ardle took him to a tiny attic room on the fourth floor. As he swung the door open, he waved his arm to usher Seamus in. The room was tiny! A sloping ceiling covered half of the room and a small window, smeared in grime, overlooked the busy and noisy Scotland Road. It had a shabby looking single bed, a threadbare chair and a small, badly scarred table. An empty beer bottle still lay on its side under the table from the previous occupier. 'There's a small kitchen at the back on the ground floor,' Ardle informed him whilst casually kicking a ceramic pot under the bed. 'Your pot is to be emptied each morning into the culvert running at the back of the yards. You may hear some noise from the second floor; there's a family of ten sharing one room.' Ardle stepped back onto the landing. 'I'll let you settle in. Shout if you need anything. Tomorrow, I'll take you down to the docks and introduce you to the bloke who gives out the jobs. I've already spoken to him, and he tells me there's work, but you'll just have to convince him you're strong, reliable, teetotal and trustworthy.' He hesitated slightly, 'I'll see you tomorrow then.'

The next day Seamus was up and about early, mainly due to the uncomfortable bed. He knocked on Ardle's door. 'Shan't be a minute,' a voice came through the door, 'give us a tick.' A few seconds later the door opened, and Ardle emerged. He wore a shiny, threadbare, ill-fitting suit, a striped shirt and a tie. He noticed Seamus appraise what he was wearing. 'I work in the office, Seamus,' he said as way of explanation. 'Come on, I'll take you down to the foreman before I start work.' They turned right out of the building and were immediately hit by the noise and the constant pervading odour of horse manure which was spread across the full width of the road. A five-minute walk then a right took them into the dock area itself. The quayside was already busy with dockers running backward and forward with trollies and small carts delivering the unloaded goods to the warehouses. Ardle headed for a ramshackle shed at the far side of the loading area and knocked on the door. The door creaked in protest as it was opened by a giant of a man. He was as broad as he was tall. He had a bald head, walrus moustache and hands like shovels. Ardle introduced the two men to each other. 'Seamus this is Tom Carter, Tom this is Seamus Quilley.'

Tom tentatively nodded. 'So, this is your friend from the old country is it Ardle?' he boomed. He remained at the door of his office and weighed Seamus up and down. 'Used to hard work, are you?'

Seamus nervously nodded. 'Yes sir, I worked on a farm.'

'Ever been in trouble with the police?'

'No sir.'

'Are you teetotal?'

'Er yes,' Seamus stammered.

Tom stepped back and began to shut his office door. 'Report to me tomorrow, seven o'clock sharp.' The door rattled shut.

At precisely seven o'clock the next morning Seamus arrived for his first day of work. A stiff breeze from the Mersey added an extra chill to Seamus's already cold body. Tom Carter must have seen him through the shed window and met him at the office door. 'Hello young Seamus. Ready?' Seamus nodded. 'Follow me.' Seamus almost had to trot to keep up with Carter's long strides. Carter swiftly took a quick left into the warehouse where he grabbed hold of one of the young workers. 'Where's your boss?' The startled worker pointed to his boss talking to another man who was stacking bales of cotton. Carter shouted over the echoing vastness of the warehouse. 'Jack!' When Jack looked up at the sound of his name Carter beckoned him over. Jack Belmont was the warehouse manager; a squat man with a red face and glassy eyes who limped over to the two men. 'This here is Seamus Quilley, over from the old country. I've taken him on. I want you to show him the ropes.' With that he marched off blowing his nose hard as he disappeared out of the warehouse.

Jack was a less intimidating character. 'I'll team you up with Ronan Sullivan, he's one of the porters who unloads onto trollies.'

Another Irishman? Have they all deserted the old country for a better life?

It was acknowledged at the time that 20 per cent of Liverpool's population was Irish, and most had settled in the immediate vicinity of the docks. Ronan was an open, friendly man and Seamus immediately felt comfortable in his presence. As Ronan directed Seamus across the wide expanse of the quayside, he set up a conversation. 'I assume you're new here. Where you from?'

'Limerick. You?'

Ronan laughed 'Not far from you. A few miles up the coast.. Ennis.' If Seamus thought Scotland Road was noisy, this was even worse. The quayside was hectic. There were noisy porters shouting instructions and friendly banter to each other, horses and carts to-ing and fro-ing, rigging on the clippers slapping against the masts in the blustery wind and creaking of wooden hulls as they moved up and down with the swell of the river. The three-masted ships were moored directly alongside the dock, within a short stride of the warehouse. Seamus could see some seamen unfurling sails as they prepared to sail off again to some exotic port on the other side of the world. Ronan pointed out the various jobs the dockers were employed to perform. One team of porters were down in the holds controlling the hooks for the crude cranes which lifted bulky cargo out of the hold and onto either the dockside itself, or onto a ramp leading from the ship. From there the porters would either load the goods onto low trailers, hand-held trollies or onto horse-drawn wagons, to be delivered further afield. On another ship Seamus observed men carrying large bunches of green bananas on their shoulders to be stored in warehouses. It was an exciting scene playing out in front of Seamus's eyes, but it was also overwhelming. He was used to the slow life of the countryside, the peace and quiet of the fields and the birds singing. At the end of the quick tour of the quayside they were back in the warehouse, where Ronan grabbed two trollies. 'Here, take this and follow me.'

Pushing the heavy trolley in front of him, the wheels squeaking and wobbling as they went, Seamus dutifully did as he was bid and followed Ronan to the side of a ship. There were dozens of large hessian sacks. Ronan heaved one onto his trolley and indicated that Seamus should follow suit. Four sacks were loaded onto each trolley and then they started the short journey back to the warehouse. This process was repeated numerous times before the large pile was stored in the warehouse. The heavy sacks contained coffee beans; a name Seamus had heard but had never tasted. The aroma from the sacks smelled so good to him. The next job involved shifting more sacks, this time containing ginger. This was something completely new to him.

Day after day, week after week, Seamus religiously arrived at the docks to start his day of moving heavy sacks, boxes and barrels. Over several months he began to recognise the contents of various containers from the aromas, sometimes it was coffee or tea, sometimes cereal or, on occasions, turpentine and tar. His favourite were the spices. Over the weeks and months, he became used to the multitude of aromas. Occasionally ships would arrive, and the crude dockside cranes would reach into the holds and pick out large bales of wool from Australia or New

Zealand to be transferred onto waiting horse-drawn wagons. Whilst Ronan and Seamus were sitting on an upturned casket enjoying a quick break, Ronan pointed out a warehouse further along the quay. 'That's a secured, 'bonded' warehouse. It's where customs store tobacco and rum brought in from the West Indies.'

At the end of each gruelling day Seamus would reluctantly trudge back to his unwelcoming room. He had a few provisions in his cupboard and would make himself a meagre meal and eat it at his badly scarred table sitting on his uncomfortable chair.

The autumn was drawing in. The evenings were getting darker and the cold wind from the river whistled through gaps in the window frame. He would sit on the side of his bed and think of Dervla and home. He really missed it, but at the same time felt ashamed that he had not yet been able to afford to send any money home. He accepted he was in this strange city for a purpose, but it didn't lessen the loneliness.

Earlier in the month he had news that his father had died. He was distraught and frustrated that he couldn't afford the ferry fare home to attend the funeral. It preyed on his mind, particularly on these cold dark nights. He would sometimes lie on his bed with his eyes shut and remember the open fields of Limerick, the Shannon River, knowing that if he walked down the main street, he would see people he knew. Sometimes tears would form in his eyes before falling asleep.

* * *

In recent weeks he had been joining Ronan for a drink in The Unicorn pub. It was a depressing pub in some respects – many were in the bar to try and forget the daily trudge of their work and their miserable lives. The drink helped them to get through each day. The location, the low gas lights and the depressing interior of the pub, attracted the poor end of society. Most nights Seamus was able to identify prostitutes plying their trade, especially to the many foreign sailors who came ashore to drink and find company after many weeks at sea. Seamus and Ronan sat at a small round table facing the main bar. They watched the comings and goings of the customers, the conversations between friends and strangers alike. They recognised many who worked along the quayside. Seamus turned to Ronan with a wry smile. 'Why does Tom Carter bother to ask if we're teetotal?'

Ronan laughed mockingly. 'Tom? He likes to think he lays the rules down, nobody takes a blind bit of notice of him.' Ronan quickly swilled down the last few drops of his beer and made to go. 'I've someone to see, I'll have to go. See you tomorrow.'

Seamus nodded and once Ronan had disappeared out of the doors he rose and made his way to sit at the bar. He ordered another beer and sat with both hands around the glass. There was a good deal of background noise and two customers who'd had too much to drink started an argument. People moved out of their way as fists started to fly until the landlord, a colossus of a man, swiftly crossed the room and dragged them both out. He bawled after them to not come back until they were sober, or they were better able to take their liquor. He obviously couldn't afford to bar them for any length of time. Seamus mulled over what his life had been like since arriving in Liverpool, his thoughts always going back to his sister Dervla in Limerick. He was jolted back to reality by a gentle voice which seemed to be aimed at him. He looked up to see the barmaid smiling at him. She was a dark haired, beautiful young woman.

'You look deep in thought, missing home?' Seamus looked up, smiled and nodded. She began to pull on one of the pumps. 'Let me treat you.' She finished the action and pushed a large glass over the bar. 'What's your name?'

He raised his glass as a thank you. 'Seamus, Seamus Quilley.' She leaned forward on the bar and smiled again. 'Megan Thomas. I'm the new barmaid.'

Seamus smiled. 'Not Irish then?'

'No, Welsh.' She suddenly noticed someone was waiting to be served. 'Oh, excuse me, Seamus.'

As she walked away, he called after her. 'Are you free one night to go out somewhere?'

'I'm free tomorrow night. Maybe meet here?'

He nodded, a broad grin across his face. 'Yes. I'll look forward to that.'

The next day Seamus had a spring in his step as he went about his work. He'd been working in the docks now for nearly five years, and each day had been hard graft, but today he felt the sun was shining even though there was a fine drizzle. The trollies didn't seem as heavy as they had done the previous day. He looked forward to meeting Megan. She seemed so easy to talk to. Perhaps she may help him stop thinking about home so much.

They met up the that evening at the pub and had a quick drink. They then moved to another pub round the corner along Scotland Road which was a little more genteel. After several months had elapsed, they were still enjoying each other's company. Love blossomed and they would spend nights in Seamus's room, wrapped in each other's arms.

* * *

Megan's parents had come to Liverpool to work in one of the processing plants when she was ten years old. That was eleven years ago. Seamus told her of his life in Limerick; how it had been devastated by the famine and how he'd decided to come to England to find work so that he could send money home. One evening, they were sitting in the pub when she noticed he was unusually quiet. He looked pensive.

She held his hand. 'I know it must be hard being away from home for so long. How are you feeling?'

He laughed. 'Better since I met you.' Then he stared off into the distance.

She squeezed his hand. 'You, okay?'

He shook his head and brought himself back into the moment. 'Sorry, I was miles away.' He looked her directly in the eyes. 'To be honest I miss Limerick, the people, the countryside, the open air. I'm not sure city life is for me.' This time it was Megan's turn to look pensive. Eventually she turned to Seamus, but hesitated before she spoke. *Am I going to speak out of turn. How would he take it?*

'Seamus,' she started, 'I received a letter from my mum today. She received a letter from her sister in Wales.' She stopped and pursed her lips before continuing. 'My mum's sister and her husband have a farm just outside Denbigh. Mainly sheep, but they also grow a few vegetables. According to my mum's letter neither of them is in good health.'

Seamus looked at her quizzically. 'And?'

Megan leaned back in her seat and thought, *in for a penny, in for a pound*, and blurted out what she wanted to say. 'They're looking for someone, a couple in fact, to help run the farm and do jobs around the house.' She looked at Seamus expecting a response. But before he could respond she added. 'Do you think it would it suit you...us,' she asked hopefully, 'it would mean you'd be back in the countryside. And there's a cottage included.' On seeing Seamus's face, she quickly added. 'I know it's a bit sudden, but we could start the job almost immediately.'

Seamus picked up his glass and showed no emotion as he finished off his drink. He then turned to Megan. He looked serious. 'I agree, but on one condition.'

'Which is?' she asked curiously.

'That you'll marry me.'

She slung her arms around him. 'Of course, of course. I'll write to my parents today.'

* * *

1856

Wales

Thomas Roberts and his wife Rose had run Mydyff Farm in Llanrhaeadr, for fifty years. They were both now approaching eighty and needed to slow down. They welcomed Seamus and his new bride with open arms.

It had taken Seamus and Megan several days to travel from Liverpool to Wales. A kindly local farmer had spotted the two newcomers in Denbigh town, carrying what few possessions they owned and asked where they were heading. He then offered to give them a lift to the farm on his horse and cart. The short journey was painfully slow, due mainly to the heavy rain which had fallen the previous day, turning the lanes into mud, and partly due to the ageing mare pulling the cart. Nevertheless, they were both extremely grateful for the offer, which allowed them to rest. He dropped them off at the end of the lane leading down to the farm. The farmhouse was at the end of a long, rutted track overgrown with brambles and thistles along the verges; large trees formed a shady canopy across the track.

As they turned a bend in the dirt lane, immediately in front of them was the farmhouse, their new home, their new life. It was a small square house with an open porch, covered in ivy. Chickens picked at the ground in their endeavour to find something to eat, a dog emerged from a kennel at the corner of the house and barked. A dilapidated barn stood to the left of the house, its wood silver-grey with age.

Alerted by the barking, the front door opened and there stood Thomas and Rose Roberts, looking aged and pale. Thomas had a thick head of white hair and a walrus moustache, Rose was leaning on a walking stick and appeared frail and petite. They stepped out into the yard, broad smiles across their faces, arms outstretched in welcome. Thomas was the first to speak. 'Come in, come in.' Seamus and Megan followed them into the house which was dark and sparsely furnished. The living room had a sofa and two easy chairs, a Welsh dresser stood along one wall and alongside it, hanging from the wall, were several beautifully carved Welsh loving spoons. A clock which emitted a loud tick, took pride of place on top of the mantelpiece over a roaring log fire. The two travellers were exhausted, but the elderly couple insisted on a celebration...a meal of lamb and potatoes.

Rose stood back and looked at Megan. 'Haven't you grown! You were only knee-high last time I saw you. It was the week before you moved to Liverpool with your parents. Ah, that was a sad day when you all left.' She shook her head and looked sad as she remembered. 'Excuse me while I go and prepare lunch.' She disappeared into the kitchen and the sound of pans and cutlery could be heard. Within what seemed like just minutes, she returned carrying large dishes of steaming vegetables which she placed on the large, sturdy wooden table. The plates were filled with extremely generous portions of meat, strategically placed to allow vegetables to be added. They all sat down and helped themselves to boiled potatoes, carrots and steaming white cauliflower.

'So, Megan, how are your mum and dad in Liverpool? Are they well?'

'Yes, they are very well, thank you,' Megan replied. She fell silent and continued with her meal.

After the large lunch, Rose and Thomas explained what duties the couple would be expected to perform. Seamus was to help with the sheep and Megan the household chores. It was obvious that neither Thomas nor Rose could run the farm with its heavy workload and long hours. 'We're so glad you both agreed to come and help.' Thomas glanced at Rose before continuing. 'We're not able to do the manual work anymore and we have no children of our own.'

Seamus smiled at them. 'We're pleased to help. I'm from a farming community and if I'm honest, I couldn't wait to get back to working on the land. All my family farm one way or another.'

Later that day, Thomas and Rose took Seamus and Megan across the farmyard and through a five-barred gate, alongside a hedge and around the perimeter of a field to a small building. Seamus and Megan were rather shocked at its appearance. It had several broken windows which had been covered in hessian sacking and the door was hanging off its hinges. The roof was covered in lichen. However, the inside was surprisingly dry and clean. It was dusty, but didn't have much detritus on the floors. It had a tiny kitchen, a living room containing a sofa, an easy chair and a table pushed against one of the walls.

Rose smiled at the couple. 'This is your new home. It's for you to have whilst you're with us, which we hope will be a long time.' Seamus forced a smile to show he was grateful. At the same time, he recognised the enormity of the task of putting their new home into a liveable condition.

Thomas patted him on the shoulder. 'I know it needs some work but I'll help where I can, and we do have a handyman that comes in from time to time from town. I'm sure he'll be able to help you with some of the work.'

Seamus smiled. 'Thank you.'

'I'm sure you'll soon have it ship-shape,' Rose added.

'Concentrate on getting your new home fixed up, then we'll talk about the jobs on the farm.' Mr and Mrs Roberts left. When they got out of earshot Seamus and Megan looked at each other, then burst into laughter.

'It's not what I expected at all,' chortled Megan….'but it's all ours. We'll soon have it right and I'll enjoy making it homely.' They both flopped down onto the sofa and began to plan.

* * *

Mydyff Farm was fifty acres set in a valley between the tiny villages of Llanrhaeadr and Pentre with a dense pine forest on the northern side which sloped down to a large lake. Wales mainly consisted of sheep farming, the hilly countryside being unsuitable for growing crops. Most farmers had a small area set aside for their own use, but hill farming sheep was the mainstay in the area. The sheep were left to graze for most of the year, but twice a year they were driven via the narrow country lanes to the sale yard in Ruthin, where farmers hoped to get a good price for their stock. The trip to Ruthin was a significant event for all the farmers in the area and the town bustled. It enabled the isolated communities to meet up, engage with each other in local gossip and stock up on their requirements, whether it was food for the home or equipment for the farm.

Within weeks Seamus and Megan had settled into their new home. Thomas was as good as his word in offering to help renovate the tiny cottage, which was now, they thought, a cosy home. Seamus had no experience of sheep but, with Thomas's help, he quickly built up his skills and knowledge.

1857

Megan gives birth to twin boys, Seamus jnr and Liam.

1858

Tragedy struck Mydyff Farm. Thomas had a heart attack and died in March only to have Rose die in the September from tuberculosis. Seamus and Megan were devastated. They wondered what would happen to them now. Would the farm be sold? Would they have nowhere to live to bring up their two boys?

Seamus was staring out of the window watching two magpies picking at the ground, whilst Megan was feeding the two boys. There'd been a keen frost the previous night and however nice it looked, the unavoidable worry of what would happen to them as a family was constantly on his mind. Megan called to him to come and get his breakfast. At least in the countryside they ate well. From time to time, they would think about the people living in the overcrowded cities: the poverty, poor health, lack of good food and the appalling smells which cities had made all of their own.

Megan poured him a cup of tea. 'What are we going to do? We've heard nothing and it's been nearly a month since Rose died. What's to happen to the farm?' They knew Thomas and Rose had no children and weren't aware of any other relatives who could take over the farm. Each day Seamus would go out into the fields, as he did when Thomas and Rose were alive. He undertook all the jobs, but now there was no pay. Fortunately, the cottage was free, and they had access to food to eat and wood to burn to keep themselves warm.

It had been six weeks since Rose had died. Seamus had completed his daily rounds of the farm and was closing the gate to the yard, when he was startled by a sound he hadn't heard for some time. He latched the gate and turned to see a horse drawn cab stopping in front of the house. A gentleman alighted and, straightening his top hat, strode purposefully up to the farmhouse door. As he was about to lift the fox shaped knocker with his gloved hand Seamus called out. 'Can I help you?'

The well-dressed man turned and raised his hat to Seamus. 'Good morning. I'm looking for a Mr Seamus Quilley.'

Seamus wiped his mucky hands down his trousers which didn't improve them and responded. 'That's me. Who am I addressing?'

The man bowed slightly and pointed to the door. 'May we go inside?'

'Of course.' Seamus stepped past the stranger opened the door and waved him through. Once inside Seamus shouted for Megan. 'Megan, we have a visitor.' Megan came through from the back room undoing her apron at the same time. She looked first to Seamus and then to the stranger. The stranger took off his hat, undid his cloak and, reaching inside his jacket pocket, retrieved a card which he handed over to Seamus. It read:

Jasper Williams, Attorney, High St, Denbigh

(The term attorney was used until 1875 when the term solicitor became more common.)

'May we sit?' The stranger asked politely.

Megan rushed around and cleared some of the boy's toys from the sofa and plumped up the cushions. 'Please,' she said indicating the sofa. Mr Williams took his time sitting down, then, picking up his case, slowly opened it and took out a sheaf of papers. Seamus and Megan looked at each other wondering what was coming next.

Mr Williams smiled. 'I understand you've been working for Mr and Mrs Roberts for some time?' They nodded. 'I represent them and some time ago they asked me to draw up their wills.' He gently waved two or three sheets of paper. 'I have good news for you.' He paused for effect. 'You are the beneficiaries of their farm and everything they own. They have left everything to you in appreciation of all your hard work in helping them to run the farm.' In a theatrical voice he added. 'Mr and Mrs Quilley, as of today Mydyff Farm is yours.' He handed them a piece of paper before putting the rest of his papers back in his case. 'I have taken the liberty of transferring the house and land to you both. Here are the deeds.' Rising from the sofa he tipped his hat before placing it back on his head and bid them good day.

The new owners of Mydyff Farm were lost for words and didn't speak until they watched Mr Williams' cab disappear down the track bobbing from side to side as it clumsily traversed each set of ruts. Seamus and Megan looked at each other with tears in their eyes.

They hugged each other. They couldn't believe what had happened. Then Seamus put his hands on Megan's shoulders and looked at her. 'I think this calls for a celebration Mrs Quilley.'

She nodded. 'It'll have to be a cup of tea.'

They would often stand leaning on the yard gate and stare out at their newly acquired property. They would scan the horizon taking in the rolling hills and the grazing sheep. During this time Seamus spent time formulating his plans for the future. At breakfast one morning he held his mug of tea in his hands to warm them up and looked at Megan. 'We have been handed a business and I think we need to develop it, not just for us, but for the two boys. I want to be able to hand a successful farm over to them.'

She nodded enthusiastically. 'What do you have in mind?'

He hesitated then continued, 'I want to change the farm from sheep to crops.'

Megan held her cup of tea half-way to her mouth stunned, 'Change it? But why?'

He leaned forward across the table, 'As much as I've been happy moving here, I'm not really a sheep farmer at heart.'

'But Wales is hill farming. Sheep is what they do. They all do!'

He sighed. 'Precisely! And they are all susceptible to varying wool prices, disease and the long hours involved in lambing.'

She couldn't disagree and nodded in acknowledgment. 'So, what do we do instead?'

'Potatoes,' he replied.

'Potatoes!' her voice lifting an octave.

'Potatoes.' The enthusiasm increased in his voice as he explained his idea for the future. 'We'll sell the sheep then get all the lower fields ready for potatoes. I'll remove the rocks and trees, buy a plough and level the ground. We'll keep some acreage for a few other crops too.' He looked pleadingly at Megan. 'That's what I know. All I know! That's what my family in Limerick have done for years. Potatoes are in my blood.' He continued excitedly. 'I'll get a couple of flat carts and horses so I can deliver fresh vegetables to the outlying districts...it will save them having to stock up on their rare visits to Denbigh or Ruthin. They'll have access to fresh vegetables on a weekly basis. And we'll sell to the shops in the surrounding area. Nobody else is doing that.'

A broad grin spread across Megan's face. 'Okay, Seamus. Let's do it.'

Little did they know that this initial decision would be the start of the Quilley empire.

* * *

Their first crop of five acres of potatoes proved to be successful. The locals loved the service and would look forward to him calling...not just for the potatoes, but also for the news he carried around the valleys. Mydyff Farm quickly expanded into supplying carrots and beans in the summer and cauliflowers and sprouts in the winter. Within a few years Seamus had bought up an adjoining farm and expanded the business even further. Each year he would leave one field fallow which he would rent out to farmers who required grazing space for their sheep. The Quilley name would become synonymous with the supply of quality potatoes and vegetables.

One of the farms he bought out was handed over to his two boys to run under his supervision. The experience they gained from running their own operation came unexpectedly into focus.

October 1890 – Seamus Snr dies

Megan was devastated at Seamus's passing and took a back seat in running the business. Sadly, her health rapidly declined after her loss. She would sit in her chair each day and stare out of the window. She and Seamus had enjoyed a long and happy life together; from their days in Liverpool, to running the farm for Thomas and Rose Roberts, and finally to Seamus developing a successful business, which had now been handed over to Seamus jnr and Liam. Under their stewardship the business went from strength to strength. They were now supplying most of North Wales and the border regions.

* * *

1910

Business was booming. The two boys decided to reappraise where the business was going. They'd hit saturation point. The Quilley business was supplying as much as the market would take. Over a glass of home brewed beer, they laid out a plan for the next ten years. Whilst Seamus snr had been alive the Quilley household had been a 'dry' house – strictly no alcohol. However, Seamus jnr and Liam were now able to enjoy the odd glass of beer. Liam was concerned. 'No farms are coming up for sale any time soon, Seamus, mainly because the farms are being handed down to the children. We need to expand outside Wales.'

Seamus took a long drink of his beer before answering. 'I know. I reckon we need to look at the whole of the UK. Locations that are within delivery distance of a major conurbation. We need to look at possibly acquiring a site in England.' After several weeks of enquiries via land agents, Liam was dispatched to check out the market. He arrived in England as spring was getting into its stride. The trees were beginning to bud, giving a beautiful green cloak to their silhouette. The fields and grass verges were showing signs of new growth and wildflowers were popping their heads up. New lambs were gambolling around the pastures. There was definitely a feel of spring in the air. Liam looked at several farms which were suitable for their needs. He eventually decided on a farm in the Cheshire countryside between Goostrey and Chelford. The owners of the farm, who had no family successors, were the Grevilles, Tom and Clarice.

Liam was fascinated by the name of Goostrey. He was curious about the name and decided to do a bit of local history digging. He discovered the village was first named in the Domesday Book in 1086 and the spelling of the name was originally Gostrel, meaning Godhere's tree. Goostrey was a farming community and boasted a well patronised pub, The Red Lion, no doubt in reference to Le Coeur de Lion, Richard the Lionheart. Melrose Farm had two hundred acres of gently undulating fields. It had several barns, one housing an impressive Saunderson tractor and several large farming implements. In an adjoining barn was a

Leyland truck. The truck was a real find and absolutely vital if they were to deliver to the wholesale market in the city of Manchester. Alongside the eastern perimeter was the River Dane, which would be a useful source of irrigation. He walked the perimeter of the farm alongside the river, through a copse of beech trees and back to the large farmyard. Every so often he would stop and scan the fields. Already he was seeing what great potential it had.

Within a few months, Liam and Seamus jnr had secured the purchase of Melrose Farm and Liam moved in. Within a year he had purchased an additional truck, a good old reliable Austin. The Quilley organisation now had two centres, one in Wales and one close to the conurbation of Manchester. The Quilley Potato Merchant, now known as Quilley Enterprises, whilst rapidly widening its markets, had seen the world change. There had been the death of Queen Victoria in 1901, the subsequent coronation of Edward VII and his short reign of only nine years.

* * *

1914

Quilley Enterprises was expanding at an exponential rate, when the great disaster hit Europe, WWI. Both Liam and Seamus jnr were classified as being in a reserved occupation and didn't go to war. Their contribution was in making sure the valuable work of producing food for the population, the forces and hospitals, was maintained. They supplied most of the vegetables necessary for keeping the forces at full strength.

During the war years, the local Goostrey community made great efforts in keeping the morale of its community high. There were weekend dances, quizzes in The Red Lion and homes were opened for convalescing airmen, away from the continual bombing of the cities. At one of the now regular Saturday night dances which Liam attended, he met Mary, a nurse who was on leave for a few days from the front line. Liam and Mary jitterbugged to the sound of Glenn Miller and the Harry Roy orchestras. The evening came to an end all too soon. Liam walked her home to her parents' house, Dane Bank Farm, three miles from Melrose. 'Can I see you tomorrow?' asked Liam.

She looked at him, her eyes saddened. 'Sorry, I'm back at base to-morrow, maybe next time.' After seeing Mary home, he walked back to Melrose Farm along dark country lanes which he knew like the back of his hand. During the day they were so familiar, but at night they looked so different. It was a pitch black sky. The north star was shim-mering overhead. An owl hooted in the distance. The silhouette of the trees with arms outstretched looked eerie. He strode purposefully with a smile across his face, convinced Mary was the girl for him. He had no doubts when the war was over, he and Mary would marry. With that in mind he increased his stride and arrived back at Melrose with a re-newed passion for building the business. He put his heart and soul into the Quilley Enterprises and his hard work continued to achieve results.

It was a difficult courtship; Mary was very rarely at home. However, the love between them survived and blossomed.

1920 – Liam and Mary marry
1923 – Patrick is born

Mary's parents had died during the war leaving their property Dane Bank Farm, to Mary. The farm was sold, and the proceeds were used to buy more acreage to add to Quilley Enterprises. The same year Sea-mus jnr, who had been running the Welsh operation, also died. He had contracted tuberculosis. Due to the hard work he had been putting into the farm, it had left him weakened and unable to fight off the disease. He had never married, so the Welsh enterprise went to Liam and Mary. Liam was devastated by Seamus jnr's passing and it took him many months to muster the enthusiasm to continue running the business. The property and land in Wales were finally sold and the proceeds used to buy more land in England, more trucks and to employ more labourers. It ensured a great future for them both. Quilley Enterprises was now a million-pound business, a household name within the vegetable industry.

1946

WWII was over and many parts of England had been reduced to rubble, particularly London. England was desperately trying to get back on its feet. The general population was still experiencing rationing and difficulties in obtaining supplies of food and many household items. Any surplus industrial production was being exported. The government hoped this would generate money to enable them to start the rebuilding process. France had been decimated. Their once pristine farmland was now acres and acres of bomb craters, it would be some time before their food production would return to pre-war levels.

1948

Liam decided that Quilley Enterprises could fill a much-needed gap and set off to France to discuss the possibilities of exporting potatoes and vegetables.

Mary's maternal aunt Madelaine had lived most of her life in France. On the death of her husband, Madelaine had moved from Calais to England to live with her sister, Mary's mum. She had taught Mary the language as a child knowing it would be useful to her when she was older. It turned out to be a huge asset.

On Liam and Mary's journey home from France, the plane crashed in the Channel as it approached the coast near Dover. All passengers and crew perished.

1948

Patrick, now twenty-five was the sole custodian of Quilley Enterprises. He had grand and far-reaching plans for the future of the company.

The 1950s was a boom time for many companies. The population was tired of austerity and wanted a better life, an easier life. It was the beginning of the consumer society. People wanted to buy "things" – if only they were available. The government was still trying to get England back on its feet, so many products were still only available for export. During this time Patrick had expanded the business into supplying even more of the larger establishments, such as hospitals and prisons, and his latest coup was a contract to supply tons of potatoes on a weekly basis to the growing crisp market. Amid all this to-ing and fro-ing in expanding and developing the business, Patrick somehow managed to acquire himself a wife. Patrick was so driven in developing Quilley to even greater heights that most of his romantic relationships fizzled out because of his obsession with the business. Whilst dealing with the law firm Shaw and Crossman in Manchester city centre, regarding yet another contract, he was introduced to Teresa who was his lawyer's PA. She would organise appointments, produce the contracts for Quilley and keep him appraised of any up-and-coming changes.

She was super-efficient and appeared to be well organised. Teresa was a tall slim lady in her late twenties. She had short blonde hair, grey eyes and wore immaculate make-up. Whenever he arrived at the prestigious offices for an appointment, she would always welcome him with a warm smile. Whilst Patrick waited to see Mr Gerry Crossman, one of the partners in the firm, the two would have a pleasant and easy conversation. As a consequence of these chats, he discovered she was an avid walker, particularly in the Lake District.

'Ah, so am I,' responded Patrick enthusiastically, 'usually, around Grasmere.'

Teresa raised her eyebrows, half disbelieving. 'Well, I'm surprised I've never seen you tramping up and down the fells. That's where I usually go. Maybe we'll meet up there one day.'

Over the weeks of visiting the office, he had been waiting for an opening such as this. 'Well, how would you feel if we made a weekend of it?' He ventured. 'Go up Friday afternoon straight from work, come back Sunday afternoon.'

Her eyes lit up and she opened her mouth to reply, when Patrick heard his name being called. 'Mr Quilley?' He turned to see Gerry Crossman standing in the doorway gesturing for Patrick to join him in his office.

'Good morning, Gerry.' He stepped toward the door, but not before glancing at Teresa who gave him an imperceptible nod which Patrick took as a yes.

1960 - Patrick and Teresa were married

1963 - Declan was born

Teresa was a godsend in helping to run Quilley Enterprises. Whilst Patrick organised the every-day running of the business, including the planting, the harvesting and the daily contact with his customers, Teresa kept the office running smoothly. She was superb at rooting out any new regulations that may have come out and kept Patrick up to date. She liaised with his accountants at tax time and dealt with any financial hiccups.

Quilley Enterprises was now acting as an agent for other growers in the area. Patrick had built a processing shed that enabled him to not only wash and bag his own produce, but also to do the same for other farmers who had not been able to finance such facilities.

* * *

1964-1984

Quilley Enterprises diversified the business from being a producer and supplier of potatoes and other vegetables, to opening a chain of retail outlets. Over a three-year period, they opened six shops, all within the catchment area of the main business. The retail shops were simply called Q Vegetables. The retail business boomed and over the next two years he opened seven more outlets. Things were moving fast.

In February 1967, he met with Shaw and Crossman and later that same week, his accountants Jessop and Buston. The purpose of the meetings was to set up Quilley Retail as a franchise business. By 1969 Quilley Retail had nearly three hundred franchised shops across the UK. Quilley Enterprises was now a multi-million-pound organisation. Their name was as well known in the average household as Kellogg's and Cadbury.

Kellogg's, Cadbury, Quilley – all well-respected names on the high street. All family owned.

Over the next twenty years the business went from strength to strength.

Patrick now controlled a fleet of thirty lorries, employed nearly one thousand people and four hundred franchised retail outlets. During dinner one evening sipping a glass of Merlot, Patrick thought back over the last hundred years to the Quilley's simple beginnings. He raised his glass to Teresa. 'The Quilley family has done okay, Tess. It's up to us to continue the good work.'

She raised her glass in return. 'You'll have to back off at some point Pat. You're not as young as you were. It's about time you took a break, we should have a holiday abroad. You need a rest.' Patrick nodded and smiled, he had no intention of backing off, the business needed him.

1999

Lightening his workload was forced upon Patrick. His arthritis, which had hovered for some years, was now causing him considerable pain. He struggled to climb on and off the tractor, chainsaw fallen trees and generally get around the farm. Teresa constantly nagged him to retire. 'We're not short of money. You can hand over to Declan. He's running the other farm quite well.'

Patrick pursed his lips. 'I'd be happier if he found a wife, settled down. It takes two committed people to run the enterprise.'

She nodded in agreement. 'I know, but you've got to retire sooner or later. You need to hand over to Declan.' He nodded back. Even with a good accountant and lawyer in the background, he had serious doubts about Declan's business acumen.

2003

Patrick's arthritis was now so bad he struggled to get out of bed in the morning. Teresa presented him with a brochure showing new houses. 'I've been making enquiries,' she held her hand up to stop him interrupting, 'just enquiries.' She handed him the brochure. 'This company has been building a new development near Alderley Edge.' Patrick raised his eyebrows; he knew Alderley Edge was a prestigious area and very expensive. She saw his look. 'We can afford it. You've worked 24-7 for God knows how long, it's time we reaped the rewards. Retire. It's time for you to do what you want. Read a book. Go out for lunch whenever you want.'

'I don't know Tess; work is all I know.'

'Precisely. Anyway, I've made enquiries to go and look at the show house, this afternoon.'

He laughed. He'd just go along with it; he didn't want to make a fuss.

The show house was beautiful. It was a five-bedroom mock Georgian bungalow with a double garage. The rear garden led down to

Throsby mere which was edged by weeping willows and had several ducks paddling their way to the small island in the middle. As it happened, the show house was for sale, the development now almost completed. Teresa and Patrick agreed to buy it and within one month they were the proud owners of an enviable home, surrounded by open land, their nearest neighbours a good distance away. The outlying view of heather-covered hills was magnificent. As they walked out of the solicitor's office Teresa kissed him. 'You'll love it you know. No more getting up at four in the morning. No more going over the books at eleven at night. No more stairs to climb. Come on let's go and celebrate with lunch at the Warlock pub, it's just down the road.' Patrick climbed into his beloved Jaguar and turned the ignition.

CHESHIRE COURIER
New managing director

It was announced today that Quilley Enterprises has a new managing director. Declan Quilley will take over from his father, Patrick, on the first of January. An insider has said that the retirement of Patrick Quilley was due to ongoing health issues.

Quilley Enterprises has been in business for over 150 years. It was founded by Seamus Quilley who came over to England during the Great Irish Famine. The business has gone from strength to strength and is now one of the largest businesses in the UK. On the eve of his retirement Patrick Quilley said:

'I'm confident that, under the leadership of Declan, the business will continue to grow and have a long-standing presence on the high street.'

Declan also commented saying:

'My father has built up a successful organisation from humble beginnings to the mammoth business it is today. I hope I can continue the standards my father has set and see the business grow even further.'

It is rumoured that Quilley's retail arm is contemplating opening up their franchise to the French and German markets.

Declan moved out of the farmhouse he'd been living in and moved into the home that Patrick and Teresa had shared for forty years. His first day in the office as MD was a momentous occasion for him. From now on he could make all the decisions – and get rid of some of what he perceived to be, the "hangers on". He could spend a bit more of the profits on enjoying himself. What was the point of amassing vast profits if there was no personal benefit. Things will change! Must change!

He leaned back in his plush upholstered chair, balancing it on the back two legs as he surveyed the office. Black and white grainy photos hung on the wall depicting the history of the Quilley name. His desk was a large walnut piece of furniture with an antique lamp on one corner. He pictured his dad in this chair. All his dad thought about was the success of the business, making sure his employees were happy, never treating himself with any personal rewards for all the long hours he put in. He sat up and pressed the intercom to the outer office. 'Brenda, can you get me a coffee, black.' *What were PAs for if not to make coffee.* He'd seen his dad on numerous occasions offering to make Brenda a coffee because she was busy.

Why? That's what you had staff for, wasn't it? Within minutes his coffee arrived. 'Do you want me to go through the appointment book with you, Declan?' He shook his head. 'Maybe tomorrow.' He glanced at his watch. 'I'm popping out at lunchtime to meet someone.'

Brenda had her pen poised. 'Who would that be so I can put it in the file?' He waved his hand at her. 'It's nothing to do with business.'

Brenda hadn't taken to her new boss. She knew him, of course, because he'd been around when his father was running the business. She had few personal dealings with Declan, but there was something about him she didn't like. It could have been his moodiness, his supercilious look or his dismissive attitude. Maybe all those things. She didn't know, but what she did know was that he was very different from his father. Brenda was not impressed.

Declan was a tall, slightly overweight individual, with short dark hair, stubble, red cheeks and an inappropriate sense of occasion in terms of dress. He would meet customers in his office or visit the accountant wearing jeans and a sweater. *Was it an arrogance or simply a couldn't-care-less attitude?* He didn't walk, he strutted.

For the first few months Patrick came into work two or three times a week to provide an overview of the business to Declan, but as the weeks and months went by it became more and more difficult for him to attend due to the increasing impact of his arthritis. In addition to Patrick's painful condition, Teresa had suffered two nasty falls, the second one resulting in a short stay in hospital. As a consequence of his parents' disabilities, Declan was left alone to run the business. Patrick and Teresa stayed out of the way by booking themselves on a three-month cruise around the Mediterranean.

One of Declan's first decisions was to look at the franchise contracts Quilley had with its four hundred outlets.

He called Brenda into his office. 'These contracts,' he said waving one of them in the air, 'they seem over generous in favour of the franchisee. I see the royalty to us is ten per cent.'

Brenda nodded. 'That's what your father thought was fair. That figure, I think, is the norm throughout the franchise industry.'

Declan shook his head in annoyance. 'It's too generous. Ten per cent is not giving us a fair return for having established the Quilley name.' He turned to Brenda. 'Can you get the list of franchisees out and mark off which ones are due for renewal, say within the next six months. I'm going to give them a new contract and up their royalty payments to us to twelve and a half per cent.'

'Right,' said Brenda reluctantly, 'that's upping the royalty by twenty-five per cent. Is that right? Isn't that a bit steep?'

Declan dismissed her concerns. 'They can either sign the new contract or not. We'll soon find someone else who would be prepared to take on the franchise at twelve and a half per cent.'

As she went to close the door behind her he called her back. 'I won't be back this afternoon; I've got something I need to do.' She returned to her desk, shaking her head in frustration and went to retrieve the franchisee list from the file.

Declan's lunch break consisted of an afternoon in the Rope and Anchor pub. It was a country pub on the outskirts of town backing onto a canal and a small marina for the leisure barges that used the waterway. It had the reputation of being the meeting place of the 'Cheshire Set', a hub for the well-to-do. The car park was always crammed with Jaguars, BMWs, Mercedes and the odd Roller. Declan parked his BMW, noticing his mate's Porsche was already parked. He entered via the rear door that led into the bar. Declan knew Jasper Tierney from his university days. Declan never applied himself at university, dropping out halfway through his Business Studies degree course. He was most likely to be found propping up the university bar. He had always had a privileged upbringing and was secure in the knowledge that money would never be a problem. Jasper was already seated in their favourite corner, two glasses of red wine waiting in front of him. He was a tall stringy individual. He had sandy hair which hung over his collar, a pasty face and had a panatella in his right hand. He wore a thin green wool polo neck sweater and beige chinos; a jacket was slung on the seat beside him.

'Hello mate, how's things?'

Declan sat down, picked up one of the glasses of red wine and took a sip. He raised the glass. 'Thanks, I needed that,' he laughed, 'after a hard hour in the office.' He reached inside his jacket and discreetly pulled out a small white packet which he pushed over to Jasper.

Jasper sat back in his seat. 'Great.' Then, passing some folded notes to Declan he resumed the conversation. 'So, how's the new role. Settled in?'

'Slowly, but surely. I need to make some changes. Dad was a bit soft. The business needs a shake up.' He went on to explain his intention of upping the royalty paid to them by the franchisees. 'It's about time, they've had a good run at our expense.' He went on to say how he was going to change the company, bring it into the twenty-first century.

'On a lighter note, Declan, are you in town on Friday night?'

"Town" meant Manchester, viz-a-viz clubland. The place to be seen at this time was The Indigo Club in Canal Street.

'Of course. Chelsea will be back on Friday.' Chelsea was Declan's girlfriend, a stewardess with British Airways.

'Where's she been this week?'

'The US. I think she's getting tired of the Atlantic run. I'm tempted to find her a job at Quilley, not sure what.' He broke a wry smile across his face. 'If only Brenda would leave, I could bring in Chelsea as my PA.'

Jasper rose up from his seat and stretched. 'I'm back to work mate. See you Friday.'

Declan waved his hand. 'Yeah, Friday, see you.'

He watched his friend disappear through the doors then got himself another drink. He had no intention of returning to the office this afternoon. Whilst he sat there his imagination began to run wild. Maybe he could engineer Brenda out. Make things difficult for her so she would leave of her own accord.

Friday night arrived and Declan picked Chelsea up from her apartment. She lived in a three-storey block of up-market luxury flats overlooking Kendal Park. 'Have a good trip?' he asked as he opened the car door for her.

She nodded. 'It's tiring and it's the same routine as usual. Same obnoxious passengers. Business Class is no better.' Chelsea epitomised a caricature's depiction of air stewardesses. She was a chirpy thirty-year old. She had a head of curly blonde hair that bobbed about as she spoke, blue eyes, and immaculate make-up.

'Thought we'd go to the Indigo, then for a meal in Chinatown later on.'

'Suits me,' she replied straining into the sun-visor mirror to check her false eyelashes, pout her lips, then add even more lipstick

The Canal Street area was the place to be seen. There were a multitude of warehouses, which at one time serviced the cotton industry that Manchester was so famous for. The upper floors had now been turned into sought-after apartments and on the lower floors were cafes, bars and clubs. The streets were abuzz as they strolled hand in hand from the car park to the club. Declan was well known to the doorman who greeted them with a 'good evening, sir, madam' and lifted the rope across the entrance to let them in. Once inside they were hit with the noisy, heady atmosphere and flashing strobe lights. The place was packed with people either dancing, drinking or straining their voices to have a conversation over the noise. 'Grab a table Chels, whilst I get the drinks.'

She wandered off, acknowledging people she knew as she negotiated her way through the throng. Declan joined her with two brightly coloured cocktails. 'Cheers, Chels.' They clinked glasses.

'Where you off to next week?'

'Same again, Manchester, New York.'

Declan nodded then leaned across the tiny table in order to be heard. 'Have you thought of giving up your job and having another career?' Over the weeks she'd become used to Declan and their frequent visits to the Indigo. She had learned to deal with the noise by studying his lips as he spoke.

She nodded and shouted, 'Yes, often.'

'How would you feel working for Quilley?'

'Working for you?' She laughed, then looked serious. 'I don't know.'

He tried to lighten his question. 'Just a thought, nothing more.'

She touched his arm. 'But now you've asked, yes, I think I would.'

He smiled and raised his glass. 'Another?'

She handed her empty glass over to him and watched him push his way to the bar. He was about to turn away from the bar with two glasses in his hand when he stopped to talk to someone, a tall cadaverous man who stood close to Declan. She could see Declan nod, put one glass back on the bar, dip into his jacket pocket then exchange something with the stranger. He came back to Chelsea and placed the glass in front of her.

She ignored the drink and questioned Declan. 'Who was that man?'

He tapped the side of his nose and smiled. 'It's on a need-to-know basis sweetheart.' She didn't pursue the question and picked up her glass. She was convinced there would be other occasions when she could try to find out what he was doing. She was a girl of the world, not much got past her and it didn't look kosher to her.

They wandered along to Chinatown and to Declan's favourite restaurant, The Beijing. After the waiter had taken their order and delivered the drinks, Chelsea, elbows on the table and her hands folded underneath her chin, stared Declan directly in the face and asked, 'Who was that man you were talking to in the Indigo. I think I possibly recognised him from somewhere?'

He smiled. 'He's just a mate.'

She returned the smile disbelievingly. 'You were buying drugs, weren't you? I saw you exchange something.'

His face turned ashen. 'What makes you think that?'

She picked up her drink and spoke over the top of her glass. 'I recognise small packets...and money!'

He looked embarrassed. 'And?'

Her smile broadened. 'I want some of the action.'

Declan relaxed visibly. 'I've got enough for two Chels, more than enough.'

Chelsea nodded and raised her glass. 'Good.'

He leaned forward. 'I've got some I need to deliver to a mate of mine, then we can go back to my place and...well...enjoy ourselves.'

'Sounds good to me.'

On the way home they called in at Jasper's place, a detached house in a leafy suburban street. 'Shan't be long Chels, stay in the car.' Declan trotted up the gravel drive and pressed the doorbell. A light came on in the hallway, then the door was opened. After a two- or three-minute conversation, Declan returned to the car, switched on the ignition and headed to his place.

Chelsea was quiet for some time then. 'How come he doesn't get his own supply?'

Declan turned to her. 'No reason. I just have better contacts, so I buy for him.'

'And make a profit!'

He shrugged and didn't answer.

'D'you supply anyone else?'

His answer was short and sweet. 'A few.'

As Declan arrived at work on the Monday morning around ten o'clock, the phone was ringing as he entered his office. He snatched up the phone and shrugged off his jacket at the same time. 'Hello?'

'Declan, it's your dad. How's things?'

He didn't need this conversation before he'd had his coffee. 'Fine. All good.'

'Good. Just checking.'

Declan, keen to switch the conversation away from work asked. 'How's mum...and the cruise?'

'The cruise was fine, mum's not so good. Her hip's playing up. It's been iffy since her fall. Are deliveries on time?' asked his father, keen to steer the conversation back to business. 'Are payments coming through OK? Have there been any customer complaints?'

'No dad, everything's okay.' God, did he never stop thinking about the business!

'Right son. I'll speak to you again soon. Don't forget, if you have any problems, I'm only a phone call away.'

'Right, cheers. Say hello to mum.'

'Will do.'

The phone clicked off. Declan put his head in his hands and leaned on his desk. *Why, oh, why can't dad leave me alone to get on with it.* He was returned to the moment when he heard his door open. 'Ah, Brenda!'

'Good morning, Declan. There're a few issues to deal with. We've had a few people phone back in response to the royalty fee increase.'

'Well, I half expected that. If they don't like it, we'll hand the franchise over to someone who wants it,' Declan said, exasperated.

'Right,' she replied unsure how to take the conversation further, 'do you want me to confirm their option to terminate their agreement?'

'Yes! Anything else?' he asked brusquely. Brenda hesitated slightly.

'A couple of the contractors who supply us with their crops want a meeting with you.'

'What about?'

'Something to do with increasing the price we pay to them.'

'No chance. Leave it with me.' Without looking up he muttered 'Bren, can you grab me a coffee before you get bogged down at your desk.' Brenda half-smiled and left the office. She wasn't happy with the way things were going since Patrick had handed over the reins. By the end of the month out of a total of fifty franchises that were up for renewal, seventeen had opted to terminate their agreement. Brenda knew in her heart this was potentially the start of a downward trend for the business.

Declan arrived at the pub as his mate Jasper was reversing his Porsche under the shade of one of the large beech trees that ringed the perimeter of the car park. As they entered the pub Jasper whispered, 'That coke you brought round the other night was good. I'm up for some more.'

Declan slapped him on the back. 'Good as done my friend.' Armed with their drinks they sidled their way to the back of the room that was a little quieter.

'Still busy, Declan?'

'Never stopped. Dad keeps phoning. I don't think he trusts me to get on with it.'

Jasper laughed cynically. 'I don't blame him, you've not exactly been burning the midnight oil as far as the business is concerned and your track record doesn't say much for your commitment, to anything.' Declan raised an eyebrow, so Jasper explained. 'Remember? Expulsion from school, threat of expulsion from boarding school, drugs at Uni and you didn't even complete your degree...need I say more?'

Declan laughed. 'Since you put it like that you're probably right. Anyway, I've got some news to tell you.' He glanced down at the empty glasses. 'Another?' Jasper nodded and handed Declan his empty glass. When he returned with the drinks Jasper was curious.

'Come on mate what's the news?'

Declan looked smug. 'Do you happen to be doing anything tomorrow?'

'No, why?'

'If you're free for the morning I want you to come with me.' He stopped his flow to grab his drink. 'I'm picking up my new car tomorrow.'

'Which is?'

Declan slapped a brochure onto the table.

Jasper's eyes bulged. 'A Ferrari? Bloody hell mate, you don't do things in half measures do you.'

Declan leaned back in his seat with a satisfied look.

'Well, you've got to treat yourself occasionally, haven't you.'

Jasper shook his head. 'Nice one!'

* * *

The next morning Declan woke with butterflies in his stomach. It was a crisp autumn morning. He had a leisurely breakfast, followed by a line of coke to get him through the morning. He then picked up the phone. He waited several minutes for someone to answer. *She must be away from her desk, Blast!* 'Oh, hello Brenda. Just to let you know I won't be in this morning; I've got an appointment with a customer.' Before Brenda had a chance to question him as to who the customer was, or what time he would eventually be in, he finished the conversation with, 'I'll be in some time tomorrow.'

It was a good thing he couldn't see the look on Brenda's face. She shook her head. She didn't believe a word he was telling her. Immediately after speaking to Brenda, he picked up the phone once more.

A sleepy voice answered. It was Chelsea. 'Hello? Oh, it's you. I'm still in bed we didn't get home 'til late, we had a delay at La Guardia airport.' She slung her legs out of bed. 'Did you want something?'

'Yeah. D'you fancy lunch? I've got a couple of things I want to show you.'

'Er, okay. Sorry, I'm still half asleep. What time?'

'I'll pick you up at twelve.'

'Right.' She slowly put the phone down and ran her hands through her hair. *I wonder what he wants to show me.*

The doorbell rang. 'Hi Declan, come in.' Chelsea looked stunning. It was second nature to her to make sure her appearance was immaculate. 'This is a surprise...lunch on a weekday.'

He gave her a hug and a kiss. 'Ready?'

She stepped back into her flat and held up her hand, fingers splayed, 'five minutes!'

As they took the lift down to the ground floor she gave him a playful dig in his side. 'So, what is it you want to show me?'

He smiled at her. 'You'll see in two minutes.' As they exited the building's double doors, he held her arm and pointed to the kerb side. With a flourish of his other arm in the direction of his new car he announced, 'Ta da.'

There, parked in front of her was a red Ferrari. A low sleek mean looking beast.

She was impressed. 'Wow. When did you get that?'

'Yesterday. Come on, climb in.'

She glanced down at the front of the vehicle. 'Oooh, and vanity plates!' The registration plate was DQ 10. 'How come 10?'

He chuckled, 'One to nine were already taken.'

She had to bend down to climb into the machine, glad that she'd taken the decision to wear trousers. She didn't want to flash her somewhat brief underwear to the neighbours, new Ferrari or not! Declan turned the ignition and the engine emitted a loud raucous roar. He put it in gear then shot off down the street. 'I thought we'd go out towards Knutsford – The Blue Unicorn.'

She nodded enthusiastically. 'I love that place,...almost as much as I love your new car.'

The Blue Unicorn was a restaurant well known for its superb cuisine and cosy ambiance. Declan parked well away from the main door and other cars in the car park. 'I don't want any cars near mine. I don't want it scratched on its first outing.' As they walked across the car park and entered the restaurant via the rear door Declan couldn't help glancing back at his latest purchase. Yes, it felt good to treat yourself.

The pub had been a coaching inn two hundred years previously and still retained its original exterior. The interior had low beams and lots of brass on the walls. Unobtrusive, light orchestral music was being relayed through the restaurant speakers.

Declan ordered a bottle of champagne. 'It is a special occasion Chels,' he explained seeing her raised eyebrows at the price of the bottle. The conversation was easy, relaxed and centred on Declan's plans for the future of the business.

'Business must be good if you can afford a Ferrari,' Chelsea observed. Must be a lot of money in the simple potato.'

He looked at her and smiled. 'And my sideline.'

She frowned. 'D'you mean the drugs?'

He put his finger to his lips. They finished off their lunch with a black coffee. Declan paid the bill and winked at Chelsea. 'With the compliments of Quilley Enterprises,' he announced as he produced the company's credit card with a flourish.

Once back in the car Chelsea turned to Declan. 'That was wonderful.' She leaned across the car and kissed him. 'Thank you.'

'My pleasure sweetheart, my pleasure.' He revved the car and was pleased to see several heads turn as he exited the car park.

'On the phone you said you had two things to show me.'

'Yes, I have. That's where we're going next.'

'What is it?'

He spoke gently to her. 'Just be patient.'

He turned the car into a familiar gate and followed the dirt track until Chelsea could see his farmhouse looming ahead. 'Your house? I have seen it before you know.' He held his hand up as an indication she should be patient. He drove to the right of the old farmhouse, round the back of the large barns and continued down another dirt track which cut across one of the fields. This section appeared to have been widened and the fences along each side appeared to be newly installed. The grass verges, normally overgrown with both weed and wildflowers, were cut within an inch of their lives, manicured to bowling green standard. 'Where are we going?' No sooner had she asked the question when they were confronted by hive of activity ahead of them. It looked like a building site. It was a building site! Tradesmen scurried backward and forward pushing wheelbarrows, climbing ladders, sawing, nailing. Chelsea looked again at Declan and shook her head. 'What's all this?'

He stopped the car. 'Come on, I'll show you.'

As they approached, a voice rung out from one of the workers. 'Morning, Mr Quilley.' Declan acknowledged him with a wave. He directed Chelsea around the back of the building, the view was stunning. The new building overlooked the large lake that was on the property where Declan's family had lived and worked for so many years. The lake was lined with weeping willow trees, on the far right was a well-established reed bed, and in the distance, the low hills which in summer were covered with heather. Declan looked at Chelsea's smiling face. 'Welcome to my new home.'

She was taken aback. 'Your new home? What was wrong with the one you've already got?'

'It was mum and dads. They lived in it for forty years. They never had any ambitions. I do.'

Chelsea was almost lost for words. 'A new car and a new house! I say again, potatoes must be big business.'

He didn't respond.

2007

Declan continued his extravagant lifestyle...and his drug dealing.

He'd been stopped for speeding in his Ferrari and breathalysed on three occasions. On one occasion he hadn't been drinking and was only fined for the speeding offence. He now had points on his licence, and one more misdemeanour would have seen his licence revoked. His drug taking and dealing, so far, had not been discovered.

Chelsea was sacked from her job as air stewardess after being routinely tested for drugs which proved positive.

Brenda was still PA to Declan, more from loyalty to Patrick and Teresa than to Declan.

2008

Declan was still working 'part-time' at Quilley Enterprises, and the business was beginning to suffer. Brenda had tried to contend with the increasing number of phone calls from dissatisfied suppliers complaining about non or late payment for their goods.

One morning, Brenda approached him with updated figures. 'Declan, we've now lost nearly twenty per cent of our franchisees, they just can't absorb the royalty increases you've imposed on them.'

He dismissed her concerns. 'Brenda, it's their job to manage their own business. Maybe we do a promotion to recruit new franchisees.'

Brenda shrugged her shoulders knowing it was futile to expect Declan to take her concerns seriously. 'And', she said, handing him an invoice, 'we still haven't paid this invoice for the new shed you had erected. It's now more than three months overdue.'

He sighed deeply. 'Leave it with me. I'll deal with it.' Brenda left his office and made her way to the kitchen. She made herself a cup of coffee and sat at her desk. *Should I phone Patrick?* She eventually decided against it and carried on with her work.

Over the next few months Brenda received more and more phone calls from franchisees terminating their contracts, or suppliers complaining of late payment or extortionate service bills.

In the meantime, Declan was increasing his involvement in drugs. Because his Ferrari was too high profile on the streets, Chelsea began to act as courier in her bland, beige Citroen. She would pick up the supplies from Declan then set out on her prescribed circuit, sometimes around the council estates, and some of the more salubrious areas. The recipient would know the day and time of Chelsea's deliveries and would have payment ready. Within minutes of the drop-off, she was gone and on to the next customer. Declan was gradually spending less time in the office and more time in the pub with his mate Jasper, and had recently taken to cruising the red-light district in Manchester.

* * *

Following a tip-off from an informant regarding Declan's drug dealings, DI Les Mulbury of the Manchester Drugs Squad, called a briefing session. Les stood tall at the front of the room and commanded attention. He was well respected in the force and had many high-profile arrests to his name. He didn't chase recognition, he just got on with the job in hand. He scanned the room and smoothed his dark moustache out before welcoming his team. One of the fluorescent lights in the briefing room flickered as Mulbury was about to commence his briefing. He looked up and tutted. 'Can someone sort that bloody light out, it's been like that for the last three weeks. Oh, don't tell me, it's not in the budget!'

On the whiteboard was a photo of Declan, his car and the farmhouse. He pointed to the whiteboard. 'This, ladies and gentlemen, is Declan Quilley, MD of Quilley Enterprises. Some of you may know Quilley Enterprises is one of the biggest employers in the area. Mr Quilley here took over as MD some years ago from his father Patrick. We've had tip-off from one of our informants that Quilley is dealing drugs. I intend to have surveillance put on Quilley over the next two weeks. I'll organise you into three teams of two to follow him on a roster basis.'

He turned to two female officers. 'DCs Jo Crisp and Andrea Lowton you're first off the block. His home address is in the folders you've all just been given. Check out when he leaves home. As soon as he leaves, report to DCs Jeff Collins and Tony Burton. Stay in radio contact at all times. Collins and Burton, be ready to take over from Crisp and Lowton as soon as they have informed you he's left the property.' His DS, Philip Watson, wrote DI Mulbury's instructions on the board. 'DCs Simon Matley and Mal Gresty, stay on call should his movements dictate a different strategy. Are we all okay? Good. Let's see where this leads us.'

At 7 o'clock the next morning DCs Crisp and Lowton parked discreetly behind some low-growing bushes at the far end of the lane, where they had a good view of anyone leaving, or entering the Quilley property. Builders' trucks were constantly entering and exiting the lane. 'This could be a long day, Jo.' She nodded keeping her eyes on the narrow lane, binoculars at the ready. For the first hour or so, the only movement was the trucks, but as the morning went on, cars started arriving and returning within 10 minutes.

'That's a good sign Andrea. Ten-minute sessions often mean quick drug purchases. I'll radio it in.' Three hours after they'd arrived for their stint they saw a red Ferrari DQ 10 screaming down the lane, turn left and race off.

'Radio Jeff and Tony tell them which direction Quilley's gone.'

DCs Matley and Gresty had based themselves in the local Tesco car park, on the road leading to Quilley's office. They were casually dressed, Matley wearing a T-shirt, sports jacket and jeans. Gresty had decided to go a little more up-market with an open neck shirt, chinos and a windjammer. Gresty looked at Matley, smiled, then screwed his nose up. 'I know we were asked to blend in, but don't you think the T-shirt is a bit too low key?' Matley looked down at his T-shirt. 'It's my favourite; it's got ACDC written on the back.' They both chuckled. Within minutes they spotted the red Ferrari. 'Here we go. If he's going to the office he'll turn right, towards us...oh, bloody hell he's gone left. Where the hell is he going?'

They followed at a safe distance until Quilley turned into the Rope and Anchor, parked, then trotted into the pub.

'Come on Mal, radio in first then we'll go in. We might see who he's gone to meet.' They took their time and ambled into the pub several minutes after Quilley had arrived, made for the bar, ordered two drinks then scanned the room. 'To your right, over by the fireplace.'

Simon pretended to take a photo of Mal who was overtly posing at the bar, drink in hand. The photo also managed to take in the two who were sitting in the corner, Quilley and A.N. Other.

At the de-briefing DC Matley showed DI Mulbury the photo that had been taken inside the pub. DI Mulbury asked. 'D'you know the other guy?' Matley nodded.

'Yeah, Jasper Tierney, he's an informant.'

'Really? They look like mates.'

DC Matley took a deep breath. 'They are. They're both in the same game so maybe they share the turf, who knows with these bastards.'

'What now boss?'

'Same again tomorrow. We need to build up a picture over several days.'

After meeting up with Jasper and providing him with his drugs, Declan finally decided to show his face at the office. Brenda looked frazzled as he passed her desk. 'You okay, Brenda.'

She looked at him with disdain. 'No, I'm not! I'm inundated with constant phone calls. You've had one from the accountants. They want a meeting. They said it's urgent.'

'Okay, I'll give them a ring.' He had a sneaking suspicion as to why they wanted the meeting, however, he had no intention of giving them a call. Instead, he went in his office, closed the door and dialled a number, keeping the conversation down to a minimum. 'Bogdan? It's Declan. I need some more stock. Usual place? Thanks.'

Bogdan Cajocaro, a Romanian, was Declan's supplier of cocaine and occasionally, amphetamines. Unknown to Declan, Cajocaro was also involved in people smuggling and sex trafficking.

At 6.00pm, Declan left the office and drove in the direction of Manchester city centre. DCs Jeff Collins and Tony Burton were now the team following Quilley. 'He's keeping to the speed limit, Jeff. Either he's got points on his licence, or just doesn't want to get stopped. A red Ferrari is a bit conspicuous, isn't it?' Quilley drove into the city centre, round Piccadilly Gardens onto City Road, in the direction of the red-light district.

Jeff raised his eyebrows. 'Could be interesting.'

The Ferrari slowed even further as it arrived in a sleazy area. By day it was a dismal area with boarded up shop windows and row upon row of terraced houses due for demolition. But, by night, it became a vibrant area with people doing 'business', most of it illicit. There were numerous pubs within walking distance, all noisy and busy. Bright lights could be seen from the windows; business appeared good, despite the grimness of the surroundings. Several cars could be seen slowly circling the back streets. Collins and Burton dutifully followed the rest of the parade of vehicles. The Ferrari suddenly stopped, and a young woman stepped out of the shadows.

'Photo, quick Jeff.' The woman in her mid-forties was dressed in a short, black leather skirt, leopard skin top and stilettos. She had bleached blonde hair and was carrying a red handbag.

Tony joked. 'At least she's colour-coordinated her handbag with the car. Let's radio in, see what they want us to do now.'

The next day Brenda was surprised to see Declan arrive on time at the office. She handed him a handwritten note. 'The accountants have been on the phone again for you to arrange an appointment.'

'Right,' he said distractedly, then continued walking past her desk, 'can you grab me a coffee, Bren.' Brenda shrugged her shoulders in defeat as he disappeared into his office.

At the police station DI Mulbury was updating the team. 'I'm getting a warrant prepared to search Quilley's home. From what DCs Crisp and Lowton saw it appears that Quilley is dealing from home. He's also been cruising around the Moss Vale area, and we now have photos of him picking up a prostitute. Quilley's dealings from home was also confirmed by our informant. But our informant may have an ulterior motive for wanting Quilley off the streets.'

A hand went up at the back of the room. 'Ulterior motive boss?'

'Yes, don't forget, our informant is allegedly helping the police by being an associate of Declan's in his drug dealing in the area, but it could be he wants Quilley off the scene to allow himself to take over Quilley's turf. We won't know until we get Declan off the streets.'

At the same time DI Mulbury was briefing his team at HQ, a Mercedes pulled into the Quilley Enterprises car park. It parked directly in front of the reception doors. A well-dressed man with a trimmed moustache and carrying a bulky briefcase stepped out of the car. He entered the reception area where he was met by Brenda and presented his card. 'Martin Cowdray, Mr Quilley's accountant. Please tell him I'm here to see him.'

'I will, please take a seat.' Mr Cowdray preferred to stand; he thought much more quickly standing up. He wandered around the reception area looking at photos of various franchises and the farms. He heard his name being called and turned to see Declan Quilley, a broad smile across his face. He invited Mr Cowdray into his office.

'Sorry, I've not been in touch. I've been run off my feet. Would you like a tea or a coffee?'

'Yes please, coffee, white no sugar.' Quilley nodded and popped his head around the adjoining office door where Brenda was hard at work.

'Couple of coffees please, Brenda.' Brenda was shocked; it was the first time he'd said please. No doubt it was to impress Mr Cowdray.

Mr Cowdray slowly removed his hat, placed it on the desk, opened his briefcase then sat down. 'So, how's business, Mr Quilley?'

Declan steepled his hands. 'Absolutely fine...and it's Declan, please.'

Mr Cowdray continued unabated. 'All divisions of the business achieving targets, Mr Quilley?'

'Spot on.' He continued in a more serious tone realising his initial response sounded a little glib. 'More than achieved. In some areas we're up fifteen per cent.'

Mr Cowdray continued in his monotone voice. 'How did your franchisees react with your move to increase the royalties they pay you?'

Declan leaned back in his chair. 'Some decided that franchising wasn't for them. I've organised a promotion to help rebuild the number of franchisees to its previous levels.'

Mr Cowdray sighed and pulled some paperwork out of his case. 'Mr Quilley, I have to tell you that you are trading illegally.'

Declan's voice rose an octave. 'Illegally! That can't be right.'

Cowdray continued. 'You've been trading illegally for the past six months. You owe more than your assets are worth.' He gave Declan a few seconds to absorb the information before continuing. 'We've also had notification that several of the farmers that supply you with their crops to process have not been paid.'

'Ah, yes, I have been a little lax over those payments.'

Cowdray ignored the excuse and continued. 'The bank with whom you have an overdraft is withdrawing its support.'

Quilley was shocked. 'What? They can't do that!'

'I'm afraid they can, and they have.'

Cowdray then delivered the final blow. 'We have no alternative but to place Quilley Enterprises in the hands of administrators as of tomorrow.' He handed Declan a manila folder containing all the pertinent paperwork. 'I am sorry to see such a good business end up in this position, particularly as our relationship with your family goes back many, many years. Good day Mr Quilley.' He closed his briefcase, retrieved his hat from the desk, nodded goodbye to Brenda and let himself out.

At six-thirty the following morning, several police officers arrived at the Quilley farmhouse. The DI rapped on the door, which was opened after several minutes by Chelsea, looking sleepy, her hair tousled, her make-up smeared. 'Yes?'

'Is Mr Declan Quilley at home?' DI Mulbury asked.

A voice from behind Chelsea rang out. 'Who wants to know?' Mulbury held his warrant card and the search warrant over Chelsea's head to the person standing in the gloom of the hallway.

'We have a warrant to search these premises.'

Quilley stood his ground and became abrasive. 'What's this about? You can't just come in here and start sniffing around the house.'

The DI put his foot on the threshold. 'We can actually, we have a warrant. We have reason to believe drugs are being kept on these premises.' He turned to the other officers waiting behind him. 'In you go. You know what to do.' Four officers pushed past Chelsea and Quilley, two headed upstairs, the other two headed for the kitchen.

Mulbury guided Quilley and Chelsea into the lounge. 'You must remain in here whilst we complete the search.' The DI stood by the door. Background noise could be heard as the officers opened and closed wardrobes and drawers, turned over mattresses and searched through books on the shelves. Two officers who had been searching downstairs came into the lounge and shook their heads at the DI, then went into the garage to check the Ferrari. Declan panicked.

'Hey, be careful, I don't want any scratches on my car, or I'll sue.' After more clanking and banging from upstairs one of the officers came into the lounge and showed DI Mulbury a quantity of white packages. The DI held one up to the light then sniffed at the contents.

He turned to Quilley. 'We'd like you to come down to the station for questioning.' As the DI escorted Quilley out of the house he turned to Chelsea. 'We may want to interview you at some future date. Please make yourself available.'

Back at the station Quilley was put into an interview room. It was small room, with high, rectangular windows along one of the walls and a pervasive smell of disinfectant. Quilley fidgeted whilst he waited for the DI to reappear, constantly aware of the blinking light in the top corner of the room. Mulbury eventually appeared. He sat down and opened a file before looking up at Quilley. 'Would you like a drink?' Quilley shook his head, his face black as thunder. 'You have been arrested on suspicion of dealing in prohibited drugs. The packets we took away from your house are currently being analysed.' He took a second before continuing. 'What do you think the lab will find?'

'No comment.'

'The packets were found concealed behind the bath panel. Do you know how they came to be there?'

'No comment.'

'We do have a written statement from a witness who says he has been buying drugs from you for the past four years. Have you anything to say?'

'No comment.'

'The witness tells us he's prepared to give evidence in a court of law.' He gave Quilley a little time to digest that snippet of information, then changed the subject. 'Do you know the Moss Vale area of Manchester?'

'No comment.'

'Just to jog your memory, Moss Vale is the red-light district. You were seen and photographed in the area on the nineteenth of this month.'

'No comment.'

'Have you ever procured the services of prostitutes?' At this question the DI could see Quilley's leg bouncing up and down. 'You look nervous...are you nervous?'

'No comment.'

The DI took a deep breath. 'We have a photograph of a prostitute getting into your car. The Ferrari is very noticeable, isn't it?' He glanced at his file as though checking his facts. 'Er, registration DQ 10, that's your car, isn't it?'

'No comment.'

'We understand Quilley Enterprises may have serious financial problems.'

This time the DI got a heated response. 'We're not in trouble, just a medium-term cash-flow problem.'

Mulbury closed his file. 'Thank you. We may want to question you again once we have the result of the contents of the packages.' He nodded towards the officer standing by the door. 'The constable will show you out. Make sure you're available for further questioning. Thank you again for your co-operation.'

Almost at the same time as the police were searching Quilley's home, the accountant's administration team arrived at Quilley Enterprises' headquarters. Mary Costin, the team leader had spoken to Brenda the previous day to inform her of their intention to check the files and accounts. Brenda had organised a room for them and, being the thoughtful individual she was, had organised a coffee machine. Mary Costin introduced herself to Brenda on her arrival and asked to see Declan. Brenda shook her head. 'I don't know where he is. I've tried his mobile several times and he's not picking up.' Costin tried not to show her annoyance.

'Don't worry,' she replied, knowing it wasn't Brenda's fault, 'can you make the company's accounts books available to us which show all outstanding invoices?' Brenda nodded. She'd guessed what documentation they would require, and all the files were already piled up on top of one of the filing cabinets. She picked up the phone and tried Declan's mobile once more. It went to message bank, so she tried his home landline.

It was answered on the fourth ring. 'Hello. It's Brenda at the office, is Declan there?'

The person at the other end hesitated for a second. 'Er no, he's not here. I'm Chelsea, his girlfriend, can I help?'

'Oh, hello Chelsea, no I don't think so. It's just that the administrators have arrived at the office and need to speak to him.'

Chelsea hesitated for what seemed like an eternity. *What the hell? Administrators? The guy's bankrupt?* She blurted out hysterically, 'He's down at the police station!'

'Police station! What's he doing there?'

'I don't know. The police arrived this morning, searched the house and took him away.'

Brenda slowly put the phone down and panic started to set in. *I knew it! I knew it! Sooner or later, he'd be in trouble.*

After giving herself a few minutes to decide what she should do next, she then picked up the phone once more. 'Hello Patrick, it's Brenda.'

'Oh, hello Brenda,' he replied jovially, then his voice changed. 'Is something wrong?'

'I'm not sure. Has Declan spoken to you?'

'No.'

'Well, the accountants have brought in an administrator. Apparently, the business has been trading illegally for several months. The administrators are checking all the invoices. I think they may try to find a buyer for the business or...' Patrick knew what 'or' meant. If a buyer couldn't be found the business would go under with all the consequences that would follow.

He was furious. 'And where is Declan amid all this?' Brenda didn't want to be the harbinger of more bad news and hesitated. 'Brenda, where's Declan?' His voice now slightly raised.

'Apparently he's helping the police with their inquiries.'

'What! Police! What the hell has he done?'

Brenda was on the verge of panic. 'I don't know,' she quickly added, 'Patrick, you need to be here.'

'Brenda, I can't. Teresa is going through cancer treatment; I daren't leave her.' There was silence, then, 'and I'm not well either. Bottom line Brenda, neither of us can come over. I'll speak to Joe Crossly.' Brenda knew he was a solicitor and close friend of Patrick's. 'He'll keep us in touch. Hang on I'll give you his phone number, just in case.'

The lab report came through and landed on Mulbury's desk. He scanned to the bottom line – cocaine. Got him! Within the hour the DI and his sergeant were knocking once more on Quilley's door. It was answered again by Chelsea. 'We'd like to see Declan please.' She resignedly opened the door further and waved them in. They found Quilley sitting in the lounge. His demeanour subdued. 'We need you down at the station again, Declan.'

He pushed himself off the sofa and quietly followed the officers out to the car.

Back at the station the evidence from the lab was presented to Quilley.

'The packets we removed from your premises have been confirmed to be cocaine. Do you have any explanation as to why we would have found them in your bathroom?' Quilley shook his head. 'For the tape, please.'

'No!'

'We have traced the prostitute that was seen getting into your car and she also tells us that she's been supplied with drugs by you for the past two years. Have you anything to say?'

'No'

'We have presented all the evidence to the CPS and they have agreed we can charge you. Do you have a response?'

'No.'

'Please stand up. Declan Quilley I'm charging you with dealing with intent to supply illicit drugs. You do not have to say anything, but anything you do say will be taken down and may be used in evidence in a court of law. Do you understand?'

'Yes.'

Mulbury turned to the officer by the door. 'Take him down.'

The administrators spent three months at Quilley Enterprises trying to decipher what had happened to all the profits. Further investigations showed that large amounts from the Quilley business accounts had been siphoned off, to pay for Declan's lavish lifestyle. The accounts also showed large sums of money deposited on a regular basis, generated by the illicit drug dealing, then subsequently withdrawn. An order was given to seize Declan Quilley's assets, which included his Ferrari and his new house. They were also able to identify investment properties in France and Spain, which were also seized. The administrators struggled to find a buyer for the Quilley business, placing staff, customers and suppliers in a precarious position.

At the eleventh hour they found a buyer for Quilley Enterprises. It was a company based in France who were keen to develop their business into the UK. In a humiliating move for Quilley, the French were able to buy the business for one pound and take on the debts.

After nearly one hundred and seventy years of the Quilley name, which was synonymous with hard work, commitment, fairness and self-sacrifice for the betterment of the business, it was at an end.

From penury to riches, then back to penury in 170 years.

This was the Rise and Fall of the House of Quilley.

EPILOGUE

Declan Quilley was found guilty of dealing in illicit drugs and sentenced to ten years imprisonment. He was also found guilty of procuring the services of a prostitute and sentenced to two years jail. In addition, he was also charged with embezzling funds from Quilley Enterprises and sentenced to five years imprisonment.

Chelsea was charged with aiding and abetting Quilley and sentenced to three years imprisonment.

Brenda chose to retire early and went to live with her sister in the Yorkshire Dales.

Teresa Quilley did not survive the cancer treatment and died during her son's trial.

Patrick developed serious heart problems and now lives alone in the home he hoped would be their retirement home for many years.

Bogdan Cajocaro, who was named by the police informer, was intercepted and arrested by Interpol and is in jail awaiting trial.

Jasper Tierney, the police informer, was found dead in his apartment three months after the arrest of Bogdan Cajocaro. His badly mutilated body was categorised by the police as "typical of a drug cartel killing".

Declan Quilley's hedonistic lifestyle and his dependence on, and dealings in, drugs, had resulted in his best friend's gruesome death. No arrest has been made.

The French company which had bought the Quilley business decided in 2019 to pull out of the UK after the Brexit decision.

None of the original business now exists.

The House of Quilley is no more.

5

The Pub Lunch

Sid Upthwaite peered out of his kitchen window at the deteriorating weather. It had started gently snowing around eleven o'clock in the morning, but had now developed into a blizzard, straight from Siberia. The weather bureau had forecast the worst storm in thirty years and it was looking like they may have been right. Although it was only three-thirty in the afternoon, the fading light was creating an eerie, ghostly scene. Earlier in the day he had been out in the fields which were next to his tiny stone cottage. Together with his dog, Shad, the pair had rounded up his flock of nearly one hundred sheep and herded them safely into a warm dry shed in the lee of the forest running alongside the field. The storm was increasing by the minute and the snow was beginning to drift. A howling gale blew across the cottage chimney, flickering the flames in his fireplace and rattling the window frames. He was aware there were still a dozen or so sheep half way up the top field, on the now, white slopes. There was shelter for them in a small copse of conifers and a dry-stone wall. At first he thought they would be safe, but as the storm intensified, he was now having second thoughts. As the shepherd for Curlew Farm, it was his responsibility to ensure the well-being of the flock.

He looked out of the window once more and could see the weather wasn't abating. The snow was now drifting in the lane alongside his cottage and up against the barn doors. He decided to phone his sister to let her know what he was going to do, before venturing out. In this type of weather, it was always best to notify someone. Grabbing his great coat and cap from the back of the door he called his dog.

'Shad! Come on! Time to go to work.'

Shad was curled up asleep in front of the roaring log fire. He opened one eye and lifted one ear as if to say, *are you sure about this?* Sid stepped out into the bitterly cold snowstorm, battling against the wind to close the door. As he walked, he leaned against the wind, holding onto his tattered cap, and made his way to the barn.

The trailer, large enough for a dozen sheep, was already attached to the large red tractor. Shad, who was well-practised as to what was required of him, jumped into the cab beside Sid as he drove out of the farmyard and up the lane. The top field was a good mile away, through the village, then a quarter of a mile up a pot-holed dirt track. Fortunately, he knew the lane well as the large drifting flakes were now creating a complete whiteout. Man and dog finally arrived at the top field. Sid struggled against the wind to prise open the rickety gate. Then they both began to search for the sheep. The snow was now up to Sid's knees and the dog was having to jump and leap about to make its way through the snow. All the sheep were found sheltering among the trees close to the stone wall. With the help of Shad, he successfully managed to gather up all the sheep and return them safely to the shed at the farm. He made sure they had clean straw, food and water before securing the doors.

* * *

The Dalesman was one of three pubs in Lower Crumpsall and the only one that offered accommodation. It was a traditional country pub, with a history going back to the mid-eighteenth century. The interior consisted of what some would call 'quaint', exposed rough brick walls and low beams. The beams were adorned with an abundance of brass including horse brasses, bed warmers and hunting horns. Before foxhunting was banned The Dalesman was where the famous Critchley Hunt met.

Bob Clampitt, the landlord, was an ex-rugby player, complete with cauliflower ears and a broken nose, which had not been professionally set, giving is face a skewed look. His size and demeanour ensured that there was never any trouble at the pub. His wife, Audrey, was a rough diamond, originally a rugby groupie who had latched onto Bob. She was a buxom, peroxide blonde, with a penchant for bright red lipstick and trashy costume jewellery. She was popular, particularly with the male customers, because she usually wore a low-cut top. They made it their mission to tell her jokes that would encourage her lively bosom to wobble whenever she laughed. If anything, she was more feared than her husband Bob. They were a good team and had been married for ten years.

Bob turned to his wife, Audrey. 'We'll have a quiet night tonight. Nobody in their right mind would be out in this weather.' The door suddenly crashed open as two of the regulars, Ted and Josh, spilled into the welcoming warmth of the pub, stamping their boots and knocking surplus snow off their coats. 'Well, if it isn't the two objectionable snowmen,' chuckled Bob. 'You two must be desperate for a drink to come out on a night like this.'

In unison, they both gave him the V sign. 'Two pints, please landlord, if you don't mind.'

Ted Booth and Josh Winterbottom were farm labourers and spent most nights in The Dalesman. They made their way over to the large open brick fireplace and ensconced themselves in their usual seats. Ted shouted back towards the bar. 'The main street's completely white and some of the side lanes are blocked. Lucky for us we live in the village.'

Bob strolled over to throw a couple more logs on the fire causing a shower of sparks and responded, 'aye, and there's more to come.' The main door opened, allowing the unwelcome Arctic gale to blow through the lounge. The three men looked up to see Sid Upthwaite enter the pub. He was well-known in the village and not particularly well liked.

'Bloody hell! What a night!' he muttered to himself as he unwrapped his scarf, exposing his weathered face and several days' stubble.

Bob whispered to the other two. 'Smarmy Sid. That's all we need tonight.' Sid strolled over to the bar, nodding to the three men standing by the fire as he went. He leaned on the bar. 'Hello gorgeous,' he said, leering at Audrey. 'You look ravishing tonight.'

Josh shouted over to the bar, sniggering. 'Evening Sid. I thought you'd be tucked up in bed with a warm sheep on a night like this.'

Sid gave him the finger and turned back to Audrey. 'I'd rather be tucked up with the warm Audrey! The usual please.'

Audrey pulled a pint of Ram's Blood. 'One pound fifty, please.' He gave her a five-pound note and held onto her hand a little too long when she handed him his change. He made her skin crawl.

The pub slowly filled up which was surprising on a night like tonight. The snowstorm had subsided a little, but the roads and pavements were treacherous. A couple of customers got up to have a game of darts and Bob turned on the Muzak. Audrey went around the lounge collecting empty glasses. She leaned past Sid to reach glasses that had been left on a table. 'Excuse me.'

He put his arm around her waist and drew him to her. She tutted and pushed him away. 'Oops, sorry Audrey. I thought you said squeeze me,' he said with a supercilious smile. He chuckled to himself as he went through to the gents. Bob then followed Sid into the toilets. Once inside he grabbed Sid's lapels and lifted him up against the tiled wall.

'You touch my wife once more and I'll kill you. You're a sleazy bastard, so just watch it. Anymore stunts like that and I'll bar you.'

Sid held up his hands in submission. 'Sorry Bob. It was only a bit of fun. No harm meant,' he said in a nervous voice.

Bob slowly let him down. 'Just remember what I've told you. Watch your back!'

* * *

Several days later the snow had almost disappeared. The sun had reappeared and was quickly melting what was left of the snow, turning it into a dirty, grey slush. There were still small traces of white where there had been shade and some of the lesser used lanes remained blocked. Ted and Josh came into the pub chattering excitedly. 'Bit of excitement out there Bob.'

'Oh aye? What's that then?' Bob responded nonchalantly.

'The cops. Bit of a kerfuffle by the looks of things. They're over in the supermarket car park. There's quite a few police cars, and what looks like a communication van. It looks like they've got the full Monty out there. Apparently, Smarmy Sid's gone missing. His sister tried to contact him a few times by phone and got no reply, so she went round. Everywhere was locked up and the dog was on the doorstep, but there was no Sid.' Before Bob could comment, two men marched up to the bar, easily identifiable as plain clothes police officers due to their natty dress and short haircuts.

'Morning gentlemen,' the tallest of the two officers announced their arrival to the customers before turning to Bob behind the bar. 'Are you the landlord?'

'I am.'

The officers showed their warrant cards. 'I'm DS Jones and this is DC Fleming.'

Bob nodded and held out his hand. 'Bob Clampitt. How can I help you?'

DS Jones continued. 'We're investigating the disappearance of a Mr Sidney Upthwaite. We understand he was a regular.'

Bob nodded. 'Not every night, but certainly a few nights a week.'

'When was the last time you saw him?' he asked taking out his notebook and licking his pencil.

Bob pursed his lips and rubbed his chin. 'I think it was Monday night. The night of the storm. He'd been out rounding up his sheep and then came in here.'

DS Jones made a few notes, then hesitated before speaking. 'It seems rather odd. Apparently, Mr Upthwaite phoned his sister to say he was going out to move the sheep, which he appears to have done. The sheep were all safe, the tractor was back in the shed and the dog was back. Sat on the step it was, but no Mr Upthwaite.'

Bob shook his head. 'Any idea what's happened to him?'

DS Jones sighed. 'I'm afraid not. Nobody's seen him. If it was Monday when he was in here, then you're the last one to have seen him. He seems to have disappeared into thin air. We don't know if he's alive or dead.'

DS Jones glanced at his watch. 'Wow! Is it lunch time already? A couple of orange juices please Bob. Nothing stronger, we're on duty, but we're starving. We'll have a quick lunch before we carry on with our investigation. What have you got on for lunch? Any specials?'

Bob slowly continued to dry the newly washed glasses with his red and white chequered tea towel and, avoiding eye contact with the two officers, coughed to clear his throat.

'Er, shepherd's pie, okay?'

6 |

The Disappearance on the A492

2022

Glossop, Derbyshire, UK

'Fire sweeps northwest England'
'Hottest day on record'
'1650 die in Western Europe'
'Water shortage warning'
'Wildfires hit France and Spain'
'41 Degree warning'
'Reservoirs dry up'

The newspaper headlines had been highlighting the dangers of not taking precautions during the current heat wave. Hospitals were reporting that admissions for heat related illnesses were up 50 per cent.

* * *

Carol Burnett always felt a little apprehensive approaching the Peak Care Home where her mum had lived for the past two years. Visiting her mum was always a lottery; she never knew what mood she would be in.

Entering the main lounge, she could see her mum sitting at the bay window which overlooked the manicured lawns. She was in deep conversation with two other white-haired ladies. As she approached, her mum, sensing someone close by, looked up and smiled. 'Ah! Carol,' turning to her companions she proudly informed them, 'Carol's taking me out for the afternoon.' Her daughter smiled back and sighed with relief. Her mum was in a good mood!

Carol drove out of the care home for the afternoon drive. It was partly to give her mum a break from the home and partly so that she could enjoy the benefit of the car's air conditioning. The home either didn't have the air conditioning turned on or it was very inefficient. The rooms were stifling.

Out in the open the sun was blistering, the air too hot to breathe. The whole community was suffering from the extreme heat as they tried to complete their daily routines. By mid-morning the shops had emptied, the locals having completed their shopping early to hurry home before the midday heat intensified.

The modern, double-storey care home was situated on the outskirts of the market town of Glossop, an area heralded as the gateway to the Peak District. With a population of thirty-one thousand, the town had passed its heyday when it had enjoyed full employment producing cotton products from its two large mills, Peak Mill and Blossom Mill. They were long gone, and the town now had a tired feel to it. Several shops had closed and sported large 'For lease' signs at the front or were boarded up. Many other towns had experienced the same demise due to the collapse of the cotton trade. Nevertheless, for all its difficulties the town still had a great community spirit.

Having had a salad lunch at the Dog and Partridge in the town centre, they made their way up the A57 onto Woodhead Road, passing an old derelict engineering company on the left. Its stonework now blackened having suffered from many years of industrial smoke and grime. Eventually Carol and her mum were out into the countryside. Woodhead Road was the main road between Manchester and Sheffield. It wended its way through the wild moorland that stretched between the two metropolises. Sheep and cattle could be seen munching their way through what little grass there was which was now burnt brown; some finding shade in the shadow of a few sparce trees. The fields, traditionally separated by dry-stone walls, were today shimmering in the heat. In the distance she could see a grass fire burning on Saddleworth Moor, the thick brown-black smoke smeared across an otherwise perfectly blue sky.

'It doesn't seem long ago since the road was blocked with snow drifts', her mum observed, 'this is always the first road to be closed. Ever since I can remember it's been the first one to close.' She seemed very chatty today.

Carol's parents had spent their whole life in this tight-knit community, running a small farm at the foothills of the moor. Carol and her sister had been born here, went to school here, worked here. Carol stayed, her sister, Helen, went on to Uni to study law and now worked and lived in Bristol.

Carol smiled to herself as she waited for the story she'd heard a million times; of when she was two and, together with her parents, had been trapped in their small farm for over a month before anyone could reach them. 'We were trapped in the farm for over a month when you were little, the snow drifts were so deep. You were just two if I remember correctly. Did I also tell you about the time we were trapped in our farm because of the snow when I was a child? Our neighbour died when he went out looking for his dog out in the fields.' Carol nodded and smiled to herself,

'Yes, you did mum.'

'I was only seven years old. Seven years old!' she emphasised, 'dad was out most of the day digging our sheep out of the drifts.' They continued in silence for some time before her mum continued. 'I remember one year we lost a lot of sheep and newborn lambs. My parents were devastated.'

Carol eventually slowed the car and pulled into a lay-by where there were two cars already parked, the owners out for a mid-week drive and no doubt also reaping the benefits of their vehicle's air conditioning. The small car park had a wonderful view overlooking the Derwent Ladybower Reservoir.

'Stay in the car, mum, I'll just get a bottle of water out of the boot.' She returned with two bottles of water and a white box. 'I've got you a vanilla slice, your favourite.' They ate the slices and slowly drank the cool water. Carol stared out of the window then turned to her mum who was trying to keep the vanilla slice from falling apart whilst she tackled the custard filling. Carol smiled to herself. 'This car park is heaving at weekends, so I thought it would be better to have a ride out mid-week, it's much less busy.' As she looked down onto the reservoir, the surface reflecting the sun's rays, Carol remembered the history lessons from school. Derwent Ladybower Reservoir was built to supply the cities of the East Midlands with water. Two villages were sacrificed to make way for the dam, Derwent and Ashopton. In previous years, when there had been droughts, the reservoir levels had dropped considerably, exposing the old villages. First to emerge was always the church spire with a cockerel weathervane still attached to the top, defiantly showing itself to the world. In years of extended drought when the reservoir dropped even lower, the walls of the farms and the submerged village streets could be seen. Carol reached onto the back seat and grabbed her binoculars. Placing them to her eyes and adjusting them she remarked, 'I love it up here, it's so open and peaceful.' She scanned the open fields leading down to the rippling water and the dense woodland in the background. The last time she visited this beauty spot curlews were soaring above in an azure sky and swifts were skimming across the surface of the water searching for insects. But not today. There was not a bird to be seen. Carol turned to her mum. 'They must be hiding away in the trees to escape the heat.' She took a deep breath. 'It's hard to believe that they used the dam in WWII for the Lancaster bombers to practise low level flying in preparation for bombing the Ruhr in Germany.'

'I remember the practice runs,' sighed her mum, recollecting her childhood, 'I can still hear them as they came low over our farm.'

Carol was silent for a few seconds as she concentrated on scanning the low water level. 'There's something sticking up out of the water, mum, on the far shore. Not a building. It's not part of the old village. It looks like a car or a vehicle of some sort.' She handed the binoculars to her mum. 'I'm going down to the side of the water to get a closer look.' Minutes later she returned to the car, breathing heavily with exhaustion having climbed the slope from the water's edge back to the car park, her T-shirt sticking to her body with sweat. Wafting away some persistent flies from around her eyes, she flopped back into the car, using her hand as a fan to create some draught across her face. She grabbed her bottle of water and took a long swig. 'It's a van,' she said, wiping her lips with the back of her hand, 'it looks as though it's been in an accident of some sort. We'll pop in at Glossop police station on our way back and report it, they need to know.'

2021

Newtown, Mid Wales

Afan and Bronwen Davies lived in the tiny village of Llanwyddelan, part of the close-knit community of Newtown, in the county of Powys, Mid Wales. Newtown, situated on the River Severn, had a population of around twelve thousand and was only a few miles from the Welsh-English border. The Pryce Jones building, the home of the world's first mail order company, still dominated the town as it had since 1850.

Afan Davies worked as a supervisor at the Celtic Knitwear factory, the last remaining wool company in the area producing Welsh tweed. In years gone by the Welsh tweed factories had employed most of the people in the town, but now, mainly due to the more efficient Lancashire factories, the town had only one factory left. Bronwen Davies was the receptionist at the local sawmill. Afan and Bronwen Davies had lived in the village for nearly five years. Their stone terraced cottage was one of twelve, collectively known locally as the Mill Cottages. On the opposite side of the road the cottages overlooked farmland, today bright yellow with rape seed. In the distance were the Cambrian Mountains, snow-capped in the winter and covered in a glorious purple heather in the summer. Today it was just a brown vista, the result of a grass fire two weeks ago. The row of cottages had originally been built for the workers at one of the wool factories, but over the years, as the industry declined, the owners of the factory had sold off the cottages to private buyers. The Davies property was at the far end of the terrace. They had spent considerable time and effort updating their home by installing central heating, new modern window frames, a fully fitted kitchen and bathroom with shower.

They sat watching the television, but Bronwen noticed Afan was distracted. He had been like that all through their evening meal. She put it down to a hard day – she knew the factory had been under pressure to increase its sales in recent months.

'Cup of tea Afan?'

He looked up as though surprised to see her in the lounge. 'Oh, yeah, please.'

She muted the television as she sat down beside him on their new sofa. 'Hey, what is it?' He was reluctant to make eye contact, but when he did Bronwen could see tears in his eyes. She put her arm around him. 'Whatever's the matter?'

He was silent for several minutes then blurted out, 'I've lost my job. I'm being made redundant. The factory's closing.'

Bronwen sat back in her seat stunned at the news. 'How come? When? Why?'

'They tell us we're not competitive,' he sniffled, 'Welsh tweed isn't the seller it once was so we're not making money.' He leaned forward, his head in his hands, 'there are no other jobs in the area, Bron. What'll we do? How will we pay the mortgage?'

Bronwen sprang up. 'Let me get you that cup of tea. There's always an answer.' She returned with his tea in his favourite mug. 'Let's talk this through rationally. When is it going to happen?'

He blew out his cheeks. 'They tell us we'll all have gone by September, that's three months off.'

'When did you first know about it?'

'About a month ago. I didn't say anything in case it didn't happen or something else came along. What else could I do?'

'Afan,' she hesitated slightly, 'think of it as a golden opportunity. Haven't you always wanted to work for yourself?'

He looked at her with a wan smile. 'Yeah, I have, but doing what?'

She smiled. 'Let's go to bed and tomorrow we'll look at all the options, okay?'

He nodded and gave her a hug.

* * *

When Afan came home from work the next day Bronwen had notepaper and pens lined up on the kitchen table. She saw the surprised look on his face and chuckled. 'We're going to look at what skills you've got and how we put them to use.' She saw scepticism across his face. 'Afan, this could be the first day of the rest of your life.' They each had a piece of paper to write down what skills they thought he had, then cross-referenced the two lists to see where they agreed. 'What have we got then?' The two lists identified that he had few practical skills, but had very good organisational, communication and time management skills. 'We also need to identify what you don't want to do.' Bronwen's enthusiasm was infectious.

He added to his list with a flourish, sounding out the words as he wrote them; 'Not factory work again. I want to be in front of people each day not sitting at a desk. I want to be rewarded for my hard work.'

Bronwen nodded enthusiastically. 'Right!' she continued, being unable to hold back what she wanted to say. 'Well, I had an interesting conversation today with a products rep that came through the door at work and, whilst he was waiting for my boss Jerry Williams, we had a chat. He covers the whole of Mid and South Wales and he'd noticed that the towns he was visiting were all experiencing the same problem.'

Afan waved his hands for her to continue. 'And,' Bronwen took a deep breath, 'over the last few years villages have seen their post offices and grocery stores gradually closing.' Afan nodded wondering where this was going. 'So, when they want to shop, where do they go?' She held up her hand to stop him saying something she already knew, 'I know, I know, more people buy on- line now. However, there are a hard core of people who don't.' She then held up her finger ready to count off what she was about to say. 'One, some people can't or don't want to use a computer, in fact they may not even have a computer, and two,' she raised another finger, 'perhaps more importantly, they miss the chat, the local gossip in the corner shop, it's possibly the only contact they have with another human being. And,' as another finger went up, 'three, they want the convenience. Any thoughts?'

He shook his head. 'I'm not sure what you're suggesting.'

Bronwen's face lit up. 'A mobile grocery shop! I know it will cost money to set up and a lot of market research needs to be done, but on paper it fits your skills and your temperament.'

Afan slowly smiled and pursed his lips. 'I think you've got something there. Where would we start?'

'We start with market research. We'll put out some leaflets in the villages, within say, a thirty-mile radius of Newtown.'

'Asking what, exactly?'

Bronwen took another piece of paper. 'Let's think of some questions.'

She headed her sheet of paper Research Questions:

Where do you shop?
How often do you shop?
Where do you go if you only want a pint of milk?
Now that the post office has closed how do you receive your mail?
Would you use a mobile shop if it called in the village twice a week on a regular day and time?
Would you be prepared to pay a little more for the convenience?
Tick any products below that would be of interest to you.
> *Groceries*
> *Meat*
> *Fish*
> *Fresh vegetables*
> *Postal services*
> *Prescriptions pick-up.*
Any other comments

The following Saturday, they awoke to a beautiful sunny day which lifted their resolve. They visited the relevant villages and asked various outlets to distribute their questionnaire. They handed out their leaflets to organisations which wouldn't be negatively impacted by a mobile grocery shop, such as libraries, garages, town halls and any clubs or institutes within the community. They arrived home as the sun was setting and both flopped into their easy chairs. Afan was exhausted. 'Phew, what a day.'

Bronwen nodded. 'Next Saturday we do the whole thing again, this time collecting the answers. Then we wait and see.'

* * *

The response to their questionnaire was well received. Afan couldn't keep the smile from his face as he read the replies. 'Wow! This is brilliant.' He gave her a hug. 'They're all so positive, and for all the reasons you predicted. You're really clever .' Bronwen was just glad to see him happy again.

* * *

It was a sad day for the whole village when Celtic Knitwear finally closed its doors. For many families it was even more traumatic as both members of the household worked at the mill, some with small children, many with financial commitments.

* * *

Afan had already put their plan into motion prior to closure of the factory. He'd sourced a suitable vehicle, a Renault Traffic, which had been used as a mobile library operated by Newtown Council prior to updating their vehicles. It was more expensive than Afan had planned, but it was close to their specifications. Based on the costings provided by Afan and Bronwen, and their enthusiasm, the bank finally agreed to loan them the money. The light cream van, having been re-sprayed to cover the Newtown Council emblem prior to its sale, was already furnished with shelving and needed little modification to suit the couple's needs. With welcome help from a friend who had more practical skills than Afan and Bronwen, the Renault was ready for business after five weekends of hard work. The final touches included fitting a freezer for the meats and magnetic signs for the side of the van. Afan stood back to admire the finished vehicle before polishing the signs with the sleeve of his jacket: *A and B Mobile Grocery Service*.

* * *

Afan's first day on the road should have been an auspicious day, but it started with the van's engine hesitating when Afan turned the ignition, causing his stomach to do a flip, but finally, to his relief, it fired. The weather forecast was threatening high winds and squally showers.

He was concerned the inclement weather may stop potential customers coming out to the van. As he eventually drove off along the A492, the winds increased, bending the branches of the small trees and hedges. The low clouds appeared to become lower and blacker before large spots of rain were deposited on his windscreen. As the wipers screeched back and forth smearing his screen, Afan made a mental note to replace the wipers as soon as possible. He made his way in the direction of Llanidloes, the wind constantly buffeting the van, the greasy windscreen obscuring his vision. He pulled into a lay-by for a planned coffee and bacon sandwich at Bruno Sabatini's Food Van, just outside Caersws, his first planned stop. He smiled to himself as he enjoyed his snack. *Self-employment! I'm my own boss!*

* * *

As expected, business for the first few months was slow. It took time for his potential customers to develop the habit of buying from his van, but week by week the takings improved. As people asked for different products and brands he endeavoured to satisfy their needs. He now had a contract with the post office to pick up mail from Newtown Post Office and deliver to a designated outlet in each village. In some cases, it was the local garage, in others the library, or the hardware shop. In turn, he picked up mail from his customers and delivered it to the main post office in Newtown for distribution. Eventually he was more than able to pay his loan back to the bank. As he got to know his customers better, they provided him with gossip and he would arrive home and regale some of the news to Bronwen.

'Did you know, Dai Thomas in Cefn Cogh is the current sheep dog trials champion for South Wales? Mrs Parry from Llanwnog is going into hospital next week to have a hip replacement. Her daughter will leave her mum's shopping list on our mobile phone, and I'll deliver it to the garage to be picked up by her daughter after work. The Williams from Beulah farm had twenty sheep rustled over the weekend. Bwlch-y-Fridd has got its annual agricultural show in a couple of weeks' time, maybe we go over there for the day. Mrs Davies was telling me that there's been a similar service to ours for some time north of Welshpool. Mr Roberts from Pentre suggested I fit a coffee machine in the van as there was no café in his village. I think that's a good idea because the service could be used by a cross-section of businesses that don't have access to a café.' His chats with his customers were relayed to Bronwen each day over dinner.

Business was steadily increasing.

One morning he was about to start his round when he found the near side tyre flat. On looking around the van he saw the off-side front tyre was also flat. Both had been ripped by a knife or some other sharp instrument. As luck would have it Afan's close friend was the village mechanic who was able to come out and change the tyres. Within the hour Afan was on his way. Over dinner he relayed the events to Bronwen. 'Honestly Bron, who would slash the tyres? And why?'

Bronwen shook her head as she cut into her chop. 'Goodness knows. It looks to me like someone doesn't want you continuing your rounds.'

The next few weeks went by without further incident, when one evening as Afan and Bronwen were quietly sitting, watching television and enjoying a glass of Merlot, the phone rang. 'I'll get it.' Afan got up from his chair. He came back after only a minute or two, his face ashen. Running his hand through his hair he looked at Bronwen and shook his head in despair. 'I don't believe that!' He flopped back into his chair and picked up his glass of red.

'What? What's happened?'

Afan waved his hand in the direction of the hallway. 'That phone call. Somebody was threatening me.'

'What do you mean? How?' Afan took another swig of his wine.

Bron sat on the edge of her seat and muted the television. 'What did they say?'

'Whoever it was said, stop trading or you'll come to some harm.'

Bron was lost for words for several seconds but finally found her voice. 'So, what are you going to do?'

Afan poured another glass. 'First, report it to the police, then continue as normal.' Several more weeks passed without incident.

* * *

In a quiet corner of the Wheatsheaf pub situated on the north side of the Newtown market square, sat three shady characters. Two decidedly scruffy-looking, menacing individuals and a well-dressed gentleman. The 'gentleman' was tall, had thick dark hair slightly peppered with grey, a thin moustache and a tattoo on the back of his left hand. He wore a tailored suit, pale blue shirt and navy tie. His name was Dafyd Williams. He was the 'W' of L&W Supermarkets. Williams and his partner, John Lorrie, owned several supermarkets in Welshpool, Rhayader, Hereford, Shrewsbury and Oswestry. They also ran a mobile service for the small villages around the English-Welsh border. Williams clicked his fingers for the barman to tend to them. He lowered his voice as the two thugs picked up their pints of beer. 'This Afan Davies, I want him stopped. He's impacting on our business, especially as we had planned to extend our mobile service to the areas he's covering. He hasn't reacted to the tyre incident or the phone call, so we need to be a bit more, shall we say, persuasive,' he waited whilst the other two nodded to acknowledge what he was saying, 'so, I want you two to put a bit more pressure on him.' Williams looked around to ensure no one was close enough to hear. 'I want him roughed up. You understand what I'm saying, just roughed up. Enough so he gets the message. Okay?' They nodded. Williams got up, threw a note on the table for them to have a few more drinks then disappeared out of the pub.

* * *

Williams' henchmen sat in their van, muffled up in anoraks and peaked caps, smoking their third cigarette of the morning. The sun was just beginning to peek through the bare branches of the trees casting a pale glow over their parking spot. Robbo glanced up through the windscreen at the dark clouds building in the sky. 'Typical. Weather forecast says fine, cool but with a stiff breeze, it's more like bloody Siberia sat here.' Spence ignored his grumblings and inhaled a deep breath of nicotine, his eyes firmly set on the main road. Robbo was never happy doing the dirty work for Dafyd Williams and his tapping foot gave away his stressed state of mind. 'If we get caught, Spence, we'll do time,' he took a long drag on his cigarette, 'particularly me, I've got form.'

'Stop your bloody tapping Robbo, it unnerves me.'

The two thugs had monitored Afan's movements over the last few weeks and knew he followed a routine. They were parked in The Crown pub car park one hundred yards from the lay-by where they knew Afan would arrive a few minutes later. He arrived, regular as clockwork. Second Thursday of the month he covered the Caersws and Llanidloes outlying areas, stopping at Bruno's Food Van in the lay-by just outside Caersws for his usual coffee and bacon sandwich around 7:30am. Spence blew his cigarette smoke out of the open window whilst looking in disgust at Robbo who flicked his ash in the footwell. 'Don't do that Robbo, chuck it out of the window for Christ's sake.'

Robbo, having been suitably admonished, opened the window a little further and flicked the butt onto the gravelled surface. 'It's bloody annoying Spence. Ceri and I had planned to go to my brother's place up in the High Peak this weekend.' He sniffled. 'And here I am waiting for Afan bloody Davies to arrive just so we can have a few words.'

'You're being well paid, so stop grumbling. Anyway, where's the High Peak?'

Robbo wiped his nose with a grubby handkerchief. 'High Peak, it's in Derbyshire. My brother's got a small farm there. Twenty acres or so.' He suddenly stiffened and pointed to Afan's grocery van driving past on the main road. 'Here he is. We'll follow him into the food stop, let him get his coffee and get back in his van then we'll sort him out.' They followed him, keeping their distance, one vehicle between themselves and their target.

Afan turned into the lay-by and parked his van. There was no movement for several minutes when, at last, Afan climbed out of the cab, stretched his arms, turned up his collar against the cold breeze and half ran to the food truck. Minutes later he was back in his van. The two heavies were about to leave their own van when they saw Afan open his cab door, jump out and make his way to the back of his vehicle, his sandwich in his right hand. He opened the customer door at the back and disappeared inside.

'Come on, now. We'll have him trapped in the back of the van,' urged Spence, opening his door. They quickly made their way across to the rear door of Afan's van and yanked it open.

It took Afan by surprise. 'I'm not open yet gents.'

Spence took a step forward. 'We're not here to buy anything. We're here to give you a message. One that you should take note of,' he added menacingly. In that instant he grabbed Afan by his overall and punched him in the face. Afan immediately pushed him back knocking Spence into Robbo who in turn crashed into the counter knocking a pile of tins from the shelf. Spence stepped forward again, swinging his fists. 'You don't learn do you! Stay out of a business that you shouldn't be in.' In trying to deflect the oncoming blows Afan slipped on tins that were rolling around the floor and he went down, cracking his head on the corner of the till. He went down like a lead balloon. He lay still. Blood poured from his temple. His eyes open but not seeing.

The world for Robbo and Spence went into slow motion.

'What the hell have you done Spence?' Robbo hissed in a panicky tone.

'Nothing! I hardly touched him! He went for me and slipped.' The two men bent down next to Afan, blood soaking into the knees of their jeans. Robbo checked for a pulse. He shook his head and looked at Spence.

'We'd better get out of here. He's dead.' They returned to their van and sat in silence whilst lighting cigarettes. After a minute or two Robbo broke the silence. 'You'd better phone the boss.'

'Christ, what am I going to say?' Spence dialled and listened to the phone ringing at the other end. It rang for what seemed like an eternity.

Finally, their boss picked up. 'I hope you've got a bloody good reason for this early phone call.' Spence remained silent not knowing how to approach the subject. 'Hello. You still there?'

Spence coughed. 'Er, yes boss.' There was no point in delaying it – he barged straight in. 'There's been a stuff up.'

Williams shouted down the phone. 'What sort of stuff up? The job I asked you to do was straightforward. What's gone wrong? Didn't he turn up?'

Spence stammered. 'Yeah, he turned up. He's dead!'

'What d'you mean dead?' cried Williams, 'I told you to just rough him up.'

'Yeah, I know, but we got into a fight. He slipped, banged his head.'

Williams exploded. 'You bloody idiots. You'd better sort it. Distance yourselves. Get rid of him and his van before he's reported missing.'

'Where to?'

'I don't bloody care!' his voice rising several octaves, 'just get rid of it. Away from the area. Out of Wales if necessary. Ditch it, burn it, do whatever it takes, but make sure it doesn't get traced back to you or me. Now piss off and don't phone again 'til the job's done. Get shut of it NOW!'

The two thugs sat in silence. Finally, Robbo spoke up. 'Well?'

Spence told Robbo what their boss had said. 'Get rid of it he says. Easier said than done. Bloody hell Robbo. What a bloody mess. He wants it out of Wales before the local cops become involved.' Robbo sat blowing smoke out of the open window his leg bouncing up and down for several minutes. Suddenly he sat up and spoke.

'Got it! I know where we can ditch it. Nobody will ever find it.'

Spence looked at Robbo and raised his eyebrows. 'What do you have in mind?'

Robbo swivelled in his seat to face his partner in crime. 'Easy. We take it to my brother's farm up in the High Peak.'

'And then what? Feed it to the pigs?' he added sarcastically, 'have you actually thought it through?'

Robbo was becoming impatient. 'Just shut up for a minute and listen. We drive to my brother's farm now, before he can be reported missing. He won't be missed until he fails to return home tonight.'

Spence was shaking his head. 'And then what. Hide it in a barn. It's a bit big.' He said pointing to Afan's van.

'No! His farm backs on to woodland which in turn backs onto the high edge of Ladybower Reservoir where it's at its deepest. Nobody will see us drive through his woods, then we run the van over the edge into the reservoir. It'll never be found.'

'Do you think that'll work?'

'Yeah, I know it will. Trust me.'

Desperate for a solution, Spence turned the ignition on their van. 'Come on then,' he stammered realising there was no choice, 'you drive Afan's van and I'll follow in our van. How long will it take?'

'Probably three or four hours. We could be there and half-way back before anyone notices he's missing.' Robbo swung himself into Afan's cab and, pulling his cap low over his forehead, drove out of the lay-by, the tyres crunching over the loose gravel, dipping in and out of the potholes caused by recent flooding. Avoiding eye contact with the Sabatini's food truck, he turned right heading back towards Newtown, closely followed by Spence.

Two miles into their journey Spence urgently flashed Robbo down. He jumped out of the van and ran to Robbo. Pointing to the sides of Afan's van he stammered, 'the signs! The bloody mobile shop signs are still attached to the sides. We need to take them off so it won't be recognised while we drive around Newtown.' He ran to the sides and prised the magnetic signs off, throwing them into the back of the van then giving Robbo the signal to continue.

They finally reached Robbo's brother's farm.

* * *

Bronwen looked at the clock on the mantelpiece for the umpteenth time. It was now 8:30pm. Afan hadn't arrived home, nor had he phoned to tell her he was going to be late. She paced up and down the lounge, wringing her hands then running them through her hair in frustration and continually checking through the bay window to see if he was coming. At 10.00pm she jumped in her car and drove to Newtown police station. It was a new three-storey brick and glass edifice on the outskirts of town, the sign Heddlu Powis standing proud above the portico entrance. She explained the situation as best she could regarding the threatening phone call and slashed tyres. Now sobbing and shaking, she was starting to panic as to what might have happened to Afan. She explained that today was his round covering the outlying villages around Caersws and Llanidloes and that he usually stopped at the food truck around 7.30am before heading for Caersws. The desk sergeant took copious notes and explained to her what would happen next. 'We'll check all the hospitals first. It's rather late now and the food truck will have gone, so tomorrow we'll send a patrol car to check that he arrived. We'll also check with his customers in the outlying villages.' He smiled to reassure her. 'I'm sure we'll find him. It could just be something as simple as engine trouble and his mobile phone may not be charged up.'

She returned home feeling better for having reported his disappearance to the police but found it impossible to sleep that night.

* * *

PCs Whitworth and Clovelly were on the early shift the next day and arrived at Sabatini's food truck at approximately the same time Afan would normally have arrived. Whitworth bumped the car through the puddles and came to park a few yards away from the truck. He turned to Clovelly. 'I'll have a chat with the owner.' He referred to his notes. 'It's a Bruno Sabatini. You have a wander around the customers in the car park to see if any of them were here yesterday. Check if they saw Afan or if they noticed anything unusual.' Whitworth climbed out of the patrol car, placed his cap on his head and sauntered over to the truck which was painted bright red with an awning showing the Italian colours of red, white and green. Whitworth waited whilst the owner served a customer at the counter, then held up his warrant card. 'Mr Sabatini?' Sabatini nodded.

'Mind if I ask you a few questions. We're investigating the disappearance of Afan Davies. Apparently, he regularly pulls in here for a coffee. Do you know him?'

Sabatini nodded once more. 'I know him well. He comes on a regular basis. We usually have a quick chat then he's on his way.' Whitworth made a few notes.

'Was he here yesterday?'

'Oh yes. I saw him arrive and he bought his usual coffee and a bacon sandwich. We had a quick chat about the weather and the up-coming agricultural show in Welshpool. It was starting to rain, so he went back to his van. Yesterday it was busy. I remember his van turning out of the lay-by and a couple of things registered.' Whitworth continued writing in his notebook.

'A couple of things?' prompted the officer.

'Yes. He turned back towards Newtown. Why would he do that, he'd only just come from there. It seemed strange.'

'Did you notice who was driving the vehicle?'

'Not sure. I was busy and didn't see who it was. I presumed it was him. Who else would it be?'

The officer prompted again. 'You said a couple of things.'

'Oh, yeah. Not sure if it's relevant but just something I noticed. It was followed out by a Merc Sprinter van. Over the years I've got into the habit of noticing which cars my customers drive, particularly my regulars and I hadn't seen this van before.'

'And why would that register?'

Sabatini spread his arms wide. 'It was the same model and year as this,' pointing to his own van, 'I noticed because it looked as though it had been re-sprayed. It was shiny.'

'And what colour was it?'

'Black. It looked good.'

'Did you happen to get the registration?' The owner shook his head.

'Not fully. I know it was a local registration 'cos the letters were the same as mine.'

'Anything else?'

'Oh yeah. Its rear near side indicator light was broken.'

The officer folded his notebook away. 'Thank you, Mr Sabatini, you've been a great help.'

As he walked away Sabatini shouted after him, 'Can I get you and your colleague a coffee?' adding quickly, 'on the house of course.' Whitworth nodded and returned to the van.

'Two flat whites, thank you, they'll be very welcome.'

Back in the car he radioed the information to the station, whilst a cloudburst dropped a deluge of rain on the roof of the car.

* * *

The next day Bronwen still hadn't heard anything from the police as she sat in the lounge hugging a mug of tea, now tepid. Just after lunch, as she was checking through the window yet again, a familiar yellow and blue chequered police car drew up outside the house. She ran to the door as the two officers were opening the wrought iron gate. 'Have you got any news?' she cried hopefully. The female officer took the lead.

'May we come in Mrs Davies?'

Bronwen nodded and ushered them through to the lounge. The male officer spoke. 'Sit down please Mrs Davies. PC Roberts will explain to you what we've discovered so far.' He smiled. 'Do you mind if I use your kitchen to make a cup of coffee for the three of us?' She nodded. He disappeared whilst PC Roberts proceeded to explain what they knew so far.

'Mrs Davies, what we've found out is that Afan arrived at the food truck at his usual time, but beyond that we can find no trace of him or his vehicle. His customers we spoke to hadn't seen him.' PC Clyde returned after rummaging around in the kitchen to make the coffees. He placed the three cups on a small mosaic coffee table. PC Roberts continued. 'The petrol station where he parks for his stay in Caersws said he didn't arrive. They just assumed he'd changed his route. He seems to have disappeared after his visit to the food truck.'

2022

Glossop

Whilst Carol's mum stayed in the car, Carol popped in at Glossop police station, its blackened Victorian stonework yet another victim of the industrial era. It still had the original blue lantern over the doorway which made Carol smile. It reminded her of the *Dixon of Dock Green* series on the television from when she was a child. She reported to the desk sergeant what she'd seen at the reservoir. He pulled out a yellow report form from underneath the counter, took her details and promised he would pass the information on to the relevant individuals.

* * *

The next morning DI Geoff Maddox, along with his DC, Helen Chisworth, arrived at Ladybower Reservoir at almost the same time as a low loader. The driver and his mate proceeded to secure a chain to the underneath of the vehicle that was sticking out of the water. The blistering sun was already burning, even though it was still early morning. The forensics team arrived minutes later just as the recovery vehicle began to slowly pull the van out of the water. Maddox shouted to the truck driver. 'Just pull it out as far as firm ground, forensics need to do their job before it's moved away from the area.' As the van emerged from the dark waters, they could see it had been submerged for some time. The sides of the van were covered in algae, the windscreen broken, and water was pouring from every outlet. The vehicle was carefully secured on dry land and was immediately pounced on by the forensic team. On opening the rear doors, they immediately stepped back, the forensics team leader shouted to Maddox.

'There's a body in here.' It was lying among piles of tins, cartons and other detritus that had entered the vehicle whilst underwater.

DI Maddox called a team briefing in the afternoon. The large windows on the main wall of the briefing room, although covered in traffic dirt, still allowed the sweltering sun to invade the cramped room. Within minutes most of the team had removed ties and undone shirt collars. 'I'll be as succinct as possible. We have a vehicle that has been recovered from Ladybower Reservoir this morning. Inside was an, as yet, unidentified body. What we do know is that the vehicle has a Welsh registration, ACX 428. I've contacted Powis police for them to check if they have any outstanding van thefts or missing persons. From the number of tins and a till still in the back of the vehicle it does suggest it was a mobile shop of some sort. From their initial examination forensics have identified a deep cut on the deceased's right temple which they think was the cause of death. Further examination may flag up other leads for us to follow. I've organised a house to house around the immediate area although I don't hold out much hope. There's only one or two farms and a couple of pubs, but that's about it. We'll have another meeting tomorrow morning at eight. By then I might have had a response from Powis police and forensics might have more info on the victim.'

By eight o'clock the next morning the sun reappeared as hot as the last few weeks. The troops gathered in the briefing room, many with their hands wrapped around a take-away coffee or iced tea. Maddox coughed to gain their attention. 'It'll be a quick meeting this morning. The case is being passed to the Powis police. It's now in their jurisdiction. They had a missing person reported about twelve months ago and believe it to be the one we pulled out of Ladybower yesterday. Forensics have managed to lift some latent fingerprints from the rear door handle and the edge of the back door of the van. Good and bad news regarding their usefulness. One set we can match, one is iffy. All the information is being sent to Powis. The vehicle is being transported to Mid Wales as we speak. Sorry it's not ours but Powis are now taking control of this investigation.'

Newtown
Mid Wales

DI Parry Evans, a short wiry man with unruly white hair and a thin moustache, stood at the front of the meeting room, one hand leaning on the whiteboard, Texta pen in the other. 'Morning everyone. Many of you will remember the disappearance of Afan Davies approximately twelve months ago. After an extensive investigation we hit a brick wall. He seemingly disappeared into thin air after stopping off at a food truck on the A492. We now have an update.' He referred to the whiteboard and pointed with his pen. 'Yesterday, Derbyshire police pulled a van out of Ladybower Reservoir. The van was registered to Afan Davies. The body found inside appears to be Afan's but forensics are doing further dental checks. The report I've received from Derbyshire police shows there were two sets of prints they were able to lift from the vehicle's rear doors. One set on the door handle was so contaminated as to be of limited use but the other found on the edge of the door gives us a match. The national database shows the prints to be those of Robert Anthony Rogers, aka Robbo! Surprise, surprise. That thug is still around.' He moved to the right of the whiteboard and began to write up a list of critical actions. 'We need to speak to Robert Rogers and any associates.' He scanned the group in front of him. 'Talk to anyone who had any dealings with him recently. Who did he hang around with? Who did he work for?'

A hand went up at the back of the room. 'DC Jones sir. I do know he has been linked to Dafyd Williams, as in W&L Supermarkets. Shall I have a word with Williams?'

Evans nodded. 'Yes, good idea. Take DC Connor with you.' He noted the action on the whiteboard.

DCs Jones and Connor drove to Welshpool through a sudden downpour, a welcome change after weeks of unrelenting heat, and arrived at the headquarters of W&L Supermarkets to find the car park partially flooded. Carefully parking the car so as to avoid stepping in large puddles, they made their way into the impressive double-storey building. The young lady on reception greeted them with a well-practised smile. 'Good morning. How can I help you?'

DC Connor smiled back. 'We'd like to speak to Mr Williams please.'

The receptionist, still smiling, replied, 'Up the stairs, turn right and Mr Williams' office is at the end of the corridor. Mr Williams' secretary will let him know you're here.' They politely returned her smile.

'Thank you.'

Williams' secretary was a middle-aged woman. She wore a pale blue business suit, a single layer of pearls and a pair of spectacles hanging around her neck. She wore a lanyard threaded through an electronic key. She politely enquired, 'do you have an appointment? Mr Williams only sees people by appointment.' In unison both officers produced their warrant cards.

'I'm Detective Constable Jones and this is Detective Constable Connor. We'd like to see him now, please.'

Having been forewarned by reception of the arrival of the police, Dafyd Williams met them at his office door just as his secretary was about to knock. He had removed his jacket and tie and was smoking a cigar.

'Please, come in,' Williams said gesturing to two chairs, 'take a seat. What can I do for you?' As Jones started his prepared questions Connor took out her notebook and pen.

'Mr Williams, we're investigating the disappearance of an Afan Davies. Does the name mean anything to you?'

Williams frowned and pursed his lips. 'The name rings a bell. I seem to remember reading something about him in the newspaper, about a year ago?' Jones nodded.

'That's correct, but he has now re-appeared.' He waited and watched for a reaction on Williams' face.

'Re-appeared?' repeated Williams as he cleared his throat. 'Well, that's good isn't it?' Jones noted his voice was at a slightly higher pitch and he wasn't as confident as at the start of the conversation. 'But what has it to do with me?'

Jones looked at Connor before continuing. 'Well, it's possible there may be a link to a Robert Rogers in the investigation and we understand he's occasionally worked for you. Is that right?'

Williams shuffled in his chair, his voice now sounding even more uncertain.

'Not sure, possibly. I have a good many people working for me, I'd have to check my books.'

Connor pushed him further. 'Can you remember what you would have used him for?'

'Er, no, unless it was during a move to new premises when we needed extra pairs of hands to shift stock.'

'Any other times?'

Williams bit his bottom lip and slowly shook his head. 'No, I don't think so.'

Jones suddenly jumped up from his chair. 'Well, thank you Mr Williams you've been a great help. We'll show ourselves out.' The two officers both politely nodded to the receptionist as they pushed through the revolving doors and out into the car park. The rain had stopped and bright patches of blue sky were showing through the remaining wispy cloud. As Jones turned the ignition he turned to Connor. 'He knows more than he's saying, doesn't he.'

Williams was squinting through the Venetian blinds in his office and watched the officers disappear out of the car park.

At the same time as DCs Jones and Connor were visiting Williams, DI Evans and DC Clem Dooley were on their way to interview Robert Rogers together with the forensics team.

* * *

Rogers lived six miles from the centre of Newtown on what had once been a successful market garden supplying vegetables to local shops. It was now overrun with weeds and discarded machinery. Evans slowly drove up the narrow dirt track to Rogers' place, past a deeply wooded area and a small pond currently covered in green algae. The Rogers' house had at one time been a beautiful stone cottage but was now looking worse for wear, neglected, tired and in need of an enthusiastic DIY job to restore it to its former glory. To one side of the cottage were several dilapidated wooden sheds. One of the larger ones directly in front them had a broken side window and a rusted corrugated roof leaning to one side. The two wide wooden doors were silver with age. An old hen coop was lying empty to the right of the shed.

Evans rapped sharply on the door and it was immediately opened by Rogers. 'Yeah?'

Evans and Dooley flashed their warrant cards. 'Robert Rogers?'

'Yeah.'

'I'm DI Evans and this is DC Dooley. Can we come in?' Rogers nodded and resignedly stepped to one side to allow them in. The house was dark and dank and smelled musty. Several chairs were parked in the hallway piled high with old newspapers. Rogers led the way through to the kitchen.

'How can I help you?'

They seated themselves on high bar stools up against a kitchen unit. 'We need to ask you a few questions.' Getting no response from Rogers he continued. 'D'you mind if my colleague has a look around your sheds?' Rogers shrugged his shoulders as Evans gave a nod to Dooley before continuing. 'Do you know an Afan Davies?' Rogers nodded.

'Yeah. I think he runs a mobile shop.'

Evans smiled. 'The very same. When did you last see him?'

'Er, months ago.'

'Have you ever used his services?'

Rogers shook his head. 'No, never. I shop at the supermarket.'

Evans let silence fill the next few seconds. 'Then, could you tell me how your fingerprints came to be on the rear door of his van?'

Rogers looked panicked. 'Dunno, must be some mistake.'

'No mistake Robbo. Is that what your associates call you? Robbo?'

Before Rogers had time to answer Evans changed his line of questioning. 'What do you keep in your sheds?'

Taken aback by the switch in questioning he faltered. 'Er, odds and sods.'

Evans stood up. 'Let's go and have a look inside, shall we?' He was out of the back door so quickly Rogers had to run to catch up.

'I just keep my van in the big one,' he shouted after Evans. Dooley was stretching across the overgrown brambles to look through the broken window, his hand shading his eyes from the bright sun.

'Come and have a look in here boss.' Evans wrenched the door open, the bottom edge scraping on the ground.

'Ah! What do we have here DC Dooley?' He lifted a badly stained canvas cover. 'Well, what a surprise! A Mercedes Sprinter van! A black one no less! The same model that a witness said was in the lay-by at the same time as Afan's disappearance.' Evans walked around the van lifting the cover as he went. 'Same colour, resprayed I would guess, and the same broken rear light as reported by our witness.' He took his time strolling round to the rear doors and yanked them open and peered into the dim light. Reaching in he pulled out two sheets of metal. 'Well, well, what do we have here, Robbo, magnetic business signs from the side of a vehicle?' He turned them round to face Rogers. 'Oh look, A and B Mobile Grocery Shop.' He looked up thoughtfully with his hand on his chin. 'Now, where have I heard that name before? What do you have to say Robbo?' He received no response so let the silence continue, before asking a blunt question. 'Tell me, Robbo, do you know anything about the abduction and ultimate demise, ahem death, of Afan Davies?'

Rogers looked sullen and muttered. 'No, nothing, and no more questions without a solicitor.'

'Very wise Robbo. Robert Anthony Rogers, I'm arresting you on suspicion of the abduction and murder of Afan Davies. Anything you say will be...'

As he escorted Rogers back to the car, he requested Dooley organise forensics to pick up the van.

* * *

Rogers sat with his back to two small, frosted windows, his solicitor sat next to him. A faulty fluorescent light flickered giving the room an eerie atmosphere. 'Please take a seat,' invited Evans. He sat opposite Rogers and deliberately, slowly, flipped through a thick file in front of him, occasionally looking up at Rogers. 'Robbo, Robert,' he smiled, 'you're in a lot of trouble my friend. Would you like to tell me where you were on September the eighteenth last year?'

Rogers' solicitor piped up 'You don't have to answer that.'

Rogers shook his head. 'I've no idea. It was a long time ago. I've had a few sleeps since then.'

Evans slowly nodded then continued. 'I'll ask you the question I asked you when we saw you in your home. Can you explain how your fingerprints came to be on the door of the van Afan Davies was last seen driving?'

Rogers remained silent.

'Let me try and jog your memory. The van has just been pulled out of a reservoir in Derbyshire.'

Rogers glanced at his solicitor and continued the silence.

'Investigations by Derbyshire police have identified that, from the location of the van in the reservoir, it must have been dumped via land owned by a Geoff Rogers. Any relation?'

Still more silence from Rogers. Then he suddenly became aggressive. Leaning forward, his eyes black with venom he screamed, 'Are you telling me that after twelve months under water you've found my fingerprints. I don't believe you. You bastards, you're trying to set me up. It's impossible.' His solicitor placed his hand on Rogers' arm, closed his eyes and shook his head as if to say, 'Don't go there'.

Evans leaned back in his chair and calmly responded, 'Sadly for you, it's not impossible. You see Robert, fingerprints leave grease marks that don't easily get erased.' He flicked open the file in front of him. 'I can show you the forensic report if you like?' At that point there was a knock at the door and a head poked round.

'Got a minute, boss?' Evans stood up, picking up the file as he went outside.

'Shan't be long Robert. Don't go away.'

The constable took Evans to one side away from the interview door. 'Forensics have analysed the mobile phone you took from Rogers to check his calls. It's thrown up some interesting calls.' He produced sheets of records and pointed to the highlighted ones. 'Several around the time of the disappearance are to an associate of Rogers, a Spencer

Coalville. He was charged three years ago for possession and has been interviewed in the past for various misdemeanours.' He paused. 'The really interesting calls are those.' He pointed to several highlighted in luminous yellow. Evans read the sheets and grinned at his colleague. 'Well, what a turn up for the books, thanks.' He returned to the interview room placing the file back on the table. 'We've been checking your telephone calls and there are quite a few, to say the least, to a Spencer Coalville. Mate of yours, is he?'

Rogers fidgeted in his seat. 'I know him, yeah, so what?'

'Well, we've looked at the number of calls. Nothing for weeks then a sudden flurry, all around the time of Afan's disappearance. Coincidence?' Silence. There was a knock at the door once more and the same constable slipped Evans a piece of paper. Evans quickly read it then slipped it into the file. With no warning he changed his line of questioning. 'Forensics are looking at your van. How come it has been resprayed?'

'I hit a gate post.'

'Mmm, okay. How long have you owned it?'

''Bout four years.'

'We've identified that it's registered in the name of W&L Supermarkets. So that tells me the supermarket is the official owner of the van, is that correct.'

Rogers nodded.

'So, why tell me you own it.'

''Cos, I drive it most of the time.'

'Doing what?'

'Picking up goods and delivering them to the various shops.'

'So, you work for Dafyd Williams?' Rogers hesitantly nodded.

'Here's another question for you. Can you explain why there are numerous phone calls to Dafyd Williams around the time of Afan's disappearance?' He let the silence hang in the air. He then continued. 'No calls to Dafyd for weeks then a flurry, again, just like the Coalville calls. Can you see why we don't believe you when you say you have had nothing to do with Afan's disappearance?' He stood up to leave. 'Think about what we've discussed Robert, it's not looking good for you. We've got your fingerprints on the van and on the metallic signs which were found on your premises. Lots of phone calls to Spencer Coalville and Dafyd Williams, we'll see what they have to say. In the meantime, you'll stay with us.'

* * *

The next morning DI Evans had a spring in his step as he briskly hurried to the briefing room, a thick file tucked under his arm. He had a tingle of excitement as he always did when cases began to come together.

He nodded a good morning to his team, then sat behind a table and made a few notes on his notepad. After a few minutes he stood up and the murmur of chatter subsided. 'Ladies and gentlemen, I need to brief you on where we're up to in the Afan Davies disappearance.' He smiled briefly. 'It isn't often we get the pieces of the jigsaw coming together so early in our investigation,' he paused for a second then continued. 'Identification of Robert Rogers' fingerprints place him at the scene of the crime. He swears blind he's never been in Afan's mobile shop and yet his prints are on the rear doors. The other fingerprints which were found on the door handle were contaminated and therefore can't be used as evidence. However, there was enough of a partial match between those prints and our database to put a Spencer Coalville in the frame too. Fortunately, a good set of his prints were clearly identifiable on the two magnetic signs taken from Afan's van and found in Rogers' shed.' He looked to the back of the room at DCs Jones and Connor. 'Liam and Sophie, I want you to pick Coalville up and bring him in for questioning. The van we discovered in the shed at Rogers' place matches the van described by the owner of the food truck, a Mr Sabatini, as being in the lay-by on the morning of Afan's disappearance. He described it as a Mercedes Sprinter, black with a broken rear light.' He continued, unable to contain his excitement. 'The evidence gets better. SOCOs were able to pinpoint where the van was pushed into the reservoir. It was at a point in woodland bordering the reservoir on land owned by a Mr Geoff Rogers. Ah, I see from raised eyebrows that some of you have made the connection, he's none other than Robbo Rogers' brother. Coalville and Rogers, in making their way to Ladybower Reservoir, avoided the obvious and quicker M5/M6 and went via Mid Wales on country roads to Chester, then from Chester on the A56 to Manchester and from there onto the A57 Woodhead Road to Ladybower. We know this because they were pinged near Wrexham, Northwich and Glossop by the ANPR. Glossop's only a few miles from where they dumped the van with Afan's body still inside.' He paused before asking. 'Any questions?'

A hand went up. 'How does this Dafyd Williams fit in with the big picture?'

Evans pursed his lips. 'It's not clear at this stage, but I'm going out to see him again. He may be good enough to clarify a few things!'

* * *

Jones and Connor slowly drove through the rabbit warren of the new housing estate where Spencer Coalville lived. Sophie suddenly pointed out, 'There it is, Carson Close. We want number eleven.'

Number eleven was a non-descript bungalow, similar to hundreds that were being churned out by various developers. They pulled up by the oil-stained grey flagged drive. 'Obviously not a gardener Sophie,' he said pointing to the frontage which consisted of a small square of lawn badly in need of a cut and one dead rose bush. They noticed dead flowers in the flowerpots which were placed either side of the front door. The plants were so far gone it was impossible to identify what they might have been in their heyday. Connor pressed the doorbell; a tune reminiscent of a TV commercial could be heard coming from inside the house. It was opened by, they assumed, Coalville's wife. She was dressed in ill-fitting trackie bottoms and a grubby top.

'Yes?'

In unison they both flashed their warrant cards. 'Does Spencer Coalville reside here?

'Er yes, why?'

'Is he in?'

She turned and shouted toward the rear of the house. 'Spence! Someone to see you.' She disappeared into the house as he arrived at the front door. They flashed their warrant cards once more.

'Yeah, what d'you want?'

'We'd like to ask you a few questions.'

'About what?'

'About your mate Robert Rogers. We just need to clarify a few things. D'you mind coming with us to the station?'

* * *

DI Evans parked conspicuously outside the headquarters of W&L Supermarkets. He pushed through the revolving doors and headed for reception where he received the practised smile. He held up his warrant card. 'I'd like to see Mr Williams please.' She picked up the phone, had a mumbled conversation then returned her eyes to DI Evans.

'His secretary will come to get you.'

'Thank you.' He waited until she arrived in the reception area.

'Mr Williams will see you now, I'll show you up.' She stopped outside the teak door, gave it a gentle push and stepped to one side. 'Please go in.'

Williams was sat behind his desk surrounded by files and paperwork.

'What can I do for you? I've already spoken to a couple of your colleagues.' He sounded exasperated, trying desperately to hide his annoyance but his body language gave him away. Evans sat down without being asked.

'Just a few questions to clarify things.'

Williams sat back in his chair; his arms folded defiantly.

Evans referred to his notes. 'It says here that from time to time you have employed Robert Rogers, is that correct?'

Williams leaned forward. 'Possibly. I did tell your colleagues that without checking the books I couldn't be sure.'

'Can you remember the last time you spoke to Mr Rogers?'

Williams slowly shook his head. 'No, I can't. Must have been months ago. I can only vaguely put a face to the name.'

Evans nodded. 'Mmm. Can you explain why there was a flurry of phone calls between yourself and Mr Rogers around the time of our initial investigation?'

'Was there? Must be a coincidence,' replied Williams, twisting his wrist to ostentatiously look at his watch.

DI Evans continued. 'Do you know a Spencer Coalville?'

Williams re-folded his arms. 'Well, like Rogers, I think I may have employed him from time to time to shift stock from one branch to another.'

'Can you remember the last time you spoke to him?'

Williams wrung his hands nervously. 'Again, probably months ago.'

He was suddenly thrown by Evans' change of questioning. 'Do you own a Mercedes Sprinter van, recently re-sprayed black?'

'Er, I don't think so.'

Evans took a deep breath before continuing. 'Would it surprise you to know our forensic team is currently analysing a van of that description, found at Rogers' premises...' he referred to his file, 'and registered to W&L Supermarkets.'

Williams remained silent.

Evans stood up. 'I think we should continue this conversation at the station. Please tell your secretary you may be away for some time whilst you are helping us with our enquiries.'

* * *

DCs Jones and Connor escorted Coalville back to the station and placed him in Interview Room 2. He was still waiting in the interview room when DI Evans entered the room.

'Good afternoon, Mr Coalville. Many thanks for agreeing to come in.'

'As if I had a choice!' he responded churlishly.

Evans smiled and sat opposite him. He opened a manila file and pushed a photo in front of Coalville. 'Recognise that person?' It was a photo of Afan Davies.

Coalville looked at it, shook his head and sat back in his seat. 'Never seen him before.'

Evans left the photo in place. 'So, you don't watch the television or read a newspaper? His photo has been in the papers almost every day for a year.' He let silence fill the gap. 'Humour me, have another look.'

Coalville leaned forward. 'Oh, yeah. I think I've seen him.'

Evans smiled weakly. 'Good.' He returned the photo to the file then pushed another photo across the table. 'Recognise him?'

Coalville nodded. 'Yeah, it's Robbo. We often do work together.'

'Who do you work for?'

Coalville squirmed in his seat. 'Lots of people.'

'Ever work for Dafyd Williams?' Coalville nodded. 'For the tape please'

'Yes!'

Evans continued. 'When did you last work for him?'

'Months ago.'

'When did you last speak to him?'

'I just said, months ago. We didn't often work for him.'

Evans returned the photo to the file. 'Can you explain to me why there was a sudden increase in phone calls between yourself, Mr Rogers and Dafyd Williams around the same time as Afan's disappearance?'

'Yeah, coincidence. Around that time, he wanted us to shift a load of stock from the Welshpool shop to Newtown.'

'Us?'

'Robbo and me.'

'Okay. Can you explain to me why we found your fingerprints on the magnetic signs from Afan's van?' The colour drained from Coalville's face. He was taken aback by this revelation. 'Do you realise that our evidence puts you and Rogers at the scene of the crime. That's a life sentence facing both of you.' Coalville was sweating and subconsciously wiped his top lip with the back of his hand. He was silent for some minutes. He finally succumbed to the pressure.

'It was Dafyd Williams' bloody idea,' he stammered, 'he wanted a clear run to expand his mobile business into the area that Afan Davies had established. He paid us to have a word, but it all went wrong. We got into a struggle with Davies, he slipped, banged his head on the counter. He was out like a light. It was an accident. You must believe me.'

Evans stood up. 'Thank you. A constable will be along in a minute to take your statement.'

Evans headed to Interview Room 3 where Williams was impatiently waiting, pacing backward and forwards. As Evans entered the room Williams stepped towards him, his face red with anger. 'I hope this isn't going to take long. I've got a business to run. Do I need a solicitor?'

'I don't know, do you? You have a right to one, but the choice is yours. If you've done nothing wrong, why ask for a solicitor? Please sit down Mr Williams.' Williams reluctantly sat down and Evans positioned himself opposite. 'I'll cut to the chase. We have a statement alleging that you were the initiator of a meeting between Afan Davies and two of your employees, Coalville and Rogers. They've told us you paid them to, shall we say, 'make arrangements' that Afan Davies ceased trading his mobile business.'

Williams scoffed. 'Rubbish.'

Evans opened his file, took out a photo then pushed it across the table to Williams. 'Do you recognise that vehicle?'

Williams pursed his lips and shook his head. 'Nope.'

Evans pursued his line of questioning. 'It's a Mercedes Sprinter, black, recently re-sprayed.'

'I told you, no, I don't recognise it.'

'If you look carefully, you can just about recognise the number plate.' Williams squinted and tried to look closer. 'The plate tells us it's registered to W&L Supermarkets.'

Williams sat back in his chair. 'Means nothing to me. I don't deal with the everyday admin.'

Evans took a deep breath. 'I have to tell you that we can place this vehicle at the scene at the time of Afan Davies' disappearance,' he added quickly, 'along with a swathe of phone calls between yourself and your two helpers around the same time.'

Williams smiled. 'Ah, now that rings a bell. That was the time we opened the new store in Newtown and they were taken on to shift a fair bit of stock over. Yeah. I remember now.' He looked at Evans in anger and pointed his finger at the DI. 'I hope you don't think I had anything to do with Davies' disappearance. I had a team meeting that day. All the shop managers were there. All day! I can give you their names to corroborate what I'm saying is true.'

Evans ignored the theatrics and continued. 'Any reason why we should have found the vehicle hidden away in a shed on Rogers' premises? There's a twelve-month gap between the incident, when you say they were working for you, and today's investigation, and yet the van is still in Rogers' shed.'

'Yeah, we use Rogers and Coalville on a regular basis and it seemed to make sense for one of them to keep the vehicle, ready to go, as it were. There's no room at Colevill's house, so it was kept at Rogers' place.'

Evans smiled and stood up. 'I think that's it for now Mr Williams. You can go for the time being. Thank you for being so helpful.'

At the next briefing an atmosphere of anticipation was palpable, everyone in the room expectantly waiting for their boss to inform them the case was completed. 'Morning ladies and gentlemen. Thank you all for your hard work. I have some good news and some bad news.' The team looked at each other wondering what was coming next. 'The good news is we're charging Robert Rogers and Spencer Coalville with the murder of Afan Davies. Sadly, the CPS say we don't have enough critical evidence to charge Dafyd Williams with conspiracy to murder. His alibi of a team meeting on that day stacks up.' There were murmurs of frustration around the room and a shaking of heads. 'Once again, thanks to the hard work by all of you, we have solved another case and we can finally provide closure for Mrs Davis. It'll be drinks all round, on me of course. Usual place.'

* * *

EPILOGUE

Spencer Coalville and Robert Rogers were both found guilty of murder and sentenced to twenty years each.

Robert Rogers' brother, Geoff, was charged and found guilty of aiding the perpetrators in the murder of Afan Davies and sentenced to five years.

Even with further intense investigation, no damning evidence was found to directly link Williams to the murder. Within twelve months of the finalisation of the investigation Dafyd Williams had expanded his mobile business to include all the geographical areas that Afan had developed for his own business.

Bronwen Davies, Afan's wife, sold the house near Newtown and moved to Llanelli in South Wales to be near her mum. They opened a small café called Bistro Afan.

Just Desserts

2010

Tony Howard successfully negotiated his way across two lanes of traffic to arrive at the doors of The Loxley pub.

It was a wonderful balmy evening. He'd spent the day doing, well, doing nothing. It was a welcome change to get up in a morning and be able to do just what he wanted. No pressure, no timetables, no cramming. Yesterday had been the last day of his A-level exams and tonight he was catching up with a group of friends to celebrate. He'd wandered around town, had a coffee, and bought himself a new pair of trainers and a novel, a relaxing change from textbooks. It had been a couple of stressful years studying economics and maths.

He pushed through the pub doors to be met with noise and the inevitable stale odour of beer. The pub consisted of a large room with three smaller rooms on either side. The room he was heading for was next to the bar, one that the group of friends had made their own over the past two years: The landlord wasn't too fussy about underage drinking. Acknowledging some school mates with a wave, he made his way through to the back room where he'd agreed to meet his friends.

Candice and Dave were already there, a glass of white wine and a pint in front of them. Tony grabbed a pint from the bar and was making his way back to the small room when Evie joined him at the bar, ordered her drink, and they entered the room together. They were all in a boisterous mood, as were many other students in the pub. The release of tension due to the end of exams was on full display. They had been a cohesive group, supporting each other whilst studying and revising. Candice and Dave were chuckling away at something that Candice had said and she snorted with laughter. 'Tony, I was just telling Dave. I felt so embarrassed when I came out of that economics exam. D'you remember the question on economic policy?' Tony nodded, wondering what was coming next. 'Where it asked you to compare monetary and expenditure policy?' Tony nodded again. 'Well, I knew it was to do with Milton Friedman and John Keynes,' she could hardly tell him for laughing, 'I only realised when I'd come out of the exam and was walking down Cubitt Street that I'd got confused and referred to Milton Keynes. I felt myself go red at the thought.'

Tony chuckled. 'Easy mistake to make when you're under stress. Was the rest of the exam, okay?' She nodded; her laughter now subsided.

He leaned forward and turned towards Dave and Evie. 'How did your history exam go Evie?'

She rocked her hand from side to side. 'Okay I suppose.' Evie wouldn't commit one way or the other. She would rather wait until the results came out.

'Dave?'

Dave blew his cheeks out. 'The phphysics was okay bbut the mmaths exam was a bit of a sstinker.'

Tony nodded and raised his glass. 'Cheers everyone. Glad to have got to the end of all that studying, at least for the time being. Fingers crossed we all get the grades we need for Uni.'

They all clinked glasses. 'We'll drink to that.' They sat in silence as they all pondered what could happen to them once the results came in.

Tony broke the silence.

'In four- or five-weeks' time our lives could change for ever.' The others looked at him and frowned. 'The results!' he prompted. 'The results will dictate whether we go to Uni.' He took a sip of his beer then continued. 'Whatever happens we will no doubt all go our separate ways and start new lives.' In unison they all responded with a forced smile and raised glasses. 'Cheers.'

The group consisted of a diverse selection of individuals.

Tony Howard: a tall lanky young man with unruly wavy hair and horn-rimmed glasses. He was very measured in the way he spoke, and his friends looked to him for advice and reassurance when situations got somewhat tricky. He very rarely wasted words. He was the steady, calm influence in the group. His main A-level had been economics.

Evie Marshall: was a chirpy, fun-loving girl. She was pretty, with soft, grey eyes and long blonde hair, usually worn in a ponytail. The other members of the group looked to her for morale and reassurance that 'things are never as bad as they seem'. She was studying history with the intention of teaching.

Candice Tully: was a reserved girl with dark, short, bobbed hair. On occasions she was her own worst enemy, seeing good in everyone only to be frequently let down. The other members thought she was rather naïve, bordering on scatty. She was studying economics.

Dave Grisholm: was a practical, down to earth individual. His dark brown hair was in the Boris Johnson style, his stubble slowly giving way to a beard. He kept to himself partly because of his slight stammer. Nothing seemed to bother him as he took each day in its stride. Nobody would have been surprised had he taken an oily spanner out of his jacket pocket or produced a carburettor for a 1938 Morris 8 series 4. He was studying the sciences, mainly physics.

Occasionally a fifth member joined the group, Carlton Williamson, who was studying accountancy. He was from a very wealthy family and tended to look down on the others. They didn't encourage him to join the group, but for some reason he hung out with them. Nobody really liked him. Dave often referred to him as an 'entitled git', and when he did voice his opinion, it came out as, 'He's an entitled gggit.' Dave thought Williamson was 'stuck up', snooty, a toff. Williamson was a lanky individual with a pale face and fair hair that constantly flopped over his eyes which he annoyingly flicked away with his hand. He had thin lips and when he spoke his top lip curled upward giving him a supercilious look. He'd been to public school and his accent exaggerated his upper crust demeanour, no northern flat vowels for him!

* * *

Away from the classroom the group were relaxed and at this moment were enjoying an evening out, revelling in each other's company. They were slowly becoming merrier and louder by the hour. Dave suddenly nudged Tony. 'Bbbloody hell, see wwwhat's walked in through the ddoor?' They all looked up to see Carlton swagger across to the bar. He must have passed some facetious remark to the barmaid from the look of disdain on her face. He impatiently pushed through the crowd to the group's table. The conversation immediately became subdued. The bubbly atmosphere disappeared. Carlton grabbed a chair and joined their table, a broad grin across his face, his usual annoyingly arrogant demeanour on full display.

'Hello losers. Wondering what you'll be doing in September once you've got your results,' he winked at Evie, 'Uni or flipping burgers at McDonald's?'

They all ignored him. It had been suggested on more than one occasion by Dave that the only reason Carlton tagged along was because they were never outright rude to him, whereas some of the other cliques he forced his way into often were. Williamson continued, determined to hog the conversation. 'Can't wait to get to Uni. Dad's had a word with a mate of his and lined me up with a job at an international bank.' He tapped the side of his nose. 'It's not what you know it's who you know.' He gulped down the last few dregs in his glass then pushed his chair back. 'Another? Come on Evie, give us a hand.' Evie reluctantly followed him to the bar, turning to the rest of them and raising her eyebrows. Dave was predictably the first off the mark.

'Wwwhat a ppain in the arse. Wwwhy he hovers around us I'll nnever know.'

Candice put her pennys-worth in. 'He's okay, just a bit full of himself.'

Tony stepped in to try to diffuse the situation. 'It's only a few weeks before we get our results then, hopefully, off to Uni and with a bit of luck that's the last we'll see of our friend...who's now coming back with the drinks.'

There was chorus of 'Cheers Carl.'

After another hour of barbed remarks and taunting from Williamson he suddenly jumped up from his chair. 'Gotta go guys. Sorry to leave you. People to see, places to go. That friend of dad's from the bank is coming round tonight for dinner and I'd like to catch him before he leaves. Ciao.'

Once he had disappeared through the door there was a sigh of relief.

'Phew, thank god he's gone.' The atmosphere immediately changed for the better.

They didn't allow the presence of Williamson to spoil the rest of the evening and continued enjoying themselves.

'Time gentlemen, please,' the landlord's voice called. Although he wasn't too fussed regarding under-age drinking, he was a stickler for closing on time. 'Please drink up, thank you.' Already the bar staff were doing the rounds collecting empty glasses and wishing the customers a safe journey home.

Evie stood with tears in her eyes. 'This could be the last time we meet. I'm off on hols next week with my parents down to Cornwall.' She scanned the faces staring up at her. She coughed to clear her throat. 'Once we've got our results, Tony's right, we'll all go our different ways.' She sniffled, her voice trembling. 'So, this could be it.' She reached down for her handbag. 'I wish you all the best.'

The others remained silent whilst taking in what she's said. They'd all come through O levels together, then A levels, but this really could be the end of their close association. As they all began to collect their belongings to make their way home, Tony suddenly spoke, holding up his hand.

'Whoa, sit down for a minute guys.' They looked questioningly at each other. Tony made eye contact with them all one by one then took a deep breath. 'This shouldn't be the end of our friendship.' He hesitated as though thinking through what he was about to say next. 'D'you remember the weekend school trip we had up in the Lakes after our O levels? Mr Burnham took us, remember?' The group imperceptibly nodded. 'We had a great time, didn't we?' Without waiting for a response, he continued. 'I've got a mad idea.' He put his arms on the table and leaned in closer to them. 'How about we make a commitment today. Right now. Tonight!'

Dave spoke up. 'And? Wwhat are you ssuggesting?'

Tony pursed his lips. 'I'm suggesting we all make a commitment to meet up together at that same hotel in the Lakes in ten years' time. Wouldn't that be good?' The others looked at each other not sure how to respond to what Tony was suggesting. Tony could see the hesitation on their faces and continued. 'We'd have loads to talk about after ten years. We will have been to Uni...or not, found work, maybe married, lived abroad, who knows, perhaps found fame and fortune! Come on, think of all the people who let their friendships drift. It'll be a milestone for us all.' That last statement clinched the deal. They all nodded with enthusiasm. Tony had a broad grin across his face. 'Look, it'll take a lot of pulling together, which I'm prepared to do. All I ask of you is that you promise to keep in touch with me. Let me know if you change email or phone number, that's all I need. When the ten years is up I'll organise the reunion.' He checked with them. 'Same one, The Belvedere, okay? Nearer the time I'll phone or email you to give you the details. Okay?' They raised their empty glasses which hadn't yet been collected and gave a resounding 'Yes!'

Tony leaned back in his chair and gave them a smile and a thumbs up.

2020

Ten Years Later

Tony sat in his office finalising a report on behalf of UK's largest wine importer, Bothy Wine Distributors.

Having left uni with a degree in economics, he had decided to take a year off and broaden his horizons by travelling. His intention was to tour south-east Asia via Australia, but he only got as far as Australia. During his time working in a bar in Sydney he made friends with Charles Wigmore, a regular at the bar. As luck would have it, Charles worked in the personnel department of a large bank in Sydney. Once he discovered Tony's qualifications, he suggested Tony come to his office for an interview as he thought would be well suited for work within the bank. Tony successfully negotiated a rigorous interview and was offered a position. Within a short time, he proved himself to be more than capable of working within the financial markets and quickly advanced through the organisation.

* * *

He was now back in the UK working on the fifth floor of the recently opened branch of the Aussie bank in Manchester. Since Brexit, the UK had no restrictions with whom it could do business, and the bank was keen to develop its UK presence. Business boomed between the two countries. The bank opened an office, first in London, then Manchester which had given Tony the perfect opportunity to move back to his home town.

The report he was working on was finalising the deal which Bothy Wines had established with a large West Australian wine producer. He smiled to himself as he stared out of the floor-to-ceiling windows which overlooked Piccadilly Gardens on one side and the Primark store on the other. Low clouds were forming across the skyline promising rain later in the day, so different from the almost constant sunshine of Down Under. His computer dinged. It was his calendar reminder: Ten-year catch-up! '*Wow, so soon. That crept up on me,*' he muttered to himself. His mind quickly did a mental check. Was his contact list up to date? He expertly clicked his way through the list then sat back and smiled. Yes, it was. His next job was to email them all to remind them of their promise all those years ago and give them some alternative dates for a weekend in the Lakes. Fingers crossed.

Within a week the group of friends had been successfully contacted. They'd all replied and enthusiastically agreed to the reunion. According to the emails they were all well, and keen to let each other know how well they were doing.

That same day Tony contacted the hotel which was now owned by a Mr and Mrs Braithwaite. The hotel had changed its name to Coniston Villa. He confirmed the booking for the second week in September. His final task was to confirm the date to the group, along with the new name of the hotel.

He sat back in his chair, his arms behind his head and indulgently imagined what the weekend would be like. The main tourist season would be dying down and thankfully would be less crowded. Hopefully, at that time of the year the weather should still be reasonable, the leaves on the trees would be a glorious gold, red and yellow. He thought about the camaraderie, the walks up the hills, the smell of heather, the calling of the curlews as they glided across the sky. He particularly remembered the welcoming hot evening meals after the strenuous walks. He sighed. *It's going to be a great weekend. Can't wait! Curious to know what they've all been doing for ten years.*

One by one each member of the group emailed their confirmation of the date.

* * *

The weekend finally arrived. Tony set off mid-morning on the Friday. He planned for a leisurely drive up the M6, to arrive at Coniston Villa by lunchtime to organise a welcome party for when the others arrived. He drove slowly up the driveway to the hotel, the gravel crunching under the wheels of his car. The lakeland weather was living up to its reputation; a slight drizzle covering his windscreen causing the wipers to screech. He'd been hoping for better weather than this. The hotel was a large Victorian mansion built from local granite blocks. It had large bay windows and dense ivy growing up the walls. The hotel was the same as he remembered, although the grounds had been further landscaped, the lawns were well-manicured and a topiary had been added. A rose garden had been created and it appeared the new owners had built an extension on the side of the hotel. He remembered noticing on their webpage that they now catered for weddings. As he made his way to the entrance he could see a gazebo at the far side of the garden, suitably shaded by a large elm tree. Several stone steps, with two pots of geraniums guarding either side of the lower step which led up to an impressive entrance hall. Tony pushed the door open to find himself in a bright and light reception area. Gentle piped musac played in the background. A receptionist, Patti, according to her name tab, was sitting behind a low desk and she welcomed him with a warm smile. 'Good afternoon, how may I help you?'

Tony placed his suitcase down and replied. 'Tony Howard. I have a room booked.'

She checked her computer and then looked up. 'Ah yes, you're part of a small party, is that right?'

He smiled, relieved that the computer system hadn't let him down. 'Yes, that's right.'

She handed a form to him. 'Would you complete this reservation form please.' He dutifully completed the form and handed it back. In return she gave him an electronic key and pointed to the lift. 'You're on the first floor, number 110. Enjoy your stay.' He carried his case into the lift, pressed the button for the first floor and within seconds he was slotting the key card into the door. The room was as airy and light as the reception area. The window overlooked the River Cluey and beyond that the heather covered hills. He stared for some time at the typical Lake District scene. Although the rain was now heavy and blurring the window he was always pleasantly surprised that, whatever the weather, the Lake District always looked beautiful. He smiled contentedly. *This is going to be a great weekend.*

Whilst waiting for the others to arrive he'd organised a champagne welcome in the communal lounge. It was a spacious lounge with a replica Adams fireplace, already laid with large logs should the weather suddenly take a turn for the worse. Paintings of the Lakeland area hung on the walls and a chess set was laid out on a large coffee table.

The rest of the party arrived in dribs and drabs and finally congregated in the lounge. There were lots of hugs, handshakes, laughter and excited chatter as they tried to talk over each other. Although it had been 10 years since they last met, it seemed like only yesterday that they were agreeing to this event, the passing of the years having had no negative impact on their friendships.

Tony raised his champagne flute. 'Welcome. It's good to see you all. Let's make sure we have a good weekend. Cheers.' The small group responded with a clinking of glasses, a loud 'cheers' and more chatter and laughter. Tony tapped his glass to attract attention. 'I've organised dinner here tonight. I thought we'd have an evening catching up on what we've been doing since we last enjoyed a drink together. Dinner's booked for seven.' Slowly the lounge emptied as they made their way back to their rooms to unpack, shower and prepare themselves for the evening.

Dinner was superb. Dave raised his fork to Tony, his mouth still full. 'You ddid wwell bbooking here, Tony, thththanks.' There was a chorus of 'cheers' again.

Tony smiled slightly abashed. 'I thought after dinner we'd stay in the hotel and tomorrow, after breakfast, head for the hills. An easy walk to start with. Are you all okay with that?' There were more positive responses. 'Back in here around nine this evening for another catch up session.'

By nine o'clock everyone was back in the lounge and prepared for a relaxing evening. 'I think we ought to have a quick round robin, an abridged version of what you have been doing over the past decade.' Tony glanced around him for agreement. 'I'll start.' He coughed to clear his throat. 'I'll keep it as succinct as I can. After uni, I had a year off and ended up in Oz, Sydney in fact, with the intention of spending maybe six months there, then off to south-east Asia.' He pulled a face in apology. 'Sorry to say I only got as far as Oz, where I was offered a job in one of the banks. Took it, moved up the ranks and eventually was offered a post in their new office in Manchester, of all places. End of story.'

Evie queried. 'Married? Engaged? Divorced?'

Tony laughed. 'None of the above, although there were a few near misses.' He looked at Evie. 'And you Evie?'

She reddened at having to speak. 'At uni I got better results than I expected. Did teaching practice in Cardiff Tech. They offered me a permanent position and that's where I am now, teaching history.'

Dave butted in. 'Mmmarried? Divorced?'

She shook her head and smiled. 'Neither, but I am engaged. His name is Pete, and he teaches drama.'

Dave offered his verbal resumé next. 'Quick sstory. Uni, Rrrolls Rroyce in Derby wworking on aerro engines, sshort engagement then sshe bbbuggered off with a mmarketing guy from Grrimsby. I ask you, Grrimsby!'

Tony turned to Candice. 'Candice, what's your story so far?'

She blushed and looked sheepishly at Evie. 'Not a lot to tell really. uni, like the rest of you. A sociology degree, then became a social worker in Greater London. I'm now a probation officer.' She took a second breath. 'It's really satisfying work. Some of the people I'm helping have had some lousy childhoods. It's my job to support them, help turn their lives around after they've come out of the prison system.'

Dave, displaying his cynical streak, had to ask his burning question. 'Don't a llot of ppeople have ddifficult childhoods bbut don't go on tto commmit crimes?' He glanced round at the others looking for support in his argument. 'Are there ssome ppeople you can't tturn around?'

Candice thinned her lips; no doubt having been asked this question many times. 'Everyone deserves a second chance.'

Dave couldn't leave go. 'Do yyou have sstats to sshow how mmany re-offend after ttheir pprobationary pperiod?' It was obvious from Candice's body language that she didn't want to pursue this line of questioning.

'A few,' she whispered.

Tony could feel the atmosphere in the group suddenly go cold and felt he had to change the subject. 'Can you all remember the last time we met?' he said jovially, 'it was on the last day of our A level exams. We were in The Loxley, remember?'

It lightened the cooling atmosphere in the group.

Candice continued, 'Oh, yeah. I was fretting over my economics question. D'you remember, Tony, when I got economists mixed up and referred to Milton Keynes.' They all had a good long chuckle.

Dave stepped in once more. 'Wwhat I ddo remember is tthe bbastard Ccarlton Wwilliamson tuurning up. What a ppain that gguy wwas.' There was a collective groan from the rest of them in agreement.

Tony's face suddenly blackened. 'Don't talk to me about that bastard.' The other three looked at him hoping he would elaborate. Tony looked at the group undecided whether to tell them what had happened. Dave raised his eyebrows and Evie and Candice looked at him curiously as to say, 'Why?'

Tony bit his bottom lip before deciding to tell them. 'He killed my sister!'

Candice put her hand to her mouth in shock then said, 'He did what?'

Tony leaned forward so he didn't have to raise his voice. 'He was home from uni at the Easter break and took my sister out for a drink with some other pals. Long story short, he was drunk, speeding, took a corner too fast and hit a tree. He was hardly injured, my sister died on the spot.'

Evie spoke with genuine concern in her voice. 'Was he prosecuted?'

Tony scoffed. 'He was charged but his dad's fancy lawyer managed to get him off.' He shook his head and stared at the floor desperately avoiding eye contact with the others who remained silent.

Evie spoke again, this time with some venom in her tone. 'He should have gone to jail. He's evil!' The others looked askance at her. She looked embarrassed, but then realised the rest of the group expected her to explain her outburst. She made direct eye contact with Candice and gave an imperceptible shake of her head.

Only two days prior to the reunion, she'd confided to Candice in an email that Williamson had raped her. A year ago, a close friend of Evie's had invited her to a birthday party; little did she know Williamson would be there. He hadn't changed: he was still the obnoxious, overbearing snob he'd always been. After a few drinks he was out of control and having seen Evie heading to the toilet, on her way out, he took his chance.

She didn't want Candice to embarrass her in front of the two boys by saying that she knew what had happened to Evie. Candice returned the eye contact to reassure her that her secret was safe. Evie felt obliged to say something to justify her outburst so quickly. 'Er, remember when we all went to the Lakes after our exams?' She looked around her for acknowledgement then continued, a tremor in her voice and tears in her eyes. 'I can't remember now what caused him to hit me but something triggered his temper. He hit me and knocked me over. I slipped down a step and twisted my ankle.'

Tony asked, 'Why didn't you report it?'

Evie looked away. 'I don't know, I just didn't.' Tony put his arm around her but didn't say a word.

Dave cleared his throat. 'Ahem, if it's any cconsolation, he rripped me off for tten ggrand. The bbastard!'

Tony looked angry. 'How? What happened?'

Dave shook his head. 'It doesn't mmatter, the ffact rremains hhe did.'

Candice looked sheepish then looked pleadingly at Tony. 'He's coming this weekend.'

'He's what?' he barked.

She began to panic. 'I'm so sorry, I phoned him two weeks ago to invite him.'

'You did what?' He shouted even louder.

'He was part of the group at the time. He used to hang around with us. I just thought it would be nice to invite him.'

Tony was livid. 'But you should have known he wouldn't be welcome!'

'I know nobody liked him at the time, but people do change. He's older and, hopefully, more mature. I phoned him to tell him we were planning a weekend away. He said he's coming. He phoned me earlier to tell me he would be arriving late; he had a meeting or something.' She held her hands to her face. 'I'm sorry.'

Dave stood up. 'Christ, I'm ggoing to bbed. See you in the mmorning.'

Tony nodded. 'Maybe we all call it a day. Make an early start tomorrow. The brisk climb will do us good.' They all trooped up the stairs together, their mood at an all-time low.

* * *

Tony had a disturbed night's sleep. The long-awaited weekend he'd organised was about to be ruined by the appearance of a man they all detested. At breakfast the next morning the sour atmosphere could still be felt. Their breakfasts were eaten in silence, the conversation restricted to monosyllables. The fun had been drained from what was supposed to have been a joyous weekend. Candice sat next to Tony and leaned into him. 'I waited up last night after you'd all gone to bed, but he still hadn't arrived by ten, so I decided to go to bed. I checked with reception first thing this morning. Carlton checked in just after we'd all gone to bed. Another two minutes and I would have caught him.' Tony nodded but didn't respond verbally.

* * *

There was an urgency amongst the group to quickly finish breakfast and get out onto the surrounding hills before their nemesis appeared. They were eager to start the day and headed for the car park. Candice called after them. 'Don't we need to wait for Carlton?' They ignored her question and continued walking out. She felt embarrassed, shrugged her shoulders and reluctantly followed them.

The rain had stopped and there was a cool, brisk wind whipping across the car park as they piled into Tony's car. The climb he'd suggested was a five-mile drive away. It was one they'd done on their last visit ten years ago. The conversation warmed up as they drove along the winding lanes. The leaves on the trees were turning a beautiful kaleidoscope of colour. Those that had fallen were strewn across the lanes and swirled into the air as Tony's car glided past. Candice continued to apologise to her friends. She realised she'd made a grave error in inviting Carlton Williamson, a man she knew in her heart was not the most congenial of people. Her training in social work, one of seeing good in everyone, had influenced her decision, putting Williamson ahead of her friends. She'd ruined their weekend.

Tony filled the silence. 'We're nearly there, just around the next corner is the lay-by where I'll park. It's a good base for us.' The sky had cleared by the time they'd arrived at Mumfty Mount, a comparatively easy climb with wonderful views from the top. They all clambered out of the car whilst Tony opened the tailgate and began to extract rucksacks and waterproofs. 'We need to do another check before we start off, guys.' He waited until the others had sorted out their belongings, then continued. 'Check - thick socks and boots, waterproofs, hats.' He looked to see if they were all nodding, then he referred again to his checklist. 'Check your rucksacks – lunch, water, compass, choccy, additional sweater. Are we all tickety-boo?' They called out in the affirmative. 'Sorry to be so pedantic, but you know as well as I do that within minutes of getting close to the top, low cloud or mist can come down or we might get separated, so we need to be prepared. I told reception this morning approximately what time we'd be back. They'll notify the appropriate authorities if we're not back on time.'

They all stood for a minute to look up at the hill in front of them. The top was already in cloud. It was possible to see the path they intended to take as it snaked, twisting left and right, making its way to the top. Already there were other walkers half-way up.

'Pphew, tthey're up early,' Dave exclaimed. 'I ccan't wwait to get going, ccome on, llet's enjoy the dday.' Dave, as cynical as he was, put the group in a better mood. His come-day, go-day attitude, annoying though it was at times, was good when friends were at a low ebb...and the thought of Williamson arriving had certainly put the damper on things. They crossed over an old, well-worn, wooden bridge which took them to the base of the hill. The path underfoot was stony and lumpy with tree roots, but well-worn with years of heavy boots tramping up and down. The climb provided them with an adrenalin rush, of pushing the body and stimulating rarely-used muscles. They might suffer the next day from aches and pains or blisters on their feet, but that was part of being able to appreciate the wonderful views from the top. By the time they reached the summit the clouds had dispersed and the sky was a clear blue. Exhausted, yet exhilarated, they dropped to the ground and shrugged off their rucksacks, then urgently delved into them to retrieve their water bottles and chocolate bars...the reward for the climb. Evie leaned back, her head resting on her rucksack, watching the black silhouette of a buzzard circling above them.

'I could come here very week. I just love it.' Tony swigged from his water bottle and stared out over the pastures below and the hills in the distance. Lake Keswick to the right shimmered in the sunlight. Sheep grazed on the upper slopes of the hills. Large outcrops of rock appeared a dazzling white against the lush green of the fields. More walkers arrived at the top, some panting and wheezing, acknowledging the group with just a wave of their hands. The friends sat to enjoy their lunch and chat. The trek up the hill had been good for them. It had dispersed some of the gloom that seemed to encircle them at the start of the walk. Even Candice, the unwitting source of their anxiety, began to relax.

'I'd forgotten how beautiful the Lakes are. Living in London doesn't give me the chance to pop up for the weekend, maybe I should make the effort.'

Tony butted in. 'Maybe we should have another reunion, but not leave it so long. Five years?' he asked tentatively.

'Fffive years is okay with mme,' said Dave as he glared at Candice, which made her feel uncomfortable. 'Bbut just ffor the ffour of uus...not ffive.'

Candice reddened. 'I have apologised. What more can I say?'

Once more Tony tried to lighten the mood. 'Hey, the four of us are more important to each other than to let past events by one individual get between us, no matter how ghastly they were.' He checked his watch. 'It's time we made tracks.' The steady walk downhill was treacherous in places, the loose stones causing their feet to slip and twist. Tony called from the back of the line. 'Take your time, we don't want any mishaps going down.' Silence descended once more as the group concentrated on their footwork. There was also a noticeable drop in the air temperature.

The conversation on the drive back to the hotel was limited as they were each immersed in their own thoughts of what or rather, who, awaited them on their return to the hotel.

* * *

Tony swung into the hotel car park, then suddenly stopped. 'What the...!' They all stared through the windscreen to see several police vehicles spread across the car park. Several people dressed in hazard suits were coming in and out of the hotel, some carrying bags and placing them in a large plain white van. A gurney carrying a body was being placed into the back of an ambulance. Thick low clouds had suddenly appeared. The purple-black sky was a stark contrast against the yellow and blue chequered police cars and their flashing lights. Tony repeated, 'What the..! What's happened?' Their concentration on the scene in front of them was suddenly interrupted by a knocking on the driver's side window. It was a police officer who was wearing a hi-vis jacket and circling his hand as an indication to roll down the window.

'Excuse me, sir. Are you a guest here?'

Tony nodded. 'Yes I am, we all are.'

The officer waved them over to the far side of the car park. 'Please park over there and as you enter the hotel give your names to the officer on the door.' Tony indicated he understood and slowly drove his way around the police vehicles to the far side. As they made their way to the front entrance lugging all their belongings, they looked around them. People were standing in small groups, others were staring out of the upstairs windows, all wondering the same thoughts. *What the hell was going on?* They gave their names to the officer on the door as instructed who ticked off their names on the clipboard he was holding and instructed them to wait in reception.

'A police officer will escort you from reception to your rooms to leave your rucksacks and coats then show you into the lounge. You will be asked to stay there until you are called to be interviewed.' They all nodded and stood quietly. The receptionist emerged out of the door next to the reception desk. She looked flustered, her eyes darting wildly around her.

Tony leaned into her and whispered. 'What's going on?'

She shook her head seemingly reluctant to answer, but eventually blurted out. 'It's your friend Mr Williamson. He was found dead in his room this morning.' She burst into tears and retreated back into the office she'd emerged from just as an officer came down the stairs. The female officer turned to the four after referring to the clipboard then smiled, at the same time flicking her hair over her ear.

'Tony Howard and Candice Tully?' They nodded. 'Please follow me.' She turned to the other two. 'I won't be a minute, please wait here.' Tony and Candice picked up their belongings and trooped behind the officer up the stairs. Within a few minutes the officer had escorted Tony and Candice back downstairs and into the lounge. She then turned to the other two. 'Evie Marshall and David Grisham?' They already had their belongings in their hands. They nodded and obediently followed the officer.

Other guests were already waiting in the lounge. The silence was unbearable. No one was speaking, avoiding eye contact with each other. They looked like figures frozen in time. Some were leaning back in their seat, eyes closed, legs crossed. Others leaned forward their head in their hands, awaiting their turn to be interviewed. The group of four friends were identified as a priority for interview, the victim being one of their party. The silence across the room was broken when a strong voice called, 'Mr Tony Howard?'

Tony half-raised his hand, half-rose from his seat. 'That's me.'

'Please come with me.'

Tony was shown into a small room, no doubt used by the hotel as a meeting room. In the middle of the room was an oak table and four chairs. On the far side of the room was a large fireplace, a fire prepared, but unlit. Blinds at the window were half-closed. In the corner was a narrow sideboard with tea making facilities. 'Please take a seat.' The voice belonged to a rotund man, slightly balding with a ruddy face. He wore a white shirt and blue tie. Standing to Tony's left, DI Mick Donovan introduced himself. His DS was already seated. She was Sally Downy, who gestured for him to take a seat. Mick Donovan repeated the command, 'Please, take a seat.' Tony sat down and put his hands on his lap and waited for what was coming next.

Donovan opened a file which he had in front of him. 'What was the purpose of you all meeting up?'

'We hadn't seen each other for ten years...since our A levels. It was a reunion'

The DI nodded. 'I understand Carlton Williamson was one of your party, is that correct?'

'Yes.'

'How long have you known him?'

Tony shuffled in his seat. 'About 15 years. We were at school together.'

'Was he a close friend of yours?'

Tony hesitated to the point the DI looked up from his writing notes to prompt him. 'Er, not really.'

'Then why was he a member of your party. You say the weekend was a reunion.'

Tony nodded then continued. 'Yes it was. I organised it, but I didn't invite him. Another one of the party did.'

'Who?'

'Candice Tully.'

The DI referred to the list of names in front of him and nodded. 'Why didn't you invite him?'

Tony hesitated even longer.

'Mr Howard, could you answer the question please?'

Tony coughed then. 'I don't like him,' he blurted out knowing sooner or later the police would find out the true relationship between himself and Williamson.

'Why?'

Tony looked angry. 'He killed my sister.'

Mick Donovan put his pen down and leaned back in his chair. 'Like to tell me a bit more about that?'

Tony took a deep breath. In for a penny in for a pound! 'Whilst he was at uni he came home for one of the breaks, took my sister out, got drunk and crashed his car. My sister was killed.'

'Oh, I see, I'm sorry. Was Williamson charged?'

'Yes, but his parents' fancy lawyers got him off.'

'If you don't like him then why did…' he referred to his list again, 'Candice Tully invite him?'

'He was always hanging around on the edge of our group and Candice thought he should be invited. I think she felt sorry for him.' Before the DI had time to ask the next question Tony continued. 'She's a probation officer – thinks there's good in everyone. She thought maybe he'd changed.'

'Did he need to change?'

Tony nodded. 'Nobody liked him. He was an obnoxious character.'

'Was there no one in the group that liked him?'

Tony shook his head. 'Candice maybe, more out of pity, but no one else.'

'Can you tell me what time you all went to bed?'

'Er, around nine-thirty…except Candice she wanted to wait up for Carlton.'

The DI smiled. 'Thank you. That'll be all for now.'

Next to be called was Dave. An officer called out, 'David Grisham?'

He stood up, followed the officer and was shown into the meeting room that had just been vacated by Tony. The DI introduced himself and DS Downy then offered Dave a seat. Dave looked more confident than Tony and sat up straight, smiling to the two officers.

'How well did you know Mr Williamson?'

'Nnot tthat wwell. He wwas alwways on tthe pperiphery of our ggroup. He was a ppain in tthe arse tto bbe hhonest.'

'In what way?'

'Mmouthy, a ssmmart arse and, oh bboy wwas hhe a nname drropper. I'll nnever uunderstand why hhe tagged allong with our llot...and hhe sscammed mme out of a llot of mmoney.'

The DI raised his eyebrows. 'How?'

'He cconned mme into invvesting in a ccompany. Hhe ttold mme it wwas on advvice ffrom his empployers, a llarge internnational bbank. I ttrusted him beccause it sseemed to bbe bbacked bby his bbank.'

'And yet you didn't go to the police?'

'Nno. It wwas my own ffault...ccaveat emptor and all tthat.'

'So, you didn't like him and yet he was invited to the get-together. Why?'

'Yyou'd bbe better aasking Ccandice. She's tthe ddo-ggooder.'

'Thank you, Mr Grisham. Don't go too far we may need to speak to you again.'

Next in was Candice. The DI went straight in. 'I understand you were the one who invited Mr Williamson to the reunion.'

She teared up and nodded. 'Yes. I wish I hadn't.'

'So why did you?'

'I know he was a pain when we were all at school, particularly during our A levels, but I thought he might have matured, you know, grown up. The others were furious when they knew he was coming.' She wiped her eyes with a tissue. 'I wish I hadn't.'

'Did you like him?'

She shrugged her shoulders. 'I didn't dislike him, I thought he was just okay, I felt sorry for him.' Then she added something that alerted the DI. 'I can see why all the others had reason not to like him.'

He sat back in his seat tapping his pen in the palm of his hand. 'Does that include Evie Marshall?'

'You'd be better asking Evie.'

Donovan stood up. 'Rest assured, we will. Thank you.'

Evie was shown into the room. She looked pensive. 'Please take a seat Evie. We've just got a few routine questions to ask you.' She sat down, twisting a handkerchief through her fingers. The DI smiled. 'It seems that no one liked Mr Williamson, is that correct?' She nodded, taking a deep breath. 'Did you like him, Evie?'

She shook her head and answered quite firmly. 'No. I did not.'

'Could you explain why?'

Evie looked first to the DS and then to Donovan. She started to become tearful then blurted out. 'He raped me!'

The two officers looked at one another before the DI continued. 'When? Whilst you were here in this hotel?'

'No. about a year ago...at a party...he was drunk.'

'Did you report it to the police at the time?'

She shook her head. 'No.'

'Why?'

'I knew he was well connected. His family had access to good lawyers.'

The DS could see Evie was becoming upset. 'Can I get you a coffee or a tea?'

She nodded. 'A coffee, please.'

Downy stood up. 'Stay here Evie, I'll go and get you a coffee. The DI and I are done here for the time being.'

Once Evie had had her coffee and settled down again she returned to the lounge where the rest of them were waiting for her. In the meeting room DI Donovan turned to Downy. 'So, what do you think?'

'In a nutshell, three of them have a motive.'

The DI agreed. 'I'm going to suggest the other guests return home. Make sure we have all their contact details. We'll close the hotel whilst the forensics team do what needs to be done. Once we've got something from forensics we'll haul the four main suspects in again. Where do they all live?'

Downy checked her notes. 'Just our luck sir. They're spread all over the place. Tony is in Manchester, David in Derby, erm, works at Rolls Royce, Candice in London and poor Evie lives in Cardiff.'

'My gut feeling – and my money – is on one of the four we've just interviewed. It's too much of a coincidence for one of their party to die and all have their own motives for seeing the back of him, apart from Candice Tully. We'll eliminate the other guests. How many others are there by the way?'

'Twelve.'

The DI continued. 'Double-check to make sure there isn't a link between the victim and any of the other guests. If not, we'll leave them for now and concentrate our efforts on those four.'

Downy added. 'I did speak to the receptionist who told me Mr Williamson didn't arrive until just gone 10pm when she was about to finish her shift. She also said the others had gone to bed by that time, or at least she assumed they had. Apparently, they'd been in the lounge all evening, but when she went in later, they weren't there, only Candice Tully. Tully said the others had gone to bed and she was waiting up to check that Mr Williamson arrived and booked in okay.'

The DI hesitated for a second. 'Do we know why Mr Williamson was late in arriving?'

'All he said to the receptionist was that he'd been held up on a video call to New York.'

He straightened his back as though with renewed energy and clapped his hands together. 'Right. Let's hope forensics move quickly and have something for us. You go home for the weekend; I'll shout if anything urgent comes up.'

'Thanks, boss.'

'Before you go please remind forensics to check the cars.'

'Will do.'

'Cheers, see you Monday.'

* * *

The next day Donovan and Downy, with high expectations, made their way to the single storey building a block further down from the police station, the home of the pathology and forensics departments. They grabbed a couple of take-aways and arrived at the science block after a ten-minute walk. It was an old crumbling block due for replacement. No money had been spent on it for the past decade and it showed. The paintwork was peeling, the windows decidedly grubby and the limited car park was overgrown with weeds which had emerged between the cracks in the concrete. They pushed through the main doors and headed down the corridor pushing through several badly scratched, thick plastic, double doors to one marked 'Pathology'. As they entered they could see Michelle Aston at the far end of the room talking to a group of her colleagues. She waved and held up one finger to indicate she would be with them in one minute. Michelle was one of a team of three pathologists. The two officers were relieved when they saw it was Michelle on duty. She was a no-nonsense individual and could be trusted to double-check every detail.

'Morning, Mick, Sally, come into my office.' Her office was somewhat cramped, consisting of a desk and two visitor chairs pushed close together. Along one wall were several grey filing cabinets and on top, a pile of boxes and a large plant which trailed almost to the floor.

'I've not got a lot to tell you. The deceased died of a blunt force trauma to the back of the head. I would suggest that the weapon was a hammer or something similar, one with a flat face. There was a mark on the skull in the shape of the weapon.' She looked up from her file. 'Have you found the weapon? Have forensics found anything on the clothing?'

Donovan shook his head. 'Sadly, no, and we haven't found the weapon.'

Michelle continued. 'If you can find the weapon I can match it to the mark on the head.'

'Anything else?'

She took a deep breath. 'Only that his arms showed signs of drug use. He was a user, but that's not what killed him. It was the hit to the back of the head....sorry, that's all I've got.'

Donovan thanked Michelle for the information. 'We're off to see your colleagues next door.'

Colin Preston, head of forensics, acknowledged them as they entered his domain. He had a serious look on his face and met them half-way across the room shaking his head.

'What have you got for us, Colin?'

'Nothing. Absolutely nothing.'

'Seriously Colin, nothing?'

'No. We've checked for DNA, fibres, all the usual checks, both in the room and in the cars you asked us to prioritise. Nothing! There's nothing on the guest room door handle either. Whoever did this must have been wearing gloves. There was blood everywhere but no definable prints. It's as though nobody had been in the room. Whoever is guilty of this act was thorough. No trace of anything. My gut feeling is whoever did this was wearing a hazard suit. Last time we spoke you hadn't found the weapon. Has that been found?'

The DI shook his head, his lips firm. 'No,' he said frustratingly.

Back at the police station, Donovan and Downy sat re-reading the statements from the four friends. 'Let's look at the facts. Williamson arrives, late I might add, to a reunion to which he wasn't welcome. He was invited by our Miss Tully, a probation officer who knew he wasn't liked by the rest of them, but took it upon herself to invite him anyway. Agreed?'

'Yes, agreed.

The other three have very strong motives to have committed the offence. We still need confirmation as to why Williamson checked in late.' Donovan sat back in his chair. 'Look, while I go through their statements again will you get in touch with Williamson's firm, get confirmation he was on a video call. See if it would justify his late arrival.'

'Will do.' She jumped up and left the room. She was back before the DI had read through the first interview and planted a cup of coffee in front of him. 'We've hit a brick wall again boss.' Whilst he struggled with the sealed top on his coffee cup, she explained, 'I spoke to the security guy at the bank and he confirmed that Williamson was still in the building until late. He knows for sure because he helped set up the video call for him. He says it was to New York. Williamson's explanation stands up.'

Donovan ran his fingers through his hair. 'Bloody hell Sally. We've got nothing.' He blew out his cheeks in frustration then counted on his fingers. 'We've got three, possibly four, if we include Candice Tully, dead cert motives and nothing else. No DNA, no fingerprints, no fibres. It sounds like a professional hit, but the three on our priority list are not professionals. Not even close. So, what are we looking at?' Sally Downy didn't have any answers to offer. Donovan sat up straight having decided to send forensics in again to look at all the rooms and outlying grounds. They needed to check litter bins on the roads leading to the hotel where a weapon could have been ditched and had them check the sewers. Williamson's background needed checking out regarding his drug taking. Did he have contacts with pushers who are on the police databases? Anything that could give him a lead!

The group were eventually dismissed by the police as they had nothing to hold them on, but were warned they may need to be re-interviewed. Dave suggested the four of them call in at the local pub before heading home. They drove into the large car park of the Rose and Crown. There were already a few cars parked. A coach at the far end was disgorging what looked like a pensioners' day out. 'Come on, let's get lunch. Some of you have a long journey ahead.' The main area inside the pub was spacious, having several smaller rooms off the main dining area. A young waitress welcomed them and showed them to a table at a bay window. The window was at the rear of the pub and overlooked a pond and beyond that, a small copse. They studied the menu in silence and only spoke when the waitress came to take their orders. The drinks arrived first which the group welcomed if only to have something to do rather than having to talk.

Candice eyed the others one by one, in silence.

Which one did it? Or was it all three? Or was it someone else entirely.

Did Tony organise the trip with an ulterior motive? Did Dave do it? He was the most impetuous. How about Evie? They say the quietest ones are the worst.

Tony broke the ice. 'Well, that wasn't the weekend I had in mind.' The others murmured in agreement. Candice put her drink down and cleared her throat.

'I know some of you didn't like Carlton, but he didn't deserve what happened to him.'

Dave couldn't resist voicing his opinion. 'I ffor one am gglad he's ggone. I have nno ssympathy for the gguy.'

Candice stepped in again. 'You can't mean that Dave. He is a human being you know!'

Dave looked at her with contempt. 'A nnasty pperson yyou mean. Hhe's got his jjust ddesserts. He nnever gave a thhought ffor the ffeelings of others.'

Evie reddened. 'I have to say I think he deserved what happened to him.'

The others looked at her amazed at her outburst. It was most unlike Evie. She was the shy one who usually kept her views to herself.

Candice shouted. 'Evie! Please!'

Evie looked around the table for support. 'Well, I do. He did get what he deserved.'

Tony leaned across and held Evie's hand. 'She has a point. That guy did the dirty on all of us.' He saw the look on Candice's face. 'Maybe not you Candice, but the rest of us have suffered one way or another. How many other people has he cheated or ruined that we don't know about?' The meals arrived and were eaten in silence.

* * *

As they said their goodbyes with hugs and kisses, devoid of the usual banter, the atmosphere was stilted. A brisk wind had set in whisking dust and loose paper across the car park. Patrons ran to their cars fastening their coats and pulling up their collars. Dave had the last say as he climbed in his car. 'I still say hhe ggot wwhat he deserved. His jjust desserts!'

Tony was the last to leave, he stood by his car and watched Evie, the last of them, disappear down the road. He sat in his car and pondered over the last forty-eight hours. As he turned the ignition he spoke out loud to himself.

'Just desserts! That sums it up exactly!'

DI Donovan and DS Downy were becoming increasingly frustrated as they'd hit brick walls whichever way they turned. The investigation into Williamson's drug taking went nowhere. His contact was a small-time pusher. After more extensive searches of the hotel grounds the weapon had not been found. Neither the path lab nor forensics could offer them any new leads. Donovan was convinced he was looking at a professional hit. There was no critical evidence that directly linked any of the four main suspects to the murder of Carlton Williamson. Other priority cases came across the DI's desk and so the murder of Carlton Williamson was put on the back burner.

Five years on and still no one had been charged. The case was relegated to the cold cases file. Hopefully another detective, another time, another investigation, could review the files and resolve the case.

Just desserts, indeed!

8

Killer Code

2023

A small queue was excitedly gathering outside Rosco's Book Emporium in Hay-on-Wye, some were pressing their faces to the window to see if they could get a glimpse of the person they were all so excited about. In the darkened window was a full-size cut-out of their hero. They were all here for the book signing by Jack Rosario, crime writer. This was the famous annual book festival. The weather was perfect. A typical English spring day, clear blue sky, a slight breeze and the promise of a hot day.

Hay-on-Wye pronounced Y Gelli Gandrill in Welsh, boasts a Norman fortified castle known as Hay Castle which overlooks the town. It was built in the twelfth century after the Norman invasion and was rebuilt after severe damage during the Welsh rebellion led by Owain Glyndwr in 1401 and again in 1460 during the War of the Roses. It was subsequently converted to a mansion house in the late seventeenth century. Its neighbouring towns include Symonds Yat, Ross- on-Wye, Clun, Bishops Castle and Ludlow. It has a population of only two thousand which explodes to eighty thousand during the ten days of the festival. Sponsored by the Daily Mail, it takes place during the last week in May and first week in June. Hay is situated in the Wye Valley in the county of Powys, Wales. Half the town is in Wales the other half in England. It sits at the edge of the Brecon Beacons, an area of outstanding beauty. However, it's also the training ground for the UK military.

Rosco's Book Emporium is snugly situated in a granite stone building whose origins are lost in the mists of time. The shop was originally located on the opposite side of the road in a three-storey building which dated back to 1835, known as the Cheese Market, but some years ago it had been converted to luxury apartments. If only walls could talk.

At the hallowed entrance of the famous Rosco's Emporium is another full-size cut-out of Jack Rosario leaning against a small desk which was piled high with his latest book, *Death Wish*. The walls are lined with black shelving from floor to ceiling, the walls themselves are painted a deep red to match the carpet. In a corner by the window was a large table and chairs which allowed customers to peruse any potential purchase in comfort.

Jan Crecy, Rosario's agent, having scanned the queue, returned to Jack's side. She had been the push behind Jack's success. She was a doer, a brisk, no-nonsense woman. She was rather rotund which was accentuated by her short stature. Her blonde hair was pinned up in a chignon and she had startling grey eyes. Rosario was sitting at the back of the store behind a large desk surrounded by his books. He was checking that his pen was working by scribbling on a spare piece of paper. Jack was a wiry, white-haired character. He had discovered his gift for writing later in life, his background originally being in high finance. He smiled as he saw her approaching. 'How do they look? Hostile? Friendly? Do they look the type that have thick wallets?'

She sat beside him, her face grim. 'Not as many punters as we'd like.' She stood up and patted his shoulder. 'I'll talk to you about it when we've finished here.'

The doors were finally opened and the queue flowed into the shop. Some already had books in their hands to be signed, others grabbed copies from the shelves, queued to pay for them, before queuing again for the signing. Jack didn't enjoy these sessions. He was happy writing books but shied away from the public. It had to be done and he approached each session stoically, putting on a front, a façade. Each signing was virtually the same dance. A forced smile from Jack, a nervous smile from the fan, the obligatory question: 'What would you like me to write?'

'Just my name, 'Mary'. He would scribble: *Best wishes Mary, Jack Rosario,* another smile and the fan was gone and on to the next one. He appreciated his fans; after all, they'd made him a name to be reckoned with in the world of crime writing. However, he felt very uncomfortable when dealing with his public face to face. The allotted three hours of signing came to an end. There hadn't been as many fans as in previous years and Jack sadly recognised the fact. His agent returned to his side.

'Finished?' He nodded wearily and sighed. He was acutely aware that sales weren't going well. She put on a smile. 'Cleo's?'

'Cleo's?'

'The coffee shop round the corner.'

He put his pen away and tidied up the desk then followed her out. Cleo's was on the north side of the cobbled market square between a deli and yet another book shop. There were now over twenty bookshops, selling both new and second-hand books, in this tiny town. Jack found a quiet corner, at least as quiet as it could be on this busy weekend, while Jan organised their coffees. Jack hoped he wouldn't be recognised and concentrated on looking down at the table until Jan returned.

She dived straight into the conversation. 'I spoke to your publisher yesterday, they're not happy with the sales of the last two books.'

He scoffed. 'And d'you think I am?'

She ignored his comment and moved on. 'They're getting cold feet and are reluctant to re-new your contract.'

Initially he'd been given a six-year contract, six books in six years. The last two for a variety of reasons had not sold in the volume the publisher needed. He nodded resignedly. 'I know,' he looked at her pleadingly, 'but you already know some of the reasons.' She nodded and took a sip of coffee.

* * *

Jack Rosario, his real name James Mumford, had originally worked within a large financial institution. Unfortunately, it was discovered that two members of staff had been involved in fraudulent dealings. The indictment said, 'money laundering.' As the boss, he was responsible and was sentenced to five years jail. He was released after three years as new evidence was presented to the courts which showed he was innocent of any involvement. During his time in Strangeways jail, he kept a diary of his experiences and later converted these into a novel. It was his first foray into writing, and it was an instant success. The next few books constantly hit the best sellers list. At the same time as his increased success, his wife surprisingly commenced divorce proceedings against him. This shook him to the core and his writing suffered. He couldn't eat, sleep, or concentrate on his work. In his progressively worsening emotional state he repeatedly missed the publishing deadlines for book number four. In a desperate attempt to give the publishers a book to be ready for the Christmas rush, he retrieved out of his 'bottom drawer' half an idea he'd thrown together several years earlier, dusted it down, padded it out and presented to the publishers what he knew only too well was a weak effort. It deservedly received very poor reviews. Book number five followed the same track. He shook his head in despair and appealed to Jan.

'That TV series didn't help. Lousy script, casting, acting, and worst of all, lousy directing. It was panned by everyone and I don't blame them.'

She attempted a smile and drained the last few drops of coffee from her cup. 'Let's hope *Death Wish* does better.' She collected her belongings and stood up. 'I've got to get to Bristol this afternoon so I'll be off. I'll give you a ring during the week.'

As Jack watched her go, he slowly picked up his cup to sip his now cold coffee, when he sensed someone standing to his right. He looked up to see Della Mitchell, wife of John Mitchell, aka David Kutzi, his main competitor in the world of publishing. Depending on which propaganda you read both were acclaimed 'King of Crime'.

Della was an attractive woman. She appeared to be in her mid-forties, slim with short dark hair, olive skin and coal-black eyes. 'Mind if I join you?'

Jack, who'd always had a soft spot for Della, now had a broad grin across his face. 'Of course, please do.' She sat next to him. 'Can I get you a coffee?'

She placed her hand on his arm. 'No, it's okay, I've ordered. How did the signing go?' David, Della's husband, was currently doing his signing at another book shop in town.

Jack swivelled in his seat to face her. 'Good.' He said as enthusiastically as he could manage, knowing she'd be aware of his plummeting book sales. He quickly changed the subject. 'It's good to see you Della.'

She smiled in agreement. 'Good to see you too. I thought you might need some company. You looked to be in a world of your own. Everything okay?'

He silently nodded. She placed her hand reassuringly on his arm again. 'Things will turn round. They always do.'

He returned a weak smile, then tried to make a joke. 'It would be helpful if your David would stop writing such bloody good books.' He subconsciously always referred to him by his nom de plume. Jack found David irritating, not because of his writing, which Jack acknowledged was brilliant, but because of his boasting. Only last week he'd taken a phone call from David. He remembered the pompous tone. 'Hi Jack, I see you're not in the top ten again. My *Blue Cross* has topped *The Times* hot list again!' David lowered his voice and added admonishingly, 'You really must try harder, Jack.' He signed off with a chuckle. 'See you next week in Hay.'

'Jack!'

He shook his head. 'Sorry, Della, I was miles away.'

'Another coffee?'

Jack and Della went back a long way. There had always been a chemistry between them, although neither had admitted to having any strong romantic feelings for each other. He didn't look forward to these festivals and the signings, but the one thing he did look forward to was the chance to catch up with Della. He knew she would be there. Jack suspected it was more for the attention than the support for her husband. He knew from the grapevine that her marriage wasn't good. Jack suspected she was rather neglected at home. David was controlling, demanding and from what he'd heard, occasionally physically abusive towards Della. He warmly remembered the time she had been particularly supportive towards him during his acrimonious divorce, when he'd lost everything: house, money, respect and, even more distressing, his motivation for writing best sellers. As he didn't want to leave the café while he had the chance of being with Della, he agreed to yet another cup of coffee. He could see her expertly sashaying her way around the tables with two coffees. 'Thanks Della, you're good to me.'

She squeezed his hand. 'That's what I'm here for Jack. If ever you want to catch up, have a drink, a grumble, whatever takes your fancy, give me a ring.'

He relaxed and smiled. 'I'm back home in Chester tomorrow for a couple of weeks then I'm on the circuit again, but thanks, I'd look forward to that. I know you're not far away.'

* * *

The following week he received a phone call from his agent. 'Morning, Jack, have you seen the review in the *Sunday Chronicle*?'

Jack went cold. 'No. You know I don't read reviews, particularly in the Sunday Chron.'

There was a pause at the other end of the phone. 'You need to read it. I'll call you later when you've had time to go through it, suffice to say your publisher is not a happy bunny.'

Jack reluctantly pulled the Chron out of the bin and turned to the book reviews, critiqued ruthlessly, as usual, by Carole Arnold.

Yet again, another dismal effort from Jack Rosario. His new book Death Wish is an insipid attempt to recreate his earlier successes of the DI Mick Flanagan series. This latest effort is predictable, lacking in credible characters and contains several police procedural mistakes. Rosario is going to have to up his game if he wants to compete with the likes of David Kutzi, Peter James, or David Baldacchi. No doubt his publishers will encourage him to take a long break from writing in the slim hope that he will re-charge his batteries and return to the page turners of his earlier books... And so it went on. She was vicious in her condemnation, no holds barred. Jack sank back into the sofa not in the least bit surprised at Arnold's comments. Whereas he recognised his latest offering was not in the same league as his earlier books, the review was predictable. Arnold was known within the industry as Carole Cobra, she spat so much venom. Rosario was not the first author to succumb to her caustic, biting reviews.

He immediately returned Jan Crecy's phone call.

'Hello Jack, did you read it?'

'Yeah. It's what I've come to expect. I'll try to ignore it, but it's almost impossible when I'm being hit from all sides.'

Jan's voice softened. 'Your publisher is getting even more iffy. They said they're not going to renew your contract, but I've got them to agree to at least *read* your next novel.' She hesitated. 'That's the best I can do.'

'What about another publisher?' He was clutching at straws.

'That won't work. They'll query why your current publisher has dropped you.' She quickly added, 'Look, why don't you take a break. Go somewhere quiet and relax for a while. Give yourself a chance to rethink what you do next.' Without waiting for a reply, she put the phone down.

He sat with the phone still in his hand, staring out of the lounge window at his neat garden. His garden was the only thing currently keeping him sane. By getting stuck into the weeding and trimming he could forget, at least for a short time, the severe stress he was under. The tiny garden was just coming into bud. The lone apple tree was covered in lush foliage and white blossom. A wren sat on the handle of his wheelbarrow which was leaning against the wooden fence. He could see his meagre two bright green rows of carrots bobbing in the breeze in his mini veggie patch. He suddenly shook himself out of his self-pity and nervously dialled a number. It was answered almost immediately.

'Hello, Della Mitchell.'

He relaxed at hearing her velvet voice. 'Hi Della, It's Jack.'

'Ah! How wonderful to hear from you.'

He hesitated but then blurted out 'I need someone to talk to. Can we catch up over the next few days for a chat? Perhaps lunch somewhere?'

He heard her giggle at the other end of the phone. 'It's your lucky day. David's away all week in Bristol. If you'd like to come round today I'll make lunch.'

'Wonderful Della, that would be great. I'll be about an hour, okay?'

'I'll be ready and waiting.'

Jack lived in Chester, about thirty miles away from Della in Collington which meant, taking into consideration the traffic and possible road works, it would take at least an hour. He had a spring in his step as he showered, shaved and spruced himself up and hit the road. He had the window down and his Spotify tuned to French café music as he took the A419.

Della's house was a mansion. A detached limestone, double-fronted mock Georgian house with large double wrought iron gates opening up to a wide gravelled drive. A well-manicured lawn spread either side of the drive with the odd weeping willow planted at regular intervals. He turned off the ignition and quickly walked up to the red front door which boasted a large brass knocker. Before he'd had chance to knock, the door was opened and Della emerged bare foot. She wore a peach dress which superbly contrasted her olive skin to great effect. She looked stunning. She kissed him lightly on the cheek and took him by the hand into the hallway. It was a very spacious, circular hall with several doors leading off to various rooms. Ahead was a wide oval staircase. Impressive masterpieces hung on the walls. He was no connoisseur, so couldn't decide whether they were genuine or fake. She guided him into the lounge. 'Please.' She arched her arm toward a comfortable sofa. 'Wine? Whiskey? Beer?'

He smiled. 'A white wine please.'

He sat and looked around him. The décor was minimalist. Abstract paintings hung on the walls. It had two large white leather sofas and a glass and chrome coffee table. A large television hung on the main wall and a large bay window with French doors opened to a large rear garden. The immaculately manicured garden had obviously been created by a professional landscaper, not a blade of grass was out of place. She poured two glasses then sat down beside him tucking her long legs underneath herself. 'I've got lunch on. Pasta, okay?' He nodded and they chinked glasses.

'You said David was away, anywhere special?' He ventured.

She sighed. 'Yes he is, thank God – more book signings. He's in Bristol and Bath today and tomorrow, then he's driving to Plymouth for more signings Thursday, coming back Friday.' Jack relaxed at the news, then hesitated as he remembered why he'd phoned her. 'Thanks for asking me over. I needed to talk to a friendly face.'

She pressed her fingers on his lips to stop him talking. 'After lunch. Just enjoy a wine first.' He nodded enthusiastically and relaxed back into the leather sofa. After a couple of glasses of wine and a relaxed, lightweight conversation which centred mainly around holidays, family and restaurants, Della abruptly scanned her watch then jumped up. 'Come on, lunch will be done.'

He followed her into the kitchen. It was as equally expensively furnished as the lounge. It had a central unit with several high stools along its length. All the white goods, albeit in stainless steel, were of German manufacture.

Della spooned out a deliciously smelling pasta into two bowls which she placed on the central unit. Turning back to the worktops she grabbed a bottle of red and waggled it in front of Jack. 'A Malbec?'

Jack beamed and nodded. They ate in silence enjoying the meal. It left a warm glow inside him and it wasn't just the food. It was so good to be with someone who seemed to care. He glanced at Della – if only things were different. Jack finished first and patted his stomach. 'That was superb, thank you.'

She smiled and poured out another Malbec. 'Now, Jack, what did you want to talk about?'

He hesitated slightly, shook his head not knowing where to start, then continued. 'I just need to get some demons off my chest.' He took a deep breath. 'I'm sure you know my sales haven't been good recently.' She gave a sympathetic smile which implied she knew. He continued. 'The divorce didn't help; it was brutal. In fact, that was the start of the downturn as far as my writing's concerned. I couldn't think straight. I couldn't formulate any new ideas. I also found out later that the reason for her wanting a divorce was that she'd been having an affair. Added to that I got negative reviews in the Chron.'

Della frowned before speaking. 'Yes, I read the article. Carole Arnold seems to have a personal vendetta against you?' Jack nodded without comment as she patted his knee and continued. 'My, ahem, 'loving' husband constantly tells me how good he is. Unfortunately, he also takes every opportunity to remind me of your, shall we say, misgivings, as far as your writing goes.'

Jack told her about the phone call he'd received from David recently and the acerbic conversation. Della smiled knowingly. 'He often said to me he was worried in case you got your creative juices going again and that if you were out of the market completely he would do even better.' Her eyes glazed over as she stared into space then returned her eyes back to Jack. 'He's a bully. He says things to undermine you. He's very good at it, as I know only too well.'

Jack looked at her, concerned. 'Is he physically or mentally a bully?'

She looked down at her glass of wine. 'Both.'

Jack reached and held her hand. 'I'm sorry.' They both sat in silence for a few minutes not sure what to say next. Jack stifled a laugh. 'I'm not sure what the answer to all this mess is, but it sure is good to talk to you,' he held her hand once more, 'I'm very fond of you, Della,' he took a deep sigh, 'if only things were different, I reckon we'd make a good team.'

Della looked him straight in the eyes. 'Different, as if Carole Arnold and David weren't around perhaps? Hmm, life would be good wouldn't it.' Jack nodded. She took him by the hand and had a wicked look in her eyes. 'Well, that could be arranged...in the meantime let's go to bed.'

* * *

Carole Arnold slowly put the phone down and shook her head in frustration. She'd been on the phone to Pan Macmillan regarding several authors' new release dates which had been delayed on at least two occasions and fans were becoming frustrated. She turned to focus on the almost completed review in front of her which was due on the editor's desk by end of business today. It was the latest Michael Connolly book and, as with all Connolly's books she reviewed, the back cover was full of superlatives and commendations. She could almost write the reviews without even reading the book. His offerings were consistently of the highest quality. She grabbed a coffee before scanning the reviews once more prior to planting it on the editor's desk then made her way home. Arnold was a talented reviewer, albeit she had her favourites. Any author, and there had been several, who crossed her, were probably in for some venomous barbs, not the least of whom was Jack Rosario.

Carole Arnold had unkempt mousy hair, light brown eyes and almost never wore make-up. Her questionable fashion sense added to her rather dishevelled look. Today she wore her signature long brown tweed skirt and green polo top. She seemed determined never to become a slave to fashion.

The traffic going home was light. The road works she'd encountered on her early morning drive into the office were now finished enabling her to be home in under thirty minutes. She lived in a pleasant suburb on the border of England and North Wales. Number 39 Kyffin Terrace was in a row of Victorian houses, originally home to timber workers in years gone by, but over the past ten years had been gentrified: It was now a much sought-after area. The street was tree lined and had easy access to the nearby café and restaurant strip. Due to her busy schedule, she ate out most nights which bestowed her with rather more excess weight than she would have liked. Dieting was not on her shortlist of things to do, but she did manage to get to her yoga class on a regular basis!

As she pushed open the white picket gate to her house, she paused for a second to look at the azalea bush which was coming into bud. She stuck her key in the lock and, balancing several bags of shopping, she kneed open the door. Arnold was completely oblivious to the fact that someone had been stalking her for the last three weeks. The person in the silver-grey Mazda had followed her to work each morning and on the return journey each evening. By the end of three weeks the car's occupant had a complete picture of Arnold's movements: what time she left for work and what time she returned, which evenings she went out again and where she went – Tuesday for yoga and Thursday for catch-up with friends. Each evening the person in the silver-grey Mazda would park in her street and observe what time her lounge light went out and her bedroom light was turned on. However, tonight was Wednesday. Carole was always at home on a Wednesday. Tonight, the stalker was not parked in the street. Instead, the car had been parked two streets away. They had walked the short distance from the car, sneaked along the alleyway running behind the row of houses and climbed into number 39's small back garden. They then took out a balaclava, pulled it over their head and grabbed a wooden crate lying against a lean-to and stood on it to peer in through the kitchen window. Taking a knife to prize open the window, it was only seconds before the window was open.

Arnold dropped the bags on the hall floor, shrugged off her jacket and casually threw it on the newel post at the bottom of the stairs. As she walked down the hall she could feel a draught and turned to check that she'd closed the front door. The nearer she edged to the kitchen area the stronger the cool breeze became. Pushing open the kitchen door she could see her kitchen curtains lifting with an incoming breeze. She rarely had the kitchen windows open, so it struck her as odd. Why would they be open? She didn't remember opening them. Had she had burglars? She felt a cold shiver run down her spine as she backed out and went to check the study and the lounge. Standing at the door and scanning each room she could see nothing out of place. Her heart started beating faster and she felt frightened. She quietly inched her way back down the hall to the kitchen. Pushing the door slowly open with her foot she then warily stepped inside. Suddenly a pain shot across her head, then everything went black.

* * *

Chester police station was a new three-storey construction of glass and concrete. It had been open for three years. It looked incongruent, sticking out like a sore thumb sandwiched between the beautiful Victorian Town Hall and nineteenth-century church school. DI Ray Crispin was sitting at his desk on the top floor wading through the files he had stacked on his desk. The year so far had been particularly busy. In addition to the usual burglaries and domestics there had been some more serious crimes: three murders and an investigation into people trafficking. He stood up to stretch his legs, removed his rimless spectacles, rubbed his eyes and ambled slowly over to the window. His office overlooked the market square, and down below he could see the market traders setting up their stalls. Several buses parked at the bus station at the far side of the square were disgorging crowds of people from outlying areas coming into town to do their weekly shop. He smiled to himself and mused, *it wasn't a bad town, this year had been a bit of a bugger, but overall, not bad.*

He was snapped out of his daydreaming as the phone rang.

'Hello, DI Crispin.'

'Morning Ray, it's Jeff.'

Crispin relaxed. 'Morning to you Jeff. How's things?'

Jeff Bannister was the editor of the *Sunday Chronicle*. He and Ray Crispin went back a long way. Over the years they had done each other various favours. They worked well together and trusted each other. Ray knew Jeff could keep to an embargo on information. Likewise, Jeff would feed info to Ray on anything that came across his desk via the newspaper's contacts. It was a symbiotic relationship.

'Busy, as usual. I need a favour if you can. You know I wouldn't ask unless it was really important.'

Crispin's mood changed from welcoming to one of concern. Jeff was good at his job and didn't ask for favours unless it was absolutely necessary.

'What is it?'

'It's one of our journalists. She's not come into work. She hasn't phoned in and isn't responding to either her mobile or her landline which is unusual for her. One of the staff has been round and knocked on the door but got no reply. She wasn't due to go on holiday and she didn't have an assignment somewhere. Could one of your guys call in on their patrol, see if they can find out if anything untoward has happened.'

Ray grabbed his pen. 'Sure. Give me the address. I'll give you a shout once we know something.'

'Thanks, Ray.'

PCs Adele Thompson and Colin Wilcock, after completing their drive around the industrial estate, arrived at Arnold's house. They knocked on the door, looked through the letterbox and the lounge window, but could see nothing. 'I'll go round the back, Col.' Adele went down the entry leading to the backs of the houses, turned right then worked out which was number 39. She found the backyard gate open. Immediately she saw the broken window frame and peered inside. She could see Carole Arnold lying on the floor covered in blood. She spoke into her radio. 'Col, we've got a break-in and the occupier is down. I'll call an ambulance.'

Within minutes an ambulance arrived but it was too late. Carole Arnold was pronounced dead.

* * *

DI Ray Crispin arrived on the scene within half an hour, accompanied by DC Gail Hampton. The two PCs who had discovered the body had already taped off the crime scene. The only people inside the house were the forensics team. The two detectives quickly donned protective clothing and entered the house where they were met by Peter Craven the forensics team leader. 'Okay if we come in Peter?'

'Aye,' he beckoned them through to the kitchen area. 'I've got something to show you.'

As they followed, the DI asked Peter if he could give them any indication of time and cause of death.

Peter spoke over his shoulder as he went. 'I can give you a more accurate assessment once I've got her back at the mortuary, but I reckon fifteen to twenty hours, so, sometime last evening. The cause of death was probably the blow to the back of the head.' He stepped into the kitchen and pointed to the body. 'What do you make of that?'

The DI crouched down to look closely at the body, which was lying on the right side, her head covered in blood. He glanced first to the DC then to Peter. 'Mmm, interesting. Have you taken a photo?'

Peter nodded then pointed to the victim's head. 'Ring any bells?'

The DI stood up and shook his head. 'No, it doesn't.'

* * *

Back at HQ Ray Crispin addressed his team. 'We have the murder of a well-known journalist.' He hesitated. 'But I want you all to look at this photo.' A colleague at the back of the room flicked a switch that projected a photograph of the murder victim onto the screen. Shown clearly across the victim's forehead was a large blue cross. The DI let the team digest the photo for a few seconds. He held up his hand as a sign he had more to say. 'Now we don't yet know what this means, but it's obviously significant to the perpetrator of this crime. Let me give you all some background on our victim. She is Carole Arnold, a journalist with the *Sunday Chronicle*. She's 42 years old and single. She's the literary reviewer for the Chron. According to Jeff Bannister, the Sunday Cron editor, she's quite vehement in some of her reviews so she could have made a few enemies over the years. That will be one line of enquiry.' He turned to one of the team, DC John Mason. 'John, go and speak to Jeff Bannister, he may be able to give you more detail regarding some of her more recent reviews, and her work colleagues. Marnie, can you make enquiries regarding her friends, family, does anyone hold grudges? Gail and I will pursue the significance of the blue cross.' He looked round the team. 'Any questions, no? Right, back here at four o'clock for a de-brief.'

Everyone was exhausted by the time they arrived back for the after-noon briefing. It had been an unseasonably hot day and several of them immediately went to the water fountain before taking their seats.DI Crispin cleared his throat before starting, 'How did we get on John?'

DC Mason sat up. 'I've made a start. Work colleagues thought she was rather hard-hitting in her reviewing, but they also thought she was extremely good at her job. One of Carole Arnold's recent reviews was very negative for Jack Rosario. There had been negative reviews for his last two books, and sales bombed. I delved a little deeper into Jack Rosario and Carole Arnold...and guess what?'

DI Crispin looked frustrated. 'And?'

Mason looked smug as he delivered his next piece of information. 'They were married. They were, at one time, Mr and Mrs Mumford! Divorced four years ago and apparently it was very acrimonious.'

The DI smiled and nodded. 'Good work John, we'll make a detective of you yet.' The rest of the team applauded. 'So, a potential suspect. Gail and I will follow that up. Anything else? Marnie, what have you got?'

She shook her head. 'Nothing so far. Her family are spread throughout the UK so I've only spoken to them on the phone. They revealed nothing significant. Her family gave me the names of a couple of friends, but when I spoke to them on the phone, they told me they hadn't been in touch with her for quite some time.'

'Okay. Keep asking questions, Gail and I will visit Jack Rosario.'

* * *

The DI and DC parked a little way from the row of town houses that were home to Jack Rosario. Its boxy architecture, typical of the 1970s, looking a little tired and more like a Lego brick set. Shabby net curtains hung at some of the windows. The ground surrounding the townhouse was brown and bare. There were no signs of well-kept pot plants or even the odd shrub. Gail Hampton squinted at the tired-looking row. 'I didn't expect him to live in a place like this. Maybe the divorce was worse than we thought. Looks like his divorce really impacted on him.' She sighed. 'It's sad really, I read some of his early books and they were good.'

Ray looked at her with a questioning smile. 'You're a detective and you read crime books?'

She laughed. 'Well, yeah. Come on boss, let's see what he has to say.'

Rosario lived in the end house. They rapped sharply on the paint-flaked door.

In seconds it was opened by Rosario. 'Yes?'

The officers flashed their warrant cards. 'Jack Rosario? real name James Mumford?' Mumford nodded. 'Can we come in, we'd like a quick word?'

Mumford stepped aside then led them down a narrow hallway and into a square lounge. It had a well-worn two seat floral sofa and a single easy chair. Pushed up against one wall was a small dining table. A television in the corner was showing some breakfast show. A small card table against the window held a computer and a few files. Crispin moved across the room glancing out of the window and could see a rather bare but tidy rear garden. Mumford picked up the remote and turned the TV off. 'How can I help you?' as an afterthought he added, 'sorry, can I get you a tea or a coffee?'

They each held a hand up in a 'stop' sign to indicate 'no'.

DI Crispin led the conversation. 'We're investigating a murder. The victim is Carole Arnold.'

There was a sharp intake of breath from Mumford. He looked shocked and nodded hesitantly. 'Oh God. What happened?'

Crispin looked at Hampton before continuing. 'We understand your divorce was acrimonious.'

'Yes, and still is,' he added with venom, 'but what has it got to do with what's happened?'

DI Crispin added, 'That's what we need to ask you about. Her reviews of your books weren't exactly glowing, were they? When did you last see Miss Arnold?'

'Years ago, since the divorce. We stay out of each other's way. I know my last two books haven't been that good, but even so there was no need for her barbed outbursts in her reviews. Reviews often dictate whether sales go up or down. Unfortunately for me, it meant sales of my most recent book have not been good. But surely you don't think that's a reason to kill her! The less I had to do with her the better, but this news is just awful.'

Hampton stepped in. 'You mean the book *Death Wish*.'

'Yes, have you read it?'

She shook her head. 'No, not yet. I've read most of the others.'

Mumford smiled weakly in appreciation.

Crispin pulled the conversation back to the job at hand. 'You see, because of these reviews you would have a reason for holding a grudge against Miss Arnold.'

'Yes, I admit I bear a grudge, but I've got too many things going for me to do something stupid, if that's what you mean. I let her get on with her life and I try to get on with mine.'

Crispin nodded. 'Can I ask you where you were on July the seventh?'

He answered without hesitation. 'In Leeds. I was doing a book signing.'

'Can anyone confirm that?'

'Well, no doubt the hotel could.'

DI Crispin clicked his pen. 'And that was?'

'The Queens Hotel, Victoria Street. I stayed two nights as I had another signing the next morning.'

Crispin finished the informal questioning. 'Thank you, Mr Mumford. We may need to speak to you again.' As they went down the hall Crispin halted and turned for a last question. 'Does a blue cross mean anything significant to you?'

Mumford looked puzzled and shook his head. 'No, sorry.'

Back in the car Crispin turned to Hampton. 'What do you think? D'you believe him?'

She hesitated. 'Yeah, I reckon I do, but let's talk to the hotel and look at CCTV. Chester isn't that far from Leeds. If he finished signing late afternoon it wouldn't be difficult to hop over to Arnold's place, just outside Chester, and then back to Leeds.'

Crispin nodded in agreement. He turned on the ignition. 'Come on, let's get back, I'm due to deliver a debrief in half an hour.'

The team were already waiting for him when he rushed into the room. 'Thanks, guys.' He plonked his file on the table then went straight into the debrief. 'Gail and I interviewed Mumford, aka Rosario, and on the face of it we're not convinced he's guilty of the crime, perhaps just a victim of over-zealous book reviewing! However, we will check his alibi.' He switched his attention to Marnie. 'Anything new?'

'Sorry boss. I checked out the relatives again - nothing. Apparently, she's been estranged from them for several years. Just a thought boss. Rosario's competitor in the crime market is David Kutzi.'

'Right. So, what are you saying?'

'Well, I was skimming through Rosario's books on WH Smith's shelves when Kutzsi's new release sprung out...it's called, wait for it, *The Blue Cross*. Coincidence or what?' She looked around the room for support. They were impressed.

'That, DC Marnie, is what we would call critical evidence. Good work.' He made a note in his pad. 'I'll follow that up.'

* * *

The next day DI Crispin and DC Hampton parked outside the home of David Kutzi, real name John Mitchell. They were sitting in the car whilst they surveyed the Kutzi residence. 'Bit different from yesterday's home viewing boss.'

'Mmm, just a bit. He's obviously more successful.'

'And maybe he hasn't gone through a divorce...or had negative reviews from Carole Arnold.'

They strolled up the driveway taking in the surroundings, then rang the bell. Inside they could hear the pleasant chimes of an electronic non-descript tune. It was opened after a few seconds by, they assumed, Kutzi's wife.

They flashed their warrant cards. 'Mrs Kutzi?'

The very attractive lady smiled. 'Mrs Mitchell, actually. Kutzi is David's pen name. How can I help?'

'May we come in?'

As they walked down the hall Crispin asked, 'Is your husband at home?'

'Yes, I'll show you into the lounge then give him a call. He's upstairs in his den.'

The two officers made themselves comfortable on the plush sofa whilst she quickly tripped up the stairs and returned seconds later with Mr Mitchell in tow.

He entered the room sporting a false tan and fashionable stubble. He held his hand out. 'John Mitchell, how can I help?'

Crispin shook hands. 'I'm DI Crispin and this is DC Hampton. We'd like to ask you a few routine questions regarding a current investigation. I'm sure you're aware of the tragic murder of Carole Arnold?'

Mitchell nodded. 'Yes, it's very sad. She was a great friend of mine.'

Mitchell's wife appeared at the door. 'Coffee or tea?'

The two officers chimed, 'Coffee please, white, no sugar.'

Crispin leaned forward on the sofa. 'Mr Mitchell, that's your real name, isn't it?' Mitchell nodded.

'Could you tell us where you were on July the seventh?'

Mitchell grinned and leaned back in his seat. 'Just routine questions are they? Where's this leading?' The DI smiled to himself remembering Mitchell wrote crime novels for a living and was familiar with police terminology and tactics.

'We need to eliminate from our enquiries anyone who knew Miss Arnold, particularly those within publishing.'

'Why in particular within publishing?'

'We understand she had, on occasions, upset certain authors.'

"Yes, she did. She was brutally honest in some of her book appraisals.'

'Do you know of anyone who would hold a grudge against her?'

He vigorously shook his head. 'Jack Rosario had a few bad reviews, but you can't think he's responsible surely! I can't think of anyone who would hold that sort of grudge. It's all part of the rough and tumble of publishing,'

'We understand your new book is called *The Blue Cross* – does that symbol have some significance for you other than the title of the book?'

'No. It's one I invented as the MO of a criminal in the book.'

'Can I ask you again, where were you on July seventh?'

He looked surprised at the return to the previous question. 'At a book signing in Leicester.'

'And where did you stay?'

'The De Beaufort Hotel, Northampton Road and the next night I was at the County Hotel in Cambridge for another book signing...at Marlow's. You can check if you like.'

'We will.' The two officers stood up to leave. 'Thanks for your co-operation, we'll leave it for now, but we will probably need to ask you a few more questions at a later stage, just to clarify things as the investigation progresses, you understand.'

Back in the car DI Crispin asked, 'Any thoughts?'

Gail was quick to respond. 'He's a bit smarmy and self-centred. The hotels and book shops will be easy to check though.'

The debrief at the station started bang on time.

'Gail and I have interviewed both Rosario, real name Mumford, and Kutzi, real name Mitchell. Mitchell seems to be in the clear so far. He was in the East Midlands for two nights including the one in question, but we still need to check the hotels and bookshops to confirm his alibi. John, can you do that? If necessary, go over to Leicester and get hold of the CCTV footage of the two hotels, have a good look, okay?'

John Mason gave him a thumbs up.

Crispin continued. 'At this stage Rosario also has an alibi, although it's possible he could get from Leeds to Chester within the time frame in question, particularly if his book signing was in the morning or early afternoon. Marnie, would you go over to Leeds, get the CCTV for July seventh and check whether he left the hotel either late afternoon or early evening. Today we're going to check with Peter Craven at forensics, see if he's uncovered anything. Back here tomorrow morning, eight o'clock sharp.'

* * *

The Forensics Department was in an old pre-war building behind the hospital. Crispin and Hampton pushed their way through the double doors and were immediately hit by the familiar smells of the mortuary. Both put their hands to their noses simultaneously. Would they ever get used to the pungent odours that permeated every pore of one's body and every stitch of clothing?

Peter met them at the door to the lab. 'Come in. I haven't got a lot for you.' He took them into his small office that contained a desk littered with files, his lunchbox and myriad pens and pencils. He directed them to sit on two hard plastic chairs on the opposite side of the desk and opened a file. 'We got no prints so we can assume the perpetrator wore gloves. No weapon's been found but, if we could find it, we may be able to salvage something.'

'Such as what?'

'We photographed the damage on the window frame and it appears that the knife or blade used was distinctive. It had a couple of broken pieces along the blade. If we could find that knife we could match the damage on the blade to the window frame,' he leaned back in his chair and steepled his hands, 'there's no doubt the cause of death was from being struck by a blunt object. So, if the weapon that struck her could also be found we would be able to do further tests, but other than that...' he shrugged his shoulders, 'nothing, sorry.'

Ray and Gail left, disappointed but not surprised.

As they sat in the car Gail tentatively put forward a suggestion. 'I've had a thought...with regard to the blue cross. Lots of organisations use symbols to differentiate themselves from others. Someone at one of the universities may be an expert on icons, symbols, whatever you want to call them. Maybe we contact them.'

The DI responded with a nod. 'Great. Good Idea. Can you do that this morning, see what you can find whilst I go back to HQ and have another wade through statements; see if there's anything that's been missed and at least try to put some kind of strategy together.'

'Will do.'

Gail's visit to Bristol University didn't produce any really useful information. The Head of the Psychology Department thought it may symbolise a personal motive rather than representing an organisation or group. The killer might be using it as a personal tag. Could this be the start of a serial killing?

* * *

The next day at the briefing Gail Hampton explained to the team what she'd found out at the University. 'I've contacted the other forces to see if they've had any murders involving a blue cross and I'm waiting for them to get back to me.'

Crispin stepped in. 'We've not got much to go on, so I want to review what we do have.' He pulled a whiteboard across so everyone could see what he was about to write. 'We've only got two potential suspects at this stage, Rosario and Kutzi, aka Mumford and Mitchell. On the face of it Kutzi has a good alibi. However, we still need to keep him on our radar. What I want to do now is have a brainstorming session in relation to those two.' He wrote two names at the top of the whiteboard, Rosario and Kutzi. 'First Kutzi. Motivation and opportunity?' He scanned the team. 'What motivation does Kutzi have? What would he gain? Any offers?'

A voice called from the back. 'The obvious suspect is Rosario having had bad reviews from Arnold, so if Kutzi could make the police look in Rosario's direction he could eliminate his main competitor from the crime book market.'

The DI nodded in agreement and wrote it on the board. 'Ok, next - opportunity?'

John spoke up. 'I've checked with the hotels in Leicester and Cambridge and his alibi stands up so, unless he persuaded someone else to do his dirty work it looks as though he's in the clear.'

'Okay, let's look at Rosario. Motivation?'

Marnie spoke again. 'His sales of the last two books have been really poor. And his reviews haven't helped...get rid of Arnold and maybe his sales would increase. There still seems to be bad blood between the two of them after the messy divorce, so I reckon his motivation is high.'

Crispin quickly wrote on the board. 'And opportunity?'

Again, it was Marnie who spoke up. 'The hotel in Leeds confirmed his booking, but it wouldn't be impossible to drive from Leeds over the M62 to Chester and back within the time frame.'

'Did you check the CCTV at the hotel in Leeds? Was he seen leaving in the afternoon and arriving back late in the evening?'

She shook her head. 'No, I ran the tape through from three hours before our time frame to three hours after. He didn't leave.'

Crispin stood back and surveyed the whiteboard. 'We're no further on, are we? We need to look further afield for the tool used to crack the window and the actual weapon that killed her. Forensics tells me if we could find those crucial items, they can do further tests which may help us. There's some wasteland up the road from Arnold's place, I know it's been searched once, but let's have another look.' He stood in silence for a few minutes whilst he pondered then blurted out in frustration, 'my gut tells me there is a connection to Rosario. I don't know what, it's just a feeling. John and Marnie, have another look at the CCTV from Leeds. Was there a back entrance...or side one?'

'Aye, will do guv.'

* * *

Ray Crispin was out with his wife at an Italian restaurant, Cuppello's, to celebrate their wedding anniversary. They'd finished their main course, declined a dessert and opted not to have a liqueur. His phone rang. His face screwed up in apology to his wife as he answered it. 'Hello, DI Crispin.'

'Evening guv, sorry to bother you, Marnie and I have re-run the CCTV from Leeds and there's something you need to see.' As he put the phone back in his pocket his wife was already at the counter paying the bill. She'd spent all their married life living with his crazy hours.

Crispin felt frustrated. 'Sorry love, you know how it is.'

He was back at the station within half an hour and raced up to the briefing room where he found John and Marnie sipping a coffee. John apologised again. 'Sorry to bring you out boss, but you need to see this.' The three of them sat round the screen whilst John re-wound the tape to the three hours prior to the crime taking place. 'The tape is a twenty-four hour one and shows everything until the next morning.' John clicked the button and the tape started running showing the time. 'Rosario isn't on tape leaving, but keep watching,' John explained. He fast-forwarded the tape to the critical point. 'We Googled David Kutzi's bio and a photo of his wife came up.'

At the 7.00pm point John stopped the tape. 'Now this is the interesting bit.' He clicked again and re-started the tape. It ran for a few minutes then Crispin got excited.

'Stop the tape, John! Bloody hell!'

Clear as a bell coming in through the revolving doors was a face they recognised from the Google photos. Della Mitchell!

'Keep watching guv.' John and Marnie looked a little sheepish. 'Sorry guv, we weren't aware of Della Mitchell's involvement the first time we ran it. We were too busy looking for Rosario.'

Crispin dismissed their apology with a wave of his hand. 'This is a great step forward.' The tape continued until it showed 8.00am the next morning. Two people were seen leaving the hotel – Jack Rosario and Mrs Kutzi, aka Della Mitchell. 'Wow. Great work you two, brilliant!' He rubbed his hands together. 'Guess where I'm going tomorrow morning? I think an interview with Della Mitchell is in order, don't you?'

Crispin phoned Gail and picked her up at home. On the drive to Della Mitchell's home, he explained what John and Marnie had found. 'This is a big step forward. If they're having an affair, and it looks as though they are, then that's motivation in my book.'

Although it was early morning the temperature was rising rapidly. The forecast for the day was for high 20s. The sky was a clear blue with very little breeze. Crispin wasn't looking forward to the hot day, he preferred cooler weather. Already he was sweating. They arrived at the Mitchell home to find Della washing her silver Mazda on the drive. She was wearing very short denim shorts and a white blouse tied under her chest.

'Morning Mrs Mitchell. May we have a word? We just need to clarify a few grey areas.'

She dropped her sponge into the bucket of water by her side and beckoned them inside. Once inside she smiled and nodded. 'How can I help?'

Crispin led the conversation. 'Is your husband at home?'

'No, he's up in Dumfries until Thursday.'

'Do you know James Mumford, otherwise known as Jack Rosario?'

'Certainly. I know him well. He's on the book circuit as is every other popular writer.'

His next question took her by surprise. 'How well?'

A frown creased her forehead. 'Meaning?'

The DI took a deep breath. 'How well do you know him? To put a finer point on it, are you and Rosario having an affair?'

'No!' she spat, a little too defensively. 'I've seen him from time to time around town and we may have a coffee but that's it.'

'Can I ask you where you were on the evening of July seventh?'

She placed a finger on her head and looked skyward as she feigned thinking. 'July seventh? Mmm, not sure.'

Crispin smiled. 'Maybe I can help. You were seen on CCTV entering the Queens Hotel in Leeds at approximately seven o'clock in the evening.'

'Ah yes. I remember now. I was in Leeds.'

'Why were you in Leeds?'

'Shopping! Harvey Nicks and all that.'

'And what time did you leave the Queens Hotel?'

She gave a stifled laugh as she realised Crispin knew! The game was up.

'I stayed at the Queens...with Jack. All night.'

'Did you know Jack Rosario and Carole Arnold had been married until a few years ago?'

She looked shocked. 'No! I didn't know! But I do know she gave him a bad time. He blames his low book sales on her. I felt sorry for him.'

'Sorry enough to do her some harm?'

She shook her head and remained silent.

'When was the last time you saw Carole Arnold?'

Della avoided eye contact by looking through the window. 'Don't know, can't remember.'

Crispin nodded to Gail who took up the next stage of the conversation. 'Mrs Mitchell within the hour we will have a search warrant for your house and garage.'

'You don't think I had anything to do with it do you? That's ridiculous. OK, we were having an affair, but that's all, I swear.' Tears welled up in her eyes.

The search team arrived and the warrant was served on Della Mitchell. Gail sat with her in the lounge. Crispin joined the search team as they began looking in every drawer, cupboard, loft space, even behind the panels in the bathrooms. Two officers searched upstairs whilst two were concentrating on the downstairs and two in the garage. The DI returned to the lounge after a few minutes and joined Gail and Della Mitchell. It wasn't long before an officer knocked at the lounge door. 'Have you got a minute guv?'

Crispin went outside with the officer who took him over to the Mazda still parked on the drive. The officer pointed to the wheel-well in the open boot. A knife! It brought a smile to Crispin's face. 'Good work. Stick in an evidence bag.'

Another officer came out of the garage and called to the DI. 'Guv!' In his right gloved hand he held a stick, resembling a baseball bat. 'Found it behind the shelving.'

The knife in the bag and the heavy stick were immediately dispatched to the forensics lab.

* * *

The next morning Peter Craven from forensics phoned Crispin. 'Good news Ray. The marks on the knife blade match the damage done to the window frame.'

'Great. Any luck with the stick?'

'Well, we can confirm that it's actually a snooker cue, but sadly no prints. However, the blood on it matches that of Carole Arnold, so I can confirm that the cue was the weapon used to kill her. It also has traces of a cotton fabric. If we could match it to a piece of clothing we may have something for you.'

'That's great. We can do another search, but what should we be looking for in particular?'

'It's a quality cotton, a Sea Island cotton to be precise and it's a lemon shade. Probably female clothing, a T-shirt or at least a lightweight top.'

'Thanks, Peter. Leave it with me.'

The search continued at Della Mitchell's home. They again searched her wardrobe and drawers in the main bedroom and guest room, much to her annoyance. An item found was removed and delivered to the forensics lab by patrol car.

Peter Craven phoned the DI with some positive news just as the debrief was commencing. Crispin couldn't wait to tell the team.

'The garment we took from Della Mitchell's home yesterday matches exactly the cotton fibres found on the snooker cue. And the exclusive manufacturer's brand has limited outlets, only one in Chester, and another at Harvey Nicks in Leeds. It might help if you could find the receipt for it.'

Another search proved fruitless; no receipt was found.

'Gail, come on. I think Della Mitchell has a bit of explaining to do.'

Della was in the back garden lying on a sun lounger by the swimming pool when the DI and DC arrived. They got no response knocking at the front door so undid the side gate and wandered into the back garden.

'Hello, again, Mrs Mitchell.'

She removed her sunglasses and sat up on one elbow. 'What this time?' she said showing her annoyance.

'Please stand up.'

She slowly did as she was told.

'Mrs Della Mitchell. I'm arresting you on suspicion of causing the death of Carole Arnold. You do not have to say anything but anything you do say may be used in evidence...do you understand? She reluctantly nodded.

'I need to hear you.'

'Yes!' she shouted.

EPILOGUE

Della Mitchell was found guilty of murdering Carole Arnold and was sentenced to twenty years imprisonment. She admitted that she'd daubed the blue cross on Arnold's forehead in the hope to link the murder to her husband's latest book and in turn to her husband. Her warped thought process was that if Arnold was dead and her husband in jail, she and Mumford would be free to be together.

No evidence was found against James Mumford (Jack Rosario) of having been involved in Miss Arnold's murder. Mumford's (Rosario's) creative flare returned, and he went on to write several more successful books followed by great reviews. Two of his novels have since been turned into TV series.

9 |

The Country Run

2023

She scurried across the road from Piccadilly Gardens to the station desperately trying to avoid the traffic and hold on to her hat at the same time. It had been a pleasant morning when she'd left home, but as she arrived in Manchester city centre, a brisk wind had suddenly developed and the dark clouds above were threatening rain.

The multi-storey where she had parked her car was some way from the station. She'd had to park almost at the top level which hadn't helped her timing and she was in a rush not to miss the train. She half-ran half-trotted up the long slope leading to the station's main entrance which was lined with black taxis. The heavens suddenly opened and the pavements and unfortunate pedestrians were drenched in seconds. She was wearing jeans with short Chelsea boots, a lightweight top, a short cream zip jacket and was carrying a Guess handbag. Her hair, now wet, stuck to her face as she pushed into the concourse. A train had just arrived and she was trying her best to avoid the avalanche of people swarming in the opposite direction heading for the city.

Piccadilly station was always busy. It never stopped. There were porters everywhere, some directing people, some pushing trolleys piled high with parcels. There were harassed mums with kids in tow, business-men armed with briefcases, marching, trying to imply they were on an important mission. There were the obligatory daydreamers sauntering along checking their mobiles and those who simply lingered within the station trying to stay warm.

She made her way to the main arrivals-departure board to check the arrival time of the train from Glasgow. She was disappointed, or rather, annoyed, to see the train from Glasgow had been delayed. No explanation. Shaking her head in frustration she headed for the coffee shop unimaginatively called 'The Coffee Shop'. As usual, it was busy. All the customers had their reasons for being there, some no doubt filling in time before being taken to whichever far-flung reaches of the country they needed to be. 'A flat white please.' She leaned to one side to view the chilled cabinet, 'Ooh, and a friand thanks.' Just then someone got up to leave, so she grabbed the table and settled herself in for the wait.

Carol Mason was thirty-five-years-old, married to John Mason. She was a petite woman with shoulder-length dark hair and a pale complexion. As she took her first sip of coffee, her mobile phone rang.

'Hi, it's me. There's been a delay.'

'I know,' she replied trying hard to disguise her annoyance.

'We've just come through Preston station. The guard tells me we'll be another twenty minutes or so…just thought I'd let you know.'

'Thanks love. I'm just enjoying a coffee. See you soon.'

'Cheers.'

As she finished the last few drops of her coffee she glanced through the café window at the large clock above the arrivals board. Her husband was due in five minutes. She picked up her handbag from under the table and leisurely made her way to the barrier on platform 4. The train stopped within metres of where she stood and within seconds the passengers began to alight. She stood on tiptoe to try to identify her husband among the hundreds of fellow travellers, straining her neck from side to side. Eventually the throng of people thinned and the platform became empty once more. She looked around her a little bewildered. *Where is he?* She peered down the far end of the platform, but there was no-one there. *That's odd!* At a loss of what to do next she approached a porter who was standing by the barrier. 'Excuse me. My husband was on this train but he seems to have disappeared. Is there another exit for this platform?'

He shook his head. 'No ma'am, this is the only one. Are you sure he was on this train?' It suddenly struck her that maybe she was at the wrong barrier. She pointed to the train still stationary at the platform.

'This is the Glasgow train, isn't it?'

'Yes it is. Maybe he caught the next train.'

'No,' she replied in a panic, 'he phoned me when the train was coming through Preston, but he hasn't come through the barrier.' She had another thought. 'Perhaps he's fallen asleep, could someone check for me, please.'

'That will have been done, ma'am. Once everyone has disembarked we have someone to walk the length of the train to check for people and baggage. Nothing so far has been reported. The cleaners are now working their way through, sorry.'

She thanked him and turned to face the concourse, looked left and right and along the row of shops. *Where could he be? Could he somehow have walked straight past her without her seeing him?*

She wandered over to the coffee shop in a trance and looked through the window just in case he was having a coffee, perhaps thinking she hadn't arrived to pick him up. *No, he wasn't there.* She decided to walk the full length of the concourse and back, checking in the various shops, WH Smiths, The Sock Shop, the newsagency, telephone boxes, she even stood outside the gents for a few minutes in case he came out. *Nothing.* Almost in a panic she hurried to the exits. Perhaps he was outside waiting for her! The area outside the entrance was almost as busy as the inside. People were grabbing taxis or climbing into cars which had been arranged to pick them up. Couples were hugging and kissing like long lost friends. *But no John!* She stood there checking and double-checking everyone who came past. Eventually she decided to make her way home. There had to be a rational explanation.

As she reached the bottom of the station ramp leading to the main road, she halted as a police car and ambulance, lights flashing, flew up the ramp to the main entrance. A realisation struck her. *Oh, no! Maybe he's been hurt.* She turned and ran back up to the station, pushed her way through the doors and back to platform 4 where a crowd had gathered. Several officers were holding the crowd back as the ambulance medics, pushing a gurney, ran along the platform. Carol grabbed the porter she'd spoken to earlier. 'What's happened?' she cried hysterically. He instantly recognised her as the woman he'd spoken to earlier.

'A man has died. I don't know any details.'

At that moment the paramedics returned to the main concourse pushing the gurney. She collapsed at the sight. On the gurney was a body bag.

She knew! She just knew!

* * *

2021

John Mason was a thirty-year-old engineering supervisor. He'd been married to Carol for eight years. John worked for Coleman and Helsby. It was the UK division for a Swedish based organisation which supplied parts to the car industry and, more recently, to the EV industry.

He turned up for work one morning to find some of his colleagues in a huddle in the coffee machine area. He dumped his bag in his office, hung his jacket on the wooden coat stand and wandered over to the huddle. 'What's up guys?'

Ted Webster, another supervisor, turned to him and shook his head. 'Bad news mate. Apparently some redundancies are on the way...or at the very least an even shorter week looks likely.'

'How come?'

'Not sure. The rumour, if it is one, came from one of the sales guys from one of our subsidiaries. Let's hope it is just a rumour.'

John wandered back to his office. He slumped into his chair and put his head in his hands. *Please let it just be a rumour. We're already on short time.*

He'd been with Colemans since the age of sixteen and eventually completed his apprenticeship. He'd started work on the shop floor, working hard to prove to himself and to management what he was capable of. He was popular with his peers, who discovered him to be particularly adept whenever there were machinery problems. He gradually gained promotion.

Their main contract with Toyota could always be relied on. However, the smaller contracts were the ones that often let the business down, particularly the EV industry, which had taken a nosedive, hence the shorter week.

* * *

John and Carol Mason lived in a modest semi on a small housing estate in the village of Grenton, twenty miles south of Manchester. Grenton was a leafy suburb and was still essentially a farming community. They'd bought their house only two years previously after living in a flat in Broadly, a busy suburb close to the city. They'd stretched themselves to the limit for their mortgage which had been just about manageable at the time, but since the recent interest rate increases it had become a struggle to make their monthly payments. Any further impact on their expenses would be a disaster.

Over dinner that evening he gave Carol the bad news. 'We're all hoping it's just a rumour. To be honest some of us have been half expecting it. The EV industry hasn't taken off like everyone hoped, for all sorts of reasons.'

Carol looked pensive. 'John, we've been struggling to pay the mortgage since you've been on a four-day week, so how will we go on if you go onto a three-day week or even worse, redundancy?'

John forced a smile to try to lighten the conversation. 'It's a good job you're working, eh?' His face didn't match his words.

Carol did have a secure, reasonably well-paid job. She was employed as the receptionist at a finance company in the town centre. Their joint incomes allowed them to have a modest lifestyle. They had a new-ish car, which Carol used for work. They went on holiday every year and, very occasionally, went out for dinner. Life had been quite good until John had gone on a four-day week. The drop in their monthly income made a big difference to their bank account balance. Covid hadn't helped and the massive increases in the interest rate had pushed them to the very edge financially. Unknown to John, they'd already received a letter from the building society regarding their mortgage arrears. Carol had kept that little 'gem' to herself knowing how much he worried. She just hoped that John's work would get back to normal and would enable them to catch up on their mortgage payments. Any further erosion of their income would potentially push them under.

'When will you know for sure?'

John shook his head. 'Not sure, the rumour mill suggested by the end of the month.'

Carol stood up to clear away the dishes and called over her shoulder as she went into the kitchen, 'We'll really have to tighten our belts if you go down to a three-day week.'

* * *

The next few weeks went by without any further news to either quell or confirm the rumours. The company was still on a four-day week and John had noticed some high-level meetings taking place in the boardroom. Several visitors were from the company's Swedish headquarters.

The men under John's supervision were getting nervous seeing all the comings and goings of top management and approached John. 'What's going on? Is the company in trouble? We need to know, most of us have mortgages and kids.'

John would shrug his shoulders and apologise. 'Sorry guys, I'm in the dark as much as you are. I promise, as soon as I know something I'll let you know.' Everywhere he went along the production line or in the canteen the topic was the same: redundancy or further reduced working hours.

Another two weeks passed and still nothing. John was ploughing through the production paperwork on his desk when he was aware of someone at his door. He looked up. It was his boss, Malcolm Plessey. 'When you've got a minute John, can you come up to my office.' John's stomach did a somersault. He guessed what was coming. He quickly finished off his paperwork and made his way up to the second floor of the building to Plessey's office.

John's own office was a hurriedly constructed box-type room squashed into a darkened corner of the shop floor, with a half-window from which he could view the production line. Plessey's office on the other hand had large windows which at this moment in time enjoyed the luxury of the sun streaming through, giving the office a warm, light atmosphere. John tentatively knocked on his door.

Plessey looked up to see John hovering. 'Come in John, take a seat.' He grabbed a chair and sat down opposite Plessey who was sitting behind a wide mahogany desk. Plessey was a large man with watery eyes and a red face. He always wore a suit and a colourful bow tie. Plessey held up his hands. 'I don't have a lot to tell you yet regarding the organisation's future, but I thought you deserved to be put in the picture.' John mutely nodded and Plessey continued. 'As you're probably aware, the last few weeks have been busy with meetings between the management here and our Swedish counterparts. They, understandably, are concerned about the drop-off in contracts and production, particularly around the EV production.' He held his hands up once more. 'No decisions have been taken yet, John, but I have to say, it doesn't look good. Quite a few of the top car brands are reported to have put EVs on hold. I'm updating you because I'm sure your men are asking you the same questions.' John mutely nodded again in acknowledgment. Plessey leaned forward. 'They've promised me a decision will be made by the end of the month.'

John wandered back to his office and sat at his desk unable to concentrate on the work in front of him. He glanced up, looking through the half-frosted glass in his office at the shop floor. He could see the men working at the production lines. Most of them would be devastated if the worst outcome eventuated.

Tom Webster, married with two children, one at university; Dave Pollit, about to be married; Colin Dempsey, married with three children, one of whom was autistic; Joe Mullet, Brian Sackett, Miles Marchington, Ellis Leah, Norman Dewsbury. All had massive commitments. *How would they manage?* The 'lucky' few: Basil Aldbury, Martin White and Eric Hurst, were all due for retirement within the next twelve months. The redundancy payments for them would no doubt be welcome. But the rest? John couldn't concentrate for the remainder of the day.

At the end of the month Plessey summoned John to his office once more.

As John entered, he could see the look of embarrassment on Plessey's face. Even before John had time to sit down Plessey gave him the news.

'John, I'm so sorry. It's the news we hoped wouldn't come. Sweden has decided to close this facility by the end of the year. We'll complete the contracts already started but then...' he paused for a moment, 'then that's it. They're shifting all our production to a new facility they've built in Sweden. I'm sorry. After seventy-odd years of production on this site there will be no more production.' John remained silent not knowing how to respond. Plessey stepped in to break the silence. 'Do you want me to tell your men?'

John shook his head. 'No, I'll do it. They're my men.'

Plessey nodded in agreement.

At home that evening, after John had given Carol the bad news, the atmosphere was understandably subdued. She saw the look of panic on his face. She grabbed a pen and pad from the kitchen drawer. 'Let's not panic. Let's look at this and think it through rationally. First, we'll itemise all our commitments and highlight areas where we can cut down. Don't forget we'll still have my wage coming in, it's not as though we'll be on the dole. Some of your men are in a worse position than we are.'

He reluctantly nodded. 'I need to look for another job love; that has to be a priority.' She squeezed his hand trying to reassure him. She knew unemployment in the area was at an all-time high, particularly in engineering. John hesitated before he spoke. 'I'll have to tell the men tomorrow. I'm not sure how I'll do it.'

Carol tried to put his mind at rest. 'John, they're men, just tell them how it is, they'll thank you for your honesty.' He silently nodded and drank his coffee.

* * *

The next day, the weather was bleak, rain spattering on the windows. John called Geoff, his deputy supervisor, into his office. 'Can you gather the men into the canteen at break time; I need to speak to them.' Geoff raised his eyebrows. John looked him directly in the eyes. 'It's not good news.'

The men gathered in the canteen. Some had cups of tea in their hands, some were eating, some pacing, they were all expecting the worst. John cleared his throat. 'There's no easy way to tell you. The factory is closing by the end of the year. We'll all be out of work.'

A voice from the back of the group called out. 'How come, I thought we were doing okay?'

John took a deep breath. 'The Toyota contract is solid. It's the smaller contracts that are drying up, mainly due to the downturn in EV sales worldwide. Apparently it's no longer cost effective to produce the parts here. The plant is outdated and too costly to maintain. They're looking for more modern, cost-effective facilities so they're shifting all the production over to the new Swedish plant.' The men, although fearing the worst, were at least hoping for reduced hours. 'I'm sorry, guys.' Several held their hands up acknowledging it wasn't John's fault and wandered off in small groups to discuss what their futures might hold.

John was sat at his desk and could feel himself panicking. He had been hoping all would go well, but he knew in his heart, the evil day would inevitably arrive. *How would he and Carol cope? Would the building society be sympathetic? Would he find work?* All their plans were now on the back burner.

* * *

John was now at home full time, something he'd never experienced before. He'd been in work from the day he left school. Unemployment hit hard.

Over the next few weeks he became more and more morose. He would reluctantly roll out of bed in the morning, force himself to have some breakfast with Carol before seeing her off to work, then sit on the sofa and bore himself silly watching breakfast television. Occasionally he'd pick up a book and read a few pages before putting it down and wandering around the house.

Carol was increasingly worried about him. He was becoming more and more introverted, his conversation limited. She knew what a strong work ethic he had, and it wasn't being satisfied. One morning she ventured a suggestion. 'Why don't you go into town, have a coffee. You could meet me for lunch. It'll do you good to get out.'

He shrugged his shoulders. 'Yeah, I might.'

She was slightly irritated at his negative attitude and pushed for a more positive commitment. 'Lunchtime. I'll meet you in the White Swan around one o'clock, okay?'

He looked at her and forced a smile. 'Okay, one o'clock, White Swan. I promise.' She leaned into him and kissed him.

After Carol had left for work, he did his best to try and snap out of his negative frame of mind. He showered, put on a clean sweater and jeans, and set off for town.

The White Swan wasn't the best pub in the world, but it offered convenience for both him and Carol. In the evening it became a pub where younger people gathered to meet and have a drink, before moving on somewhere else. He was annoyed with himself for being so negative, so depressed; It wasn't the real him.

Arriving at the pub at a quarter to one he found it busy. Of course, it was a Friday, the day when those with a job began to relax in preparation for the weekend. He could hear snooker balls clunking in the adjacent room and raucous laughter from a bevy of young girls in the corner. He half-smiled to himself as he strolled to the bar and ordered a pint from Jen, the barmaid. Carol arrived a second later. He gave her a squeeze and a smile. 'What are you having love?'

She slipped her arm through his, pleased to see him looking a bit more like himself. 'A prosecco, please.'

He grabbed a couple of menus from the bar then the two of them navigated their way between the tables to the area reserved for dining. He playfully nudged the top of her arm. 'Thanks for forcing me out. I don't seem able to snap out of this depression.'

She raised her glass. 'I know. It's understandable. You've never been out of work before, but things will work out, you'll see.'

Carol ordered linguini and John a Guinness pie. Much to Carol's relief the conversation was so much lighter than it had been over the past few weeks. She lost track of time, then suddenly realised. 'Oh my god, I should have been back at work ten minutes ago.' She quickly finished off her prosecco, gathered her belongings, kissed John goodbye and dashed out of the pub. John, now feeling a little more upbeat strolled back to the bar and ordered another pint from Jen. Jen was an ample woman in her mid-forties. She wasn't particularly attractive, having a 'boxer's nose and large jowls. She almost always wore a black or red V-neck top covered in lots of bling. She looked fearsome but, in fact, was a very pleasant softly spoken woman.

She pulled the pint and put it in front of John. 'Are you okay? You sound a bit down.'

He glanced up at her with a wan smile. 'Yeah, I'm okay,' he said dismissively.

She leaned on the bar. 'Weren't you at Colemans?'

He nodded. 'Aye.'

She shook her head in frustration. 'The closure has affected the whole town, so many worked there.' She waved her arm around the room. 'It's been quieter in here since the redundancies. Any other jobs around town?'

He shook his head. 'No.' She realised that he was not in the mood for conversation so moved away to serve someone else. He stood, one foot on the brass rail which ran along the bottom of the bar and stared into his pint. He could feel panic rising again. *Where would he find another job in the area? Everyone else would be looking for work too. And the bills, the commitments!* He suddenly realised someone was standing by his side talking to him.

'Sorry,' John queried, 'were you talking to me?'

The man next to him was well dressed in casuals, a charcoal grey lambswool sweater, black cords and black tasselled shoes. He had a Scottish accent. 'Sorry to intrude, but I overheard your conversation with the barmaid. You were one of the unlucky ones made redundant I presume? It's tough, isn't it?' John nodded, reluctant to get into a conversation with this stranger. 'I'm from Glasgow.' The stranger continued. 'The redundancies in the shipyards are frightening. All the work is going to South Korea. It's tough,' he repeated, then took a sip of his drink and continued. 'Kids?' John shook his head. 'That's a blessing.' The man finished off his drink and handed John a card. 'I could offer you some well-paid work.' For the first time John looked him in the eyes and raised his eyebrows. 'Er, deliveries.' the stranger said in response.

'What sort of deliveries?' John questioned.

A wry smile crossed the man's face. 'All sorts of things. It would pay well. Pay the bills. Stop the worrying.' With that pointed remark the man made his way to the door, but not before pointing to his card that he'd left lying on the bar for John. 'I'm in here tomorrow night, seven-ish. If you're interested I'll give you more details then.'

John took the card and put it in his pocket.

After dinner that evening, Carol plucked up the courage to tell John about the outstanding bills that had accumulated since he'd been working a four-day week. She placed a piece of paper on the coffee table and turned it towards him listing the expenditure.

She went through it line by line. 'The arrears are mounting.'

'Arrears?'

She paused before continuing. 'We had a letter from the building society pointing out we're two months in arrears.' Before John had time to respond she pointed out, 'and three months behind on the car.'

He put his head in his hands. 'Christ! How come?'

Her voice rose in exasperation. 'Because we had other bills to pay. I had to prioritise which ones got paid...I've been robbing Peter to pay Paul.' He began to hyperventilate so she placed her hand on his. 'Take some deep breaths; it will all get sorted. I've put a plan in place to get us back on track.' She paused to check he was listening to what she was saying. 'It'll be tough, but we'll get there. The sooner you can find some employment the quicker we'll come out the other end.' She turned his face toward her and smiled. 'We will, I promise.' He didn't respond, he was just thankful that Carol had the strength of mind to look at the problem logically and come up with a practical plan. She saw him visibly relax. 'We will have to cut back drastically. I know we're not extravagant, but even so, there's areas where we'll have to pull our belts in.' He was no longer listening; his mind had jumped to the conversation he'd had with the stranger in the bar.

'Carol, I met a guy in the pub just after you'd left and he suggested he could give me some work.'

She frowned. 'What sort of work?'

John shook his head. 'He wasn't specific. Deliveries of some sort. He said if I was interested that I should be in the pub tomorrow night, seven-ish.'

She pursed her lips. 'Sounds iffy. You need to find out what sort of deliveries.'

'I know, but if it clears our debts, what does it matter?'

She took a deep breath. 'What do you mean "what does it matter"? What if it's illegal?'

John shrugged his shoulders not wanting to face that possibility. 'I don't know. I'll see him tomorrow night and find out more.'

Carol didn't comment.

John was in the pub by six-thirty. He had to admit to himself, he was rather excited at meeting up with the stranger. He felt more positive than he had for some time. *A chance of some work. Hmmm, did it really matter if it was a teensy bit illegal? It would pay the bills.* The pub was less noisy tonight; the usual crowd wasn't yet in. 'A pint please, Jen.'

She chuckled. 'You seem chirpier tonight. Good to see you back to your old self.' She pulled his pint and pushed it across the counter. Before he had time to pay, he heard a Scottish accent.

'I'll get that.'

John turned to his left. 'Thank you.'

The man nodded. 'Always happy to help people along the way.' He held his hand out. 'Robbie Kelvin.'

John smiled and took his hand. 'John Mason.'

Robbie nodded over to the back of the room to a small alcove away from the main area. 'Let's grab a seat and I'll explain a little more.' Once ensconced, Robbie looked around to make sure they couldn't be overheard, then lowered his voice and leaned into John. 'I'll come straight to the point, John. There are certain goods I need delivering from a location in Scotland to the Manchester area. What I need you to do is simply pick up the goods, take them to an address in Moss Side and, once the goods are dropped off, you will be paid.'

John looked puzzled. 'That's it?'

'That's it. Pick up, deliver, get paid and repeat it the following week.'

John pushed Robbie for more detail. 'What are the goods?'

Robbie held up his hand. 'You don't need to know those details. Your job will be to collect and deliver.'

'Okaaay...how much will I be paid?' Robbie pushed a piece of paper across the table and waited for John's response. John read it twice then looked at Robbie. 'Each delivery?'

Robbie smiled and nodded. John leaned back in his seat and smiled. That amount would pay off all John and Carol's debts in two or three deliveries! 'And the catch?'

Robbie Kelvin scoffed. 'There isn't one. It comes with a certain type of risk, but you're being well paid.'

'Is it legal?'

Robbie shrugged his shoulders. 'Depends on your definition of legal.'

'How does it work?'

Robbie knew he'd got him! 'You drive up to Glasgow...'

John interrupted him. 'We've only got one car and my wife needs it for work'.

Robbie ignored the interruption, 'or take the train to Glasgow Central and grab a taxi to an address I'll give you.' John nodded slowly whilst he processed the information. 'The work I'm offering you will help clear your debts.'

John made a quick, irrational decision. *Hmm, I might not get another chance!* 'Okay, I'll do it,' he blurted out.

Robbie smiled a wolfish smile. 'Let me get you another drink then we'll finalise things. You won't regret it. I know other people who've been out of work have done what you're about to do and have managed to pay their debts off.'

As soon as John arrived home from the pub, Carol was keen to hear all the details. 'Well, what did he have to say?' John repeated the conversation he'd had with Robbie, told her how much he would be paid and that he'd agreed to make a couple of deliveries. 'What are the deliveries you're making? Did you ask him?'

'Yes, but he wouldn't say. He said I didn't need to know. My job would simply be to collect the parcels in one location and drop them off in another location.'

'It sounds iffy to me; you don't know the guy. I'm not happy about this.'

He acknowledged her concerns. 'I know. I'm not over the moon either, but two or three deliveries will clear our debts, then we'll be back on an even keel.'

'So, where do you go from here?'

'Robbie, that's the man's name, said he would phone me with instructions.' Before Carol had time to respond, the phone rang. They looked at each other and read each other's minds. John jumped up and disappeared into the hall. Carol could hear a muffled conversation which continued for a few minutes, then John reappeared. He sat down, a surprised look on his face.

'Well?' Carol barked. He didn't speak for a few seconds. Carol saw the look. 'What?'

'Tomorrow! They want me up in Glasgow tomorrow. It's taken me a bit by surprise. I didn't think it would happen so quickly.'

Carol swirled her hands at him implying she wanted more information. 'So, what's the detail.

'Glasgow.'

'I know, you've already said.' She was exasperated at having to drag the information out of him. 'Where in Glasgow? Who are you meeting? When will you be back?'

He looked bewildered at the fast-paced questions. 'Oh, yeah, sorry.' He cleared his throat. 'I need to get an early train, Robbie suggested there was one around eight, arriving in Glasgow around half eleven.' He held up a piece of paper on which he'd written some instructions. 'I'm to take a taxi to this address where I'll meet the 'boss', as Robbie calls him, have a chat, pick up a parcel and be back on the train around two-thirty, arriving in Manchester around six.'

'Then what?'

'Ah yeah, Robbie said that someone will provide me with the phone number and location of the guy I need to meet in Manchester where I have to make the drop-off. The person will then pay me in cash.' As an afterthought John added, 'can you take me to the station tomorrow morning and pick me up off the six o'clock train?'

Carol nodded. 'Yeah, sure.' She still wasn't happy. It all sounded too *"cloak and dagger"*; too easy. It had to be illegal, iffy at best.

John could sense her negativity and tried to appeal to her. 'I need to be working, whatever it is.' Tears formed in his eyes. 'I need to take this opportunity, if only for a short time.'

She sighed and relaxed for a moment. 'I know, love, I know.'

The following morning Carol dutifully drove John to Piccadilly, kissed him goodbye and wished him good luck. 'See you tonight, love.'

The station was busy, and she was glad to get away from the noise and the swarms of people milling about. She then drove to work, mulling over what John had agreed to do, but there was a sick feeling in her stomach.

* * *

Part Two

Fiona Cavanagh had been contacted by Bill Bogle the day before John's first delivery. She was the girlfriend of Bogle's partner in crime, Donny Campbell, who was currently serving a twenty-year sentence for a drive-by shooting in the Govan area of Glasgow. Fiona was a 30-something, non-descript woman of medium height and short sandy hair. She had been recruited to gather information on John Mason's life: who his friends were, where he hung out and, more importantly, whether he had any police connections. She would be sat on the train to Manchester inconspicuously reading a magazine in the same carriage as Mason with his holdall, she reflected on the conversations she'd had with Bogle previously at his home in Bearsden. She'd been there many times, although usually with Donny Campbell. Bogle oozed charm. However, there was an underlying menace about the man you couldn't quite put your finger on.

The Bogle residence was an imposing large red sandstone bungalow set on two acres of land. Fiona arrived at the property and Bogle was already standing at the door with a welcoming beam across his face.

'Fiona, it's so good to see you. How are you?'

She pecked him on the cheek. 'Well, thank you. And you?'

'On top of the world. Come in, come in.'

He waved her through to the lounge which had a large bay window overlooking the rear garden. In the lounge were two large, white, sumptuous sofas set at right angles to each other which faced an imposing brick fireplace. On one wall were several bookcases crammed with books, on another hung a wide-screen television.

'Can I get you a coffee...tea?'

'Coffee please Bill.'

She could hear him opening and closing cupboard doors in the kitchen, followed by the gurgling of a coffee machine. He re-appeared several minutes later with a tray containing a pot of coffee and a plate of biscuits.

'Allow me,' he said as he carefully poured them each a cup of steaming coffee. He leaned back into the sofa and, smiling, raised his cup. 'I've another job for you. Did Robbie explain?'

She smiled back. 'I assumed you had and yes, he did.'

He chuckled. 'I'll come straight to the point.' He reiterated what Robbie Kelvin had already explained to her on a previous occasion. 'We've just taken on a new courier for the Glasgow-Manchester run, a John Mason. He'll be coming up to Glasgow tomorrow for his first trip. He's going to make a delivery to Jamie McKay.' She nodded; she knew Jamie well. Bogle hesitated slightly. 'I haven't told Mason what the delivery consists of. I think he's assuming it's drugs – and of course it normally would be.' He then went into more detail which Robbie wouldn't have known. 'Because Mason is an unknown quantity the holdall will contain nothing more than bags of coconut flour. The only other person who knows this is Jamie McKay at the Manchester end. Robbie doesn't know, nor do any of the staff.' He chuckled. 'And if Mason gets stopped for any reason, he's carrying coconut flour!' He leaned forward to pour a second cup before continuing. 'I want you to monitor him. Follow him back to Manchester on the train, check out where he works, who he associates with. Get as much detail as you can.' Fiona nodded knowing exactly what was expected of her; she'd done this kind of job for Bogle many times. 'If he's clear then we use him on a regular basis.' She tilted her head. 'Consider it done.'

John's train ride to Glasgow was pleasant enough and he began to relax and think about how their lives could change if he could continue the deliveries beyond paying off their debts. Who knows, after a year they might have enough to have a holiday or buy a second car, or even make larger payments on the monthly mortgage. His thoughts sounded optimistic. Perhaps the redundancy was a blessing in disguise. What a stroke of luck he was drinking in the pub at the same time as Robbie Kelvin. Very fortunate indeed.

He arrived in Glasgow Central just before eleven-thirty. As he stepped out of the carriage he was met by the inevitable smell of large stations, the masses of people moving in all directions like ants, the incomprehensible voice of the public address system and station porters busying themselves with luggage. Once outside the station he stood and took a breather and looked around him. *So, this is Glasgow.* He delved inside his jacket pocket and retrieved the piece of paper on which he'd written the address given to him by Robbie Kelvin. He grabbed the next in-line taxi, informed the driver of the address then settled back in the seat. The taxi driver, half tilting his head over his shoulder whilst he drove, kept up a flow of conversation with his passenger, most of which John could not understand. He hummed and harred hopefully in the right places trying to be part of the conversation, but whether he was offending the man or agreeing with him he had no idea – the strong, gravelly Glasgow accent defeated any meaningful understanding of the topic of conversation.

The address he'd given to the driver was in Blythswood. Within a few minutes the taxi drew up at number sixteen Blythswood Square. It was obviously an up-market area from the look of the buildings and the luxury cars parked on the road. John paid the driver and stood on the pavement looking up at number sixteen. The three-storey building was constructed of large red sandstone blocks. It had black wrought iron railings on either side of the stone steps which led to an impressive front door. He tentatively climbed the ten steps to the large red door with ornate stained-glass windows on either side. A list of residents was attached to the right-hand side of the door, each with a button and a brass plate surrounding the names of the occupants. John checked his piece of paper for the name of the man he was to meet. His finger hovered above the bell for a Mr Bill Bogle. His stomach suddenly lurched. He suddenly felt he was getting into something that was out of his league.

Was Carol correct in thinking this was too good to be true? What would be the consequence if he pulled out now and caught the next train home?

Before he realised what he was doing his poised digit seemed to have a mind of its own and pressed the bell. The intercom was immediately answered. 'Hello, the Bogle residence.'

John cleared his throat before speaking. 'Er, It's John Mason, I'm here to see Mr Bogle.'

He heard the door electronically unlock and the faceless voice gave instructions. 'Take the lift to the top floor. Someone will meet you.' The voice clicked off. He pushed the main door open and stepped into the main entrance. John felt himself perspiring. He took out his handkerchief and wiped his brow. He headed to the small lift which was located on the left of the entrance and pressed the button. When the lift finally arrived, he pulled back the metal gate and nervously stepped in. He began to feel a little claustrophobic as the lift headed for the top floor. As soon as he stepped out of the lift he was met by a giant of a man with black, staring eyes, who almost filled the gap left by the open doors of the lift. 'John Mason?' The owner of the enquiring voice had a surprisingly soft gentle lilt and a pleasant manner which helped put John at ease. He led John down a corridor then pushed open a door and waved John through. As he nervously entered, a man stood up from a large cream leather sofa from where he'd been drinking from an oversized cup. He held his hand out and had a warm smile.

'Ah, John. I've been looking forward to meeting you.' He pointed to the tray on which were several cups and a coffee pot. 'Can I get you a coffee?'

John nodded. 'Yes please, white, no sugar.'

The man introduced himself as Bill Bogle. 'Welcome to our association.' He was a large man who obviously worked out, his muscles straining at his shirt buttons. He had black hair, a swarthy olive complexion and designer stubble. As naïve as John was, he guessed that Bill Bogle was not the man's real name. He looked more East European than Pollokshields East. Bogle pointed to the sofa. 'Please, take a seat.' He nodded in the direction of the man who'd met John at the lift and who was now standing by the door. 'I see you've already met Tam.

Tam this is John Mason, he's joining our little venture.' Both John and Tam nodded to each other in acknowledgment. Bogle smiled at John. 'I won't keep you long. We can have you back on the train by lunchtime and you'll be back in Manchester by six.' His face changed from 'bon homme' to serious. 'I'll get down to the nitty gritty, John. It's all very straightforward.' He pointed to a large brown holdall which was by his side. 'You'll take this back to Manchester.' He handed over a small card. 'This is your contact in Manchester. You must phone this number tomorrow, John....tomorrow!' he emphasised, 'it's imperative, Okay? He's your end of what we call the country run.'

'The country run?'

Bogle spoke as if he was speaking to a five-year old. 'The country run, the run from here down to Manchester. We have another country run from here to Newcastle and one to Liverpool. Anyway, he will tell you when and where to deliver the holdall. Once it's delivered you get paid. You then wait for your next instruction.' He lifted the bulky holdall off the floor and handed it to John. 'Take care of it. You must, and I emphasise *must*, keep it with you at all times, okay?' John nodded, still a little bewildered. 'Okay?' Bogle repeated.

John came out of his daze and replied with enthusiasm. 'Yes, yes, of course.'

Bogle nodded to Tam then spoke again to John. 'Tam will run you back to the station. Don't forget to phone your Manchester contact tomorrow, okay?' John nodded as he rose from the sofa picking up the holdall. Tam opened the door for him and ushered him out into the corridor. As the large man closed the door he made eye contact with Bogle, both nodded knowingly. The instant the door closed Bogle picked up the phone and dialled a Manchester number.

'Hello?'

'Robbie, It's Bill. Mason's just left. I've given him Jamie's phone number who he'll contact tomorrow. I want Mason followed twenty-four seven for the next week. See where he goes, who he meets, which pubs he frequents. Have you confirmed with Fiona Cavanagh?'

'Don't worry Bill, I've got Fiona locked in on this. He'll never know he's being followed.'

'Good. He's new, remember, so I want as much info on him as you can get. At this stage he's an unknown quantity. He could be an undercover cop or an informer, or a competitor. We don't want him mixing with, shall we say, undesirables.'

'Got it.'

The phone clicked off.

Carol collected John from Piccadilly Station as arranged, just as dusk was descending across the skyline. The lights in the hotels and office buildings around Piccadilly were giving a glow against a dark grey sky. As soon as they were out of the city centre and she'd pointed the car in the direction of home, she pressed him for information. 'So, how did you get on?' She looked suspiciously at the holdall nestling between John's legs and added quickly, 'I don't want to know what's in there.'

He ignored her concerns and kept the conversation light. 'They seem a nice bunch. I've got a number to phone tomorrow to find out where and when I make the delivery. Then I get paid. Three or four deliveries should clear our debts.'

Carol glanced sideways at him. 'Three or four...before you said two or three,' she queried accusingly.

'Yeah, well, two, three, four, whatever, we'll soon have our debts cleared.'

The conversation was muted the rest of the journey home. A fine drizzle had started blurring the rear lights of the car in front of them.

John also preferred not to know what was in the holdall.

* * *

The next day he phoned the number Bill Bogle had given him.

''Ello,' came an abrupt flat Manchester accent.

'Is that Jamie?'

'Who wants to know?'

'It's John Mason. Mr Bogle gave me your phone number.'

''Ave you got it?'

'Yeah.'

'Right. D'you know the Moss Side area?'

'Er, not really but I'll take a taxi. I'll find it.'

'This afternoon. Flaxby 'eights, fourth landin', number thirty-two. We're off Corcoran Street. Three o'clock, okay. See you then.' Jamie McKay was a man of few words.

John slowly put the phone down, again questioning if he was in this too deep. *This Jamie bloke didn't sound too friendly. His conversation was a bit staccato.*

The Pakistani taxi driver queried the address when John passed it to him. 'Bin there before 'ave you, mate?'

'No, why?'

'It's an iffy area.'

'Oh, right. I won't be long, will you wait?'

The driver sniggered. 'No chance, mate. I don't stop around there fer more than a minute otherwise I'll 'ave me wheels nicked.'

'Er, okay. Right, thanks anyway. I'll get home somehow.'

He found himself at the bottom of a tall block of council flats. It must have been at least fifteen-storeys high. In the open area in front of the main doors which were badly damaged and hanging off their hinges, stood several vehicles. Two were burnt out, one on bricks. A skip, which hadn't been emptied in recent times was piled high with all sorts of detritus. Dumped on top were a supermarket trolley and a child's rusting bicycle. John decided against using the lift and made his way up to the fourth landing. Gasping for breath as he reached his destination, he peered down the length of the landing. What a sorry sight! Litter was strewn everywhere. Windows on several of the flats he passed on his way to number thirty-two were boarded up, and looking at the amount of graffiti, had been for some time. Number thirty-two had a badly faded door, net curtains sagged at the window. Two suspicious looking teens moved away as John approached. He knocked at the door which was immediately opened by Jamie McKay. He was a cadaverous man with straggly fair hair, red eyes and wearing a blue jumper which sported numerous holes, and tracksuit bottoms.

He was barefoot. 'Are you John?' John nodded and half held up the holdall. 'Come in.' John was quickly dragged in, down a narrow hallway and into a "lounge". The whole flat smelled of dirt; cooking fat and had a haze of smoke hung around the ceiling. Jamie held his hand out for the holdall, quickly unzipped it and checked its contents. He nodded to John then wandered across the room to pick up an envelope that John had seen on the table. 'Go an' enjoy yerself mate.' He headed for the front door as an indication that John should follow, he opened the door to see John out. 'See yer again soon. Cheers.'

Within five minutes John found himself once more in the open area in front of the high-rise flats and wondered how he would get home. He saw an old lady wearing a headscarf and a well-worn coat waddling across the open space, full shopping bags in her hands. John smiled at her. 'Excuse me. How do I get into the city centre from here?'

She put her shopping bags down and wiped her nose on her sleeve. 'Through there, son.' She rasped pointing to a ginnel between the blocks of flats. She spoke with the voice of a lifelong smoker. 'Through there, turn right. Across the road from the Bricklayers pub is the bus stop. Number forty-seven will take you into the city, luv.'

'Thank you.' She didn't reply, but carried on her way, waddling and sniffling. Thankfully he didn't have to wait long for the bus to arrive. From the city centre it was an easy bus ride home.

John was already home from his first delivery to Moss Side when Carol returned from work. He gave her a kiss then produced an envelope, conjurers style, from his jacket and placed it on the kitchen unit.

'Ta Ra!' A broad beam spread across his face as he went to the fridge to retrieve a bottle of wine and proceeded to pour them both a glass. She smiled with curiosity.

'What's the celebration?' she asked picking up the glass of Chenin. He clinked her glass and pointed to the envelope lying temptingly half open on the unit. She raised her eyebrows then slowly pulled the envelope toward her and peered inside. 'Oh, my god! How much is that?'

He tilted his head a smug smirk across his face. 'Enough to pay off a fair bit of our arrears...and there's more to come.'

* * *

Over the following week Fiona checked out where he lived. On a couple of occasions he went to the pub in the early evening and met up with, whom she assumed, were his friends. She followed them in and sat within earshot, quietly reading a book. None of the conversations were significant. There were no hushed voices, no looking around checking out the other customers, no passing of notes or envelopes. She even sat at the next table to John and Carol at Cuppello's on the Saturday morning. There was nothing suspicious about the man at all!

At the end of a week's monitoring she rang Bill Bogle. 'Absolutely nothing Bill.'

He sounded relieved. 'Thanks. We might do one more dummy run then let him go live. Hang on another week. Maybe a couple of weeks monitoring him should be enough. Thanks again Fiona. We'll catch up for a drink once you're back in Glasgow.'

'I'll hold you to that.' She put the phone down and smiled to herself.

That was easy money, a week in Manchester and nothing to report! One more week and more easy money!

* * *

John received another phone call from Robbie at the end of the week.

'Tomorrow John. Same routine as before.' At the thought of another pay day John readily agreed. Only Bill Bogle, Jamie McKay and Fiona Cavanagh knew it was another dummy run.

Fiona had completed her two-week stint and reported back to Bogle. 'Still nothing Bill. He looks good to go. I think your Glasgow to Manchester run is safe.'

Over the next month John completed a total of eight deliveries, albeit the first two, unknown to him, being dummy runs.

Over dinner one evening in the restaurant Le Canard Rouge, enjoying a bottle of Merlot in celebration of John's new-found fortune, Carol gave John some good news. She delved into her handbag and pulled out several sheets of paper which showed their bank statement. 'See, not only are we owing zero we've got a buffer in our bank account!' John smiled at her and raised his glass.

'Well worth the risk wasn't it? I still don't know exactly what I was carrying, I preferred not to know. How fortunate I met Robbie in the pub that night.' They clinked glasses.

By the sixth month John had made seventeen deliveries to Jamie McKay.

He was having coffee in Cuppello's one morning when he spotted someone staring at him then quickly look away as John looked up. He didn't recognise the individual and immediately dismissed it. Over the following weeks he thought he'd seen the same person watching him. It made him nervous. He'd scurry down the road only to halt around a corner waiting to see if he was being followed. He was becoming paranoid. Would he sooner or later get stopped as he was getting on the train in Glasgow or alighting in Manchester? He began taking alternative routes home, constantly looking over his shoulder.

Carol noticed his change in demeanour. 'What's the matter?' She caught him pushing his food around his plate. He looked up at her. 'I think I'm being watched.'

Carol looked worried. 'What makes you think that?'

He shrugged his shoulders. 'Just an uneasy feeling. Maybe I'm imagining it.'

'D'you think you should stop the deliveries?'

He nodded. 'Probably. It worries me that perhaps the police or a rival are keeping tabs on me.'

'Then stop. You've done what you set out to do. It was a short-term arrangement after all. We're okay now, we're on the right side. You don't need to be taking any more risks.' Carol could always put problems into perspective.

He hadn't heard from Robbie in a few weeks, when one evening the phone rang. John jumped up and almost ran to the phone. Carol could hear a muffled conversation then raised voices. He came back into the lounge, running his hand through his hair in frustration. Carol looked concerned. 'What was all that about?' He sat down flushed, shaking his head. 'John,' she barked, 'what is it?'

'He wants me to do another run. I told him no and why; that I thought I was being followed.'

'Did you tell him you wanted out?'

He looked across at her his eyes tearing up. 'Yes. He got quite aggressive. Told me I couldn't leave. Once a courier always a courier...end of.'

'How was it left?'

'I said I wasn't doing another run, then I put the phone down.'

John didn't sleep that night. He tossed and turned. The way Robbie had turned from being the amiable character he knew, into someone threatening, frightened him. The next day he wandered around the house, unable to settle. He couldn't get Robbie's hostility out of his mind. He made himself a cup of coffee, but sat staring out of the window until it went cold. He was glad when Carol came home from work. She shouted from the hallway, 'Hi John.' As soon as she saw him she could see he was worried. 'How have you been today?'

He pursed his lips. 'So, so. I can't get over Robbie's attitude. He wasn't prepared to listen.'

Carol poured them a glass of wine. 'You stick to your guns. It's your life, your decision.'

They looked at each other and held their breaths as the phone rang. It seemed to sound louder and more intrusive than usual. 'Christ! Who's that?'

Carol touched his arm as encouragement. 'You won't know until you answer it.' John nodded, went into the hallway and picked up the phone.

'Hello?' John listened to what he was being told to do then came back into the lounge.

'Was it Robbie?'

'Yeah. He's picking me up at eight to go to the pub. He wants to discuss the other night's phone conversation. It'll be busy so not much can happen to me in the pub.'

At almost eight o'clock a knock came at the door causing Carol and John to glance at teach other with worried looks. John's stomach did a somersault.

He stood up. 'It'll be Robbie. I'll see you later love.'

She gave him a kiss. 'Stick to your guns. Which pub are you going to?'

'Cross Keys on Highgate.' With that he reluctantly left, quietly closing the front door.

The Cross Keys was a town centre pub and, thankfully, from John's perspective, always busy. Tonight was no different. A darts match was taking place and John could hear snooker balls clunking in the adjoining room. Robbie marched to the bar and ordered two pints without asking John what he wanted, then walked over to a table as far from the bustle as he could get. The background noise would muffle any conversation they were about to have. John was surprised to see Jamie McKay already sitting at the table, a pint pot in front of him. Both men mutely acknowledged each other with a nod. Robbie strategically placed himself with his back to the rest of the pub to eliminate the risk of anyone lip reading what he was about to say to John. John sat down next to Jamie, his back leaning against the panelled wall, and waited to hear what Robbie was going to say. Robbie pushed his pint to one side and leaned on the table. 'Now, John. What's all this about not wanting to do more runs?'

John tried to sound confident. 'I told you the other night. I thought I was being followed. It's too risky. I took up the offer of work because I needed a financial leg up after the redundancy. It was meant to be short term. My debts have been cleared so I've decided I'm not continuing with the runs.'

Robbie sneered, his voice menacing. 'You really don't understand, do you?' He nodded towards Jamie. 'Jamie here is waiting for more deliveries, he has customers and orders to fulfil.' John remained silent and Jamie stepped in.

'I need deliveries now, John.'

Robbie moved even closer into John's body space. 'So, I'm expected to go back to Mr Bogle and tell him you want out am I?' John nodded. Robbie continued. 'When I tell him you want out, do you know what he'll say? He'll say nobody opts out without his say-so. Nobody, but nobody, leaves the organisation just because they feel they've had enough. Mr Bogle will not have his deliveries compromised. If they are, there will be consequences. They are consequences you don't want to contemplate.' John remained silent and stood up to leave. 'John, you've got two weeks to change your mind or...well, let's say you, and in particular Carol, will not be happy. Think on.' Robbie swilled back the remains in his glass and nodded to Jamie. 'Let's go.' As Jamie moved off he grabbed John's arm then mimed a knife being drawn across his throat. John was left standing in a daze as he watched the other two disappear though the pub doors.

Carol was pacing up and down waiting for John's return. When she heard the key in the door she ran to meet him. Seeing the look on his face she knew the meeting had not gone well. 'Tell me what went on.'

John went into the lounge still in a daze and flopped down onto the sofa. *Why, oh why, did I get myself into this mess.* He related what had happened in the pub.

Carol was horrified. 'They threatened you?'

He nodded. 'The threat was very clear. If I don't continue there would be disastrous consequences.'

'Did they say what?'

John looked at Carol with tears in his eyes. 'Jamie drew a knife across his throat as a threat.'

'They're bluffing?'

'I doubt it very much. I gathered that the Bogle set-up is part of the Scottish mafia. Nothing's more important than,' he used his index fingers as quotes, "the business". 'Robbie gave me two weeks to change my mind...or else!' He turned to Carol. 'What if I get caught! I couldn't cope with jail.'

Carol sunk back into the sofa. 'Bloody hell, what have we unleashed?' She started to cry and leaned against John's shoulder. Somehow they would have to get through this.

Neither of them slept that night. John got up at 3am. He sat in the lounge and racked his brain to think of an alternative way of getting himself out of this nightmare. He walked into the kitchen where Carol was already busying herself with the kettle. 'Couldn't you sleep either?' She shook her head and said she was going to make a cuppa. Whilst she was in the kitchen she began putting some thought as to how she could help John through it all. She knew he would panic and think irrationally. She was the practical one; the one most likely to come up with a solution. As she pondered various options, one in particular came to mind like a blue flash. It was so outrageous that she kept revisiting it, working it through over the next couple of days. In the meantime she didn't dare tell John, he would have thought her plan too dangerous. She knew in her own mind that it would have to work, because being locked into this insidious organisation was not an option.

Carol kissed John goodbye as she left for work. 'Don't worry, I'll think of something. Why don't you go into town and look for a book; take your mind off Robbie.'

He gave her a forced smile. 'Yeah, I might. Have a good day.'

He sat in the lounge and just stared at the floor. He couldn't think straight. His mind was in turmoil. *What is the worst-case scenario? What if they followed through with their threats? What if I get caught and serve time?*

* * *

Carol sat at the reception desk of Corball and Maine, financial advisers. It was a light, spacious area, with narrow oak Venetian blinds at the windows. The colour scheme was sumptuous black leather sofas and light oak panelling. She greeted the staff as they arrived with a 'good morning' and a well-practised smile. Her first task of the day was to tidy the coffee table strewn with magazines in the waiting area, ensure the various pictures on the walls were straight and fill up the sanitiser on the end of her desk. Having completed her tasks she could then start the day. It was always busy with phone calls and visitors. Today was no different. She had a good view of the car park thanks to the floor to ceiling windows. She watched Jeff Worrall, her boss, parking his BMW, grabbing his briefcase off the back seat and making his way to the main doors.

'Morning Carol.'

'Morning Jeff, beautiful morning.'

'It is indeed,' he replied as he swiped his electronic key card to enter the offices. She watched him disappear through the door and smiled to herself. *He's part of my plan to get us out of this mess. I'll catch up with him later.*

She said goodbye to Jeff Worrall's last appointment before lunch and a moment later made her way to Jeff's office. He was standing at a filing cabinet as she gently knocked on his door. He turned and smiled.

'Oh, hi Carol, come in.' She nervously sat down opposite him, having now had second thoughts about her approach. 'How can I help you?' She hesitated so he queried, 'Are you okay?'

She gave a stifled laugh and relaxed a little. 'Yeah, I'm okay. I just wanted to run something past you.'

He leaned back in his chair with an encouraging smile. 'Fire away.' She hesitated once more, then coughed to clear her throat before relating her story regarding John's redundancy, his time as a courier and left nothing out, right up to the previous night's meeting John had with two of Bogle's cronies.

He frowned and leaned forward. 'My god, this sounds serious. How can I help?'

'Am I correct in thinking your wife is a police officer?'

'Er, yes. In the drug squad.'

'Would I be able to have a word with her about John acting as an informer regarding a Scottish mafia-style organisation?'

He laughed. 'Wow! That's some risk to take. Your husband could be arrested.'

She looked down. 'I know.'

He suddenly looked serious then picked up the phone. 'Andrea's home at the moment, I'll give her a ring.' Carol got up to leave, but Jeff indicated for her to stay. 'Oh, hi, it's me. I've got a colleague in my office, Carol, d'you remember her, works on reception? Good. Well, she wants to have a word with you, something to do with a drugs cartel.' There was a pause then, 'No, she'll explain...okay, hang on I'll check.' He turned to Carol. 'She's free at lunch time if that suits you?' Carol nodded. 'Yeah, she's free. Right, okay.' Jeff put the phone down and smiled. 'She'll be in at 1pm. I'll book the small meeting room for you.'

Carol looked relieved and rose from her seat. 'Thanks, I really appreciate this. I'll get Sarah to stand in for me on reception.'

At ten minutes to one Andrea Worrall arrived. She was a woman in her late thirties with short blonde hair and a toned body. She wore a pair of tailored navy trousers and cream top. Her posture was one of self-confidence as she walked up to the reception desk. 'Carol?'

'Yes, it's good of you to come out Andrea. I recognise you from the photograph on Jeff's desk.'

Andrea had a warm smile. 'That's okay. I'm interested in what you have to say.'

Carol held up her finger. 'I'll just phone my stand-in, Sarah, to cover for me.'

Sarah, a sixteen-year-old trainee, arrived for the hand-over, then Carol showed Andrea into the meeting room. Andrea took a seat and opened her briefcase. 'Do you mind if I make notes, this sounds as if it could be serious.' Carol consented, then repeated what she'd explained to Jeff earlier. Andrea continued to make notes then looked up. 'Does your husband know we're having this conversation?'

She shook her head. 'I didn't dare tell him until I'd discussed it with Jeff... and now you,' she added quickly. Andrea leaned back in her chair. 'You've mentioned a few names.' She paused. 'They are names that are known to us. Two of them in particular, Bill Bogle and Jamie McKay, have come up in previous investigations. We know where McKay lives, but we can't pin down exactly where he's distributing the drugs from. And we haven't been able to home in on a courier. The information you have provided is crucial.'

Carol realised she was now in too deep to backtrack. The genie was out of the bottle. 'So, what happens next?' she asked nervously.

'First, you tell your husband, it's John isn't it? Second, I have a meeting with him.'

Andrea saw the worried look on Carol's face. 'Would you like me to be there when you tell him you've spoken to the police?'

She shook her head slowly. 'No, I'll tell him, but can we make a definite time and place when you see him. If an appointment is already made he's less likely to back out of it.'

'Of course, the sooner the better. I would suggest your house for the first meeting...less stressful for both of you. How about tomorrow evening?'

A smile returned to Carol's face. 'That would be perfect, thank you.'

Andrea continued. 'I do need to discuss this with my boss. This does seem to be a breakthrough for us, so thank you for coming forward. It took a lot of courage, Carol, but believe me you've done the right thing.'

Andrea left and Carol returned to the reception desk, not sure whether she had done the right thing or whether she'd just dug John into a deep hole.

Over dinner that evening Carol told John what she'd done.

'You've done what!' barked John, his face red with anger. 'You've spoken to the cops. Carol, for god's sake, I've been breaking the law. I could go to prison.'

She tried to plead with him. 'Just listen to me.' She stood up and started to pace. 'What choices have you got? One, you continue the deliveries, and, whether you like it or not, sooner or later the chances are you'd be caught...then you'd go to jail.' She paused to let that sink in. 'Or, two, you co-operate with the police and hopefully we are able to resolve the situation. You'll get a deal if you come forward with information.' He rested his head in his hands and thought through what she was telling him. He'd always relied on Carol to make the rational decisions. After the last couple of weeks he was too stressed to think straight. His mind was in constant turmoil. In his heart he knew she was right. Wasn't she always!

'Okay, make an appointment to see...what's her name?'

'DS Andrea Worrall, and the appointment's already been made. She's coming round tomorrow evening.'

* * *

The following evening Carol muted the television then answered the knock at the door, giving John a reassuring smile as she left the lounge. She welcomed the detective in.

She stepped in and in a quiet voice asked. 'Have you told John?'

Carol nodded. 'Yes.' Then in a whisper said, 'John's worried you're going to arrest him.' John nervously stood up as Andrea entered the lounge, wiping his sweaty hands down the side of his jeans.

'Hello.' Andrea smiled. 'Thank you for seeing me, John. I'm sure you're going to be a great help.' He beckoned her to take a seat.

'I'll try.'

She filled him in on some of the detail which she had already explained to Carol. The Glasgow end of the country run was being observed by Lanarkshire police and Jamie McKay was being monitored by her division here in Manchester. 'We think the drugs are coming in from South America into Glasgow and then distributed throughout the UK. They call them the country runs. What we're looking for, John, is for you to continue the deliveries as normal so we can build up a dossier of their activities. We need to know how McKay is distributing the goods around the Manchester area. We're working very closely with Lanarkshire police who are also trying to link the Glasgow enterprise with Newcastle and Liverpool. It would appear they have a similar set up to the Manchester operation, that is, employing a courier to drop off the goods. In other words, someone is doing the same as you.'

With a lull in the conversation John felt he needed to explain why he had got involved. He looked embarrassed, wringing his hands as he spoke. 'I feel terrible to have resorted to what did. I don't know if Carol told you, I'd been made redundant, and we had massive bills and overdrafts to pay.' He was hoping his explanation went some way towards mitigating his involvement. She nodded.

'What I'd like you do is come into the station tomorrow. I'd like to show you some photos, see if you recognise anyone.'

The next morning he arrived at Roby Road police station. He told the desk sergeant he'd come to see DS Worrall. The desk sergeant, a man with a thin moustache and a pointed nose, picked up the phone and spoke to someone, then turned to John. 'DS Worrall will be down in two minutes, please take a seat.' He sat on a hard plastic chair feeling self-conscious and let his eyes wander around the room. He briefly scanned the many posters on the walls referring to rabies, drink and drive, lost pets and the serious crime of dealing in drugs. His eyes quickly moved on. A door opened with a loud click causing him to look up to see DS Worrall beckoning him through.

'Thanks for coming in John.' She pointed to a blue door. 'Just in there please.' The sign on the door said Interview Room 4. It wasn't what he expected. He'd heard of 'soft' interview rooms and this appeared to be one. It was light and airy. It had a large opaque window on one wall, the décor was light green and cream; the chairs upholstered. 'Can I get you a coffee?' she continued with a smile.

'Er, yes please, white no sugar?' She was gone for a minute or so then returned with two coffees. She wrinkled her nose slightly as she spoke 'Sorry, they're out of a machine.' She immediately got down to business. 'I did say I had some photos to show you, okay?'

John leaned forward in an attempt to look helpful. She pulled several photos out of a green manila file. The first one he instantly recognised.

'That's Bill Bogle.'

'Good, how about this?'

He nodded. 'That's Robbie Kelvin.'

She hesitated, 'okay,' then informed John, 'that's not his real name. We know him as Graham Beaumont. How do you know him?'

John pointed to the photo. 'That's the man who got me the job. He'd overheard me telling the barmaid in the pub that I'd been made redundant, he approached me at the bar and offered me some work.' He raised his voice. 'That's the man who threatened me the other night when I told him I wanted out.'

She showed him another photo. 'And this?'

'That's Jamie McKay.'

'Is this the man you deliver the goods to?'

'Yes.'

'At what address?'

John told her. 'A block of flats, Flaxby Heights in Moss Side.'

'Anywhere else?'

'No.'

'Well, we now believe Flaxby Heights was his girlfriend's flat. Have you ever delivered to McKay at any other address?'

John looked helpless. 'No I haven't.'

She removed two more photos from the file and turned them to face John.

'And those?' He shook his head. Andrea shuffled them back into the file. 'We believe that they are the other couriers for the north of England – one of them on the Glasgow-Newcastle run and the other to Liverpool.' She changed tone. 'I'd like to bring in my boss if that's okay with you.'

She left the interview room and returned several minutes later with one of her colleagues. He was a tall man with short dark hair and a trim beard. He wore a two-piece navy suit, a blue shirt and a red striped tie. He had a Geordie accent. John nodded as the officer introduced himself, holding out his hand. 'Good morning, John. I'm DI Trevor Fletcher, thank you for coming in. We're hoping you'll be able to help us further.' John sat back wondering what was coming next. 'The information you have provided so far is extremely helpful, so what we'd like you to do, if you are agreeable, is to continue the deliveries, same routine.' He glanced at Andrea. 'I understand DS Worrall has shown you two photos of couriers we believe are running the Newcastle and Liverpool part of the organisation. What we'd like you to do, is try and get information on the two couriers you couldn't identify – their names, and ideally where they operate from.' He hesitated then continued. 'What we don't want to do is put you in a dangerous situation. Try, if you can, to glean some information during a normal conversation when you go up to collect your delivery. Obviously, you can't ask too many questions, otherwise they'll get suspicious.'

John began to panic slightly. 'I'm not sure. I don't trust any of them.'

The DI smiled knowingly. 'Could I suggest that you offer to deliver to Liverpool or Newcastle. As a cover, tell them you have relatives in those cities. Just get Bogle chatting about the other towns.' He stood up. 'I'll leave you with DS Worrall, thank you again.'

Once he'd left, John spoke first. 'I'm not sure I can do that. It sounds risky.'

Andrea thought carefully before she spoke. 'I agree, however, gathering that info would mitigate any charges that could be brought against you. I say that because it would be the CPS who make the final decision. We would argue for the charges against you to be dropped as you'd be working 'under cover'.' John felt he was between a rock and a hard place, but eventually agreed.

'I'll ring Robbie and tell him I've changed my mind about pulling out.'

Andrea looked relieved. 'Thank you. Whilst you're in Glasgow we'll liaise with Lanarkshire police to monitor you. I promise you'll be safe.'

'Okay,' John whispered reluctantly. What choice did he have?

Once home he contemplated what he'd just agreed to. It was a huge risk. It certainly wasn't in his nature to take risks, although he admitted to himself that's exactly what he'd done agreeing to be a courier. Lack of money was always a great motivator!

He heard the key turn in the front door lock and sprang up from the sofa to meet Carol. 'God, am I glad to see you.'

She popped her shopping on the floor and kissed him. 'How did you get on?'

'I'll tell you everything. It was a long session.' She sat beside him and didn't interrupt once while he related all that had been said. 'Bottom line is they want me to continue...and find out more. Not sure if I can.'

She remained silent for what seemed an age, then held his hand and asked a question which, no doubt, he'd also been asking himself. 'So how will you go about doing that?'

'They want me to have a normal conversation with Bill Bogle, offer to do the other runs if they need someone. Andrea's DI suggested I tell them I have relatives in both or either city...as a legitimate reason for going there.'

Carol wasn't convinced and responded a little more sharply than she intended. 'You're out of your depth; you're a bloody engineer for god's sake.'

'Yeah, I know. Do you think I don't realise that?'

'But?'

'They said that, if I went along with it, they'd fight my corner with the CPS and get the charges against me dropped.'

'So, it's blackmail,' she retorted cynically. He tried to justify the decision he'd made.

'But it's a way out for me. If I don't, it could be jail time.' There was a tremor in his voice. 'I have to do it, love. I've made my mind up. I'll phone Robbie, or whoever he really is, tonight.'

She squeezed his hand tighter, her voice a little calmer. 'How many more runs are they asking you to do?'

He shrugged his shoulders. 'Don't know, I think it's a case of suck it and see. The sooner I can get some info the sooner the nightmare will end.' He went to make the phone call, Carol following him to listen in on his conversation with Robbie. 'Hi, Robbie. I've changed my mind. I will continue. Let me know when the next run is.'

She heard the voice at the other end. 'Good lad, you've made the right decision. Everyone will be happy now.'

John's next run was the following week.

* * *

His day for travelling up to Glasgow arrived all too quickly. The atmosphere in the Mason household was subdued. They had a quick breakfast so that John could get to Piccadilly Station for the early train to Glasgow. 'Are you okay?' queried Carol as she spread jam on her sourdough toast. 'You look tense.'

'I am. I don't know what I'm going to come up against once I get to Bogle's place.'

Carol tried to reassure him. 'Glasgow police are monitoring you. You'll be okay.'

She drove him to the station and parked in a ten-minute zone for drop-offs, gave him a hug and a kiss and said, 'see you tonight.' She watched him disappear through the main entrance and pondered over what she'd set in motion. From a discreet confession to the local police, it had now snowballed into John being centre stage in a major drug-related operation. *Had she done the right thing going to the police? Will they honour their promise of dropping the charges? What will the reaction be from the Scottish mafia if they'd find out he'd wanted to stop doing the drops? How will she live with herself if it all goes wrong?*

* * *

John caught the eight o'clock train as on previous runs, ensconced himself next to the window and stared out at the passing scenery, seeing nothing; his stomach doing somersaults. He arrived in Glasgow around eleven-thirty. It was raining, which added to John's dismal mood. He took a taxi to Bill Bogle's city centre base. What kind of reception was he going to get?

The metal grated gate of the lift opened and he was met by Tam, the giant of a man he'd met on previous visits. 'Morning John, how are you?'

John cleared his throat. 'Morning, Tam, I'm well, and you?' No response.

As he followed Tam down the narrow and dimly lit corridor panic began to take over. He felt trapped. Within seconds he was waved into Bogle's domain where Tam knocked on a door, then swung it open in response to Bogle's 'Come!'

Bogle stood up from behind his desk, a broad beam across his face. 'Ah, John, it's nice to see you again, take a seat.'

'Thank you.'

Bogle's beam suddenly disappeared, and he looked serious. 'I believe you don't want to work with me anymore. Is that right?'

'Er, yeah. I thought it was getting too risky. Sooner or later I would be stopped.'

Bogle's face blackened, his voice low and threatening. 'You leave when I say so, Johnny lad and not before. The family don't take kindly to loose cannons.' John nodded but didn't make eye contact. 'Do you get it?' Bogle said raising his voice and pointing a finger.

John stammered. 'Yes, but...what about the police? They may be following me. I'm sure I was being followed.'

Bogle wasn't too concerned with John's paranoia. He knew John was being followed; it was one of his own people. Bogle scoffed and leaned back. 'Don't worry, leave the police to me.' With that last remark he picked up a holdall that had been sitting by his side and almost threw it at John. 'Make sure that is delivered.' He swivelled away from John and turned his attention to some paperwork which John took as a signal that the meeting was over. He got up and left, nodding a goodbye to Tam who accompanied him back to the lift. The taxi dropped him off in Buchanan Street, close to the main entrance of Central Station. He quickly paid the driver, briskly walked into the station, found a coffee shop and ensconced himself in a quiet corner of the café. He suddenly realised he was shaking and perspiring, so grabbed a tissue from the table and wiped his forehead. *Why, oh why did I start all this? I never expected all this hassle.* He was in it way too deep! He hoped the police really were keeping an eye out for him.

Carol picked him up as arranged at 6pm from Piccadilly Station. She could see from the look on his face that the day hadn't gone well. He looked ashen, and weary. There was a stoop to his gait. Once she settled him in the car she wanted to know all the details. 'You look worried, what happened?' He told her about his meeting with Bogle.

'He made it quite clear that I don't leave unless he says so. He was quite threatening. God knows who he's reporting to, but I hope the police are watching out for me.'

As she negotiated her way round some roadworks, she told John about a meeting she'd had with DS Worrall. 'She popped in to work today. She knew you'd gone up to Glasgow and had informed Lanarkshire police. She assured me that they were watching out for you.'

'Well, I never saw any of them,' he responded sulkily.

Carol laughed. 'Sorry, but I think that's the whole point. It shows they're good at their job. They're not supposed to be seen.'

'Yeah, I know,' he conceded.

The next day Andrea Worrall debriefed him.

John apologised, 'Sorry, I didn't manage to get any information for you. To be honest I was terrified.'

'That's okay. Let's take it slowly. We don't want you to do anything you're uncomfortable with. Let me assure you, as I did with Carol, Lanarkshire police are keeping an eye on you.'

Over the next month John did three more runs and with each one his confidence began to return. On his way up to Glasgow for the fourth trip in just over a month he talked himself into trying to glean more information about the Liverpool and Newcastle connections. It was lunchtime by the time he was taking the lift once more to Bogle's domain and again was met by Tam.

'Morning John. Good to see you, yet again. I understand you had second thoughts some time back.'

'Yeah, I did. I think I was getting a bit paranoid; you know how it is sometimes. I'd be happy to do other runs for you if you want, say, Newcastle or Liverpool?'

Tam scoffed. 'Del wouldn't be happy with that.'

'Del?'

'Del boy, as in Fools and Horses, Derek Collier, he does the Liverpool run.'

'Ah, okay. What about Newcastle? I've got relatives in Morpeth.'

'Morpeth! That's where Gerry lives, Gerry's the courier for that area. Owns a hotel in Whitley Bay. No, you would be treading on very dangerous toes there.'

John smiled to himself. *That was easier than I thought. Hope it's information DS Worrall can use.* Tam waved him into the room where Bogle was lounging on a sofa, his feet up on an oriental ottoman. He stood up and shook hands with John. 'I keep meaning to ask you, how's Jamie McKay?'

'Fine. He doesn't say a lot when I go round. We do an exchange then I'm off, end of story. I don't ask questions – I don't need to know. I'm sorry if I got cold feet earlier, I think I panicked a bit. If there's any other runs you want me to do I'm only too happy to oblige. This is a nice little earner for me and the wife's off my back now we can pay the bills.'

Bogle nodded knowingly. He reached down and handed John the holdall. 'There you go, another day another dollar.'

'Thanks, see you next time round.'

Tam escorted him back to the lift then immediately returned to Bogle's office. He knocked on his door then poked his head round. 'Got a minute, boss.' He related the conversation he'd just had with John Mason. 'He seemed too interested in the Newcastle and Liverpool runs. He usually never says a word, but seemed keen to do those runs...it just seemed off, know what I mean?'

Bogle pursed his lips and nodded. 'Mmm, I got a similar feeling. He seemed on edge, more chatty than usual, nervous chatter, he's usually very quiet. There was something about him that didn't ring true.' He gave Tam a nod. 'Thanks for that. Leave it with me.' The instant Tam had closed the door behind him Bogle reached for the phone and dialled. He drummed his fingers on his desk as he waited for someone to answer.

'Hello?'

'Hi, Fiona, it's Bill. I've got another job for you. Can you come in this afternoon? Good, good, see you then.'

* * *

Fiona arrived in Bogle's office around two o'clock. She was wearing a pair of jeans, a pink top and a navy jacket, her hair was scraped back in a ponytail. She had an awkward gait, her left foot swung outwards when she walked, the result of a motorcycle accident when on her ex-boyfriend's Harley. Bogle noticed her gait and thought her limp had gone worse, but just as quickly dismissed it. 'Fancy going down the road for a coffee, Fiona.'

Opposite the Bogle building was a block of very expensive apartments, the ground floor housing a top-notch restaurant and, on the corner, Mackies, a select coffee shop. It was a favourite with both the business community and residents in the area. Bogle ordered the coffees while Fiona found a quiet corner where they could converse without being overheard. Bogle placed his hand over Fiona's. 'It's good to see you. I'm sorry to call you at short notice, but we may have an urgent problem.'

She lifted her cup towards her mouth then stopped half-way. 'Sounds intriguing. Tell me more.'

He looked around him then leaned in closer. 'It's John Mason again. D'you remember checking up on him months ago?' She nodded wondering where this was going. 'Well, I have some concerns about him that require another look. Are you free over the next couple of weeks?'

She put her cup down. 'Yes. Same routine as before?'

'Yeah. I'll give you a call next time he comes up then you stay with him from Central Station back to Manchester and keep an eye on him for the next two weeks; see who he meets up with. It might be worth checking on his wife too whilst you're down there.'

* * *

John was quite excited and pleased with himself having gleaned some information for DS Worrall. He called her the day after delivering the holdall to Jamie McKay. 'I've got something Andrea, not sure if it's any use to you but I've got a couple of names. Can you come round?'

'Yes. Okay this afternoon?'

'Yeah, look forward to seeing you.'

DS Worrall arrived just after lunch. 'Hi, come in. I've got a couple of bits of info for you.'

Her eyes lit up. 'That's great news.' She took out her notebook and pen then gave him a nod to continue. John shuffled in his chair realising that giving this kind of information to the police was potentially explosive, not to mention dangerous – and it also now made him a "snitch".

He took a deep breath before giving her the two names. 'The names I was given, were Del, Derek Collier, who links Glasgow to Liverpool and a Gerry, don't know his second name, who does the same job for Newcastle. Apparently, he lives in Morpeth and has a hotel in Whitley Bay.' He sat back looking hopeful that this was new information for Andrea.

'That's great, you've done a good job. I'll circulate these names to the Liverpool and the Newcastle City police. When's your next planned trip?'

John shrugged his shoulders. 'I haven't got a date yet. That Robbie character phones me as and when.'

Andrea nodded with a smile, obviously pleased with the names John had given her. 'Thanks again John, this is just the kind of information we need. Keep in touch with any further developments.' She put her pad and pen back in her briefcase and stood up to go then shook his hand. 'I'll see myself out.'

The conversation that evening between John and Carol was a little more relaxed. John felt somewhat relieved to have provided what appeared to be useful information. 'Carol, you were right to contact the police, thanks. I feel better that I'm doing something positive. Let's hope it'll soon be over.'

John was in Glasgow again the following Tuesday. It was becoming a very tedious routine; Piccadilly Station early morning, three and a half hours on the train, Central Station, taxi to Bogle's place and pick up another holdall. Once back on the train he felt comfortable that the police were keeping him safe. His eyes wandered around the carriage questioning each person he saw. *Were they police? Or was he again becoming paranoid? Did that person with the cap low over his face stare at him for longer than necessary?* Sitting on the opposite side of the carriage was a woman wearing dark sunglasses and had a white stick – was she genuinely blind? Yes, he was becoming more paranoid. The person who didn't register with him was at the rear of the carriage, but with a clear line of sight. During the journey home the woman received a phone call. She tentatively answered it. 'Hello?'

'Fiona, it's Bill. How's it going?'

'Fine, we're nearly at Manchester.'

'Look, sorry to mess you about. We're getting Mason back up here tomorrow then sending him south on a circuitous route via Newcastle. The usual courier's partner is in hospital so can't do the job…and it's urgent. Can you rearrange your journey to stay with him all the way.'

'Yes, of course.' She smiled as she put the phone back in her handbag and her eyes once again locked on Mason.

When Carol and John arrived home from the station his phone rang. He sighed in frustration as he answered it. 'Hello?'

'John, it's Tam. Mr Bogle wants you up here again tomorrow to do two drop-offs, one in Newcastle and then your usual one in Manchester.'

'How come?'

'The Newcastle courier is indisposed. See you tomorrow.'

John put the phone down and cursed. 'Christ! I've only just got home. That was Tam, one of Bogle's henchmen, they want me back up there again tomorrow to deliver to Newcastle, then another drop-off in Manchester. God knows what time I'll be home. I'll be glad when all this is over with.'

Carol looked pensive then voiced her thoughts. 'You don't think they've caught on do you?' John looked at her questioningly. 'You know, talking to the police?'

'Christ, I hope not. Do you think I ought to phone Andrea?'

'Hmmm, maybe, just to be on the safe side.'

He made the phone call to Andrea and was reassured that there was no way the Glasgow set-up could have known of their conversations.

* * *

He was angry and a little apprehensive as he boarded the Glasgow train the next morning. *What would happen if they've found out I was talking to the police? This was a ruthless gang. Let's hope the Lanarkshire police are on the ball in keeping me safe.*

He arrived at Bogle's premises just before lunchtime and was met, as usual, by Tam. 'Sorry to drag you up here so soon John,' Tam's voice oozed fake concern, 'but Gerry's partner is in hospital. It'll be good experience for you to do Newcastle.' Tam took him into the outer office. 'Mr Bogle isn't in today, so he's asked me you give you the holdalls.' He pointed to a chair on which the two bags were sitting. 'The blue one is your usual Manchester one and the green one is for Newcastle.' He handed John a piece of paper. 'That's Gerry's phone number for when you arrive at Neville Street Station. You'll get further instructions then.' Tam grabbed some keys out of his jacket which were hanging behind the door. 'I'll run you down to Central Station, make sure you get the next train.'

When Tam arrived back in the office, he knocked on Bogle's door then entered. 'I've just dropped him off boss.' Bogle gave him a nod to say 'nice one' then picked up the phone. 'Hi, Fiona, did you make the twelve-thirty to Newcastle?

'Yes. I can see your target at the far end of the carriage.'

'Good. Look, just for your information the Newcastle bag is the real McCoy but the Manchester one is flour. Jamie knows.'

Two hours later John arrived at Newcastle's main station. He'd never been to the north-east before and wasn't sure which exit to take. He sat on a bench and checked the piece of paper Tam had given him then made the phone call. 'Hello?' It was a woman's voice, and it took John by surprise. 'Er, Is Gerry there, please.'

'Yes.'

'Could I speak to him? It's John Mason.'

'Yes, I'm Geri, Geraldine Carraway.'

'Oh right, right, sorry. I've arrived in Newcastle with instructions to phone you.' He heard a small laugh from the other end at his gender faux pas. How many other people had found out Gerry was in fact Geri?

'I need you to come out to Whitley Bay, the Beeches Hotel. Grab a taxi, it'll cost you all of sixteen pounds! An overnight stay has been organised for you and we'll have you on your way again first thing tomorrow morning to Manchester.'

'Right, see you later.'

Fiona didn't follow him to Whitley Bay as she knew Geri had organised to do the hand-over that afternoon and make sure John was on the mid-morning train the next day. She enjoyed an afternoon shopping in Newcastle city centre. So far, following John had not raised any question marks as far as she was concerned. *Was Bill Bogle getting paranoid in his old age?*

At the arranged time John met up with Geri. She was a plumpish woman with a round face, botoxed lips and tattoos on her arm. She had untidy silver-grey hair in a badly cut bob. She wore tight jeans, calf-length boots and a round-necked sweater. The hotel was a large building, originally consisting of several bay-windowed houses which over the years had been bought up by the owner of the original hotel and subsequently extended. She met him at the door and shook his hand. She had a surprisingly firm grip. 'Welcome to The Beeches.'

In these new surroundings he felt awkward and tried to make light conversation. 'I understand your partner isn't too well.'

She seemed quite relaxed about the fact. 'Yes. The silly bugger came off his motorbike and broke his leg.'

John held up the green holdall. 'I believe this is yours.'

She silently took it from him and handed over an envelope that had been resting on the coffee tray. She suddenly straightened her back and slapped her hands on her knees, obviously keen to keep their conversation short. 'Well, I take it you've had a long day. Come on, I'll get the receptionist to show you to your room.' As she stood up, she pointed to another room at the far end of the lounge. 'Breakfast is through there. I've organised a taxi for you at nine-thirty tomorrow morning to take you to the station. I shan't be here tomorrow morning, so I wish you a good journey back to Manchester. It's been nice meeting you.'

John forced a smile. 'And you, thank you.'

John was back in Manchester by late evening. He delivered to McKay then arranged a taxi home from the Moss Side flat. When he finally arrived home after his round-about journey he phoned Andrea. 'Hello, DS Worall.'

'Hi Andrea, It's John Mason. I've been on a merry-go round to Glasgow, Newcastle and back to Manchester all in twenty-four hours.' He took a breath. 'However, I've got a snippet more info.'

'Brilliant. Look I'm busy for the rest of the afternoon could you come in tomorrow morning?'

'Sure, what time?'

'Around ten-ish?'

'Yeah fine, see you then.'

Over a late dinner that evening with Carol, he gave her a non-stop account of what had happened over the past twenty-four hours. He sniggered. 'Geri, who I assumed was a man looked like a biker's moll.'

She listened intently wanting to hear everything. 'So, did it all go smoothly?'

He nodded. 'Just tiring. I phoned Andrea when I got home and I'm seeing her at the cop shop tomorrow morning.'

At precisely ten o'clock John ran up the steps of the police station just as a distressed looking old lady was coming down the steps muttering to herself. She looked at John with tears in her eyes as he came up the steps. 'I've lost my dog. He's thirteen you know.' John looked at her sympathetically but didn't say anything as his mind was on his meeting with Andrea. He pushed through the double doors. He hadn't noticed a woman standing across the road, watching the events unfold. Without taking her eyes off the police station she took her phone out of her handbag and dialled.

The desk sergeant contacted DS Worrall who appeared within seconds in the waiting area. 'Come through, John.' She showed him to Interview Room 2 and waved him in. 'Make yourself comfortable, I'll get us a coffee.'

'Comfortable' was an unfortunate term to use for Interview Room 2. The last thing this stark room offered was any form of comfort. It was a cold, windowless room painted in a miserable shade of light blue, with a hard metal table and chairs. This wasn't one of the 'soft' interview rooms.

He heard her call out to him as she went for the coffees, 'white, no sugar?' He smiled to himself. She'd remembered.

He shouted back, 'Yes, please.' Returning with the coffees she closed the door with her foot, placed a coffee in front of him and as she did so she pulled a face.

'Sorry, it's from the machine again.' She waved her hand around the room. 'Sorry about this too, the other interview room is being used.' On the severely bent and scratched table was a large file which she flipped open. 'We really do appreciate you providing us with all this information John, it's gold dust. We're making headway.' He smiled and nodded, clearly pleased that some progress was being made. He hoped that in return the nightmare would soon be over. Her face suddenly softened, and she paused before speaking. 'Are you and Carol, okay? I know it's been difficult and a worrying time over the last few months. My boss is really pleased with what you've been able to provide us with and he wanted me to make sure you and Carol were okay.' John nodded and smiled before she continued. 'So, what is this new (fingers curled into quotation marks) 'snippet'?' she asked.

He took a sip of his drink then leaned forward. 'I met up with Gerry, the Newcastle contact only to find out 'he' was a 'she' and it's Geri, G E R I, Geri Carraway. She owns the Beeches Hotel in Whitely Bay. It's where I did the drop-off.'

Andrea appeared to be making copious notes. 'That's great, thanks. I've got some good news too. I did say earlier that we were making progress, and we are. We've been observing Jamie McKay.' She chuckled. 'You were seen yesterday afternoon delivering your package. Anyway, as I say we've been watching McKay and we've identified three youths who call on him on a regular basis, we assume to pick up drugs. Those three were tailed which led us to three council estates.' She referred to her notes. 'The er, Crompton, the Fallows and the Broomwood.' She looked up from her notes. 'Do you know them?' John acknowledged her with a nod. 'And we also followed McKay back to his own residence which is in Moston Wood.' She looked up at John once more for confirmation.

'Yeah, I know Moston Wood, it's quite an up-market area.'

'And,' she said looking pleased, 'we've followed up on the Liverpool name you gave us.' Again, she referred to her file. 'Del Collier.' She sat back in her chair tapping her pen against her palm. 'Arrests are imminent...thanks to you.'

John blew out his cheeks. 'Wow, brilliant. Maybe I can finally put all this behind me.'

'It's all down to you John. You've been a great help, thank you again.'

* * *

Bill Bogle was staring out of his office window which looked out over The Square. People looked like ants from this height, cars like Dinky Toys. The overnight rain had stopped, and the welcoming sun was now throwing large shadows below. Suddenly he was kicked out of his day-dreaming when the phone rang. 'Hello?'

'Hello Bill, it's Fiona.' Her tone was low-key, not the chirpy Fiona that Bill knew.

He could tell there was a problem. 'What's up?'

'It's Mason. He's talking to the police. Only two minutes ago I saw him going into the police station.' She heard Bogle cursing under his breath. 'There's more. There's been a woman visiting the Mason home. I'd recognise a cop from a mile away. I called in a few favours, and it's been confirmed that she is in fact a cop and, what's more, she's married to a bloke who's Carol Mason's boss. Coincidence?' There was silence down the phone. 'You still there, Bill?'

'Er yeah, sorry. Christ, what a mess! Thanks Fiona, you've done a great job. Stay with him and leave it with me. Cheers.'

Bogle slowly put the phone down and pressed a button on his desk to call Tam to the inner sanctum. 'What's up, boss?' On seeing the look on Bogle's face he ventured, 'problems?'

Bogle slammed his fist on the desk shaking the art deco lamp and causing several pens to roll on the floor. 'I bloody knew it. That bastard Mason's been talking to the police.'

'What do you want me to do boss?'

Bogle, his face red with rage sneered at Tam. 'Get him up here within the week for another run. It will be his last one. Arrange a run to Jamie's, a dummy run of course. He mustn't know we're on to him.' He slammed his fist down once more. 'Bastard! Nobody informs on us and gets away with it!'

Tam phoned John that evening and ordered him up to Glasgow at the end of the week. 'It's another run to Jamie's. He's getting through product at a hell of a rate. He's desperate for another delivery.'

'Right, I'll see you Friday.'

Once Tam had confirmed to Bogle which day Mason was coming up to Glasgow Bogle picked up the phone.

'Hello?'

'Hi Fiona, it's Bill. Mason's coming up on Friday. I want you to follow him from Manchester then all the way back. Don't let him out of your sight. During the trip back to Manchester I want you to 'finalise' the job.'

'Got it. See you Friday.'

* * *

Friday came and Carol took John to what had now become the usual routine drive to Piccadilly station for the early train. He had become quite accustomed to the mindless stare out of the window for three and a half hours, the usual taxi to Bogle's lair, and up to the top floor where he would meet Tam. The walk to Bogle's office seemed to get darker and narrower each time he'd been. Again, he didn't meet Bogle on this occasion and was given the holdall by Tam, then ushered out of the building. As he sat in the taxi back to Glasgow's Central Station, he became nervous. Something didn't seem right. Tam wasn't as welcoming as usual. There was something amiss; nothing he could put his finger on...just a gut feeling.

He followed the same routine at the station. He bought his ticket and grabbed a coffee as he had a good twenty minutes before the train departed. He sat with his hands around his cup and looked around him. God, Central Station was a depressing place, even the advertising posters looked bloody miserable. The passengers hurrying to and fro all looked worried, even the railway staff. He felt the whole world was caving in on him. *Was it him? Was he panicking unnecessarily?* He was tempted to dump the bag and run. He felt trapped.

Fiona followed him onto the train and, as on previous trips, sat several seats behind him. She smiled to herself as she noted he had the holdall on the floor firmly clamped between his feet.

This would be her and John's last journey to Manchester

* * *

The briefing room was in a sombre mood. DS Worrall leaned back against the edge of the table at the front of the room, feet crossed, arms folded staring at the floor whilst the team settled themselves in. There was none of the usual banter. None of the usual camaraderie associated with close teams. Once they were settled and silence prevailed, Andrea lifted her eyes to face the team. 'What the hell happened? I thought we had covered all bases. Where were the Glasgow police who were supposed to have been accompanying him down to Manchester?' She pushed herself off the table and started to pace. 'I can't believe what's happened. I made him a promise we'd look after him.' She scanned her team. They looked sheepish and didn't offer any explanations or excuses. They knew they would have been shot down in flames, whatever they said. 'Christ! How will Carol view this. She's the one who came to me in the first place. She knew there was danger involved in what he was doing. She came to me for help for god's sake and look what's happened.' She forced a sigh. Her expression segued from anger to resolve. This was the Andrea the team knew. 'I'm determined to get these bastards, for John and Carol's sake! Thanks to John's bravery and the information he provided, several teams are at this moment simultaneously arresting the McKay set-up in Manchester, along with those in Liverpool and Newcastle. Our effort from now on is to find the person who fatally stabbed John Mason on the train, presumably in front of other passengers. I think we must assume that whoever did it was a hired killer. It looks professional. The person must have followed him onto the train and shadowed him all the way down to Manchester. A search of the track is under way as the weapon wasn't found on the train. It had to have been dumped somewhere along the line. I want all CCTV footage to be checked and double-checked at Piccadilly Station. DCs Cartmel and Pearce, can you do that. The person we are looking for must have got off at Piccadilly. He, or she, must be in the town somewhere. Go as far back as you can with CCTV, but if I manage to get specific dates from Carol, I'll let you know. So, jump to it, there's no time to waste, it's imperative the CCTV is viewed ASAP – knowing the railway companies, they might delete footage before we have time to analyse it. I'm going to see Carol to try to pin down the dates when he went up to Glasgow. I'll get the Lanarkshire police to check the CCTV at their end. I'll also ask them to check the local taxi firms. The drivers may recognise someone or have regular customers.' She clapped her hands, business like. 'Anything that gets flagged up, you call in straightaway. It may give the others something to focus on; an individual perhaps shadowing John; something out of kilter. So, any questions?' She scanned the team for a response. 'Do you all know what to do? Good, let's get the bastard who did this. Chop, chop. Debrief tomorrow morning.'

Her chat with Carol was brief and tearful. She looked weary. Carol and her sister were desperately trying to organise John's funeral and at the same time questioning why she was having to do this. It was so unfair. 'Andrea,' she pleaded, tears running down her cheeks, 'you promised me he would be monitored to make sure he was safe.'

Andrea shook her head and apologised profusely. 'I know Carol. I'm so, so sorry. I don't know how it happened. I'm determined to catch whoever did this to John. I know it's a really difficult time, but I must ask. It would really help if we knew the dates John went up to Glasgow. We're checking the CCTV at Piccadilly and Glasgow stations so specific dates would be useful. It may help us find the perpetrator.' She felt guilty asking Carol, but it had to be done. The sooner the better.

Carol wiped her eyes and rose from the sofa. 'They'll be in my diary.' She rummaged through a draw in the sideboard and retrieved her diary. She sat down again and flipped through the pages. 'Yeah, the dates are in here. You can take it if you want as long as you let me have it back.'

Andrea took it and stowed it in her briefcase. 'Thank you. I promise I'll return it.' She paused before speaking again. 'Is there anything you need? Can we help in any way?'

Carol shook her head. Andrea touched Carol's arm and stood up. 'I'll see myself out. Anything you need just call me.'

Back at the station Andrea emailed the dates to her teams. As she closed her computer one of the arresting team stood by her desk. 'We've brought in Jamie McKay. He's in No.4 interview room ready for interview.' Andrea felt angry. She'd made a promise to John and Carol and they had been badly let down.

'Thanks.' She was ready for him. She was determined to make amends.

The next day brought more good news. She had received a phone call from DC Pearce. 'Great news boss. On several occasions on the CCTV our local helpful cop was able to identify a person who is known to the Glasgow police. Apparently, she's easily identifiable as she walks with an awkward gait, on CCTV it stands out a mile. Also, on one of the shots we could see a specific tattoo on the side of her neck, an eagle and a sword, the insignia of a Glasgow gang.'

Andrea suddenly felt excited. 'And?'

'It's Fiona Cavanagh, girlfriend of a Donny Campbell, currently serving time in Barlinnie for drive-by shootings. Cavanagh has always been on the periphery of the crime scene but, apart from one occasion for soliciting, she has no charges against her. The local cop tells us from information gathered from informers, that she's a nasty piece of work, more than capable of murder.'

'Great work. Bring her in.'

* * *

Glasgow police arrested Fiona Cavanagh at her Callender flat and Andrea flew up to Glasgow to conduct the interview. Cavanagh was left for nearly an hour alone in the interview room but was watched by the investigating team through the two-way mirror. She sat chewing her thumb nail, her face sullen.

DS Worrall entered the room and sat down without saying a word. After flicking through her file, she eyed the woman sitting in front of her. 'We're investigating the murder of a John Mason; do you know him?'

'No comment.'

Andrea pushed a photo across the metal table. 'Do you recognise this man?'

Cavanagh turned sideways, away from Andrea. 'No comment.'

DS Worrall then lifted the top of her lap-top, cued in the CCTV footage, turned it toward Cavangh then waited for her to look. Andrea pressed play. 'Do you recognise anyone in this video?' She carefully watched Cavanagh's facial expression on seeing the footage. 'Isn't that you?'

She stared defiantly at the detective. 'Yes,' she responded sharply.

'What were you doing in Glasgow Central?'

'Going shopping.'

'To Manchester? The platform you are on is for the Manchester train.'

'I've got friends in Manchester. I went to visit them.'

Andrea nodded. 'Could you give us their names?'

'No comment.'

'You seem to go on a very regular basis. Very good friends, are they?'

Before Cavanagh had a chance to respond there was a gently knock at the door and a head appeared. 'A minute boss. You need to see this.'

Taking her file with her Andrea left the room. She was handed a piece of paper and a photo. 'Thought you might like to see this.'

She studied it then smiled. 'Brilliant.'

Back in the interview room she presented the information she'd just been given by the officer. 'We've found a knife on the tracks on the approach to Piccadilly station. It's a stiletto, do you recognise it?'

'No.'

'You sure?'

Cavanagh responded abruptly, venom in her voice. 'No, never seen it before.'

Andrea took a deep breath. 'Hmm, can you explain why we have your partial fingerprints on it? You see, it's no use wearing gloves just when you commit a crime if you've already handled the knife without gloves.'

'No comment.'

Andrea closed her file and slowly stood up. 'Fiona Cavanagh, I'm arresting you on suspicion of the murder of John Mason on March the fourteenth. You don't have to say anything but anything you do say may be taken down and used in evidence...' She turned to an officer who was standing at the door. 'Take her down.'

EPILOGUE

Fiona Marie Cavanagh was found guilty of the murder of John Mason and sentenced to life imprisonment for a minimum of twenty-five years.

Jamie McKay, Derek Collier and Geri Carraway were all found guilty of dealing in prohibited drugs and each sentenced to eight years imprisonment.

The 'runners' attached to the drug runs were all given two years suspended sentences.

No direct evidence linking William Bogle to the illicit trade could be found. Bogle continues, seemingly untouchable, to continue his hideous trade.

All potential charges against John Mason were dropped.

Carol Mason continued in her job. Three years later she met and eventually married David Allsop, a shop-fittings representative and moved to Devon.

DS Andrea Worrall was promoted to DI. She was presented with a Commendation for her role in breaking up, at least in part, the Scottish drug mafia.

MANY THANKS TO:

Graham Ladyman at Pick-A-Woowoo Publishing, for his prompt and comprehensive responses to my many questions.

Eddie Albrecht, for his copy-editing and useful comments.

My son, Richard, for his inspired book cover design.

My wife, Mazzie, who encouraged me to put my years of writing efforts into print. Without her IT skills my first project would not have come to fruition.

My friends who, over the years, have endured reading my efforts with enthusiasm and encouragement.